Bruised Love

A Novel By
Nanette M. Buchanan

Type of Work: Fiction
Creation Date: 2008
First Edition: June 2009
ISBN-978-0-979-3883-2-3
ISBN-0-9793883-2-5
Cover Design: Smoove Productions, CEO, Terry Smith

I Pen Books
www.ipendesigns.net

Acknowledgements

God has given me the desire and blessed me with the ability to pen.
And for that I am humbly grateful.

To my husband, your midnight input has paid off again. I want to thank you for the smiles, nods and debates on what is real.

To my son and daughters, thank you all for understanding my desire to fulfill my dreams. It is your understanding that has inspired me to continue to write.

To my readers, thank you for your support and encouraging words. This novel and all that follow are written for people like you.

As an author I am blessed to have you all, those who take the challenge and walk through the pages of my work. Whether for entertainment, reviews or relaxation, I am proud to make this journey with you.

To the book clubs and those who provide an avenue of sales, I will never forget you taking that step with faith and belief that the work of Nanette M. Buchanan was worth promotions, sales, book signings and other fabulous events and opportunities.

You all have become a part of my literary journey and I thank you.
Read, Relax and Enjoy as I Pen.

Ms. Smith

Look, there out the window, isn't that Ms. Smith?
She's so well dressed; her beauty truly a gift.
You say those children all belong to her
Oh what a blessing to a proud husband, I'm sure.
What, no husband?
One, two, three boys and the girl carrying the bags,
My, my, what happened on the path she chose?
She had blossomed to be a rose.
No, no don't say that, her life is a common fad…
Wait one minute that limp she never had!
You say she took to alcohol and drugs,
What you say the men in her life were common thugs?
Ms. Smith had potential, she had a jump on many, a clean educated start
Yes, you are right she had a giving heart.
I guess she gave her love real easy, looked for love in the wrong place.
Wait I didn't hear you. You said her last mate beat her in the face?
She's a victim of abuse and still she goes on.
To see her from this window, one would think nothing was wrong
The problems women encounter, one never knows.
To live daily as a victim diminishes one's goals.
Is she moving forward, what about her self-esteem?
It's good she's still working, but it's not exactly what I mean.
She's lost a part of her character with each violent act or blow,
without character and self-esteem, how far will she go?
I pray Ms. Smith won't surrender to the negatives she has seen.
I pray Ms. Smith remains strong to walking a path that is clean.
It is easy to make excuses or hang her head low,
listening to the criticism and ridicule as she goes
My prayers go with her for indeed she needs spiritual strength.
A comfort to her soul will see her the length.
Oh, look she's waving at us, she noticed our stare.
"Hey, Ms. Smith, how are you?" I'm not just asking; I care!

Chapter 1

Cassandra smiled and waved at her mother's neighbor and friend, Madeline Dearling. Most thought Mattie was nosy but not Cassandra. She was practically raised by Ms. Dearling, who she affectionately called "Ma'Dear", and she was pleased to see her. She hadn't seen Ma'Dear in what seemed like a lifetime. Ms. Dearling had been a mother for all the children in the neighborhood when Cassandra was young. She still sat daily perched in her rocker on her porch across the street from the house where Cassandra once lived. There would be plenty of time to update Ma'Dear on how her world had changed since she moved from Grape Street.

The neighborhood looked so different. The houses seemed smaller than she remembered. She could tell from the residents sitting on the porches, her childhood friends no longer lived next door. As she passed the last two vacant lots, she spotted 231 Grape Street, her three boys ran ahead of her. Cassandra had not been home in more than five years.

She sat her bags on the porch and helped her five-year-old Cassie up the stairs with her bag. Kyle, Christopher and Taylor stood on the porch waiting for directions from their mother before they moved any further. Cassandra rang the bell and smoothed her blouse and skirt waiting for the door to open. She reached for Kyle to stand next to her. Christopher and Taylor fell in line. The door opened slowly and the family filed in with their bags in hand.

"Sssh, c'mon in girl, your mother is trying to rest. It's been a rough afternoon for her. I just gave her the medicine the doctor told us would help. Whew, y'all sure done grew. Look at y'all. Sandra, they sure are beautiful girl and you looking good too."

"Thank you, Aunt Laura, where should we put these bags?"

Laura, a well-kept woman for the age of sixty, led them into the kitchen where they could see and smell the dinner that was being prepared. It was close to five o'clock and the heat of the day was beginning to subside. The ceiling fan was on low circulating the smell of a good meal and scented candles. Mary's sister had been caring for her off and on for months since her stroke but Laura called Cassandra to say that she couldn't do it all herself. Mary's objection to calling her daughter went unheard once she told her family the doctor said her condition was deteriorating. Cassandra agreed that her mother was more than a handful for her aunt who had her own ailments from time to time. She wasn't sure what the arrangements would be between herself and her mother, but she was there to help where she could.

"Where's your overnight bags, your suitcases and stuff? Cassie, come give me a hug baby."

"I stopped at the hotel first. You know how Mama is; I didn't know what she would say about us staying."

Cassie and Taylor stood close to their mother's leg. Kyle and Christopher had warmed up to their Aunt giving her a hug and kiss hello and returning to Cassandra's side. Laura stretched her arms outward toward Cassie and reached for a kitchen chair to sit in.

"Girl, you better give me a kiss, you too boy." Taylor smiled shyly as he gave in giving his great Aunt a kiss. It was returned with a loving hug. "They sure have grown," Laura repeated her thoughts aloud. "Sandra your mother can't say nothing; she needs you as much as she needs me. Now she'll tell us both something different, but you'll see. Child, she ain't doing well at all. We're all she's got, so as I see it, she's stuck. I can't do everything for her all day long. Thank you for stopping by the store, its things like that your Uncle Earl, and I have been doing for weeks. Someone has to be here with her and the errands still need to be run. I gave up my apartment in the senior's building last month. I told them to put me on the list to return after I tended to my sister. She don't even know it. I believe she still thinks I just stop by. I had your Uncle Earl bring all my things over. My furniture and things are in storage. The superintendent of the building said it would be fine to keep it with a few other things I had packed away. I don't know why I keep so much of that mess. Earl complains about it all the time. He said I shouldn't trust them cause, I ain't staying there. Earl don't know them, as well as I do. Yes, dealing with Mary and Earl, whew, it's been quite a job for me."

Cassandra kept her laughter to herself and gave her aunt a small smile. Her Uncle Earl was the youngest of the three, and he proved it often. Laura being the eldest and mediator for the family was the rational one. Sandra loved to hear her talk and complain about what they had or had not done. Earl called it rattling.

"Kyle, y'all go out back and play, don't go out front either. Cassie you mind Kyle now."

"Sandra they sure have grown, how old are they now."

"Kyle is eleven, Chris is nine, Taylor is seven and Cassie is five. They keep me busy."

Cassandra looked around her aunt scanning the kitchen. She began reminiscing about the times her mother would be cooking while her father read the paper at the kitchen table. Cassandra and her father had an inseparable relationship and Mary never found a place in her daughter's heart after his death. Steven Smith died when Cassandra was sixteen. Cassandra felt her mother treated him badly in his final days, and she never forgot or forgave her for his pain. Mary tried to rekindle a relationship with Cassandra, but it wasn't the same without her father. Mary hadn't spent much time mothering Cassandra. Laura and Ma'Dear had. If she needed love in a motherly way, she looked for them to comfort her. She tried to fill the void for her father by dating, often seeking to replace her missed love in all the wrong places. Cassandra mourned until she met Trevor Black her first and only love.

Trevor and Cassandra spent every free moment with each other and Mary saw her only child slip into what became an everlasting tug of war. Mary tried to stop Cassandra from seeing Trevor. Cassandra would go out of her way to be with him. Trevor put on the air of a proper young man but Mary, Laura, and Ma'Dear agreed Trevor was never good enough for Cassandra. Trevor was her senior prom date and Cassandra got pregnant with Kyle shortly after. The pregnancy and her relationship with Trevor was enough for Mary Smith to push her only daughter away telling her she would get enough of him if she had to depend on him.

Cassandra left the only home she knew at nineteen. Trevor never kept a job, money, or a roof over their head. Cassandra fell for his smooth talking, and sweet loving as often as he gave it. That was twelve years, and four children ago, Trevor still didn't have a permanent job and slept between his babies mothers. Cassandra saw him once or twice a month.

Cassandra kept in touch with her Aunt Laura and Ma'Dear by phone and would send them pictures and gifts on the holidays. She just couldn't bring herself to visit her mother. Cassandra couldn't stand the "I told you so" speech. When her aunt called, Cassandra felt the guilt and shame hit her all at once. She packed their bags for what she thought would be only a week or two. Now she knew different.

"I bet they do keep you busy. How are you going to get your things? You're not staying in the hotel."

"Aunt Laura, I need to talk with my mother. I don't want the kids feeling uncomfortable and with her being sick I don't want them getting on her nerves, or on yours, for that matter."

Laura got up to check the pots on the stove and peeked out the back door at the children.

"Pass me that box of rice there girl. Listen, you can talk with your mother all you want. There's no need for you to waste your money on no hotel. There's plenty of bed space here. The boys can have the guest room; you and Cassie take your old room. I'll sleep in the den. We'll all be fine. As for your children keeping up noise, we need some life in this house. Maybe that's what's killing her."

"Killing her, Aunt Laura is she dying?" Cassandra had put off coming to visit for weeks. She didn't know how sick her mother was.

"Go talk to your mother. You tell me. I think she's giving up. Did you have to take a leave from work?"

"Uh, uh… that's another problem. I'm not working right now. I'm on unemployment."

"What happened to your job, how are you and those kids making it on unemployment?"

"Well it just kicked in last week. I was looking into a job program for cosmetology. They'll pay me as long as I go to get the certification. I dropped everything to come when you called so I guess I'll have to check into it here."

"Well it's not like you moved out of the state Sandra, if they offered it on your side of Philadelphia it's on this side too. Why did you leave the job you had?"

Cassandra had no intention on telling her aunt how her last day on her "good paying" job went. She had been a bank teller for five years and Trevor had given her major on the job drama at least twice a month for the past two years. His last escapade was her last day at work. Cassandra could hear her girlfriend Trina saying, "Leave that nigga alone before you lose everything you worked so hard for."

She was right, the job was first, four months later it was the apartment. Cassandra had to go to a hearing to get cleared to collect unemployment, and she had just received her first check. The drama at the bank didn't stop Trevor from begging at her door a week later for her attention, and eventually he was in her bed giving her attention. Trina was disgusted when Cassandra used the excuse, "he's the kid's father" or "we started out just talking".

Cassandra lived in West Philadelphia in an apartment Trina offered to share with her and the children. The apartment was in a building, owned by her and her mother. It worked out perfect for the two young women. Trina was good company and a good babysitter for Cassandra, whenever she needed her. Her plans were to start the cosmetology class, graduate and start her own health care hair and body spa. Trina and her mother supported her dreams fully.

The distance between Cassandra and her mother made it easier for Cassandra to live in West Philadelphia. Where she lived was never a priority on her list and Mary wasn't interested in Cassandra's lifestyle or how she provided for her children. They spoke on the phone because it was a safe way to handle their relationship. The children had not seen their grandmother in two years, which was the year Kyle graduated from the fifth grade.

Laura opened the refrigerator and took out the bowl of tossed salad and the salad dressing. Cassandra watched as her aunt set the table for their dinner to be served.

"Aunt Laura, do you think my mother wants me here? I mean, I know what you and I think but, what about her feelings?"

"If you're waiting for her to say, 'Sandra, I need your help', that ain't gonna happen. Listen, your mother is sick. I don't know how long you and I can keep her comfortable, or care for her; but if we can, let's do what we need to do. Don't worry about what she'll say. What will you say later if you don't do anything?"

"Has Uncle Earl seen her, since she's been this sick?"

"No, he was here to visit her two weeks ago. She was still sitting up during the day then. Since she's been in the bed he calls her every day. She spoiled him rotten when we were kids and that brother of ours is still the baby. He's scared to death of her dying when he's around."

Cassandra went to the back door and watched her children playing in the yard. Tears formed in her eyes. She realized she had a task ahead of her; sick mother, four children, no job and the love for a man who had no clue.

Chapter 2

Ma' Dear folded the newspaper and leaned back in her rocking chair. Seeing Cassandra sent a sting to her heart. She spoke with Laura two days ago, and it was clear now that Mary wasn't doing well. Mary and Steven moved into the neighborhood when Cassandra was entering kindergarten. Ma'Dear met Mary at the grammar school as they both stood watching her older children go inside for class on their first day of school. Sylvia and Lamont were running to their classes while Terrance stood holding her leg smiling at Cassandra. Over the years, the children went to birthday parties, grammar school, high school, graduations and proms together. Steven and Joe, Ma'Dear's husband, became as close as Mary and Ma'Dear had become. Cassandra played with all the neighborhood children, but she never had what one would consider a close friend. She considered Sylvia her friend growing up since Cassandra was an only child and Sylvia was the only girl in her family. They played dolls, jump rope and house when the boys would leave them alone. After Steven died, Cassandra stayed off to herself. Ma'Dear made a mental note to tell Sylvia that Cassandra came home to help her mother.

Lamont tried for years to be more than a friend to Cassandra but Trevor Black was the one who stole her heart. Trevor was from New York, his family moved to Philadelphia when they were in their junior year in high school. Ma'Dear and Mary saw the sparkle in Cassandra's eyes, whenever she would see him passing through their street. Trevor asked her to their senior prom and that secured the love hate relationship they shared ever since. Ma'Dear became the sympathetic ear for Cassandra. Mary wouldn't listen to her whining and complaining about the boy she told her to stay away from. Ma'Dear hadn't seen Cassandra since her second child, Christopher, was born.

"Lamont will be glad to see her too, although he'll never say it to me." Ma'Dear chuckled at the thought. Terrance came out the front door with two glasses of iced tea.

"Cassandra waved back at you Ma?"

"Now you know she had better. I sure hope Mary is feeling better today. I called over there two days ago and Laura said she was looking poorly."

"Did you go over there?"

"Not this week, I try not to visit her but once a week, so she can get her rest. You know, I go over there, and she tries to keep her eyes open to talk or just to listen. Terry she needs her rest. You can look at her and tell that right off. That stroke took the wind out of her sail. I really don't think she ever got back on the right foot since she had it. I hate to say it, so I just pray on it."

"They say it takes a while to recover from a stroke. Listen, do you need anything before I go to work this evening. I think I'm going to lie down until nine. My shift starts at eleven this week."

"They done changed it again? No, I don't need anything. You go on and take your nap. Driving that bus that time of night, are you on your regular route?"

"Yeah no different just the time, if you need me, wake me."

"Thank you sweetie, I'm just fine. I guess I better find something to eat in a little while."

"Dinner's done Ma. I cooked, remember?"

Ma'Dear was becoming forgetful about things more often, and it bothered her. She tried not to tell her family, but she had a feeling they knew especially Terrance. Terrance worked as a bus driver for the City of Philadelphia's Department of Transportation. He drove the local bus and enjoyed it, especially the day shift. Ma'Dear didn't know he requested the change because he, Sylvia, and Lamont worried about her remembering small things around the house during the day. Terrance had the job that would allow a change. His being with Ma'Dear during the day until she went to bed meant her children could rest with a clear conscious. Ma'Dear didn't have any major incidents but there had been times when she forgot to turn off the bath water, forgot food while it was cooking in the oven or the stove, or forgot to lock doors.

Ma'Dear knew that Terrance wanted to save as much money as he could to buy a new home. She offered to share her home certain his new home had a room for her. She had no idea he and his siblings had other reasons for the living arrangement. Joe and Ma'Dear were still close friends, but they were separated. It was just Ma'Dear and Terrance living in her home, and she enjoyed his company.

"Boy, seeing Cassandra, I forgot you cooked. Well, let me get to fixin' me a plate then. You eating before you lie down?"

"No, I'll be fine."

Terrance sat in the chair on the porch to finish his iced tea. The chair became the place for his nap.

Chapter 3

Cassandra took the plate with her mother's dinner and told Kyle to bring the iced tea. Taylor and Chris brought the fork and napkins while Cassie followed behind. Laura had been in to check on Mary to make sure she wasn't awakened by their entrance. She rearranged her pillows in the bed preparing her sister for her dinner. Laura never mentioned Cassandra would be bringing her plate.

Cassandra knocked on the door, opening it slowly. She could see the shock on her mother's face. Before Mary could speak Kyle, Taylor and Chris sang her name.

"Hi Grandma, we brought your food." The questions began immediately after.

"Grandma, why are you in the bed so early?" Cassie couldn't understand why she was in her pajamas or in the bed. "Didn't you want to see us? You didn't come out of your room."

Taylor and his grandmother shared a hug and a loving kiss. Cassandra allowed them to question her mother for what seemed like five minutes and then told them to let her eat her food.

"They're fine Sandra. Leave them be. What did you bring me to eat Chris?"

"Aunt Laura made it. We didn't eat yet, we brought you yours first. What is it Ma?"

Cassandra took the cover from the plate and showed the children.

"Yummy, I like macaroni's"

Mary smiled at Cassie's comment and took the tray positioning it on her lap.

"Kyle, you and your brothers bring Cassie and come wash your hands so you can eat."

Laura had prepared their plates in the kitchen. She knew this would give Cassandra and Mary a few moments together.

"Cassandra, I'll bring your tray and plate. You can use the chair I use to eat in there with your mother."

"Thank you Aunt Laura. Kyle help Cassie wash her hands."

The children left the room and silence fell between the two women. Cassandra felt that uncomfortable feeling creeping upon her again. Mary felt it too.

"How's Trina and her mother?" Mary said, adjusting her covers.

"They're fine. They said to tell you hello, and they hope you feel better soon."

Mary sighed and held her head back. Cassandra watched not knowing what to do. Her mother had lost a lot of weight since the last time they were together. Cassandra noticed her left side moved slower than the right. Her speech wasn't slurred but it took a deliberate effort for her to speak. Mary had always been an attractive woman. Her hair was gray. It looked as though a beautician had highlighted it creating a beautiful sheen. She had hands of a pianist. Her long fingers were accented with manicured nails. Cassandra wondered if Mary allowed Laura to keep them up for her. Laura entered the room with Cassandra's plate.

"Mary, is everything okay?"

"Yes, Laura just fine sweetie. I was waiting for Sandra to get her plate. I didn't want to eat alone. Are you eating with the children?"

"I will, if you need anything, the two of you, just yell."

"Mama, you should have told me, I would have gotten my plate."

"Hush, child. Say the blessing over the food."

They ate most of the meal in silence. Cassandra watched as her mother carefully put the food on her spoon and put the spoon in her mouth. She could only imagine how painful it would have been to watch her mother try to eat in her early months of recovery. Cassandra wasn't sure she was ready for the task that was yet to come.

"How's your job?"

Cassandra raised her eyes from her plate and felt her mother's direct stare.

"I'm no longer employed there. I'm starting cosmetology through a program offered at the college. The state will pay for it."

Cassandra wasn't about to tell her mother why she was no longer employed. She didn't want to tell her that unemployment was paying for the schooling. It sounded better if it was a state funded program.

"So you quit your job to go to school, who's supporting you and the children?"

Cassandra knew the routine. She avoided talking about her financial needs or status at all cost. It always led to an argument about Trevor. She knew silence would not stop the questions, and if she was expected to stay, her mother would have to realize the subject of Trevor was off limits.

"I'm collecting unemployment. It's a program to get my certification, so I can work independently or at a salon. I want to eventually own a skin care and health spa. It would include the clients getting their hair done or cut, facials, manicures and health tips."

"And the state will pay for all that?"

Cassandra was stunned her mother didn't yell about how stupid her dream was, nor did she throw Trevor in the conversation.

"No, I will probably have to see about a small business loan after I get my certifications. It's a dream but I'm determined to see it through."

"Humph, I could comment by saying you should have thought about it earlier, but we know where your thoughts were."

Cassandra closed her eyes to count to ten. She knew it was coming.

"You know when you're raising children; it leaves little room for yourself. Take your time and avoid those who would see you fail. You'll be fine. I just hope unemployment won't snatch the program before you finish."

Cassandra couldn't believe her ears. She reached for her mother's plate and stacked the dishes and trays to carry them in the kitchen.

"Are you coming back to talk a while? Tell your aunt to give you my pill please. I believe it's time for one."

Laura stood from the table seeing Cassandra enter the kitchen. They met at the sink and spoke softly so Mary and the children wouldn't hear them.

"Aunt Laura, do those pills make her personality change?"

"Not that I know of, they're just for pain. You know something to make it easier for her to rest. Her therapy in the mornings is long and tedious. The therapist is here at eight thirty and doesn't leave until, whew, most times eleven thirty or twelve. She needs those pills for the afternoon."

"She asked for them. Is it time?"

"No, I give her the pills after I bathe her for the night. I guess you'll help me with that now that you're here. She does most things by herself but there are some days she can't manage a thing."

"Let me tell her it's not time for her medicine. She sure seems different Aunt Laura."

"She's not as mean Cassandra. She's slipping away and she knows it. Things will be okay between you two, you'll see. I'll call Earl to come get you so you can bring your things from the hotel. He'll be glad to see you."

"Will Uncle Earl come this late? I can get a cab over there in the morning."

"One of your cousins will come with him. He's got three there living with him. If not I'll call Larry, he should be home."

"How is Larry and his family?"

"Like yours, growing, I think his wife is due with their third child in another two weeks."

"So you'll be a grandmother again soon."

"What about Leon?"

"Leon is still in school, seems like a lifetime. He finished Penn State and went on to get some other degree. Don't ask me what he's studying, I don't know. I wish their father had lived to see them and you. Y'all sure keep me proud."

"Sandra, did you get my medicine?"

A faint cry came from the bedroom. Cassandra jumped remembering she said she would return with the medication.

"It's not time yet Mary. Sandra's bringing your water." Laura yelled in the direction of the bedroom. "Here take her this glass of water; she'll sip off it while she watches television."

"Where are the children?"

"I sent them in the yard so they could run off more of that stored energy. I'll call Earl and clean the kitchen. You go sit with your mother."

Chapter 4

Earl was glad to have a reason to come out of his house. Laura called saying Cassandra was home but needed a ride to the hotel to get her bags. Earl didn't ask questions. He told her he would come to pick her up in an hour. It was eight thirty before he stepped onto the porch and turned the key to his sister Mary's front door.

"Here's your Uncle, Cassandra. C'mon now I told you he was on his way."

Laura had little patience for people who kept others waiting, she said it was rude. The children were in the family room watching television. Cassie was the last one in the tub and Cassandra was cleaning up their mess. Laura peeked into Cassandra's old bedroom just as Cassandra was folding back the covers on the bed.

"You go on now with your Uncle before he sits too long. He's in with your mother now, that won't be long. He'll probably use you as his excuse to end his visit early."

"He didn't talk with her today?"

"I don't think so. You go ahead now."

Cassandra grabbed her handbag off the chair that sat in front of her old desk. She smiled thinking of the memories her room held.

"So it does feel good to be home huh?"

"I guess it does Aunt Laura. I didn't know what to expect, but it does feel better than when I first walked in."

"It's gonna be fine, you'll see. C'mon 'fore your Uncle gets to yelling he can't see."

"Why didn't he send Kevin or one of them?"

"Why does Earl do the things he does? That's the better question? I'll tell you why, because he's Earl."

They both laughed as they came downstairs into the living room. Earl was sitting on the couch patiently watching the children playing in front of the television.

Cassandra looked at her Aunt as they waited for an explanation.

"Earl, I thought you went in to speak to Mary?"

"I did, she was dozing off so I didn't bother her. I'll come back and see her tomorrow. It will be fine. I don't want to disturb her sleep."

"You know she'll be wondering what happened to you today. You said you would be here to visit her yesterday and didn't."

"Sandra, are you ready baby. Your aunt will spend the next few hours fussing at me about this visit. That's why I don't stay long."

"That ain't why Earl. Tell the truth if it's in you. You scared of death knocking at the door. You know your door is open too."

"Well if it's open death won't have to knock! C'mon Sandra. We'll be right back, just don't you answer no doors hear?"

Cassandra was laughing as she went in the family room to tell her children she would be right back with their pajamas and other clothes. Cassie began to cry, but Chris reassured her, they would have fun while waiting for their mother to return. Cassie followed Chris into the room. Cassandra smiled and whispered, "Thank you" to her son.

"Aunt Laura if she falls asleep you can leave her downstairs, I'll carry her upstairs when I return."

"Go on child, I'll handle these you leave here."

Cassandra went out the door spotting the interior lights to her uncle's car as he pulled up. She smiled as she got in on the passenger's side. Her uncle returned her smile, put the car in gear and adjusted the radio. Cassandra was his favorite. He often told Laura and Mary that Cassandra was the innocent one of all their children. They both looked at him and shook their heads telling him there was a lot about her he didn't know.

Cassandra had her faults like their other children, but she handled most of her problems on her own. She didn't ask for much and they all felt that was her way of admitting she had made a mess of her life in the past. What Earl called innocence was covered by Cassandra's street sense. She had done all there was to do to support herself and her children. Trina was her tell all friend. Her confidant, and in some incidents she had been Cassandra's savior. There were nights when Cassandra didn't make it home to her children or had been beat so bad she couldn't have them see her that way. Trina stepped in and watched them and her. She knew about Trevor and his hateful ways, but she also knew there was something that would always attract Cassandra to him.

Trina knew first hand that Trevor was a good lover, but his right hand was fierce. That's where her experience with him ended. She wouldn't put up with his physical threats or acts of violence. Cassandra fell in and out of love with him. Trina tried him once, during a brief separation he and Cassandra had. She didn't love him as deep as Cassandra. Now they shared his bed whenever passion called for it.

Earl asked Trina about Cassandra and Trevor, whenever he would see her in town. Trina denied knowing much, but Earl knew better. Trina understood the game, love or abuse Cassandra would always be there. She also knew there would be trouble between Trevor and Cassandra if she was to stay with her mother for a while.

"How's Trina and her mother?" Earl turned the radio down so he could hear Cassandra's answer.

"They're doing fine. Trina has a new job as a customer service representative. Her mother is still into rehabbing houses."

"That's nice. Trina still don't have no children, huh?"

"No, she says they take a lot of time to raise, and time is one thing she's short of."

"Now how would she know that?" Earl chuckled at the thought.

Cassandra caught a glimpse of her uncle and smiled. They spent time together like this when she was younger. He would always take her and her cousins to Maryland to fish. The time they shared was memorable and Cassandra loved hearing her uncle tell her how proud he was of her. That had been years before Trevor or the children, and she certainly didn't have any merits for his praise now.

"What have you been into? Are you still working at the bank?"

"No, I'm starting in a program for cosmetology in two weeks. I want to start my own business, a hair care and health spa."

"Whew, big dreamer; well, you need to buckle down to get that done. What you gonna do to support your children? I know you ain't counting on Trevor."

Earl had warned Trevor about putting his hands on his niece. Cassandra never told Earl or anyone else in the family that he had hurt her twice since then. Her uncle was a man of his word. He vowed to kill Trevor and Cassandra didn't want the trouble she lived through to be trouble for the rest of the family. She didn't tell Earl she was still seeing Trevor, even though twice a month didn't amount to much more than sex. Trevor reminded her that was all she was good for at the end of each encounter. She didn't look anywhere else for her own satisfaction.

"Trevor doesn't know yet. I didn't speak to him before I left to come see about Mama. I don't know what to tell him now. Looks like I may have to stay longer than the two weeks. I'll have to tell him and Trina the situation."

"Trina. Why do you owe her an explanation?"

"I rent an apartment with her in a building her mother owns. Well, we room together in an apartment and split the rent and other bills."

"I see. Yeah, it's best you let her know. Your mother may need you by her side for a while. I wouldn't waste time explaining anything to Trevor. It's good you don't need him for nothing."

"Uncle Earl, he is the father of my children."

"Do they know him, his ways, what he has done to you or for you?"

"Uncle Earl, please. Let's just forget talking about Trevor."

"I'm watching you Cassandra. A person doesn't have to say it constantly. I'm waiting for my flower within you to bloom. Stay away from that weed!"

Earl turned the radio back up. He didn't wait for Cassandra to reply. Cassandra looked at him in deep thought. He was a nice looking man. His features would tell he was fifty-two. Christopher had a lot of his features. His complexion was caramel and he had light brown eyes. She knew he was the choice of many women in his day. She looked out the window allowing her thought of him to drift to memories.

Her Aunt Evelyn always smiled when she spoke of the man she married. After her death, Earl spent more time with Laura and Mary seeing to their wants and needs. He never was much for socializing or mingling with any of the women in the neighborhood. There was talk that two years after Evelyn had died, Ma Dear was dating Earl. Cassandra never heard about it from her family, and she never mentioned it to her Aunt Laura or Ma Dear. She took it to be a rumor. Just as the car approached the parking lot of the Holiday Inn, Cassandra's cell phone rang.

"Hello, Trevor let me call you back. No, I'm not coming home. It's a family matter. Yes, my mother. No, I don't know when. They're with my Aunt. I'm…never mind where I am. Where are you? That's what I'm saying."

Cassandra noticed Earl looking at her, listening closely.

"Look, I've got to go. No…I'm not going to be home. Please Trevor, we're not a couple so what's that to you. Look, I've got business to handle."

Cassandra closed her phone and got out of the car heading for the hotel's front door. She called the hotel earlier telling them she would not be staying. They promised to keep her room available until she got there to check out. Cassandra walked back to the car.

"Uncle Earl, I've got to go to the room to get my bags. It may take a minute or two."

"Yeah, call that nigga back and tell him where you'll be so when I have to bust his ass, I can say he was warned. Let him know the rules are still the same."

Cassandra closed the passenger door. Her uncle knew she would call Trevor back. "Damn, is it that obvious? Why can't I shake him?" Cassandra walked into the hotel for her bags. She never made the call to Trevor.

Chapter 5

Cassandra paid her bill for one night and led the bellboy to her uncle's car. Her cell phone sounded as she was attempting to get in on the passenger side. It was Trina, she paused before answering, thinking she'd rather give the conversation distance.

"Uncle Earl this will only take a minute." She stepped away from the car and closed the passenger door.

"Hey girl what's up? Is your Mom's okay? I thought you would have called a sistah by now."

"I've been trying to get a mental hold on all this. Trina, my mother is really sick. My aunt keeps talking as though she's about to die. I don't think it will be this week, but she is really sick. I have to talk with the doctors to get all the details, my mother isn't saying much. It doesn't seem as though Aunt Laura or Uncle Earl know more than I do. I was going to call you after I went back to the house."

"Where are you?"

"I had to go to the hotel to get our luggage. We'll be staying at my mother's house. It will be cheaper for me, since I don't know how long I will be staying."

"Oh, I see. Well, what are you going to do about your things here, the rent, or the program you signed up for?"

Cassandra could hear the doorbell ring. She listened closely as Trina invited the visitor in. She could hear the muffled tones of a male's voice.

"Sandra, I've got to go. Listen, call me when you get settled at your mother's house, I'll be up."

"Okay, I'll call you then."

Cassandra got in the car thinking about the voice she heard. She couldn't make it out. If someone asked her she would have said Trina covered the phone, so she couldn't hear. Trina didn't have many male friends, and because she wasn't in a committed relationship, none of them visited. She'd ask her who the mystery man was when she called her back since she rushed off the phone for his visit.

"Uncle Earl thanks. I needed to handle this before tomorrow. It would have been another day's rate if I had waited."

"No problem sugar. Anything else, I mean while we're out you might as well get anything you may need for you or the children. There's a food store on the way back to the house. Anything those children like special might not be at the house with your mother and aunt."

Earl waited for the answer. Cassandra didn't respond. There were plenty of items she could think of, but she needed to hold on to her money until she could find out what unemployment would do about her living with her mother.

"C'mon girl. I'll tell you what, you and I both go to the store, and you get what you need. I'll pay for it and you'll owe me. Between you, and me no one has to know. Okay?"

"Uncle Earl, it's okay. Those kids can do without that stuff."

"Listen, you don't know how long your stay will be. Your mother won't tell you and neither will Laura. Your mother had a stroke, and they found out, she has cancer. I think it's in her stomach, but she thinks it has spread all over the organs. She's being kept comfortable. She refused the treatments and the operation. Anyway, I don't know all the details but the point is she seems to be living only to die. Who knows how long it will take. Let me help you and those kids. You need to be comfortable while you handle your mother's business. Laura can do the cooking and cleaning, and I'll do all the running around for you and with you."

Cassandra was stunned. *"Cancer"*? She thought her mother's condition was because of the stroke. Paralysis that would last longer than expected, something she was prepared to deal with, not cancer.

"Does Aunt Laura know my mother has cancer?"

"She sure does. Your mother told us after the doctor told her. They gave her all the avenues she could choose from. Your mother chose not to take the treatments or an operation. I don't know what she was thinking. But Laura didn't want to talk her out of it. I was angry for weeks, but it didn't change their minds. So I visit when I know I won't argue with her. She doesn't need that. I'm glad you came and decided to stay. She's changed Sandra. I guess death will do that to a person."

"So I guess we'll be going to the store and things often Uncle Earl. I'll need someone to talk to."

"That won't be a problem sugar."

The two of them went shopping. Cassandra tried to convince her uncle that it wasn't necessary to go down each aisle of the store. He ignored her. It seemed as though he was grocery shopping. Every now and then, he would ask, "What about this or what about that?" Cassandra let him have his way. The cashier totaled the bill to one hundred and fifteen dollars. Cassandra went to speak and Earl gave her the parental eye. They put the bags in the cart and wheeled it into the parking lot. Earl talked about the neighborhood and some of the changes. He promised her a city tour within the next few days.

The conversation went on until Earl drove into the driveway of his sister's house. Cassandra went in the house, bags in hand, thinking of her conversation with her uncle. Earl had given her an update on her cousins Kevin, Reggie and Veronica. She was told they all lived locally, within minutes of her Uncle Earl's home and were anxious to see her. Kevin and Reggie were her favorites. Aunt Laura's sons were older than her by four and five years. Uncle Earl's children were her age except for Veronica; she was two years older than Cassandra.

When Cassandra was club hopping, Reggie posed as her date when she didn't want another man in her ear. Her club hopping days were short lived when Trevor found out where she had been spending her weekend hours. She told him she needed space in their relationship. He beat her on the ride home to her apartment and told her if he caught her in the streets again he would kill her. That's when she took to drugs.

Kevin kept her supply of coke and marijuana. She didn't dare to keep it in the apartment. Whenever Trevor went on his weekend overnights Cassandra would have one of her friends or Veronica keep the children, and she would be high and entertained for the weekend. She never went anywhere and always said she just needed to rest.

The excuse to get the children away worked until Veronica brought the children back earlier than expected. Cassandra was high and enjoying the company of a man from the club for the weekend. Veronica told her she would keep the kids until she got herself together, but if she ever caught her again she would call Child Services on her. Cassandra loved her children and knew Veronica would carry out her threat. It took her three months to stop her weekend madness and get a serious job. She began working at the bank. Trevor dropped in often, usually a payday, threatening to kill a "nigga" if they talked to her. She never knew how he found out about the lunch dates or when she went to the moves. To avoid trouble, she avoided men at all cost. Trevor was her monthly entertainment and that was getting old. Cassandra welcomed the change being at her mother's would bring.

Trevor couldn't visit her at her mother's, and he didn't have a clue about the program she signed up for. That would have to be on hold. She had to take care of her mother first. Cassandra returned to her uncle's car for the last three bags.

"Thanks, again Uncle Earl. I owe you big time. You didn't have to get all of these things."

"You'll be here a while, this will hold you until your check comes through from unemployment. Don't worry about paying me. Take care of your mother and those children for now. Everything else will fall into place."

"Well, thank you again, will I see you tomorrow?"

"Yeah, I promised I would visit. I'll keep that promise. Listen; don't let your Aunt Laura tell you it ain't right for me to buy you this stuff either. She'll say that too. Tell her you bought it if you have to."

Cassandra kissed her uncle on the cheek and went into the house. She knew her aunt would know Earl bought the groceries.

Chapter 6

Trina smiled as she hung up the phone. She tugged deliberately at her cut off jean shorts she wore purposely for the visit. She was sure the skimpy outfit was enough to convince her guest to stay.

"Why do I sense that you're angry?"

"Babe, it's just the bullshit I go through. This bitch is nowhere to be found. I know she got her check today. Tell me you haven't seen Cassandra."

"No, I spoke to her earlier, but I haven't seen her all day."

Trina knew if she told Trevor where Cassandra was their night would be ruined. She was sick of him chasing his lost love all over the city. Trina wasn't stepping in to give him ass and cash. She wasn't that kind of fool. She'd let Cassandra give him her money. Trina would get it from him, eventually. That's the way the game was played. Trina didn't want Trevor that way, but he had four women that took good care of his needs, and she got part of what he got. Rules were she didn't ask questions.

"So, is a brother going to have to ask to get something to drink or what?"

"No, is a brother staying a while or just thirsty?"

"Both, I'm staying and I'm thirsty."

"Good, what do you want to quench your thirst?"

"A beer for now; hey, listen did Cassandra tell you her mother was sick or something like that?"

Trina thought they were past searching for Cassandra. She could feel her thighs heating up, and it had been two weeks since their last rendezvous. Her nipples were beginning to get hard. Trina knew Trevor would notice them through the tank top.

"Babe, did you hear me or what? Did she talk to you about her mother?"

"She said she was sick, but she would call me back with the details."

"So she must have went to her mother's huh?"

Trina returned with two beers and her tank top unbuttoned. Trevor saw her nipples and grinned.

"Getting hot? I got something for that but first let me think a minute."

"Trevor, if she's visiting her mother, she'll call me in a little while, especially if she's not coming home. I think her plans were to go and see her today and tomorrow, and then come home. I guess it would depend on how sick her mother is."

Trevor sat back on the couch as though in deep thought. A sly grin came across his face. Trina took it to mean his thoughts were no longer on Cassandra. She stood up and unzipped her shorts so Trevor could see she wore no panties. The shorts fell to the floor. He pulled her to his side and touched her ankle moving his hands slowly up her leg. Trina parted her legs for him as he began to feel the heat from her thighs on his hand. She moved closer to the couch so he could put his fingers where her pleasures would begin.

Trevor took his other hand and unzipped his pants and pulled out his penis massaging it as he massaged her clitoris. Trina wanted to sit on his face, and as she positioned herself the phone rang. She continued to move toward him, but he sat up.

"Trina answer that it may be Cassandra."

"What the fuck! He's got to be kidding!"

She looked at him. He had stopped caressing himself and her waiting, for her to answer the phone. She rolled her eyes and shook her head as she stepped out of her shorts that had fallen to the floor.

"Hello."

"Trina, its Cassandra. Girl, I feel like I've been here for more than one day. Anyway are you okay?"

"I'm fine."

Cassandra could sense she was interrupting. She wanted to know who the guest was, but she needed to tell her about her mother too.

"Can you talk a minute? I know you have company, must be someone special to occupy your time at home."

"No one special we're just hanging out here instead of his place." Trina lied, keeping Cassandra from questioning the visit. "What's up with your Mom? How is she coming along?"

"Trina, she's got cancer. I don't know when I'll be home; she's at her house living it out. My uncle did explain a little more than my aunt.

I don't think they really want to deal with it at all. My mother refused the treatment and the operation. How does one not want to be well, I mean if they could?"

Trina sat on the couch in shock. She liked Cassandra and was fond of her mother. Although Trina wanted Trevor more than she even understood, Trina and Cassandra were close. Trevor was an addiction, a bad habit she couldn't break. Cassandra had shared her good and bad memories about her mother with her. Trina felt numbness come over her for a moment. Trevor noticed a change in her voice, a quiver, as though she was going to cry.

"I don't know. Wow. I don't know what to say. So what are you going to do?"

Trina tried to contain her emotions. She kept a lot of Trina's secrets knowing that Trevor would still want to visit her. The less Trevor saw of Cassandra the better her chances. She wanted him to herself. She understood it would probably ruin the friendship she had with Cassandra but Trevor was what she thought she needed in her life. He was rough but she liked that about him. He hadn't been abusive towards her, and she felt that Cassandra brought on the abuse she received. Cassandra's secrets were good with her.

"I'm going to the unemployment office tomorrow. I'll see what they say about the program and transferring to a site closer to here. If they don't have it here I'll have to commute back and forth. The program is eight weeks. Four weeks after that I'll receive the certification. I'll have to check things out in this area. Trina, I can't pay you and live here too. I know we have an agreement and all, but I can't see how I would be able to afford it."

"It's all good. I'll tell my mother the situation. She ain't hurting for this rent anyway. She probably was spending it on bullshit. Cassandra, she didn't really have to charge us at all. My brother and his wife live across town free. Don't worry about it."

Trevor stood up from the couch over Trina.

"Let me speak to her."

Trina covered the phone. She waved her hand for him to back up.

"Let me speak to her!"

"Trev, she doesn't even know you're here", Trina replied whispering. "Call her back when I hang up. Damn, c'mon now back the fuck up!"

Trevor walked to the other side of the room watching Trina from the chair across from the couch.

"Trina, Trina, I forgot you had company. We can talk later. Listen thanks for the words of comfort. I thought I was putting you in a situation with your mother. You know with the rent and all."

"It's fine. I'll tell her about your mother. It will be okay. Listen, kiss the kids for me. I guess I'll see them when you visit, or I visit you."

"Who's your old friend? He seems patient. You must have him trained already."

They both laughed. Trina didn't tell her any name for Trevor to go off the deep end. She answered ignoring the question.

"I'll talk to you later. Tell your family hello for me. Take care, bye."

Trina hung up the phone before Cassandra could ask again. Trevor put his hand out for the receiver.

"You can't call her from this phone. Her cell has caller ID, I thought you said you wanted our little thing to be a secret. And besides, what's up with this extra attention to Cassandra, the bitch you don't care about?"

"You're the one that doesn't care. She's the mother of my children; I'll always care about her."

"Her or what she gives you Trevor. I could buy your ass too, I choose not to. I thought you wanted a relationship built on more than finance or material things." She picked up her shorts throwing them on the couch in frustration.

"Trina, know this sweetness. What you give me, I could get from her if I wanted it. Right now you fit my needs. If you want me to fulfill them somewhere else that can be done too. Know your place. She's the mother of my children, and I will always have a place in her life, and she will always be in mine. It's the way I want it, when I want it. Cassandra can't just walk away from me, and I don't know it. Neither can you."

"You're out of your fucking mind. I'm not Cassandra. You're a good layman and that's it. You don't give me shit else that I can't get anywhere else."

"And as long as you want me to lay you down the way I do, you'll always be around. Remember I fuck you, you can't fuck me."

Trevor stood smiling as though he had won a medal. Trina walked to the door and opened it, indicating she wanted him to leave. Trevor chuckled to himself.

"Baby, we both know that ain't happening. If this is the way you want to start the evening, so be it." He moved closer so she could feel the protrusion in his pants.

Trevor closed the door and held Trina's face gently in his hands. Their eyes met and he kissed her long and passionately. That was the spark that rekindled her flame.

Chapter 7

Cassandra got up early the next morning. The unemployment office opened at nine o'clock, and she wanted to get in and out by eleven. Her mother had a doctor's appointment at two, and she wanted to talk with the doctor. She would ask her aunt to watch the kids for her. Laura entered the kitchen and opened the refrigerator.

"You sure bought enough groceries Sandra. I guess being well prepared is good. Do the children eat eggs and grits?"

"Aunt Laura there's not much they don't eat, and they don't have any food allergies. They can eat cereal too. Don't go spoiling them."

"Well, that's just wonderful. I can sneak them goodies and not worry about the allergies telling on me. Girl that's the joy of being older, you can enjoy child rearing. When y'all were coming up, we worried 'cause we didn't know what to do. Well, the worry is on you now."

Cassandra smiled at the thought of her worrying about her children being with her aunt, that wouldn't be her trouble. Laura continued talking never looking Cassandra's way.

"Did Aunt Laura give you that? Oh, Aunt Laura not before dinner!"

They both giggled like teenage girls in high school. Laura pulled out pans and pots to start breakfast. Cassandra could tell she was not on the cooking detail. She began setting the table hoping not to be in her aunt's way.

"Baby, are you going to unemployment today?"

"Yes, and if you wouldn't mind watching the children this afternoon, I want to go with Mama to the doctor's appointment. I want to find out what's going on with her health."

Laura stopped what she was doing and faced Cassandra as she continued to put the napkins in place on the table.

"We need to be there together. We don't go to the doctor with her alone. Earl and I go together. You and I can too, but I need to be there."

The seriousness in her voice told Cassandra she wasn't prepared to handle the doctor's visit on her own. She sat in the chair. Cassandra wanted to tell her aunt, she knew about the cancer, without letting on her uncle told her.

"Listen, you got business to take care of today. Go to unemployment handle that first. I'll watch the kids while you go. Your mother's appointment is late this afternoon. I don't know why they make it so late in the day. Anyway, I want you to go by that recreation center there next to the grammar school. They have a summer day camp and registration is this week. Take your children there and register them. I got you the forms and the money to put them in. It's for the whole summer. They go on trips and have other children for them to play with. I think it starts Monday. They don't need to be underfoot. We'll have a lot of business to get together in the next few weeks. The camp hours will be a help to both of us."

Cassandra thought about it. Kyle was eleven and he had never been to camp. What about Cassie? She had never been left without her brothers being around. Cassandra knew her aunt was right. If her mother was living to die, as her uncle told her, they would have to make preparations. The children didn't need to be around listening to their business or watching their grandmother die.

"I know you're thinking this old woman is crazy. Sandra, I love your babies but your mother's business and her illness is going to need our attention for a moment. If we handle things now we won't have to rush later."

"Aunt Laura, Uncle Earl mentioned how sick Mama was, and now you're talking as though she won't be with us long. What's the truth about her sickness?"

Cassandra thought that would make it easy for Laura to talk. Her aunt was avoiding the point. Her mother was dying.

"Your mother has cancer. Please, don't tell her I told you. She'll kill me, and then die. We've been dealing with it for three months now, maybe four, yeah, four. That's when they told her they had to operate."

Cassandra thought about what Earl had told her. Laura skipped telling her that her mother refused radiation treatments.

"Couldn't they treat it with radiation?"

"Your mother waited too long for treatment. She had the stroke shortly after they told her she had cancer. She never told us. Anyway, we don't know how long it will be. I want to do all I can for her. I know if it was me, she would do the same. I know she wants you with her too."

"Cassie has never been without me or the boys. I don't know how she'll act."

"The counselors will help her through it. It's run by the church that you went to as a child. Ma'Dear helps out on Wednesday's, I believe. Your mother did too until she took ill. They worked with the after school care program, and it rolls over into the summer day camp. On Monday, go with her and sit a while. You'll need her to get used to kids anyway, it's almost time for kindergarten right?"

"You're right." Cassandra sighed.

"I hope you're sighing because all of this is a lot at one time and not because you'll miss that grown woman of yours."

"She's my baby Aunt Laura."

"Girl, please!"

Cassandra's phone rang. She looked at the clock that read eight thirty. "Who is this?" The caller ID answered her thought right away.

"Hey Trevor."

"That's all you got to say?"

"What else is there to say?"

"Where are you anyway?"

"At my mother's, if you had answered your cell when I left yesterday you would have known."

"So you couldn't tell me last night when I called you?"

"Trevor, what do you want this early in the morning?"

Cassandra had grown tired of Trevor's games. When he wasn't trying to stalk her, he was stalking someone else. She knew it. The game hadn't changed since high school. After the baby mama drama with the other women who had children by Trevor, she stopped following him. The fairytale romance had ended. Veronica, her uncle's daughter, told her once he stopped beating her, the abuse would be verbal and mental. It took her some time before she realized Trevor didn't want her to have anyone else so he always made his presence known. He was not interested in raising his children or being a family man.

"Where are you Sandra?"

"I told you with my mother, she's sick with cancer. I'll be here with her and my family. I don't know how long that will be."

"What about my kids?"

"Trevor, cut the shit. Your kids that you try to see once in a blue moon are with me. We are together. I don't need the drama. My mother is sick Trevor. Not that you fucking care!"

Cassandra walked out of the kitchen where she could say what she wanted. When she got upstairs, she gestured to Kyle and the others to go eat breakfast. They went down the stairs laughing and playing leaving her in the room alone.

"So you can talk slick when you're on the other side of town. Is that some new shit you're on?"

"Trevor, I haven't seen you in two months. You don't call or come by on a regular to see your kids. What is it with you? Now you give two shits? Please, I don't think I have the stomach for your nonsense right now. This is not a fucking game. I need to keep it together for my kids and my mother."

"Bitch, I can remember when you kept it together for me. But that shit didn't last either. You can't keep it together because you don't know what it is to keep it together. That's where I fit in or did you forget me?"

"Trevor, we are not together. Remember, when you walked out my door and told me to watch your ass leave; the night you took my money to buy that bitch you had with you some food; the money that would feed your kids? Well, Trevor, I remember. I remember promising our children that would never happen again. It won't Trevor."

"It ain't over until I say so. Don't think I won't snatch your ass right out of your Mama's house."

Cassandra thought about her uncle's warning. Just as she was about to repeat the warning to Trevor, Laura called her. Laura didn't want Trevor delaying her niece's schedule. From the sound of her niece's voice when she left the kitchen, she knew who was on the other end of the phone.

"Sandra, it's almost nine o'clock. If you want to be back in time you need to be leaving soon."

"Listen Trevor, I have to take care of some business. That's my aunt calling me now. My mother has an appointment to keep so I have to go handle this business now."

"What the fuck is up with you Sandra? Your mother never was number one in your book. Let me find out you got a nigga over my kids. I swear I'll bust a cap in a nigga's ass over my kids."

"Trevor, it's not about another nigga. It's about losing my mother. It's about growing up."

"Growing up, what are you saying; I ain't grown enough for you now?"

"Trevor, you ended our relationship. I'm just another one of your baby's mama's. I understand, maybe you don't. I'm okay with it. Maybe you're not. But right now, I don't have time to explain your shit to you. You created this. This feeling I have for you, you created. The distance will do us good, or at least it will do me some good. I need my space. Somewhere you can't invade. I'll call you later."

"I'll see you later bitch!"

Trevor hung up. Cassandra looked at her phone and laughed to herself. There was a different feeling this time. Usually she would start crying wondering what his next move might be. Then she would call Trina and tell her blow-by-blow details. Instead she sighed and grabbed her pocketbook. She checked it making sure she had all the papers and identification she would need.

"Aunt Laura, does the camp need papers on the children?"

"Just the forms I have. If they need any others you can bring them later. Girl you better let go of that phone and get into town before that line is out the door."

Cassandra looked at her watch. It was nine fifteen. The line would be long if she delayed much longer. The children met her at the bottoms of the stair. She kissed her children. Cassie smiled and waved good-bye. Laura gave her a reassuring wink.

Chapter 8

Ma' Dear cleared the breakfast dishes. Terrance ate and told her he would read the paper before going to sleep. It would take him another week to get accustomed to the night shift schedule. Ma'Dear knew he wouldn't be lying down until at least eleven. It was routine for him to read the paper and watch the television until sleep fell upon him. Ma'Dear would pick a project to keep her busy and if the weather permitted, she'd sit on the porch rocking in the fresh air. On Wednesdays and Fridays, she worked for the school monitoring the children in the aftercare program. School had just ended for the year, which meant, next week, day camp would begin. The job would be enough to keep her busy during the week. During the winter months teachers would help with the after school program but during the summer only the volunteers and the school staff from the neighborhood worked. Ma'Dear enjoyed her days because the youth always had something to keep her entertained. Mary worked the same schedule, two days during the school year and five days in the summer. Ma'Dear would miss Mary not being there with her this summer.

Ma'Dear knew now how her day would start. Terrance was on the porch reading the newspaper when his mother stuck her head out the front door.

"I'd better make my way over to Mary's house. Come Monday, those children will be looking for both of us to show up. I won't get a chance to sit with her long then. Terrance, can you run me around the corner to the florist and the drug store?"

"Who you buying flowers for Mama?"

"You know Mary is sick. I want her to see my flowers and read the card. No need waiting until death is upon her. I think I'll visit her this morning. I don't know if she has an appointment. I better call Laura to find out. Can you run me around there before you lay down?"

Before Terrance could answer the screen door closed.

Ma'Dear was in the living room dialing Mary's number.

"Hello, Laura?"

"Mattie?"

"Yes, how are you sweetie?"

"Thanks be, I'm just fine and you?"

"I'm fine too, thank you. I was calling to see how Mary was making out. If it wouldn't be too much on her, I wanted to visit and sit with her a while. Do you think a visit would be too much?"

"She would love a visit from you anytime, you know that Mattie."

"Well I told her Sunday I would see her this week, and the week is creeping away from me. Does she have an appointment this afternoon? I know she usually goes on Tuesdays and Thursdays."

"They keep us running that's for sure. Yes, this afternoon, I'll have to check the time I believe its two o'clock."

"Well its eleven-thirty now. If I got there about twelve-thirty, I could sit with her until she had to go. Maybe give you a little help if you need it."

"Bless you Mattie. Cassandra came home to help with her mother, but your company is more than welcomed."

"To be quite honest with you Laura, I miss Mary's company so much."

"Well, you're right across the street you don't have to make a set time to visit. Shucks, you can keep me company while she's resting if you don't mind me as company."

"No, No Laura I don't mind you as company at all."

"Well, Mattie we'll see you in an hour or so. I'm sure Mary is looking forward to seeing you."

"Do you need anything? Anything I can get for you?"

"No, your company is what we need the most."

"Alright then, I'll see you shortly."

Ma'Dear returned to the porch talking as though she never left.

"I should have known something was up when I saw Cassandra yesterday. Laura says she's come home to help with Mary. You know what that means Terrance?"

"What does it mean Mama? Cassandra can't be but so much help, she's barely helping herself."

"And you know all that from seeing her walk by here yesterday."

"I just know. Cassandra ain't the same as she was when she left here Mama. You can tell that by those four children she has following her."

"Terrance, just because life threw you a clean path doesn't mean others don't have to walk through dirt."

"I'm just saying, I don't' think Cassandra can be much help to Miss Mary. Cassandra came home to get what she could get. She's an only child, whatever Miss Mary has is hers."

"Well I sure pray that Cassandra is a better person than you see her to be."

"They say praying helps."

"Terrance! How bad could Cassandra's life have been that you don't think she can change?"

"Trevor Black, that no good Negro she went to her prom with. When she got with him, he took her life for a nose dive."

"That's who was beating on her?"

"Yeah, still does probably. She can't shake him. She did shake the drugs and his money but that was four kids later. Ma, Cassandra was out there. Mr. Earl's daughter, Veronica used to save her from the beatings and the street. You're right, though she looks a lot better than what I thought she would look like. Maybe she's on the mend."

"Lord, why would she stay with a man like that?"

"Love."

Terrance chuckled to himself. He wouldn't allow himself to get caught up in the love game. He had a fling with a few and Diane, his girlfriend of two years. But if anyone asked, he definitely wasn't in love.

"Well, every man loves different. She has to find the right one."

"Mama, what man is going to want her with four kids?"

"A good man, who will love her, and her four children."

"Well that won't happen. Trevor won't allow it. He follows her like a pimp."

"He won't follow her here. If he is what you say, Earl won't allow him near her or the house."

"Let's just watch and listen. She's the kind of woman that loves the abuse."

"No one loves abuse Terrance! She doesn't know love. She needs to learn the difference that's all. Enough for now about Cassandra, run me to the florist and the drug store for a card."

Terrance looked over his paper noticing Cassandra was on her way without her four shadows. Terrance smiled to himself thinking, *"Yeah Ma, here's your proof. She's slipping away, leaving her children with her sick mother and Aunt. Yeah, she sure came home to help out."*

Chapter 9

T revor picked up his boxers and went into the bathroom to shower. The thought of Cassandra living where he couldn't run in and out of her apartment when he wanted to was bothering him. Although he had other women to entertain him and pay his way, Cassandra was special. She was his first love. Trevor could remember making love to her the first time. Cassandra was scared but wanted to please him in any way he asked. She was sweet and innocent. He promised to protect her and keep her from the "nigga's" that meant her no good.

Cassandra's family was the only barrier, her uncle and cousins would interfere the most. Trevor told her to choose between him and her family. She left home. He soon grew tired of her questioning where he was and playing house. The only way to keep her home and out of his business was to threaten her.

He would stay out; bring other women around; harass her on her job; and during it all, beat her. Cassandra took it all, that's when Trevor realized he didn't love her anymore. If she stood up and gave him a fight he might have felt differently. As he got older the stronger women turned him on. He was the father of her four children and that was his holding card. The romance was short lived, but he couldn't let her go. He was certain she would be around whenever he called. Their relationship had ruined her self-esteem and her chances to be with those who showed interest in her.

Cassandra was a good woman, and although he wouldn't admit it to her, he knew it. If she bounced back and could make it without him, he would look like a fool. Trevor made sure, she was not available. If anyone asked, Trevor was her man, and she was in love. Trina walked in the bathroom putting her naked breast against Trevor's wet back.

"Are you rushing to leave me?"

"What business does Cassandra have today? And don't give me that bullshit that you don't know?"

"I don't! Damn, can we have our time together without you mentioning her name? You said it was over between you two. Well, I can't tell!"

Trevor turned to face Trina. He grabbed her face holding it tighter than she expected him to. She tried to squirm away from his grip.

"Don't try me Trina. Cassandra has some business she claims she's got to handle. Call her and find out what it is, and don't ask me no more damn questions about me and her!"

Trevor shoved her away from him and walked out of the bathroom. Trina stood holding her cheeks in shock. Looking out of the bathroom she could see Trevor putting on his shirt. The phone rang before Trina could use it.

"Hello."

"Trina, its Cassandra."

"Hey, girl. What's up?" She asked with no true concern.

"I need you to look in my room for the program code. It's on my dresser in the mirror. I think they can transfer me into the program close to my mother's house."

"So, you're going to the hospital with her now?"

"What the hell are you talking about Trina?"

"Okay, let me get the number."

Cassandra looked at the phone from the other end. Trina put the phone down and Cassandra heard silence.

"It doesn't say program code. It says, oh, here it is. The code is six, zero, nine."

"Thanks are you okay?"

"Sounds like your friend wasn't what you expected."

"Yeah, you could say that. Listen, how long will you be at your mother's. I mean, will you be coming here to get more clothes?"

"Yes, that's me. Listen, Trina they're calling me. I'll call you when I get out of here."

"Okay, later."

Trina put the phone in its cradle. Trevor walked to where she stood and kissed her on her cheek.

"So, what's the business?"

"Something to do with her job, I think she's got to sign up at unemployment, I guess she can't work where she was or something like that."

Trina was growing tired of Trevor following Cassandra's every move. She was glad Cassandra's mother's house was off limits.

"She's going to call me to let me know how long she plans on staying with her mother. It could be permanent, who knows."

"Is that what she said or are you hoping that's what it will be?"

"Both."

Trina lied to see what response she could spark. Trevor kissed her on her lips. He could feel the rise in his pants but decided to ignore the feeling. He needed to catch Cassandra at the unemployment office.

"I'll take care of this jones I got for you later. What plans do you have for today?"

"I don't know, call me."

"Shit, girl if you want this you better be where I can find you."

"Call me."

Trina watched Trevor walk out her door. Trina liked the cat and mouse games they played.

"Let the games begin."

Chapter 10

C assandra left the unemployment office pleased with her progress. Her files would be transferred from the office where she lived to the office near her mother's house. The information clerk had her wait for a processing clerk who would be able to help her.

Ms. Johnson called her in her office and explained the requirements for the program she was enrolled in. Cassandra was informed that the program for Cosmetology would begin in two weeks, what she needed and where she would report. The school offering the program wasn't far from her mother's, which would save her traveling time. Cassandra didn't have a car but there was a bus that went right pass the school. The bus stop was in walking distance.

She explained she would be living with her mother temporarily and due to her condition, she didn't think she could work. Ms Johnson assured her that as long as she attended the program her checks and benefits would continue. Cassandra signed all her paperwork and thanked Ms. Johnson for her help.

It was noon when she walked out of the unemployment office, and she still had to register the children in the day camp. Cassandra walked to the corner and waited for the next bus. Trevor spotted her walking to the corner and decided to make a u-turn and park. He watched to see where she was headed. A black Lexus pulled up to the corner. He couldn't see the driver clearly, but he could tell by the smile on Cassandra's face, she knew who the man was. Trevor felt a rush of anger taking over him. He waited to see whether Cassandra would ignore the man's attention.

"Lamont, how are you?"

Lamont smiled returning her greeting. "Can I offer you a ride?"

"I don't want to take you out of your way."

"Cassandra, you could never take me out of my way. I'm going to my mother's, there's no hurry. I wouldn't mind your company and conversation if you have the time."

Ma'Dear had called Lamont and Sylvia telling them that Cassandra was home caring for her mother. Sylvia didn't seem too concerned but Lamont told her he would see her soon. Ma'Dear knew that meant Lamont was looking forward to seeing Cassandra again. He wasn't dating and his last relationship told him he needed time before his next commitment.

Cassandra reached for the handle of the passenger door but hesitated when Lamont got out of the driver's side to open it for her. Trevor, watching from across the street, sped off making the tires on his car screech. Lamont was the last person he expected to see. Although they never had a confrontation, it was understood that Lamont had feelings for Cassandra. Trevor felt threatened.

"Thank you."

Cassandra grinned timidly, as she adjusted herself in the seat. Her dimples still showed a touch of innocence. Lamont wanted to know everything she had done, where she had been, was she married, and so much more. He waited before asking any questions. She wore a yellow sundress topped off with matching sandals and handbag. The color set off her bronze complexion. Her hair was pulled back neatly into a bun. Lamont was pleased; she still held her natural beauty.

Lamont looked just as he had the last time Cassandra saw him. She and Trina were out on the town going from club to club looking for Trina's cousin. The night was almost over when Cassandra spotted Lamont on the dance floor. Now looking at him, she couldn't imagine he stopped to pick her up. The girl he was with was all over him, and he seemed quite pleased with her presence. Lamont had always been attractive and manly. He didn't have the pretty boy features that would make girls swoon. His look was clean and sharp. Lamont could have been a model for an ad campaign. Lamont wasn't the modeling type but an ad for cars or tools would have a special touch with his look. Cassandra didn't speak to him that night, but she made a point to talk about his looks with Trina. Now sitting next to him, she kept her thoughts to herself.

"So where can I take you."

Cassandra paused before answering. She wanted to say anywhere you want to go, but she decided not to be forward. She remembered quickly her four children and Trevor, whom Lamont knew nothing about. "Too much baggage girl, he'll never be interested in you."

"I've got to go to the school around the corner from Grape Street. I'm glad it's not out of your way."

"I would have taken you, even if it was. How have you been?"

"I can't complain. Things aren't as bad as they could be."

"I can understand that."

"Do you still live on Grape?"

"No, as a matter of a fact, I was coming to spy on you."

"Spy on me?"

"My mother called and told me you were caring for your mother, I wanted to see you."

"You said spy, that means watch from a distance."

"Well, I think the last I heard you had a reason for people to watch from a distance."

"Well, there's no reason now. I'm caring for my mother and that's about it."

"No husband?"

"No."

Lamont hadn't gotten the answer he wanted to hear. Terrance had told him about Trevor and the four children. He wanted Cassandra to tell him. He could understand her being devoted to her mother and children, but she hadn't mentioned them at all. He hoped Trevor was a part of her past.

"What's up with Mr. Black?"

"Mr. Black? You mean Trevor? I've gone my rounds with him. I have to admit I waited too long to end the relationship, but he showed me his true colors, and I'm not blind anymore."

"Hmmn. I hope you don't mind my questions."

"No. How about you? Are you married?"

Lamont smiled. The thought of being married after his ordeal with Gwen seemed impossible.

"No, I'm not. I don't know if marriage is for me."

"Dating?"

"Now dating is a possibility. Are you offering?"

Cassandra smiled. She could sense that Lamont was teasing her to relieve the tension in their conversation.

"No, I mean, that's not what I was asking. Are you dating anyone? Is there someone special in your life?"

"No, we broke up about a month ago."

Lamont turned the corner and pulled up to the school stopping at the playground entrance. Neither of them wanted the conversation to end.

"What's going on at the school? Isn't the school year over?"

"Yes, I have to register my children for summer camp."

"Children? How many do you have?"

"Three boys and a girl; eleven, nine, seven and five."

Cassandra looked at Lamont when she answered to read his non-verbal response. Lamont turned off the ignition before he spoke.

"A girl, is she like her mother was when she was little?"

Cassandra smiled. She could remember Lamont teasing her when they were younger. Her mother would tell her that Lamont and Sylvia didn't want to be bothered with her company and stop being a nuisance to them. Since they were older than her, she would seem to always be in the way. Terrance didn't want to be around them much but Cassandra felt special when they paid attention to her.

"I don't know what you're talking about? Her mother wasn't that bad, was she?"

"No, not bad at all. When can we talk? I would like to visit your mother if that's possible. I think I sat with her right before her stroke. I run in and out, visiting my mother, but I haven't stopped to see your mother in a while."

Cassandra was surprised. She didn't know Lamont had visited her mother. As she turned to look his way her cell phone rang. She looked at the number and ignored it.

"Look, I know you have to go. Let me give you my business card. Call me. Don't worry about the time, just call."

"Lamont, you can visit my mother without my input. There's no need for me to have your number."

Lamont looked at Cassandra and she realized the reason he gave her the number. She could feel herself blushing. "This man can't possibly be interested in me."

"Okay, when should I call you? I don't want to call at a bad time. This is your business?"

"Yes, do you remember Sean Moore, my close friend?"

"I think I do."

"Well, he and I own the business together. It's a body shop on Eleventh Ave. We've been in business for ten years. It pays the bills."

Cassandra's phone rang again. She glanced at her watch. Lamont looked at her waiting for her to speak.

"I'm not answering it. Do you have a pen? I don't have a business card, but I will write my number down for you."

"That's fair enough. What time will you be finished here? I may still be in the neighborhood."

"This will only take a minute. I wanted to go with my mother to the doctor but my aunt warned me against it without her being there. I didn't understand it but I won't question it. I'll be at my mother's house the rest of the afternoon."

"Well, I…"

"I wasn't suggesting you should visit then or anything I was just saying you can call me when you're about to leave your mother's. Maybe I'll step outside to say hello to your mother."

"So you didn't visit your sweet Ma'Dear? How long have you been back?"

Cassandra laughed giving Lamont the paper with her number written on it. She could recall visiting Ma'Dear every day, she loved her company. Ma'Dear showed her how to knit and crochet. They sewed on the sewing machine and Cassandra even learned how to make patterns for doll clothing. Ma'Dear spent a lot of time with her, time, she thought about often.

"I guess thinking about my mother has me behind in getting reacquainted with friends."

"Listen, you handle your business. I'll call you when I'm leaving my mother's. Promise me you'll answer your phone."

His comment made them both laugh. Cassandra got out of the large truck and thanked Lamont for the ride and the conversation. As she walked into the playground she looked at her phone. It was as she thought. Trevor had left another message. Cassandra entered her code for her messages and deleted them.

Chapter 11

Mary was sitting in her bed enjoying her visit with Mattie. The two of them talked about the times they had with their children growing up and the children they had adopted working within the school programs.

"I sure wish I could see Lucille's face Monday when she sees Cassandra's children at the camp."

"Mary you know she's not gonna believe that baby is Cassandra's, and that Kyle, her oldest, is a handsome thing too."

"Mattie, Lucille loved Cassandra so, I don't think she has seen any of her children. But that Cassie is the spitting image of her mother when she was her age."

"Well, her children are well raised, that's for sure. Cassandra didn't fall short in making them respect and obey. They have such beautiful manners."

"Mattie that will soon wear off; you wait until they get used to living here. You'll be yelling from across the street."

"You know it, reminds me of how you would yell at Terrance and Lamont."

They both laughed. Mary held her chest until the pain she felt subsided. Laura walked in the room with a pitcher of lemonade.

"Refills ladies, Mary, how are you making out?"

"I'm doing okay Laura; I think a visit from an old friend is doing my spirit fine."

"Well, I'm glad I could move your spirit."

Laura set the pitcher on the standing tray that held the remains of the lunch she made for Mary and Mattie. She poured lemonade for the three of them and stacked the dishes to take them to the kitchen. She sat down to join the conversation.

"Mattie, I tell you, being this sick is rough. You know I don't want Laura and Cassandra to have to care for me like this. It seems like the more I want to get better the worse I feel. Today, I woke up with a prayer on my heart for today only. I asked God to let me be able to feel a little better just for today. I'll deal with tomorrow when it comes."

"Well, prayer works. Look how you're sitting up and talking. Mattie, we're so glad you stopped by."

"Laura, I would have been visiting more often. I've been running the past few weeks. Doctors, paying bills, you know Terrance is staying with me now."

"Terrance? Is he alright Mattie?"

"Yeah, Mary that man is fine. He thinks something is wrong with me. I have to admit I forget things now and then but what does he expect I'll be fifty five next month."

"Everyone forgets things now and again. So he moved home Mattie?"

"Laura, I don't even know when he officially moved in. I guess it was so gradual I missed the transition. He told me he was changing shifts down at the bus station to help take me around during the day. I still don't like driving, you know. Anyway, the next thing I knew he was coming in sleeping, eating and leaving for work from my house."

"Mattie, are you sure that girl of his didn't put him out?"

"Mary, you know it could be. I asked Sylvia the other night on the phone if she had seen Diane. Diane works in the same office building downtown as Sylvia. She said they spoke in passing but that was it."

"Weren't they living together?"

"Laura, at one time they were talking marriage. I haven't heard nothing about that in a while though. I don't think he was living there, you know, I think he was staying with her off and on. He was living with Lamont before he moved home, in Prospect Court."

"Lamont lives over in those condos?"

"Yeah, Mary, your heart has a condo and a new Lexus."

"Lord, I sure wished Cassandra would have taken up with him instead of that dead ass Trevor."

"Well, who knew, Mary, I can remember you telling her to stay away from Lamont."

"Laura, I told her to stay away from Trevor too. If she was going to disobey, she should have chosen Lamont."

They all laughed. Mary picked up the remote and turned the channel looking for the local news.

"It must be past noon the news is going off."

"Yeah, close to one o'clock. Cassandra should be back shortly. You and Mattie call me if you need anything, I'm going to make these kids lunch."

"Where are they Laura? I don't hear a sound."

"They're in the yard and Cassie is taking a nap. They're really no trouble, must be a blessing to have four that don't tear up."

Laura walked out of the room calling the boys in for lunch.

"Mattie, I don't know if Cassandra can handle this by herself."

"Mary don't you worry about Cassandra. Laura, Earl and I'll include myself, won't let her or you down. You just rest your mind about that. Things will work themselves out. Cassandra is moving in isn't she?"

"Laura said she was getting her business straight this morning. I don't really know what that included. Mattie, I don't want her to feel uncomfortable, but she can't have the life she had living here."

"I'm sure she knows that."

"Trevor can't even visit here. I mean that Mattie. He has beat my child; I mean bruised her physically and mentally. If I could I would kill him, and murder ain't never been on my mind for no one."

"Don't work yourself up. God will take care of all that trouble. You'll see."

"I hope I live to see it Mattie. Truly, I do. Now where is she supposed to start her life with four children and no education or a job?"

"What was she doing before she came here?"

"I think she was working at a bank, but Mattie, I don't think she has any intentions on working there anymore. She enrolled in a cosmetology program with a dream of having her own salon."

"Well, that ain't bad money. It takes long hours and work. She'll see it through if she wants it bad enough."

"I just hope that her living here will give her some balance, at least enough to leave that fool alone."

"What time is your appointment? I don't want to wear you out talking."

"You sit right here. All I do is take those pills and sleep. It will do me some good to get worn out talking. You mentioned Sylvia, how is she?"

"Still dating her boss' son. I don't know what she sees in that white boy. She's crazy about him though, and he seems to love her."

"Well, what can we do Mattie?"

"Pray that's all Mary, just pray."

Chapter 12

Lamont left Cassandra thinking about their conversation and looking forward to talking with her again. Maybe he would consider entertaining her or at least visiting her now and then. Cassandra always held his interest. In their younger years, he sat in the background and watched. He finished his thought out loud.

"They say good guys always finish last."

Lamont parked in his mother's driveway. He noticed Terrance's Explorer was parked on the street. Lamont opened the door to his mother's house with his key, letting himself in. The house was quiet. He searched the first floor for his mother or Terrance.

"Ma, Terrance, anyone home?"

"Yeah man. I'm upstairs. Mama is across the street visiting Ms. Mary."

"What's good in the fridge?"

"There's leftovers in there if you want some, if not cook."

"Come on down and talk with me. I'll heat enough for you."

"I'm good man. I'll be down in a minute."

Lamont went into the kitchen to look in the refrigerator. He pulled out three bowls and took a little of each putting them on a plate. Terrance came in smiling while towel drying his hair.

"Man, I didn't mean to rush your shower."

"I was done, what's up with you? What brings you on this side of town?"

"Your mother called saying I hadn't been over in at least two weeks. So I decided I would stop by."

"Who's at the shop?"

"Sean is there and the rest of the crew. I had to come this way to pick up a contract anyway."

"Anything long term or just one time work."

"I hope it will be long term. There's a company with a fleet of Medical Vans. You know, ambulances, medical care vans that type thing. Anyway, they need a shop to maintain their vehicles and repair them when needed."

"Good money. So the deal is settled."

"Just about, I'll talk with Sean, but it looks good to me."

"Yeah well our mother is across the street. Ms. Mary's been sick a while man. I don't think she'll recoup from this. I believe they said she has cancer. Ms. Laura has been living with her, caring for her. Mr. Earl has been by quite a bit too. That man is still crazy."

"I like Mr. Earl. For that matter, their family is pretty cool.

I went to see Ms. Mary, at the hospital and her home, about three or four months ago, right after her stroke. I told Mama I would get over here to visit her too."

"Well you can kill two birds with one stone, they're together. I think Mama said Ms. Mary had an appointment this afternoon though. So if you're going to see her today, you better run over there now."

Lamont thought to himself. Perfect, I can go over there and sit a while after Ms. Mary leaves for her appointment. That's if Mama doesn't see through my motives." Mattie would know that Lamont had another reason for his sudden visit.

"Your girl is staying there now, her and her children."

"My girl?" Lamont attempted to act surprised.

"Man, you still can't cover those feelings. Cassandra, she came home to help care for her mother."

Lamont didn't want Terrance to stop talking so he just listened as he spoke. He would wait to tell Terrance that he saw Cassandra earlier. Terrance gave him all the gossip about Cassandra and Trevor and her bumps and bruises, since she left home. The gossip told on the bus spread quickly.

"I didn't know she had been through all that with Trevor."

"I told Mama last night that Cassandra must enjoy the attention he gives her. She hasn't left him alone."

"They're still together?"

"Man I don't know. He can't come to Ms. Mary's house. Mary, Laura and Earl would whoop his ass. So if she's here I know he's not far, probably stalking her."

"But you said they were still together."

"No, I said she hasn't left him alone. The talk is that he comes around whenever she gets paid. You know, welfare, I guess. Anyway he comes to collect. But I guess she'll have to take it to him now. A couple of people I see on the bus know her. They tell me in conversation during their ride. They talk about her and everyone else. You'll see her when you visit."

"How does she look?" Lamont was fishing now to see how reliable Terrance's sources were.

"They said she was beat down. I saw her yesterday and I couldn't really tell. Makeup does wonders though. She still has that limp."

"Limp, what limp?"

"They tell me she has a bad leg. Trevor broke it once during an argument. He beat her in the face too. That's why they say she wears makeup."

"Terrance, stop. I saw Cassandra today. She's still a beauty. No makeup necessary. Now I'm not saying Trevor didn't beat her, but she healed fine. I didn't notice the limp, but I'll notice in time."

"What do you mean in time? Come on Lamont, don't tell me you saw her and hooked up with her already."

"No, I saw her and gave her a ride to the school around the corner. I told her I would call her later, nothing more than that for now."

"For now? Man, that chick has four kids! What you going to do for her other than tap her off for Trevor to get mad and kill her?"

"According to her, she's done with him. We'll see. I'm not rushing into anything. I just got out of a relationship. I'm not looking for anything. She's a friend and I'd like to rekindle our friendship."

"Watch yourself bro. You've got your own business, a house, and you don't need her to slow your roll."

"My role is slow, slow and careful. I don't intend on getting involved with trouble."

"Well she has trouble written all over her. Plus, she's been used and abused bro.; she has issues, both in and out of bed."

"How would you know about her issues in bed?"

"Abuse, man, abuse. Women that have been abused can't be good lovers. They're always reflecting back on the nigga that abused them."

"Man, take that shit somewhere. I'll let you know."

"See that's what I'm saying, in your mind you already have her in your bed."

Lamont smiled and slapped his brother on his back as he passed his chair heading for the living room.

"Watch yourself man. You know you get whipped fast. Don't get caught up in Cassandra's drama."

"Don't you get caught up in the gossip. If she's abused, she'll need a good friend that ain't scared of Trevor."

"You're going to do what you want anyway. Don't say I didn't warn you."

"I'll probably get a warning from Sylvia and Mama too. But I'm just looking to be her friend for now."

"I'm just thinking it's a dead end Lamont. She's got four kids, you have none. Even if it did work, she's not going to want more children. Then you're stuck with Trevor's girl, and Trevor's kids. It drove you crazy to see them go to the prom, and now I see it continues to drive you crazy. Trevor Black won that one over. Man, let her go. That's dirt you don't need to turn over."

"Thanks for the advice man, but for the record, if she's not with Trevor it's his lost. You and no one else can speak on the future or her wants. Look man; let's just leave it where it is. I'll be okay. My love life is about shot anyway."

"So you and Gwen are really done?"

"Really done. I don't even want to talk to her."

"Lamont, you really should. It may give you closure. That way you won't slip and rush into anything too soon with Cassandra."

"Man, I don't plan on slipping. Gwen was doing her thing for months. I just thought that if she wanted someone else she was too old for games."

"So Gwen and the dude were dating for a while."

"Terrance, they were dating, vacationing, planning, you name it. They're supposed to be getting married this October."

"Man you're joking! When was she going to tell you?"

"I guess if I hadn't walked in on their love making session, she wouldn't have told me."

"At her place or yours?"

"Her place, she wasn't totally insane. They were so busy they didn't hear me open the door. Clothes were dropped in the foyer, and they were busy on the couch. The couch I bought."

"Damn, right in the living room?"

"Man if I didn't know her I could have got my thing off just watching. They were getting their shit off."

"What did you do?"

"I threw the keys on the table. The noise interrupted them and when they noticed who I was I was on my way out the door."

"And that was it?"

"Yeah, for me that was enough."

"So how did you find out they were dating for a while and getting married."

"Her friend, what's that chick's name that lives over on Fourth Ave?"

"Oh yeah, that fine thing, uh, Tasha. I think that's her name. No, Taysha."

"Yeah, that's her Taysha. She called me about a week later asking about Gwen picking up her things from the house. I thought you mentioned a conversation between you and Gwen."

"I spoke to her right after it happened. She didn't tell me what the problem was, just that it was over."

"Well anyway, Taysha and her man came by and picked up Gwen's boxes. I had packed them already. I don't think I ever want to talk to her again. It ain't easy man to see your girl getting her shit off with another man. I can't even say that I'm mad at him. She knew where we were in our relationship, or where I was. I loved her and no one else. So I got raw love. I don't have any plans on rushing into anything with anybody. It's going to be a while before I commit like that again. I wanted to marry her. Man, I'm glad I didn't make a fool of myself."

"I wonder what she told that nigga."

"Probably some shit about me being shot out over her. It doesn't even matter. Listen; let me get across this street. I do want to see Ms. Mary."

Terrance looked at Lamont giving him a smirk. He knew it wasn't Ms. Mary he wanted to see. He walked out the front door with the newspaper in his hand and took a seat in the chair on the porch.

Chapter 13

T revor parked his car on Grape Street, two houses before Cassandra's mother's house. He spotted the same car that approached Cassandra in Dearling's driveway across the street. It confirmed his suspicions of who was driving the car that picked Cassandra up at the bus stop. He had been sitting waiting for her to come out of her mother's house for more than ten minutes but no one had entered or left the house. He dialed Cassandra's cell number for the third time, since she left the unemployment office. The phone rang four times and went into her voice mail. Trevor slammed his phone closed.

Trevor watched as Lamont came out of his mother's house with Terrance. He couldn't make out the conversation, but he could only imagine Lamont bragging about spending time with Cassandra. Lamont crossed the street and walked up the steps to the Smith home. Trevor watched, hoping to catch a glimpse of Cassandra opening the door. Laura opened the door and hugged Lamont inviting him in.

"This shit ain't going down like this. I warned that bitch! No nigga is going to be over my kids!"

Trevor sent a text message to Cassandra on his phone. He pressed each key with force. *"Bitch, ain't nobody playing games with you! Call me; I'm outside your Mamma's house watching this shit going down. Don't make me go off Cassandra!"* Trevor's phone rang and he answered not looking at the caller ID.

"What the fuck is going on!?"

"What's wrong with you?"

Hearing Trina's voice heightened Trevor's anger. He thought Cassandra was calling him back. Another idea came to him.

"I'm glad you called."

"You don't sound like it. What do you mean, what's going on?"

"Trina, do me a favor baby, call Cassandra and tell her she better call me now!"

"Trevor, I don't want to be mixed in your shit."

"You put yourself in it when you starting sleeping with me. Call that bitch and tell her to call me."

"Yeah, right!!"

"Trina, call her now."

"Trevor, when are you going to give up on that relationship?"

"I don't have no relationship with her, she's got my kids, and I want to see them."

Trina heard this excuse, whenever he was jumping from bed to bed with his other women. Cassandra had never fit into that category. Trevor always referred to her as different. Whenever he wanted to visit her, it was always that they needed to talk. Trina didn't know what to think, but she wanted him to leave Cassandra alone before Cassandra caught on to them being lovers. Although she wanted to be with Trevor, she didn't want to lose Cassandra as a friend. If Cassandra found out about them after they had separated Trina could explain them getting together as a comfort session. Trevor didn't care about their friendship. Trina was caught in the middle. She hung up the phone and dialed Cassandra.

"Hello, Cassandra."

The voice message continued, saying to leave a message after the beep. Trina disconnected the call and dialed Trevor's number.

"Trevor I didn't get her either. It went right into the voice mail."

"Shit!! Oh, wait, I got to go."

Trevor hung up the phone watching Laura, Mary and Mattie coming out of the house. Lamont was helping the ladies down the stairs and into a car in Mary's driveway. Cassandra was standing on the porch with Cassie waving. Mattie came back up the stairs with Lamont, and they watched the car back out of the driveway and head down the street.

Trevor didn't know what to do. He wanted to know what Lamont and his mother would do next. He decided if they left Cassandra, he would definitely be knocking at her mother's door. The trio and Cassie took seats on the porch. Kyle and Chris came out the door running. Taylor was peeking out from the front door. Mattie took the boys in the house, leaving Cassandra, Lamont and Cassie outside. Trevor wanted to move his car in a better position but thought twice about it. He didn't want Cassandra to spot his car.

Trevor got out of his car and opened the trunk. The view standing near the curb was better. Whenever Cassandra looked his way, he ducked behind the opened trunk. He pretended to be searching in his trunk when he turned to a familiar voice.

"Hey daddy, did you come to pick us up?"

It was Kyle. He had walked down to the vehicle without Trevor noticing. He stood up and looked toward the house to see if Cassandra had noticed him. She was standing on the porch waving her hand and smiling.

"My mother said to ask you are you sitting here waiting for us? I can get Chris and Taylor for you. Are you taking just us or Cassie too?"

"Go get Chris and Taylor and come right here to me."

Trevor watched as Kyle ran down the street and up the driveway into his grandmother's backyard. Cassandra had returned to her seat. He knew Cassandra sent Kyle to his car deliberately.

Kyle returned with his brothers. Trevor gave each of them, five dollars and a hug. He sent Cassie's money with Kyle. The children watched as he got into the car and pulled off. He slowed down when he passed the porch where Cassandra, Lamont and Cassie sat. Cassandra picked up Cassie, so she could wave. They both smiled at Trevor as the car passed. He couldn't hold his thoughts.

"That Bitch!"

Chapter 14

Cassie stayed with her mother and Lamont on the porch until Taylor came and asked her to play with him. Cassandra brought a pitcher of iced tea with two glasses and set it on a standing tray.

"How about some iced tea?"

"That would be fine. Your daughter is cute."

"Thanks, living here she's going to have to get used to being able to run around freely."

"Do you live in Philly still?"

"Yeah, closer to the University though, we're in an apartment and my kids don't have the freedom they have here. You know, a yard, the run of the house. They probably think we've struck it rich."

Lamont was glad his mother and Laura had helped him break the ice. It was their suggestion, he stay and "sit a while". They winked at him as they helped Mary out the door. Mattie agreed to stay behind also. She promised she would clean the kitchen and have it ready for Laura to prepare dinner.

"Well, they'll be spoiled rotten before it's over. What's up with Trevor? How long had he been sitting there?"

"I don't know, wait, let me get my cell phone I think I can tell by his calls."

Cassandra walked into the living room and picked up her phone. She noticed Trina had called and dialed her number.

"Hey Trina, what's up?"

"Girl, what are you doing?"

"What are you talking about?"

"Trevor was here looking for you, and then he called back saying you needed to call him right away and stop with your damn games."

Trina knew playing two sides wouldn't pay off but Trevor would be easier to deal with if he knew she had spoken to Cassandra.

"Ain't nobody playing games. That nigga's buggin'. I went to unemployment. I registered the kids for camp, and I came here to my mothers. He had the nerve to be sitting in front of my mother's house calling me on my cell."

"What was he calling you for?"

"Trina, he can't come here, nowhere near here. My mother has a restraining order on that ass. Not to mention my uncle would kill him. So, I noticed he was playing stalker, and I sent his kids to see him at his car."

"So he got to see the kids."

"Trina don't fall for that. Trevor didn't come over here to see his damn kids. Anyway, I've got company. I'll call you later."

"Company?"

"Yeah, you ain't the only one who has an unexpected guest."

Cassandra smiled and hung up the phone. She felt brand new. She didn't want to say that coming home was the best thing for her, but if it gave her time to get on the right track she could accept it.

Lamont was talking with a neighbor on the sidewalk in front of the house. He kept looking over the man's shoulder to see if Cassandra was on the porch. When he saw her come to the door, he excused himself ending their conversation.

"Cassandra, I'll be there in a moment."

"Take your time. I left something inside. I'll be right out."

Cassandra went back in the house to the kitchen where Mattie was finishing the dishes.

"Ma'Dear, I just wanted to say thank you. My mother enjoyed your visit today."

"Sandra we enjoyed each other. This ain't my last visit. I told your mother that I would be around to help you and Laura through this thing. That's what I mean to do."

"Well, I didn't want you to leave without me thanking you."

"Where's those sweet children of yours. They are pleasant to be around."

"They should be in the yard. That's where they ran off to."

"Did Lamont leave?"

"No, he's talking to the guy next door. I just wanted to tell you thank you."

"Girl, no need, no need."

Chapter 15

L amont and Cassandra met in the doorway. There was an obvious pause as they caught themselves waiting for the other to make the first move.

"The neighbors are watching." Cassandra heard Lamont's whisper, and she was quick to whisper back.

"Let them watch." Lamont smiled and held the door open for her to pass him.

"Did you want to go inside?"

"No, I was coming in to see if you were okay. I figured you and my mother were talking, she can go awhile once she gets started."

Cassandra smiled. "She's almost done in the kitchen; I was telling her how much I appreciated her help and her visit."

"So, how long will you be here with your mother?"

"I'm not sure. I just signed up for a certification program, so I guess I'll be here until the program is over. If my mother still needs me after that well, I'll make other arrangements then."

"Understandable, so, when does your program begin?"

"In two weeks; that will give the children time to get situated in camp. I'll need to get the rest of my things from my apartment, at least more clothes."

"Do you drive?"

"I do, but I don't own a car. That's something else I'll be saving for."

"How are you going to get to your certification class?"

"The bus goes right by the High School where the classes will be held."

"What time are the classes?"

"They start at nine in the morning. They said that the ending times change depending on the class for that day."

"Well, I wish you luck. You never did tell me about Trevor stalking you."

"I don't know if you can call it stalking. He just isn't used to me being at my mother's."

"You mean being out of reach?"

"Lamont, really, it's not like that anymore. We've done our share of damage to each other. His only reason for wanting to be around is he wants the kids to know he's their father."

"And they don't know that?"

"It's hard to explain."

"Yeah, I think I have the picture."

Lamont was beginning to add the pieces together. Terrance told him she had been abused. Trevor had her making excuses for him to stay around. Terrance warned Lamont of getting himself involved, but he could see Cassandra had set new goals that Trevor wouldn't allow her to accomplish. Lamont thought about their past. He never told Cassandra about his interest in her when he returned from college his first year. He should have stayed in touch things may have been different. Lamont thought about his flings, dates that never meant anything more than a quick lay. Cassandra would have meant so much more. He never thought to ask her for a date. Lamont's thoughts about Gwen and what could have been made him shake his head.

"What's wrong?"

Lamont got up from the chair where he sat and propped himself on the porch banister. He looked up the street pass Cassandra as he spoke.

"I was just thinking that things would have been so different for us if I had only asked you to the prom."

"That's been more than ten years ago Lamont. We were kids, at least I was. Besides my mother would have fell out if you invited me to your prom. I was in grammar school, no, my first year of high school. No one takes a freshman to their prom."

"No baby, not my prom, yours. I should have been there with you instead of Trevor Black. Now what senior doesn't take a college man to their prom?"

Cassandra blushed. She couldn't help herself. Lamont was right. If he had asked her she would have said yes. Trevor barely went to school, but his reputation and looks made every girl want him.

Cassandra would have passed him over for Lamont. That year was the year he began to abuse her. The thought of what she missed made her want to cry.

"I didn't upset you, did I?"

"No, I was just thinking. You're probably right. Lamont I've been through so much, my head is still spinning. I think I'll need the two weeks just to get grounded. It's like I've been away from the real world, and I have to catch up. I mean here we are talking, and you have a business, a home, a truck and probably so much more. I have four children. That's my accomplishment, no job, no home to call my own, no car, I'm so far behind."

Cassandra wiped her tears with the back of her hand. Mattie came out the front door and noticed the two talking. She decided she would just wave good-bye and not interfere with the conversation. Lamont told her he would come to her house before he left to go home. Mattie never looked back she just yelled, "Okay."

"Do you want me to leave?"

"No, I'm fine, really."

"Cassandra, let's start this over. I have always enjoyed your company, even when we were younger. Yes, I know our paths went in different directions. It's funny how fate plays games with one's life. Here you are and our paths cross again. I want us to be friends. I want to help you accomplish your other goals in life and there's nothing wrong with being a mother. Your children are beautiful. There's one thing I must ask you though before we go any further. Are you still in love with Trevor?"

No one had ever asked Cassandra that, not even Trina. She didn't know what to say, she had never thought much about it. Their relationship was a routine. They both went through the motions, and it just repeated itself over the years. No, she didn't love Trevor, but he was like an old shoe, he fit. Cassandra was accustomed to him treating her the way he did. She accepted his abusing and using her in and out of the bed. She didn't know any other love.

Cassandra looked at Lamont. He had asked his question and turned his back to look out over the street. She knew this was to give her time to think without looking him in the face. He turned to face her slowly, and it was at that moment that she knew she wouldn't deal with Trevor any more.

"No, I don't love him."

"He's the father of your children."

"Yes, that he is; our relationship, without love will ruin them if I let it continue. Kyle is old enough to understand and the others will see it too. They need to be in a loving home. Lamont, I've been with that man, no boy, for twelve years, and I had to think if I loved him. No, I don't love him."

Lamont turned back to the street to keep Cassandra from seeing his pleased expression. He decided to change the subject.

"When do you want to get your other clothes?"

"I'll probably call my uncle later and ask him."

"I'd like to take you if it's okay. We'll have to pick up my truck."

Lamont wanted Cassandra to have no contact with Trevor. He would use her two weeks to introduce her to new treatment. He'd start by being a supportive friend. Terrance was right, he was slipping, but he didn't care.

"It's okay but, I don't want to tie up your time."

"Cassandra, let me help you. Really, I want to. As a friend, that's what friends do."

Cassandra knew Lamont meant more than that but again, she didn't care. Lamont Dearling by her side was what she needed to keep Trevor away. Lamont's friendship couldn't hurt.

"When do you want to go?"

"I guess the sooner the better."

"Your mother and your aunt should be back shortly, how about, I ask my mother to watch your kids. You'll have your things here tonight."

Cassandra looked at Lamont. He smirked and turned his head as if to ask, "Well?"

"I don't want to burden your mother Lamont, I just got here."

"Believe me; she'll love to do it for you, for us."

Cassandra kept her thoughts to herself, *"For us?"*

Chapter 16

Laura and Earl followed the nurse to the waiting area where they had sat repeatedly for the past few months while Mary was seen by her physician. The room was comfortable complete with magazines and a plasma television. Most of the women loved watching the daytime talk shows. Today the show was Dr. Phil. The topic was of no interest to Earl or Laura. They buried their heads in different magazines.

The usual visits allowed time for them to consult with the doctor if they needed. Today Laura wanted to talk with Dr. Stone in private. Since Mary's stroke the doctor was familiar with Mary's family and answered their questions, whenever she could. Laura requested extra time with the doctor on the phone before they arrived. She didn't want Earl or Mary to become suspicious, so she waited until Mary came into the waiting area. Earl was always anxious to leave and stood when Mary approached their seats.

"Did everything go well Mary?"

Mary gave her brother a pert look, and before she could answer Laura spoke.

"Earl, why don't you take Mary to the car, I want to check the date for her next appointment."

"Laura, I have all the information, you don't need to check behind me. C'mon, you and Earl both. It's the same as always."

Mary passed them slow and deliberate determined not to have a delay in their departure. The valet parking attendant would have the car at the door shortly after they gave him the ticket and Mary was feeling the length of the day. She planned on sleeping throughout the night without feeling the normal aches and pains. Earl was caught between what the two sisters wanted. He looked at Laura and then Mary waiting for one of them to give in to the other.

Laura continued to walk to the office door without hesitation. She needed to talk to Dr. Stone, and she was sure it would only take a few minutes. Earl nodded, not fully understanding what was going on, but he turned and followed Mary, who hadn't turned around to notice Laura was not walking with them. Laura stepped in the door and took a seat across from the doctor's desk. She waited patiently, looking around the room at the doctor's certifications and diplomas.

"Good afternoon Mrs. Perry. My nurse told me you had questions about your sister Mary's condition. I hope I can clear them up for you."

"Good afternoon Dr. Stone, I hope you don't mind my questions. However, my sister explained her condition as hopeless. I mean she said there is nothing that can be done but make her comfortable with the medication. I'd like to know with all the treatments that are possible isn't there one that would give her a better chance?"

"Mrs. Perry I don't quite understand, perhaps you should tell me what Mary told you about her condition. There are certain things by law that I am prohibited to discuss with you. However, I'll answer the questions that I can."

Laura wasn't ready for the next five minutes of their conversation. Although the news she received should have made her feel relieved, she was stunned and growing angry.

"Dr. Stone, I don't understand. Why would Mary lie about terminal cancer? She had my brother and I believe that the cancer would spread throughout her body."

"Mrs. Perry, your sister's condition is not terminal. Yes, she has cancer. It is breast cancer. I believe her fear is a mastectomy."

"But Dr. Stone, all the medication? Isn't that to prevent the cancer from spreading?"

"Yes, Mrs. Perry. Mrs. Smith elected to take medication to shrink the mass in her breast. Most of the medication she is taking is related to the stroke she suffered. She has a long way to go for a full recovery. Both conditions have taken a toll on her."

"Why would she lie though? Why tell us it's worse than what it really is?"

"I hope I haven't caused any problems. I would like to see Mrs. Smith through this to full recovery, but I can't force her to undergo the surgery. I can only hope the cancerous tissues react to the medication.

It's a longer process and time may not be on our side. If you do reveal to your sister that you know the truth, please, talk to her about the risk she is taking."

Laura was already thinking about the talk they would have; but before she talked to Mary about her medical risk, she would explain how she was risking family trust.

Chapter 17

K yle saw his Aunt's car pull into her driveway, he waved as they walked onto the porch.

"Ma'Dear let me wait for you out here."

Kyle opened the door so the ladies could enter. Laura and Mary smiled, pleased with his manners.

"How did things go? Mary, how you feeling? Sit here I'll move to the other chair."

Ma'Dear gave Mary her seat. Mary sat back and sighed. Taylor and Chris came from the family room when they heard voices in the living room. Cassie followed the two with her thumb in her mouth.

"Mattie, where's Sandra?"

"Lamont offered to take her to pick up her things at her apartment. He said he would save Earl the trouble of having to do it this weekend. I told them go on; I would watch the children for her. I didn't have the key to lock up so here's where we've been."

Mary rolled her eyes and shook her head. Mattie and Laura looked at Mary waiting for her to speak.

"That child of mine, Laura, that's why I hesitated when you said it may be good for both of us. She ain't been…Kyle y'all go on and watch TV now, I don't need ya'll in my mouth while I'm talking."

"Kyle, there's fruit in the refrigerator for y'all if you want. I'll start your dinner in a minute."

"Laura, excuse me Mary, I started the corn on the cob for you. I saw you had it out. I wasn't sure what else you had in mind."

"Mattie, thank you honey, I didn't think we would be as long as we were. We stopped to get her medication refilled and that Earl…"

"Don't ignore me Laura! I said that's why I hesitated when you wanted to call Sandra here to help out. I agreed because I thought time away from that damn Trevor would do her some good."

"Mary, she's with Lamont not Trevor."

"I hope she's not using your son Mattie. That's what I'm saying. She knows Trevor will be around, what was she thinking? I don't want Lamont mixed up with her mess."

"Mary, I've learned with both my sons, they pick their own dangers. Lamont knows what Trevor's about."

Mary shook her head again before answering.

"Yeah, but he don't know Sandra."

"And neither do you Mary." Mattie and Mary were stunned. Laura continued.

"Listen, Sandra has been gone close to six years. She's been to hell and back, we all know that. Mattie, if you don't, I'm quite sure you can fill in the blanks. That man she's been with wasn't our choice but who are we to choose for her. Now, since she's been back she's talked about getting her act together. I'm gonna repeat to you what I told her about you being sick. Sandra won't ask us to help her. She got that stubborn streak from you Mary Smith. If we support her goals and her dreams, now that she has some of her own, I think she'll be fine. Lamont will be a good friend for her. Now if more comes of that, again, that's her choice. Mary they are grown. Trevor can't come here and if Sandra chooses to see him, I'm sure we won't know it. Sneaking off with him is what started this mess. Let's not force her to sneak again."

There was a long moment of silence.

"Well, I agree Laura. Let's just be there for her. Mary is there anything else I can do for you today dear. Terrance will be wondering where I am. His memory ain't what it used to be either. I'm going to leave you for now good people. If you need anything, call. Listen, if you need somewhere for the kids to go you know the camp opens Monday."

Mary was silent as though in deep thought. Laura's words struck a chord. She failed so many times with Sandra, and she hoped her stay would repair the damage. In time, she would tell them her fears of a mastectomy and the reason she chanced the cancer spreading. Maybe she would get the chance to tell Sandra that she thought she wouldn't come home, unless she felt her mother was about to die. Laura spoke breaking the silence.

"Sandra went and signed them up today. They'll be there."

"Good, I told Kyle about it, he seemed excited. Well, I don't want to stay too long. Mary, do you need help to your room?"

"No, thanks Mattie, I want to talk to Laura a minute."

"We can talk in the room if you want, listen, Mattie, see you, hear?"

"I'll talk to y'all tomorrow."

As Mattie walked out the front door Laura sat in the chair opposite the couch where she and Mary could talk face to face.

"Mary, we need to talk. Clear the air. I need to fix dinner too. Let me help you to your room and get you settled, when I bring your dinner in, we'll talk."

"That's not a problem Laura, I think you're right, we do need to talk."

Laura helped Mary to her room. She paid close attention to Mary's movements and how and when she complained. She was sure by the end of the talk they would touch on the subject of her condition. Laura wanted to know why Mary lied.

Chapter 18

Trina opened her apartment door after the bell rang four times. She wasn't sure whether she wanted to hear Trevor whine about Cassandra. His complaints were getting on her nerves. Trina knew Trevor was using her friendship with Cassandra to find out information on her whereabouts. She wanted to know there was a chance for her to be Trevor's full time love. She didn't worry much about the other women Trevor slept with, for most of them, he was just one on their list of men. Everybody played the game. Trina didn't want to play anymore she wanted to know where she stood. It seemed like as long as Trevor was connected to Cassandra, she still stood on the outside. Although Trevor would say during pillow talk that she was who he wanted to be with.

"What's wrong with you not opening the door? Didn't you hear the bell? You don't live in no mansion, got me waiting at the door. What's wrong, huh?"

Trina walked away from the door and returned to her place on the couch. She grabbed the remote and turned the channel on the television.

"Cassandra ain't here and she didn't call. I don't know where she is."

"I know where she fucking is, who asked you? What the hell is wrong with you?"

"I wanted to get that over with. Seems like that's all you want me around for, to keep tabs on Cassandra."

"Look Trina, she left here to see her sick mother, and now she's not coming back here for a while. My kids are where I can't see them when I want to, that's the problem. She's with that nigga Lamont. I saw the two of them on her mother's porch. That's the problem."

"What? The problem is you can't see the kids, or she's got a nigga?"

Trina wanted to smile from ear to ear.

"If Cassandra's guest was Lamont then maybe Trevor will leave her ass alone." Trina tried to remember if Cassandra ever mentioned him to her. She heard the name but nothing that connected Lamont and Cassandra as anything more than friends. It didn't matter, if Trevor thought she had moved on, maybe he would be done with chasing her.

"Trina, don't play with me. I didn't say she got Lamont, I said I saw them together."

"Okay, make me understand, not about the kids, but about seeing her with this guy Lamont."

"Now you gonna pretend you don't know this brother."

"I don't. Cassandra never mentioned him. If she did it wasn't nothing for me to remember."

Trevor thought about it. Cassandra told Trina everything, all their arguments, about her feelings toward Trevor, his love making, everything. Lamont was new on the scene if he wasn't Trina would have known.

"Bet. Cassandra has new moves now. She's trying to make it without you as a friend or me."

"You, as what Trevor?"

"What do you mean as what?

"You said me as a friend, so what are you to her now?"

"Bitch please, me as Trevor. That's all. Always there, just like I'm here for you. Don't I take care of your needs?"

Trevor leaned over to kiss Trina on her forehead. Trina moved continuing her questions.

"So you've been fulfilling Cassandra's needs lately? I thought it was about the kids. Maybe that's why you're upset about her new friend, you think he's fulfilling her needs?"

"Cassandra ain't like that. Can't no man just walk in her life and replace me. No, I ain't been fulfilling her needs. I want her to know what she's missing. She don't need nobody filling her head up with no wild ideas about her making it on her own or with them. Like I said, it's about my kids."

Trina repositioned herself on the couch, which told Trevor he had struck a nerve. Trevor knew Trina had a head on her shoulders. It would take some time to change her ways. Trina was independent. Their relationship would be different than any of the others. Trina would demand more. Trevor wasn't ready for that commitment.

"What did you cook?"

"Nothing, I wasn't hungry."

"Not even for me. I told you I would be back."

He moved on the couch inching closer until he was close enough to nibble on Trina's ear. Trina ignored his movement. There was so much she wanted to say; but saying it would only start an argument.

"Listen baby, I understand. You don't want to be in the middle of this. I don't want you to be. Cassandra makes bad decisions at times. She needs you and me to help her, you know that. Think about it. She relies on your opinion even when she's mad at me. We owe it to her and the kids to be there for her. We're the only ones who really care about her. Trina, I love you because of what you do for Cassandra and the kids. I really do."

Trina heard what he said but couldn't believe him. Her thoughts held her anger. "You love me for what I do for Cassandra and the kids? Nigga, you got it twisted. I did that to get with you!" She was angry with herself. She was the fool in the middle. She knew Trevor loved her because he could use her.

"Trevor if that's what you love me for, don't come here, just call, you can still get the damn information. There's no need for us to be playmates at night if I have to hide what I feel in the day. I got with you because I thought we stood a chance. Fuck Cassandra, and you can take care of her and your damn kids! I don't want the job no more!"

Trevor sat back. No woman had ever told him what she wanted that way. All the other women, including Cassandra, didn't show any resistance to the way he wanted to treat them. Trina was a challenge. It brought him new excitement. Trina got up from the couch and went in the kitchen. Trevor knew it would take time but, Trina would be his, the way he wanted her to be.

"Trina, listen."

Trevor stood behind her at the kitchen sink. He wrapped his arms around her waist.

"I didn't know you felt that way. Look, I'm sorry. I don't want you to be in a spot, you know, in the middle. I thought you and me, you know, it was all about sex. I didn't know about the feelings you had. You're different Trina. Now I know I'll have to treat you different."

Trina was melting. Trevor broke the ice when he told her she was different. Trina was now on an emotional high. She felt she won the grand prize. Trevor felt her giving in. He turned her around and kissed her long and passionately.

"C'mon, for starters, no more talk about Cassandra and the kids. When I'm with you that's it; I'm with you. What's that movie you're watching? C'mon baby, let's just relax, it's been enough excitement for one day."

Trevor led Trina to the couch. He sat on the couch opening his legs for Trina to sit in between them and lay her head back on his chest.

"Sit up a minute baby; let me take off my shirt."

Trevor took off his shirt and kicked off his sneakers. This gave Trina the sign that he would be staying for the night. As she leaned back, she smiled to herself. "You're right, I am different!"

Chapter 19

Lamont parked his car in front of his house. Cassandra sat waiting for him to open her door. His home wasn't far from Grape Street, their old neighborhood. The street was lined with trees in full bloom and houses with beautiful landscapes. Cassandra could remember the vacant land prior to the development being built. Lamont's home was on the same street as the townhouses. She wondered why he stopped at his house after agreeing to take her to the apartment for her belongings.

"I don't want it to sound like I want to get you in my house but, would you like a tour? I need to take a few things off the back of the truck."

Cassandra got out, trying to remember what the block looked like before the community uplift. Lamont opened the garage and began unloading his truck. The house was more than she expected with a large front lawn and yard. She couldn't understand how he could afford a home this beautiful. Cassandra met plenty of Trevor's friends that lived in homes like Lamont's, but they sold drugs. She couldn't believe Lamont was single without a woman waiting to reap the benefits of a hard workingman.

"Your mother said you owned a townhouse or condo; I didn't expect your house to be this size or this beautiful."

"The townhouses my mother was referring to sit at the end of this street and continue on the next block. She assumes because I live in this area my house is a condo too. So would you like to see the inside or do you want to wait for another time."

"It's getting a little late; I don't want anyone to think I'm taking advantage of your mother."

Lamont knew his mother would understand, but he didn't know what Cassandra intended on moving, or how long it would take. He turned, hesitating before walking toward the driver's door. Cassandra stopped and walked to the gate that separated the yard from the driveway.

"You have a lot of space here. How long have you lived here?"

"About four years, almost five. I wanted to secure a home while I could enjoy it."

"This is a lot for one person to enjoy, but it is beautiful."

"I bought it with the hopes it would be for two. It didn't work out that way. It's okay, it's mine."

"Okay, curiosity is killing me. I want to see the inside."

Lamont smiled, pleased that she was beginning to relax. They walked to the back door, which allowed Cassandra to see the deck and patio area. Cassandra wouldn't have imagined this as his house or the rekindling of their friendship. The yard was huge with lawn furniture that sent the message, "Relax, stay awhile." They walked onto the patio and used an entrance leading to the family room. Lamont put the key in the door letting Cassandra enter first.

Cassandra had thoughts of the rooms being plain, suiting a man's taste and needs. To her surprise, the rooms were decorated in natural colors with contemporary furniture. The floors on the lower level were tiled in beautiful patterns. Lamont showed her all the extras. The surround sound system and mounted plasma television, he added for entertainment as they proceeded to the first floor.

The den was the room that had the sliding doors that led to the deck. The room showed signs that indicated where Lamont spent most of his time. Papers from business deals and unfinished work were on the desk and a worktable. The room had auto body books neatly placed in a wall-to-wall bookcase, which stood from the floor to the ceiling. Cassandra was impressed; Lamont had good taste in furniture and artwork, which was displayed on the den walls.

The kitchen was a moderate size. Cassandra wondered how much cooking Lamont did. The color scheme was silver and black. The floor was covered with black speckled tile. The stainless steel appliances added richness to the room's appearance. The walls were painted white.

"Do you cook much?"

"Not every day, but I don't eat out often. I'm a homebody. I enjoy every inch of this house. I paid enough for it. There's plenty of room for family or company to come over and stay if they need to. Terrance lived with me for a while. We got into it a couple of times about his lady friends, but he understood my point."

"You didn't want them to stay over?"

"No, I didn't want them cooking in my kitchen. They cook and then they don't clean. Not here, if you can't clean, you can't cook. He understood; if they didn't clean he would. Terrance got tired of cleaning three times or more each visit. It stopped."

There was a step for the sunken living room. It wasn't much different than the family room in furnishing. Cassandra could tell he went to the same store to pick the furniture. It had a fireplace and a mantel, which displayed family pictures. The room had a feeling of family. Lamont's personality, as Cassandra remembered it, was shown in each room.

They stepped up to the hallway that led them to the bedrooms. Each room was colored and decorated with different color vertical blinds and matching bedding sets.

There was a bathroom in the hall, with a double sink, shower and tub. The master bedroom and bath were complimented in the same color scheme. The rooms were a perfect fit for a man. Cassandra was beginning to think Lamont's favorite color was black or gray. The colors gave his room an air of arrogance. One could tell immediately, upon entering, it was a man's room.

"So how do you like it? I decorated it, for the most part, on my own. My mother and sister helped with the windows, the flooring and the bedding sets. I guess you could tell the furnishing was my choice."

"Well, you're the man who lives here. It's your house. Did you ever stop to think that if you got married the scheme of things might have to change?"

Lamont smiled. Gwen said the same thing. It didn't matter; it would be a while before he would want to share his home enough to make changes.

"You're right, but that won't be anytime soon."

"I'm enjoying your tour but we need to get to the apartment. What time is it?"

"Six twenty. We can go out the front door. I'm glad you wanted to see it. Now when I tell you I want you to visit, you won't have the first time jitters."

Cassandra was pleased. She would have Lamont as a friend. *Moving home might not be so bad after all.*

Chapter 20

The children began to eat their dinner talking about how exciting camp would be. Laura prepared both her and Mary's plate and went into Mary's room.

"Has Cassandra returned?"

"No not yet, I think her and Lamont are picking up all her things, not just a few pieces to hold her over."

"Laura, the trust you have in that girl. I don't have it yet. I sure hope she will straighten out the mess she's made in her life and those poor children…"

"Mary, you must be feeling better."

"Why do you say that?"

"Because as long as you were sick you didn't criticize Cassandra, you even seemed glad to see her. Now you're picking at her, questioning her moves and motives. Concentrate on your health and leave Cassandra to me. She'll be fine."

"It's just that whenever she gets with that damn Trevor, she forgets about all else, that will include us and Lamont. Those that want to help her."

"It won't help if every time she walks out the door, we predict danger or a setback for her. She has to recognize it and handle it, herself."

"Hmmn, I just don't know if she has the common sense to leave him alone."

"Mary, why did you lie to us?"

"Lie to who, about what?"

Laura had thought twice about talking to Mary without Earl or Cassandra, but it was eating at her conscious.

"To me and Earl, about your health."

"I am sick, why do you think they're giving me these appointments, the therapy and the medication."

"Mary, the therapy and the medication is for your paralysis. You refused to treat the cancer mass in your breast."

Mary moved her tray from her lap and held her head back. She knew from Laura's statement that she knew exactly what the doctor had told her.

"I don't want you to try to change my mind about this. If I told you it was not a chance, even if they cut, remove, or butcher me; there was no cure for this cancer, then you would leave the possibilities alone. Laura, they can't guarantee anything. They'll cut me bit by bit until I'm dead anyway. The radiation will take my hair, my energy, what good am I to life when I'm hanging on to a hope each day? I don't want that."

"So why not just tell us that."

"Cassandra wouldn't come home, unless she thought I was dying."

"Who said that Mary? Look what you're taking us through. I've given up my apartment and my way of living; Earl has rearranged his daily schedule; and Cassandra…"

"Came home, that's what I wanted Laura. My child by my side for, however many days the Lord allows me to live. My grandchildren, my daughter, my family will be with me. You and Earl have your families in your life. If you should decide I am a burden, would Cassandra be here for me? It's horrible not knowing how or what your children will do when you need them the most. I needed to know Laura."

Laura stood and collected the trays. She didn't know how to comment. She needed time to cry and pray for her sister. She didn't understand what Mary was going through, but she felt deep inside it was wrong but then again, in Mary's desperation for her daughter's love, it was right. Laura needed to talk to Earl. She walked out of the room without responding to Mary's comment.

Chapter 21

C assandra went out the front door with mixed thoughts flowing through her mind. Cassandra could tell immediately Lamont was proud of his truck. The burgundy body and silver chrome of his F150 was polished and buffed, reflecting their faces as Lamont opened the passenger door. The sight of the passenger's seat and the clean interior was an invitation of comfort causing them both to smile.

"Do you need help getting in?"

"I think I can manage. I've always wondered how people get into these trucks."

Cassandra laughed as she attempted to pull herself up. Lamont smiled and shook his head waiting for her to ask for his assistance. When she finally got into the truck, he closed the door.

Lamont opened the driver's side door still ginning. The thought of Cassandra not asking for his help proved she was different. Most women he dealt with wanted a man to do everything for them, even if they didn't need their help. Lamont recognized Cassandra's actions as her new claim to independence. He quickly referred to his conversation with Terrance. "…. *She was abused.*" He hoped he could change her mind about relationships or at least friendships. He wasn't ready to get involved again, but he realized he couldn't bury his feelings for Cassandra.

"Remind me the next time to take your assistance when you offer it. Do you know where the YMCA is?"

There was a pause before he answered. His thoughts were on the possibilities of a new relationship; a serious relationship with someone who would love him. He felt Cassandra staring at him waiting for a response to her question.

"Uh, over near the minor league ball field?"

"Yes, I live in those apartments on Twenty Third Street across from the field."

"I think I know the ones you're talking about. What floor do you live on?"

Cassandra laughed.

"What's so funny?"

"You, being worried about the floor I live on. I wouldn't ask you to carry my things down flights of stairs. I live on the second floor. It's a small walk up. The building is not a high rise."

"Hmmn....Well, I could have handled it."

"So you weren't worried about the stairs?"

"No, not at all, I would have called one of the guys from the shop to meet me that's all."

"Just that simple?"

"Yes ma'am, just that simple."

Cassandra thought about calling Trina, but she looked forward to seeing her face. Trina hadn't seen Cassandra with anyone other than Trevor.

"Do you have furniture to move from the apartment?"

"Trina and I bought the furniture together. I don't need it now, so I'll leave it there. I really don't have that much, other than clothes and the children's things. A few appliances, but my mother has those at her house. I'll leave them with Trina; she'll have a better use for them."

Lamont turned onto Twenty Third Street and Cassandra pointed to the apartment building. The ride wasn't that long, and it gave Cassandra a view of the side of town she hadn't seen in years. She was surprised that she didn't have to give him any directions. He didn't tell Cassandra he knew the area. He was surprised he hadn't seen her; he had a few customers that lived a few blocks over. He parked in front of Trina's car and got out to help Cassandra. She noticed her roommate's car but didn't look across the street where Trevor had parked.

Lamont followed her up the four flights of stairs. She was right, the flights were short unlike most apartment buildings and the building was quite large on the inside. The walls were painted off white and the floors matched giving the interior a pale but clean look. There were only four floors with seven apartments on each floor. They passed the doors in ascending order until they reached the door that read 2E.

Cassandra put her key in the door and stepped inside turning her back to the couch to retrieve her key. She hadn't noticed Trina and Trevor who had dozed off together on the couch. Lamont stepped in noticing the television was on, shedding the only bright light in the room. The daylight was fading from the windows, which gave the room the dim light of early evening.

Cassandra noticed the sneakers at the end of the couch, the shirt thrown on the chair and her memory reflected on Trevor standing by his car earlier that afternoon. He had on the same shirt. She put her hand on Lamont's wrist so he wouldn't move. She put her finger to her mouth indicating for him to be quiet.

"Trina, yo' girl what's up? A sister's gone for a day or two, and you move a man in. Girl get up."

Trevor and Trina sat up. When Trevor realized it was Cassandra, he pushed Trina to the side and stood up reaching for his shirt.

"Don't get dressed because of me. I just came to get my things. Lamont, my things are in this room. I'll get as much as I can tonight, if you don't mind bringing me back another time."

"Whatever you want to do Cassandra, we can come back and get whatever you leave."

"What the fuck is this? You bring this nigga to get your shit? And you think you're gonna come back with him again?"

"Well I'll know to call first, if I ever come back!"

Cassandra and Lamont went into her room. She slammed the door and froze in the center of the floor trying to fight back tears of anger. Lamont walked closer to her, and she turned into him and put her head on his chest. He knew at that moment that she was crushed but wouldn't show signs of it to Trina or Trevor.

Trevor could be heard cursing at Cassandra through the closed door. Trina was trying to get him to calm down.

"Fuck you and that damn mechanic. That's all he is Sandra, a fucking high-class mechanic. I guess you think you've stepped up. Cassandra, it ain't over. That puck ass is gonna have to prove to me, he loves you, cause bitch, I don't think he knows what your trifling ass is about. I made you and I'll break you. That nigga don't want you, and you don't need him. Cassandra, bring your ass out here and talk to me. What the fuck is this shit?"

"Trevor, leave her alone. This is fucked up baby. She shouldn't have to find out about us like this."

Trina was scared for Cassandra. She didn't know how violent Trevor would get, but she didn't want to be the cause of Cassandra getting hurt. She realized the position she was in and had mixed feelings. She was glad everything was in the open, but she wanted to talk to Cassandra about it. Trina knew that conversation would never happen now.

"Trina, this ain't got nothing to do with you or that nigga in there with her. This is between us. Who the fuck does she think she is?"

Trina tried to hold Trevor, pulling him toward her. He snatched away from her trying to gather up his things to leave. He put on his sneakers and paced waiting for Cassandra to open the door.

Cassandra pulled herself together and got two large suitcases from the closet ignoring Trevor's outburst. She packed them with her children's clothes. Lamont followed her directions packing toys, books and other items the children had around the room. There were folded boxes in the bottom of the closet that they packed with toys, books and other keepsakes. Lamont unfolded the boxes and handed them to Cassandra. They packed the room in silence. Lamont knew Cassandra was angry by the way she threw what wouldn't be packed to the side.

"Is there another room or closet you need to get things from?"

"Lamont, I don't really want to come back here. Do you mind if we take it all tonight? What I can't take I'll just leave."

"Listen; get what's important to you and the kids. Leave the rest. We'll replace it later."

"I do have some things in the closet in the living room; our jackets and coats. We'll have to make two trips to the truck to carry all of these things downstairs."

"That's fine, whatever you want Sandra."

Cassandra gave him a small smile; she liked the way he called her "Sandra". She would tell him about it later.

Cassandra cracked the bedroom door and called Trina.

"Trina, can you come here please."

"What the fuck? Trina ain't helping you in this. What the hell is wrong with you Cassandra?"

Trina went to the bedroom once she stepped inside Cassandra closed the door. Trina stood waiting to get what she deserved.

"Listen Trina, I don't want to talk about anything other than getting my stuff and leaving. You can have what I don't take and that includes Trevor and his shit. If I had known you wanted him, we could have done this a while ago. Good luck. I don't want to hear shit about you or him once I leave. All I need from you is my things out of that front closet. I'm not going to stay up here with him while Lamont takes these things down. We're going to his truck, and you're gonna bring our coats with you while we carry this other stuff."

Trina motioned as though she had something to say.

"I don't want to hear it. You're going to do it because the shit is foul Trina, and you know it. Carry the coats and that's it. Save your guilty speech for another time, just do that for me."

Lamont closed the suitcases and boxes. He was waiting for Cassandra to say what was next. The three of them entered the living room. The apartment door was open and Trevor was gone.

"Damn!!" Trina went to the door and looked down the hall. She returned holding her head.

"What's wrong with you?"

"Cassandra you know how crazy he is about you. I don't know what he'll do."

"Well sister that's your problem now. I don't give a damn what he does as long as he stays away from me. If need be I'll file the papers for him to stay away from my kids too."

"Cassandra, you know Trevor loves those kids."

"He can't love the kids Trina, and continue to hurt their mother. Trina just in case you didn't know, I wasn't crazy, I was just in love. By the way, this is Lamont Dearling, my friend. Lamont this is Trina, Trevor's new friend."

Cassandra went to the closet. She found the children's coats and pulled them off their hangers. She searched through the other coats and clothes and turned to Trina.

"Trina, where's my leather and fur coats? My coats are missing."

Trina pushed past Cassandra and searched the closet. She stepped back and looked at the closet in unbelief.

"Sandra, I swear they were here. You know I don't play that kind of game. Trevor must have looked in the closet and took them."

"Trina, don't fall in his shit. It ain't a sweet experience."

Cassandra went to the closet and tossed coats, shirts and sweaters onto the floor when the closet was almost empty she realized Trina was right. Trevor had taken her coats and sweaters. Cassandra slammed the closet door leaving the tossed clothing on the floor. She passed Trina and rolled her eyes.

"This is the bullshit I'm talking about Trina; your bullshit now. C'mon, carry the coats, we'll get the rest."

Lamont and Cassandra walked to the truck in silence. Cassandra looked for Trevor to be outside waiting. There was no sign of him. She knew that meant he would be calling her later with some sob story. Trina was too embarrassed to walk to the truck with them. She waited until they picked up the last of the boxes to carry the coats down; she trailed behind feeling the blunt of her guilt. She passed the coats to Lamont and returned to the apartment without saying goodbye. Lamont watched Cassandra and could only imagine her thoughts.

"Are you okay?"

Lamont was watching when Cassandra went through the closet in the living room. With each item she threw, she threw it with more force. Lamont could tell she was hurt and angry. Now she was racing to and from the truck.

"I'm fine, Lamont. I'm sorry, it's just…"

"Stop, Sandra. Stop a minute. We don't have to rush, slow down; take your time. We'll be able to replace what's missing, and if you want to come back and check that's okay too."

"Lamont, I don't want you to think I put you in this mess on purpose, and I don't expect you to replace any items that are missing. If I had known this…"

"Cassandra, I asked you did you want to come get your things. I should be apologizing to you. I don't want you upset about the missing items. I mean they must be of value, but I really don't want you worry about that, they can be replaced."

Cassandra listened to words and thought of the value. Trevor had spent thousands on her coats, his way of paying her for mistreating her. Maybe it was time to get rid of them; they were constant reminders of his violence. Whenever she wore a coat or sweater, he gave her; she remembered each blow that she received prior to accepting his apology. They were attached to bad memories.

"Yeah you're right and I'm glad I found out about him and Trina; it's more of a reason for a new start. It just confirms everything. I'm just upset at Trina. I trusted her. She must have thought I was a fool. Damn, I thought she was my girl. What's that about Lamont? That's some shit, you know. I tell her the trouble in my relationship, and she talks to me like a sister, and then sleeps with my man. What's that about?"

"Was he or is he your man?"

"No, you know what I mean. Lamont some things are just off limits. You don't listen, give advice and then get with your girl's man!"

"I guess you're right. How long have they been with each other?"

"I don't know. I don't know that I want to know. Shit! Those were my only coats!"

"Baby, Trina's probably right. Trevor took them to stir your emotions."

"Lamont, I left the box with their toys in my bedroom. It's packed already I'll go get it and bring it down?"

"Are you sure?" Lamont wasn't sure Cassandra didn't want to take the opportunity to confront Trina as she would have earlier if Trevor wasn't around.

Cassandra read his thoughts. "No, seriously I'm good. I'll be right back."

She walked the stairs for what she vowed would be the last time ever. There would be no need for her to continue the friendship.

"Okay, that's another loving relationship that just died suddenly."

Cassandra couldn't help but think about how she missed her father and how she would miss Trina. She opened the apartment door with her key. Trina was sitting on the couch crying.

"Cassandra, why didn't you call?"

Cassandra fought back the words she wanted to say. She knew Trina was caught in the middle. Cassandra thought twice about reminding Trina she brought it on herself.

"I needed to call so you could tell Trevor I was on my way? How long have you been fucking him behind my back?"

"Cassandra, I know it seems that way, but we hooked up when you broke up. I was going to tell you but the time never seemed right."

Trina knew Cassandra didn't believe her, she could tell by her response.

"What time is the right time for you to tell your best friend you're sleeping with her ex; the man that kept coming in and out of her life and her bed; the man who almost beat her to death? What are you thinking Trina? Trevor is the same man, he beat me, and he'll beat you."

"I don't think so. I know what not to say or do."

"I did too in the beginning. Listen, I'm okay with myself today. While you're still okay with yourself get away from that nigga. You don't need him in your life."

"Well, I guess you have Lamont now to worry about."

Trina was hurting already. She wouldn't let Cassandra rub it in. She was surprised by Cassandra's new attitude toward Trevor; she hoped Lamont would fill Trevor's place. She knew Cassandra kept Trevor in her life fearing she couldn't find a man that would love her and four children. Trina wanted her to be happy with Lamont then she could finally have Trevor.

"No, don't get it twisted Trina. Lamont is a friend; a true friend. Thank you for another lesson Trina. It's a good thing I'm no longer a slow learner."

"Cassandra, I love Trevor and I love you. I just chose the wrong time to express my love to him. Don't hold it against me. You were right. He's cold hearted but my addiction is the same as yours, his loving. I tried to resist him when you weren't together, but I got accustomed to what he had to offer. I know I stepped over the line, but it was too late I had crossed it already. It was my intention to tell you. You said you were done with his games. When you got with him again I couldn't bring myself to let you know that we had been together. It's been on since then."

"Trina, I meant what I said. I don't need to hear the confessions. You do you. He'll do you too. All that sisterly talk you gave me; I hope you remember it 'cause I won't be around to give it back to you. I trusted you Trina. I loved you more than I loved Trevor. I guess you loved him more."

Cassandra gave her friend the key and walked out the door. A tear rolled down her cheek, she wiped her eyes but never looked back. Trina closed the apartment door and leaned on it crying. She took a deep breath realizing she still had to deal with Trevor. She hesitated as she reached for her phone to dial Trevor's number. He told her to call when they left.

Chapter 22

Terrance walked into the kitchen and noticed the stove was on. He could smell the chocolate chip cookies baking.

"Mama, who you baking cookies for?"

Terrance didn't know where Ma'Dear was. She wasn't in the kitchen, and he hadn't passed her when he came through the living room. The back door was cracked but Terrance didn't give it a second thought. The kitchen got pretty hot when the oven was on.

"Oh, those are for Cassandra's children. I promised I would bake them and bring them over to Mary's house for them tomorrow. Terrance they are the sweetest children. That Cassie looks just like her mother."

Ma'Dear entered from the back porch. Terrance smirked, pleased that his mother hadn't left the door ajar and forgot she was baking.

"What's out in the back? What were you doing out there?"

"Terrance don't start now. I hung the mop up so it could dry. I went over the floor where I made a mess. You ready to eat your dinner? I didn't make much, we had some of the vegetables left over that you cooked last night."

"Mama, I hope you're not getting hooked on Cassandra's kids. I told Lamont earlier, that girl is bad news."

Ma'Dear threw her hand in the air.

"All the gossip in the world won't make me believe that Terrance. You know why? I was with her and Lamont this afternoon. I even watched those children when she left, until Laura and Mary got back. Cassandra has had some bad times, but she's got a good head on her shoulders, and she's determined to be someone. That counts Terrance; her determination means a lot more than what these noisy neighbors may wish upon her."

"Mama, I'm just saying you're gonna get all emotionally tied up with this girl, and she'll be gone without even a goodbye. Mentally, she's done."

"So you say Doctor Terrance. If I gave up on you every bad choice you made where would our relationship be?"

Terrance thought before he spoke. In a lot of situations that Terrance was confronted with Ma'Dear was his only alliance. Sylvia and Lamont would tell him to talk to Ma'Dear for advice before even mentioning it to them. She stood in his corner, right or wrong.

"You're right Mama, but…"

"But what Terrance, trouble is trouble. No matter how it comes in our lives. Some get wrapped up in it, and it takes them a while to get untangled and free. Thank God, Cassandra's on her way to being free."

Terrance didn't think so but he and his mother could debate the topic for weeks, and she would still say Cassandra would be okay. Terrance couldn't see anything positive in Cassandra's path unless Lamont, his mother or her family stayed in her corner. Terrance dropped the conversation knowing he knew more about Cassandra than his mother did.

"Did your sister call while I was out?"

Terrance looked in the refrigerator for the iced tea. He brought out the pitcher as Ma'Dear handed him a glass.

"No, when is Family Day at the church?"

"Terrance, look there at the calendar. I think its next Sunday. Look right there, I put it with the letters and messages for your father."

"Why are you keeping messages for Daddy here?"

"Now look, that ain't any of your business. Look on that church calendar for next Sunday."

Terrance did as he was told, but he sure didn't understand his parent's relationship. They talked more now than the last few years of their marriage. Ma'Dear kept his mail, which Terrance thought was odd, and now she was taking messages. Terrance shook his head and Ma'Dear noticed.

"Don't shake your head. It ain't for you to know. Is Family Day next week?"

"No, in two weeks, I wanted to let Diane know when it was. I think she'll be visiting her family that week though. They'll be at her sisters in Virginia."

"You going with her?"

"No, I'll be here, with you."

"Well, you should go and meet her family. They don't even know what you look like."

"And they won't that weekend either."

"Hmmm. I don't know Terrance Dearling, something's strange about that."

Terrance wanted to say, *"Ain't none of your business,"* but he dared to. The phone rang interrupting Terrance's thoughts.

"Hello, oh hey Sylvia, Mama was just asking about your call. Oh, okay I'll tell her. Bye."

"Terrance! I just asked you did your sister call, why didn't you give me the phone?"

"She's parking the car, she wanted me to pull out so she could have my spot in the driveway."

"Oh, I was about to let you have it in here."

Terrance smiled and went out the back door to move his truck. Sylvia came in and kissed her mother while trying not to interfere with her taking the cookies out of the oven.

"They smell so good Mama. Are you baking for the church?"

"No, Cassandra's children, I promised them I would bake them some cookies."

"Cassandra has how many now?"

"Four. Three boys and the baby is a girl; cute and well behaved."

"For now." Terrance had returned to the kitchen and joined in the conversation, as though he knew Cassandra's children. He washed his hands in the sink before sitting at the table with his plate.

"So how's your new shift brother?"

Sylvia hadn't asked how Cassandra was and Ma'Dear noticed. She made a mental note to question her daughter

as to why. Ma'Dear left Terrance and Sylvia in the kitchen talking. She walked onto the front porch and noticed Lamont and Cassandra pulling up in the truck. She could tell by the load that they had picked up a lot of Cassandra's belongings. Ma'Dear could tell Lamont and Cassandra were getting along well. She was glad Cassandra decided to stay with her mother. She returned to the kitchen to tell Sylvia her brother was outside.

"Sylvia, your brother just pulled up. He's helping Cassandra with her things. I guess she'll be with her mother a while."

"Why is he helping her? Where's her man?"

"You know he can't come to Mary's house. They got a restraining order on him."

"They needed one for her too." Sylvia looked at Terrance when she said it waiting for him to agree.

"Why are you looking at me? Obviously, you know something I don't. Why would Miss Mary have a restraining order on her own daughter?"

"Terrance you remember that night. Cassandra defended Trevor when the cops came. She cussed Miss Mary and everyone else that was outside watching including me."

"Oh that's when she accused you of being with Trevor."

Ma'Dear turned to Sylvia. Sylvia looked at Terrance with rage in her eyes. Ma'Dear knew by her look that she had indeed had some kind of encounter with Trevor and Cassandra.

"Sylvia all that ranting and raving Cassandra did that night was true?"

"That girl was high Mama; she was looking for a way to make her and Trevor look right. What would I want with him?"

"I don't know, you're telling this story. What did you want with him?"

"Mama, you make it sound like you believe I was with him."

"I'm listening to you, but I'm gonna say this; Terrance has been bad mouthing that child, since she returned, telling me that he hears all this about her from gossip on the bus. I'm old, but I ain't stupid. Men don't listen to that kind of gossip. Not the men I know anyway. Now if he heard all that trash about Cassandra from you while you were explaining what happened between you and Cassandra that makes more sense, but you tell me Sylvia, what's the story between you and Cassandra?"

Sylvia's phone rang. She said a silent prayer of thanks. There was no way she planned on telling her mother about her Trevor Black days. She held up one finger and stepped out of the room. Ma'Dear took down a tin cookie box to put the cookies in. Terrance could tell she didn't want to hear what he had to say. He walked past Sylvia on his way upstairs. She reached out to him and pointed to the porch. Terrance went out the front door and waited on the porch for Sylvia to join him. Sylvia ended her conversation quickly and carefully opened the screen door. She closed it slowly not letting it make a sound.

"What were you thinking?" Sylvia spoke softly so Ma'Dear couldn't hear her.

"I'm sorry, I didn't remember that night. Tell Mama what you want. I haven't said a thing about you being with Trevor."

"I hadn't planned on telling her anything. Shit Terrance, what will Mama think if she found out?"

"Hey, you're grown. She can't put you on punishment. What are you scared of?"

"Terrance, I have a good reputation in this neighborhood. If Mama figured it out how long will it be before others remember that night?"

"So, what you saying Sylvia? Cassandra is here because of her mother, there's nothing we can do about that."

"Keep Mama and Lamont from over there, you owe me that."

"What? Sylvia, you're buggin'. Miss Mary is Mama's friend, and she's sick. Lamont was visiting her too before Cassandra even got here. Now that Cassandra is back, well you know your brother had a thing for her. He doesn't even know you had a thing for Trevor and neither does Mama, stop being paranoid."

"Terrance, never mind. Shit!"

"Sylvia, leave it alone. If you don't make a fuss about it believe me, it will go away."

"Trevor won't let it go away. Terrance he still calls every now and then, asking, *Do I miss him?*"

Sylvia could feel her phone vibrating on her waist. She had just told Trevor she would call him back. The drama had already begun.

"I tried to tell you about him, but you fell for his sweet talk. Everybody gets one they don't want to remember, yours is Trevor."

Terrance could tell the way the conversation was going, Sylvia still talked to Trevor. She hadn't learned her lesson.

"This is a problem. I don't know how, but Trevor will make this a big problem."

"What are you talking about Sylvia? Are you seeing him when you want dark meat with your white bread?"

"What the hell does that mean?"

"You're with your boss's son for his money right? White, bread, we both know you love dark meat. That's all Trevor can offer."

Sylvia just shook her head. She couldn't deny that Trevor was pure bedroom pleasure. If he had a job or a stable income she could have stayed with him, she could love him. Trevor didn't have Sylvia's drive, and she wouldn't let him hold her back. Carson had the money, stability and means to make her financially happy. He was average in the bedroom with no improvement in sight. Sylvia had a variety of toys she used to help meet her needs when he fell short.

"Terrance, you and I both know our brother. Lamont is crazy about Cassandra, Trevor knows it. He'll put me in the middle, just because. Terrance you've got to help me. We've got to keep them apart as much as we can."

"Lamont is his own man, Sylvia, that ain't gonna fly."

Ma'Dear stepped out on the porch. She looked at Terrance and then Sylvia.

"So the conversation continued out here? Sylvia you'll tell me in time that I'm sure of. Cause baby, what's done in the dark always comes to light."

Ma'Dear went back in the house leaving Terrance and Sylvia looking at the door.

"Terrance, I sure hope she's wrong this time."

Chapter 23

It was close to ten thirty when Lamont and Cassandra finished unpacking the boxes and suitcases. Cassandra told Lamont he didn't have to help her unpack, but he insisted. The children had been fed and were ready for bed when they returned. After bringing in their belongings Cassandra promised them they could get up early to play with their toys if they went to sleep right away. They ran up the stairs yelling good night to everyone including Lamont.

Laura was in the den on the phone when Cassandra went in to explain Lamont's presence. Her aunt took the time to assure Lamont, his help was appreciated by more than Cassandra. She and Mary appreciated his help too. Lamont passed the den door for the last time and peeked in waving goodnight. Laura, because she was still on the phone, smiled and mouthed "thank you".

Cassandra walked with Lamont onto the front porch.

"Mr. Dearling, I don't know how to thank you."

"Ms. Smith, it was my pleasure."

Cassandra smiled. Lamont knew she was relaxing more. He wanted to continue the night with more conversation but didn't want his stay to appear to be desperation.

"Lamont, I have to apologize for you having to go through this nonsense about Trevor and Trina. I mean, it's a long story, and I don't want to read over all the pages to you. It was more like a bad dream. Anyway, I want to get over that part of my life as quickly as possible. I guess things do happen for a reason."

Lamont wanted to hear more if she was willing to talk. If he understood her point of view, he could dispel the gossip Terrance relayed.

"What things are you referring to?"

"I was referring to my mother getting sick and all. If she wasn't as sick as she is I wouldn't have come home. Lamont I didn't notice the change that I needed until I came home. I would have made out okay, but Trina was with Trevor, and I lived with her and didn't know it. I'm finished with him and her, definitely! It feels like, I got pushed off the cliff, but I have a parachute. I would have landed flat on my face if I had found out about this and still had to live there with her. I don't want to think about what could have happened. And then there's us running into each other, and you suggesting we pick up my things today. It would have been hard for me to get my things without your help, and you know how my Uncle Earl is. If Trevor had been there and my uncle was with me, it would have been ugly. It's just funny how things turn out."

"I'm glad they turned out okay. You'll see things are going to get better. I believe that, even your mother will feel better with you here."

"Hmmmn, that's a separate issue. You don't have all night to listen, and I'm don't want to rekindle our friendship by dumping my load of problems on you. So let's agree to let it die."

Lamont agreed without saying so. He knew enough at the moment.

"It's your lead. I will follow. Do you need anything done tomorrow?"

"I don't think so. I got everything from the house. I won't be venturing to that side of town anytime soon. I'm registered for my program; the children are set for camp. So no, I'm good. Thank you."

"Okay, so can I interest you in an outing over the weekend? I have to go back to work on Monday and my schedule will change daily. But I would like to spend some time with you if you agree."

Cassandra looked in his eyes and knew he was serious. She couldn't believe with the drama, the kids, and her confusion in it all, he would want to spend time with her.

"Well, let me get settled with my Aunt and her schedule of things with my mother. I don't want her to think I'm just here and not helping her at all."

"Sure, I understand that, and Sandra, the invitation to spend time includes your children. We can find some things to do that will entertain them. They can come to my house and play in the yard, whatever you choose to do."

"Lamont, you don't have to do this. I'll be fine."

"No, I have to do this. We'll talk about the reasons later. Listen if your aunt wants to get away from the house, and you're here with your mom, I'll come by."

Cassandra smiled and kissed him on his cheek. Lamont froze. The kiss was a surprise, and now he wanted his lips to touch hers. He stepped closer and kissed her lips fulfilling his wish.

Cassandra felt better about herself when she was around Lamont. She definitely wanted to see more of him and didn't resist his advance. Lamont's caress and gentleness were the touch she needed.

"I'll call you tomorrow after I find out how my mother's daily schedule is run."

"That will be fine, if you need me before then call."

"Thanks Lamont, I'll talk to you tomorrow." She smiled and watched as he went across the street heading for his truck. There was a note on his windshield. It was from Sylvia. Lamont read it and shook his head.

"Don't you have anything better to do with your time? Call me, your sister."

Chapter 24

"**I** don't understand it Earl, Mary told us she was dying, I mean, led us to believe she was just about dead. Did she think about how we would feel?"

"Laura, I told you we should have called the doctor earlier. You didn't want to push the issue. Well now what? She's got that child believing she's sicker than she is. What do you want to do now?"

Laura looked at the phone. She couldn't believe Earl was leaving it up to her to decide what to do.

"I called you to see what we could do about it, not just me."

"Laura, I wanted to call Cassandra when Mary told us about the cancer, you said no. I wanted to talk to the doctor's when she told us how serious it was, you said no. I wanted to talk Mary into the treatment or the surgery, and you said no. Now what do you want to do next? I've gone along with you this far, no need for me to give any directions now."

Laura listened as Earl spoke. Each time he mentioned she said "no" she shook her head.

"Earl, I know, I know. But what can we do? This isn't fair to Cassandra just like it wasn't fair to us. I don't want her to think we agree with her mother's reasons. Maybe we need to talk to Mary and explain the position she's putting us in."

Earl wasn't up for the battle. His reasoning wasn't the same as Laura's or Mary's, his opinion never counted.

"Whatever Mary does is fine with me; that's her child and their relationship. Suppose she doesn't want to tell Cassandra the truth about her illness, what are we going to do, tell her anyway? You are right, the best we can do is explain to Mary, we don't like the position she put us in; but she should be the one who tells Cassandra her condition is not terminal."

Laura thought about Cassandra and Mary's relationship.

"Earl, I guess you're right. If we told Cassandra it could ruin the chance of them having a bond as mother and daughter. Mary will need Cassandra if the cancer does spread. I guess that's my worry. Mary hasn't beaten this cancer, it's there. The doctor said it could spread. If we don't tell Cassandra she'd never know the difference. Mary is sick, it's just not terminal."

"Well, like I said Sis, I'll talk to Mary tomorrow if you want me to. I'm not telling Cassandra anything, that's for her mother to do."

"Alright, you're right. Cassandra is better off here with Mary anyway. I don't know what Mary is going to do when her physical therapy ends."

"How is she coming along with that?"

"She handles it the best she can Earl. The therapist said she's handling the exercises better, but she still has a ways to go. I think by the end of the summer she should be walking better. I don't know about the rest of that side though. If Cassandra plans on staying here with her, I'll go back to my apartment after the summer ends."

"I think that's ample time Laura. We should know more about the cancer by then too. I'll talk with Mary and tell her how we feel. You can say I brought it up to you. She can be mad at me, I don't care. Does that make you feel better about it?"

"I guess so Earl. I just pray Cassandra stays. You know Lamont took her to get her things from her apartment tonight. That damn Trevor Black was there with her girlfriend Trina."

"Is that why she didn't call me? She knew that boy was doing Trina behind her back?"

"I don't think so Earl. Sounded like Cassandra walked in on them; Cassandra and Lamont got her things packed and brought them here."

"You said Lamont was with her?"

"Yeah, Mattie's son Lamont, her oldest boy; you know they live across the street here."

"I know Ma'Dear's son. Well, that should have been a site. Trevor didn't show his ass with him, did he?"

"No, I don't think so. Cassandra didn't say nothing happened, other than she caught the two of them together."

"They were in the bed together?"

"No, they were sleep on the couch together or something like that. Trevor tried to loud talk his way out of it and slipped out the door with

Cassandra's winter coats. That boy ain't never gonna be worth nothing."

"Well Lamont can handle him, that's for sure. You know he had a crush on Cassandra when he was in college."

"Earl, he still does. He just walked out the door. I think he helped her unpack all that stuff of hers. He'll be around, if Cassandra allows him to. I sure hope she's done with that Trevor Black."

"They'll be fine. Just let time heal her bruising."

"Bruising? Cassandra got bruised? When?"

"Her heart, Laura, her heart. She loved Trevor. Lamont will be a good change for her. He's a nice young man; got his own business too. Yeah, he's a good catch."

"I would hope she takes her time the next time she loves."

"They'll be fine."

"I'm talking about Cassandra, Earl."

"So am I. Listen, I'll see you some time tomorrow."

"Earl, thanks, I feel so much better. I'll talk with you tomorrow."

Chapter 25

Trina wasn't looking forward to Trevor's return to her apartment. She knew he was angry and the night would be filled with him ranting about Cassandra being with Lamont. Trina was glad Cassandra had moved on, maybe now Trevor would be more attentive to their relationship.

It was close to eleven o'clock and he hadn't returned her call or knocked at her door. She turned the channels on the television not looking for any particular show, she was beginning to worry. The phone rang; she answered it on the first ring.

"Hello." Trina tried to sound like she was sleeping.

"Trina, what you sleep? I told you I would get back at you later."

Trevor's voice made her feel good. Just the fact that he called let her know he wasn't angry with her.

"I must have dozed off. What time is it?"

Trina looked at the clock as she had every fifteen minutes before the call.

"It's a little after eleven. Look, did Cassandra get all her stuff or does she have to come back."

"She got everything except her coats. Trevor, did you take her coats out of the closet?"

"I paid for them. If I could have gotten some of that other shit she took, I would have. I paid for it. The bitch ain't had nothing. You know that."

Trina just listened. She couldn't imagine what type of relationship Cassandra and Trevor had. Cassandra would say at times, *"When it's good, it's good, but when it's bad, its hell."*

Trina listened to Trevor ramble as she remembered the ups and downs as her friend had explained them. Trina told herself that they just weren't meant to be together. Trevor would be different if he had a woman who knew what she wanted and put her foot down gently. Trina could be that woman or so she thought.

"How did you let them walk in on us like that anyway? What was you thinking?"

"Trevor, did you forget Cassandra had keys?"

"What do you mean she had keys? You took the keys from her?"

"No, she gave them back."

"Oh, hell no! She moved out?"

"I guess that's what you can call it. She took all their things. I don't think there's a reason for her to come back."

"What did she do about the television and the microwave, the big things?"

"She left them and said I could have them or give them away."

"So, damn Trina, why didn't you tell me that when you called?

"Trevor, do you still want Cassandra or what, this shit is driving me crazy. I don't know what to do about my feelings. I just lost a damn good friendship thinking I had something with you and you're concerned about what's up with her."

"Look baby, my concern is for my kids. I don't want Cassandra thinking she's in control, 'cause, she ain't. She ain't been at her mother's a week and she's gonna stay there. Been there two days and she's hangin' with that nigga' Lamont. I need to talk with her to let her know ain't shit changed. She needs to check with me before making decisions that involve my kids."

Trina thought about Cassandra's words. If she got a restraining order on Trevor, he would go crazy. Trina knew Cassandra had enough of Trevor's demands. That's where the arguments between them began. Trevor wanted to tell Cassandra what to do, where to go, and who she could or couldn't see. When Cassandra mentioned it to Trina, Trina listened and planned to step in when Cassandra stepped out. Trina knew Cassandra would follow through with the restraining order. Trina wasn't convinced Trevor's interest was only in his children. Trevor wanted Cassandra to need him for both her and the children.

"Trevor, leave it alone. I'm sure you can see your kids when you want to. She's just upset about seeing us together, you'll see, she still wants you to be a part of your children's lives."

"So what did she tell you about Lamont?"

"What was she supposed to say? She told me he was a friend nothing more. I guess he just offered to help her because he had a truck."

"So does her punk ass uncle. No, there's more to it than that."

Trina had heard all she wanted to hear. Her thoughts drifted. The conversation wasn't telling her he was interested in moving on without Cassandra. *"Well if he wants me, he'll have to show me. Men always want what they can't have."*

She decided to make herself unavailable just as Cassandra had. Trina couldn't be the go between for Trevor and she needed to know if that was the only reason he kept her close or shared her bed. She knew Trevor would be tracking Cassandra until he got it in his head Cassandra didn't want him. She wasn't interested in the drama.

"Trina, did you hear me?"

"No, I'm sorry, what did you say?"

"I said are you going to bed now?"

"Yeah, I'm a little tired. I'll talk with you later.

"Oh, you're not inviting a brother over tonight."

"No, the brother has some thinking to do. You need time to decide what you want to do without me persuading you."

"So you think you can persuade me to do something?"

"No, let's just say I want whatever you decide to do to be your decision, totally."

"Hmmm. Girl you scare me sometimes."

"How's that?"

"Just something about you. If you and I were to get together on the regular, I would have to change to play your type of mind games. My attention would have to be totally on you."

Cassandra smiled to herself. *"Exactly my thoughts, Mr. Black."*

Chapter 26

T he phone rang and Lamont rolled over in his bed looking at the clock on his night table that read seven thirty. If he had to go to work, the ringing of the phone would have been a perfect wake up call. He couldn't imagine who would be calling him knowing he was on vacation. The morning light peeked through the bedroom window. The birds could be heard chirping gaily. He knew he wouldn't be returning to his peaceful slumber.

"Morning." Lamont's answer lacked the good morning spirit.

"Morning, Lamont."

It was Sylvia. Lamont knew he wasn't prepared to deal with her and her imagined drama. Sylvia moved out of the area they grew up in. She had secured a job as the Business Administrator at Klein and Sons, LLC through her relationship with the CEO's son, Carson. The job paid well and she was determined that everyone would know that her status in life had changed. Lamont argued with Terrance and his mother about her airy attitude. They told him she matured and with maturity, there's always change. Lamont kept his thoughts to himself but to him, his sister was as fake as the weave she added in her hair.

"Sylvia, why are you calling me this early?"

"I wanted to catch you before you went to work. Are you alone?"

"What do you want Sylvia?"

"Listen, we need to talk. Are you alone?"

"Yeah, so talk."

"I saw your truck across the street from Mama's, you didn't stop by."

"I saw Terrance and Mama earlier. Why the questions?"

"Lamont, I hope you're not thinking about spending a lot of time with Cassandra. I mean, a lot of time has passed, that old flame can't still be burning."

Lamont sat up in his bed and looked at the clock again. He couldn't believe Sylvia had called him at seven thirty in the morning to question his intentions with Cassandra.

"Sylvia, there'd better be a reason for you asking about my personal life. I don't recall questioning you about your love interests. I am the older brother remember. Unless it is some concern of yours what difference does it make who I spend my time with?"

"It matters Lamont. You, or should I say, our family has a decent reputation in that neighborhood. I don't think that you realize what you're dealing with Cassandra could do to Mama and Terrance, since they still have to live in that neighborhood."

"Well, you make good money. Buy Mama a home and move them out of the neighborhood. Who I deal with has nothing to do with the family's reputation. Do you think those same noisy neighbors don't talk about the fact that you date that white boy? The one who visits the neighborhood for his drugs, or do you think no one notices."

Sylvia was silent for a moment. She didn't know Lamont knew about Carson's runs through the neighborhood.

"That's not what I called you for Lamont."

"Well what did you call me for? 'Cause if you're worried about Terrance and Mama you should cut your ties with your wonder boy and find another love interest who doesn't love you just for the hook up."

"What are you talking about, a hook up?"

"Sylvia, listen, I know about your drugging days. I know you met Carson at the club downtown, and you share the same love. He buys and you know where to get the supply."

"I don't get high like that anymore."

"Baby girl, your weekends are filled with it. I ain't mad at you. Keep it away from Mama and we're fine. Now your boy toy, Carson, I know he keeps you in cash, gave you a job, and probably bought that condo you live in. It's all good, but sister keep your noisy ass out of my business."

"Lamont, it ain't like that. I met Carson at the club, but I don't know nothing about where he gets his drugs or anything about who he knows in the neighborhood."

"And you expect me to believe that his being in our old neighborhood is a coincidence."

Lamont walked through his house looking for his cell phone to check the messages. He knew Sylvia was in shock and wouldn't continue the conversation much longer. Sylvia's attention would now be on who told Lamont about Carson and how much more he knew.

"Lamont, I just called to tell you that, in my opinion, you shouldn't just jump into a new relationship because of what happened between you and Gwen."

Lamont found his cell phone on the fireplace mantel. He picked it up to see if there had been any calls. He didn't comment to Sylvia's statement.

"Lamont, are you alone? Did you hear me?"

"Sylvia, I'm alone and I heard you. Thanks for the advice. Now what else do you want."

"Well, what are you going to do?"

"Do about what?"

"About you seeing Cassandra, I mean you just got out of a relationship with someone who didn't know what they wanted. Cassandra is still dealing with Trevor, right?"

"First of all, Gwen knew what she wanted. She made her choice and I guess, forgot to tell me. As for Cassandra, she's a friend, a friend that I care about. That's it for now."

"Is she still dealing with Trevor?"

"No, but what difference does that make?"

Terrance and Sylvia were similar. Lamont could always tell when they knew more than they were saying. Sylvia would hold information longer than Terrance, but he knew she wanted to tell him more.

"Trevor could be a problem for you, even if all you want to do is be her friend."

"For someone who moved on with their life and moved out of the neighborhood, you seem to know a lot about what goes on in the neighborhood. What is it, you really called to say?"

"Lamont, Trevor is dangerous. He's hurt Cassandra, I'm sure, and he could hurt you because you show an interest in her. Maybe it's not worth what could happen, I mean, just to be her friend."

"Thanks sis, but Trevor is out of the picture. He showed the last part of his ass to Cassandra yesterday. He closed his own coffin. I'm not worried about what he might do."

"What did he do, I mean, how can you be sure she won't take him back?"

Trevor called Sylvia three times and left two messages, both stated it was urgent. She never returned his call. Sylvia had no idea what he wanted to discuss. She hoped Lamont could shed some light on what the problem was.

"Let's just say he pulled a move like Gwen's with her roommate."

"Trina? He was sleeping with Trina, for how long?"

"Sylvia, what's up with the sudden interest in Cassandra and Trevor? I didn't know you knew Trina."

Sylvia had revealed more than she intended. Trevor introduced Trina to her one night when they were out together. Trina was club hopping and made it known to Trevor she was there. Sylvia questioned Trevor about who she was he told her she was Cassandra's roommate.

"I met her once." Sylvia didn't want Lamont to question how she knew her, so she quickly drew attention to Cassandra.

"I guess Cassandra was pissed."

Sylvia remembered how pissed Cassandra was when she found out Trevor was sleeping with her. Sylvia didn't have time to put on her clothes before Cassandra came into the bedroom where she and Trevor had spent the afternoon.

Cassandra never said anything to Sylvia until the night Mary had Trevor and Cassandra removed from her property.

"She handled it like a lady, and we moved her things. She's better off at her mother's. As for Trevor, he needs to move on with his life just like Gwen. I don't intend on Cassandra having a reason to need or see him."

"So what does that mean Lamont? She has his four children. Cassandra has more than just her needs to fill."

"And your point is?"

"The point is you don't need to tie yourself down with four children and their whacko father for a used lay."

"Hold up Sylvia! Do you have something against Cassandra? What's your reason for calling her a used lay?"

"Four children, no husband, duh?"

"White boy, father's company, who's using who you or him? Stay in your lane Sylvia. This is my life."

"You can't compare Cassandra to Carson or to me."

"Why not? He's addicted to drugs and you're addicted to money. Again, the question is who's using who? I don't have an addiction or motive to be with Cassandra, and she doesn't either. I just like her company."

"I don't have an addiction either."

"Sylvia, please. Since you woke me up I might as well start my day. Is there anything else I can help you with because this conversation is dead? I will see Cassandra until she tells me she doesn't want to see me, or I don't want to see her."

"Is that the same thing you said about Gwen? I just don't want you falling into the same situation. I mean, Cassandra could want to be with Trevor again."

"I can't see why or how, but I'll pay attention to the possibility. Thanks again for the advice."

"Lamont, let the smoke blow over between her and Trevor, then you'll see."

"Sylvia, what's your relationship with Cassandra like these days."

"I don't talk to her like we used to if that's what you mean."

"So, you wouldn't consider her your friend?"

"No, we haven't dealt with each other in over seven years I would guess."

"So how do you know so much about her relationship with Trevor? Do you have a relationship of some sort with him?"

There was a silence on the phone. Lamont could tell that he had stumbled upon why Sylvia had called. She and Trevor had a relationship, and she was worried. Lamont didn't know if it was just the drug dealings, or they were involved sexually.

"Does Trevor or one of his boys sell the drugs to you and Carson?"

Sylvia heard him and knew it was an open door for her to get out of telling the truth.

"Yeah, I guess you could say that. I don't want Trevor using me to get back at you."

"My sister, always looking out for her interest. I suggest you find another spot to buy your drugs. I'm going to see Cassandra until she, and I decide we're through. Give up your habit. Either your lover or your drug dealer, you decide."

"You make it sound like I'm sleeping with Trevor for drugs."

"You are, and you know it. It doesn't matter to me. I stopped watching your back when you told me it was your life, and you didn't have a habit. The same thing I told you then, I'm telling you now. Keep it away from me. If you're fucking Trevor Black, I don't want to know; if he's your drug dealer, I don't want to know. You let that nigga know if he hurts you or something happens to you, I'll kill him. Take my advice sis, leave Trevor alone and your problem goes away. But if he's another addiction for you, I don't know what to tell you."

"Lamont, you don't understand. I just don't want you caught up with his girl without knowing that he may use me as your consequence."

"I'll kill him. He better grow up. If he hurts you or Cassandra, I will kill him."

Sylvia could tell by the tone of his voice, he was serious. She also knew the subject was dead. Although her brother was a businessman and worked hard, he learned his lessons in the street. He didn't go to college and had more than the average businessman could want. There were a lot of neighborhood drug dealings and gang members that respected Lamont for that. Trevor wasn't one of them, but he never tried him. He wouldn't take Lamont's threat lightly. Sylvia would take Terrance and Lamont's advice and leave it alone.

"Lamont, I don't think it will come to that."

"I don't think so either, but if that's your worry, you give him my message. I believe everyone should live the way they want to live. I can't stop you from dipping in and out of the drug scene or dealing with that white boy, or dealing with Trevor. I don't intend on waking up each day to your phone calls telling me what to do either. So let's just agree to live and let live. I love you girl but you and no one else runs what I do or how I do it. I'm my own man. Girl, it's almost eight thirty. You've had enough of my time for this morning. Are you okay?"

"Yeah, Lamont, I don't know what else to say."

"Say you love me, have a great day and goodbye."

"Lamont, be careful. I love you. Bye."

The phone went silent. Lamont shook his head. Now that he had talked to Sylvia, he realized why Terrance was talking the way he was about Cassandra. Terrance knew about Sylvia and Trevor. Lamont looked at the clock. He would wait until about ten o'clock to call Terrance.

Chapter 27

Cassandra got up early determined to follow her aunt's detailed schedule for her mother. She went into the kitchen and found her Aunt Laura sitting at the table drinking a cup of coffee.

"Good morning Auntie, how are you this morning?"

"I'm just fine sweetie. Did you get all your things situated?"

"Yes, I feel good about it too. I thought I would feel guilty about leaving Trina with the rent and bills."

"Guilty? She should have that load to carry. Didn't you say she was laid up with Trevor when you walked in?"

"Yeah, I feel good about that too. I mean, I'm mad because I really thought she was a real friend. She had to be seeing him while I was seeing him. It just doesn't add up that they just started seeing each other. I mean for him to feel comfortable about lying around in the apartment knowing I lived there too. I guess I needed that added dose of reality to know he was out of my life for good."

"Well I always said he had more balls than brains. Trina surprised me though, but you know women just can't tell their friends about their relationships with their men and not beware. That's just one of those things. Well, its better you found out when you did. I don't know what your reaction would have been if you still lived there."

"It certainly changed my mind about going back. I mean, even if I moved from here it wouldn't be back to that situation."

Laura got up from the table to fill her cup again. She gestured to Cassandra questioning if she wanted to join her.

"No thanks, I never drank much coffee."

"Would you like tea instead? I can put on the water for you."

"No, I'm fine. What I do want though, is for you to tell me about Mama's schedule. You know the therapist, the medication times, her meals, doctor appointments, and anything else that goes on from day to day. I want to become familiar with the routine, so I can pitch in. I came home to help, so I want to learn what needs to be done."

Laura slowly sat in the chair. She took her time before answering because she really wanted to be truthful with Cassandra about her mother's needs and condition. Although she and Earl agreed Mary should tell her daughter that the cancer wasn't as bad as they thought, she felt bad about keeping it a secret.

"Well, we start the day about eight thirty. The therapist comes three times a week. If they're going to change the days they'll call. Some days they come and Mary is so stiff from the exercises they did the day before that they just massage the side for her. It all depends on them child. That lasts about an hour or more, and then I give her the medication for the pain and her lunch. It's really not that bad on the other days other than her stiffness. I think if she got out of the bed more she would feel better. You know, the bed will kill you if you let it. Anyway, Mary will tell you if she wants to sit up or get up and that's how that's been going. Maybe now that you and the children are here we can get her to spend some time in the family room or on the porch. The air and sun will do her some good. Cassandra I think your mother just feels sorry for herself, if we can get her to change her mind set, she can beat this thing."

"I thought she was really bad off; what about the cancer? How can she beat it if she won't get the surgery or the treatment?"

Laura almost gave it away, and she knew it. As she spoke the lie that Mary wanted her to uphold came to her.

"Cassandra, we have to convince her that whatever can be done is worth it. I think its fear that is keeping her from the surgery or the treatment. We can't say it that way though. Your mother is stubborn. She won't appreciate us telling her what to do. You and your children is what she needs in her life the most now. If she embraces being a grandmother, being a mother, and being loved, she may want to get treated. I think she had a fear of dying alone."

"I never thought of that. I just thought she wanted to die. You may be right. She hasn't been in our lives much. I mean, our circumstances prevented that. Now things have definitely changed. I have changed. She needs to know that and know that I am here with her."

"I think so sugar, I think the two of you need a new start at loving each other as you should."

"Hmmm. I'll try, but you know my mother loves to tell me what and what not to do. I don't know if I can deal with that."

"That's why I'll be here until the end of the summer. That should be enough time for the two of you to get to know how to get along and simply love one another."

"Thank you. That was my next dilemma. I didn't know how I would be able to attend my classes if I had to take care of my mother during the day."

"Here you start the breakfast. Let each day take care of itself. Your classes will be over by the end of the summer right?"

"Yes, I'll just have to find a job after that until I can save up for my own salon."

"Take one step at a time. Finish the classes and we'll deal with the rest later."

Cassandra went to the refrigerator and got out the bacon and eggs to prepare breakfast. She wanted to yell at the top of her lungs. She felt confident that better days were ahead for her. She would be able to think about herself and her children without worrying what Trevor's next move was. Cassandra hadn't felt as good as she did in years. She felt the urge to yell again. She settled for humming while Laura drank her coffee in silence.

Chapter 28

Earl woke up remembering the conversation he had with Laura. He wouldn't be able to bring himself to tell his children he was dying if he wasn't and that made it difficult for him to understand Mary's reasoning. Veronica and Reggie were in the kitchen discussing papers they had scattered all over the table. Earl realized the time was moving on, and he wanted his visit with his sister to be early, leaving him the rest of the day to tinker with his old pickup truck.

"What y'all doing? Whose court papers are those?"

Reggie lived with his father since the death of his mother, while Veronica lived with her fiancé on the other side of town. She worked as a paralegal in the Public Defender's Office and often did her paperwork while visiting. Reggie worked in the Prosecutor's office and had just taken the bar exam. The two would discuss cases as Veronica did her research.

"These are your son's papers," Veronica answered reluctantly.

"My son? Who? Kevin?" Earl had no idea he had been arrested again.

"I think he's going to do time this round."

"Well Reggie, the boy's been saved a few rounds. This one will teach him the lesson he should have learned earlier."

Veronica sorted through the papers and shook her head in disappointment.

"He'll never beat all these charges. They've got him for possession, distribution in a school zone, a weapons charge, eluding the police and assault."

"What was he thinking? You and Reggie better not get yourselves wound up in his mess."

Veronica began putting the papers into separate folders. Reggie went to the refrigerator and brought out the pitcher of orange juice.

"Dad, a friend of ours just thought we might find something in the paperwork that may help him out of the situation."

"Veronica is your office handling his case?"

"I'll know tomorrow. It probably will, he'll need a Public Defender if he doesn't get a lawyer."

"Girl, I don't plan on wasting my money on a lawyer for Kevin. We'll have him out today, and tomorrow they'll find him selling in front of another school on another corner. Kevin will have to wear this one, unless y'all bail him out."

"That's what we were discussing Daddy, whether or not it's worth it. Reggie and you have said no, so I guess he'll have to get a Public Defender and go from there."

Veronica sounded as pitiful. She explained Kevin's options and what he would go through. Reggie told his father what the Prosecutors would try to make stick; those offenses that would give him the most time. Earl poured a glass of orange juice for himself and left the kitchen thinking. *"And they think I'm supposed to help him, well he's on his way to self destruction, and it's his choice."*

The two of them watched their father, as though they were waiting for his permission to be excused. Earl felt their stares and ignored them while he drank his juice. He stopped and turned at the kitchen door.

"If you bail him out, he stays with you. He can't stay here and if you think about it, he won't stay with you either. He's troubled, he needs help, and we can't give him that."

Reggie understood his father's words. They all loved the wayward son.

"Let's see what the public defender's office says. If anything can be done they would know."

Earl agreed with them. They would wait until the week ended to make any decisions. He told them he had to go to visit Mary.

"If you get in touch with their office today, let me know what they say, call me on my cell."

Veronica reached and got a glass from the dish rack. She decided to pour herself a glass of juice.

"Daddy, how is Aunt Mary? I thought Cassandra was coming home."

Earl walked over to the sink with his empty glass. He was glad she asked about Mary. Reggie gathered the rest of the papers making notes on each folder for Veronica to refer to.

"She did. She's there with your Aunt Laura. Sandra's been there two days, and I believe she plans on staying. She and Lamont picked up her belongings from where she was living last night."

"Lamont, Lamont Dearling?" Veronica sounded shocked. She always thought Lamont liked Cassandra. She often wondered why Cassandra chose Trevor over Lamont.

"Yeah, Lamont that lived across the street, you both should know him."

Reggie nodded his head in agreement as he put the orange juice back in the refrigerator. He and Lamont played ball in the summer often at the gym near the auto body shop.

"Lamont owns the auto body shop over on the boulevard. I've taken my car there. We see each other at the gym that's near there."

"Well, when you get a chance, call your aunt and see how she's doing. She'll be glad to hear from either you and so will Cassandra. Listen I'm going now so I can get back here early."

Reggie told his father and Veronica, he would talk with them later. He kissed Veronica pointing to the folders and the notes he left. He promised Earl he would stop by or call Cassandra before the weekend was over. Veronica wanted to know more so continued her questions.

"Dad, exactly what's wrong with Aunt Mary?"

Earl hesitated before answering. He pulled out the kitchen chair and took a seat. Talking to Veronica always cleared his mind before dealing with his sister's. Veronica gave insight to the woman's point of view. Earl hoped she could help him understand Mary.

"She has breast cancer. I think when she found out she had the stroke that paralyzed her left side. She's slowly recovering from that, you know therapy and all. Anyway, she doesn't want the surgery or the treatment for the cancer."

"Why not? There are many women who survive breast cancer."

"Veronica, your guess is as good as mine. She led us to believe she was dying from terminal cancer. Your Aunt Laura questioned the doctor and found out it was breast cancer, and that she is scared of the effects of radiation and the possibility of a mastectomy. She told Laura she wanted us all to believe she was dying so Cassandra would come home and be with her."

"Why didn't she just ask Cassandra to come home?"

"You know how their relationship has been. Cassandra is home but she thinks her mother doesn't have long to live, she was told what we believed was true. She doesn't know its breast cancer, or that it is treatable. It's not right but Mary seems to think it is."

"You're right Daddy. So is Cassandra planning on staying?"

"Well she is so far. I don't know. I'm scared that Mary's lie may tear them farther apart. I don't understand Mary. Anyway I'm going to talk with her this morning to see if I can get her to tell Cassandra the truth. I know she doesn't want Cassandra there just because she's sick. She needs to know that Cassandra really wants to be there."

"Yeah, but Cassandra wouldn't have come home just to be with her mother, you and I both know what Aunt Mary put her through. I mean she turned her back on her so many times, just because Cassandra made bad decisions about love. It was a mess sometimes, just hearing them talk to each other. You've got your work cut out for you 'cause your sister can be stubborn."

Earl laughed at the comment. He knew Veronica was right.

"Well baby girl, I guess that's why your Aunt Laura called me. She can't get Mary to do a thing. Anyway I'll call you later. Don't forget to call me about that lawyer. Where is Kevin anyway?"

"The county, he'll be there until Monday. Daddy, I know you're right. He needs help but he won't get it in jail. I'm looking into a couple of programs that will take him in while he's in custody as a term of his release. If he's forced to be in the program maybe it will make a difference."

"Is he addicted too Veronica?"

"I don't know. I know he's addicted to selling and that could be because he owes his connections. I really don't know. I think Reggie is going to try to find out."

"I don't know which is worse."

"Yeah, Reggie said the same thing. Tell Aunt Laura and everyone hello for me. I'll call them later but I know I won't get over there this weekend. I'm supposed to go looking for a hall for the wedding with Eric."

"You guys have about ten months until the date."

"The date may change. We may have to get married in May instead. April is a bad month for a lot of his family members. I don't understand why but that's what his mother told him. Anyway, we're going to see a couple of places today and tomorrow."

Veronica put the folders in her satchel and grabbed her handbag. Earl knew it meant she was satisfied with the update and ready to leave. He stood and pushed his chair under the kitchen table as he grabbed his car keys. Veronica smiled waiting for her father to join her at the back door. He shook his head slowly, saying a silent prayer for Kevin as they walked out the door.

113

Chapter 29

Terrance grabbed the phone before it could ring the third time realizing his mother wouldn't answer it. He answered with the hopes it wasn't his job calling to ask him to work overtime. It was his day off, and with it being the summer, they filled a lot of the local runs with those who wanted the overtime as opposed to hiring part time drivers. Terrance usually wanted to make the extra money but since Diane would be out of town the following weekend, they made plans to be spend the weekend together.

"Good morning."

"Hey bro why so professional?" It was Lamont.

Terrance could tell Lamont he had been up for some time. He checked his watch before answering the question.

"I thought my job was calling for overtime. I was saying a prayer it wasn't them. I guess praying does work."

The comment got no laughter from Lamont, which put Terrance on notice that the conversation would be serious.

"So what's up with you this morning? Aren't you still on vacation? The weather is supposed to be close to seventy five degrees, are you going fishing?"

The questions showed his uneasiness.

"No man, at least not that type of fishing. What's up with Sylvia? She called here this morning with fake ass concerns about me and Cassandra. Terrance, before you answer, I just spent an hour talking with her so you know I don't intend on playing the mystery questions rounds with you."

"Lamont, man, what do I have to do with what you and Sylvia talked about? What do you want to know? Better yet, what did you and her talk about?"

"About Trevor Black and his possible threats that would include Sylvia. Terrance what's going on between Sylvia and Trevor or should I say what was going on?"

Terrance took a seat. He realized Sylvia did exactly what he told her not to do. If she just let things work themselves out Lamont wouldn't be questioning him. He thought about what he could say but it all would blow up in his face if Sylvia wasn't willing to let things go. Terrance decided to tell the truth as he knew it.

"Look man, I think they dealt with each other back in the day. Right after Cassandra and him moved from around here. I don't know how deep it got. I don't know if it even got further than him just talking to her or what. Well, from what I do know, somehow Cassandra found out about whatever they had going on. One night when Trevor came around cussing and carrying on about Cassandra not wanting to go home with him, it got crazy. I mean, the argument that started in Cassandra's mom's house came out on their porch and then into the street. Cassandra was cussing at Trevor, her mother was yelling and shouting at her, you know. Trevor called Cassandra a "trifling bitch", Ms. Mary came off the porch and told him she would kill him. Well Cassandra defended the nigga', right there in the middle of the street with everybody watching. She talked about her mother never caring about her, her father and all sorts of things. Man, I think she was so high, she didn't even realize what she was saying or who she was talking to."

Terrance paused to see if Lamont wanted him to continue. The silence on the other end of the phone let him know that Lamont knew the story wasn't over and was listening intently.

"Anyway, Ms. Mary told her to bring her ass in the house. Well, you know she didn't say her ass but. Anyway, a couple of the older ladies, you know Ms. Mary and Mama's friends tried to tell Cassandra to go in too. Trevor got to cussing at all of them. Cassandra, I guess figured if she went with Trevor it would end the argument, and since she had torn her ass with her mom it didn't do her no good to go in the house anyway. She started talking about the other women and their household issues."

"Whose issues the other women that were helping Ms. Mary?"

Lamont wasn't sure who Terrance was referring to.

"Yeah, Ms. Carrie, Ms. Jenkins, you know, Mama and the rest of the crew. Well, she talked about them all saying they all took the same parenting class. You know things like; Ms. Carrie's girls strolling the streets on the regular; and Ms. Jenkins daughter having no idea who the father of her two children could be; I think something about Ms. Stone's son being locked up for that armed robbery, and I can't remember what else she told that day. Well, Sylvia must have thought that Cassandra was going to say something about Mama."

"What could Cassandra have said? She loves Ma'Dear more than she loves her own mother."

Lamont waited for the answer knowing it would shed light on the call he received earlier that morning.

"I know that and you know that, but Lamont when you think skeletons are falling out of your closet you do anything you can to keep them in. Sylvia cut Cassandra off just as she was turning around in the crowd looking for the next woman to put on blast. Sylvia yelled, 'And I guess your ass is perfect with no husband and two children.' Sylvia would have been better off if Cassandra had beat her down in the street. Cassandra chose Sylvia as the next woman to talk about. She told everyone that if Sylvia hadn't been sleeping with Trevor, doing things to him and for him that she refused to do maybe he would be her husband. Cassandra really let her have it. She told Sylvia she knew about them sharing her bed when she wasn't home, and she had too much respect for Ma'Dear to tell her it wasn't just sex."

"Mama heard all this and didn't confront Sylvia about it?"

Lamont was caught between shock and anger. *"How could she call me knowing I would find this out, one way or the other?"*

"No man, Mama and the other women had taken Ms. Mary in the house. They must have called the cops too, cause shortly after they went in the cops arrived. Ms. Mary put a complaint in against Trevor and now from what Mama says it's a permanent restraining order. But Sylvia and Cassandra haven't talked since. Cassandra never mentioned it after that day. I don't know if anyone ever told Mama. If they did she never mentioned it to me. But, yeah man, I don't know how true it is."

Terrance felt better about the situation after telling Lamont what he knew. He didn't add that he didn't really believe it to be as deep as Cassandra stated it to be. Terrance thought it was a one-night thing after a party where Sylvia and Trevor got a little plastered and satisfied each other for the night.

Terrance always thought Sylvia regretted it. He knew Trevor tried to pursue her after, but he didn't know she liked the chase and accepted gifts, drugs and sex over and over again.

Lamont was done. He sat in his living room chair rattled. He couldn't believe his sister would fall for Trevor. Sylvia had always pretended to hate his type, calling them ignorant thugs. He should have known that was another part of her faked character.

"Every girl wants a thug, including our sister, huh?"

"Lamont, that shit ain't even funny. I mean, I don't think it was serious, and it couldn't have lasted that long, shortly after she had Carson clinging to her."

Lamont couldn't believe Terrance couldn't see the connection. He hated to burst his vision of his older sister, but she had her own motives for being with Carson and love wasn't one of them.

"Terrance, you're in for a rude awakening my brother. Sylvia was with Trevor a while. That's why she's scared of him. He's violent, she knows it. They've been around the bush a few times. I don't know if he's been violent with her, but she knows he can be. Her and Carson man, that's another piece to the story. For her to call me and tell me that Trevor may use her to interfere with my friendship with Cassandra tells me he has something over her. That could be the relationship they had or maybe some drug dealings. Maybe Carson's drug dealings, a white boy in the hood always means there's something up. Carson doesn't come across as a white boy who just loves black women that live in our section of town."

"So you believe Cassandra's story? Man you're whipped already?"

"Terrance, listen. This didn't come from Cassandra. Sylvia called with this bull. I'm not going to mention it to Sandra. I don't think I'll have to, but bro, it will resurface if I'm right. I'm going to let it go. The move is on Trevor. If the threat comes to either Sylvia or Cassandra he'll have to deal with me."

"What did she think he would do?"

"Terrance she didn't know, she wanted me to leave Cassandra alone just because she didn't want him to threaten her. If she's just dealing with Carson and there's no connection why would he involve her? There's something going on. By the way, thanks for fishing with me. Later man"

Lamont hung up the phone. Terrance looked at the receiver realizing he had been baited for information. Sylvia had alerted Lamont, which meant he would have to be on alert too. It was going to be a hot summer.

Chapter 30

L amont wanted to speak to Cassandra but decided to wait for her call. He needed to talk with Sean before he committed himself to spending his free time with Sandra and her children. He decided to shower and shave using the time to think about his sister's conversation and how he would handle what she feared would be a problem. He let the hot water in the shower steam before he stepped into what he considered a piece of heaven.

A hot shower always eased his mind and relaxed his muscles. As his thoughts drifted, he imagined showering with Cassandra. He wanted more than a friendship with her despite the warning from his brother and sister. Trevor was Sylvia's problem. He wouldn't interfere with Trevor and his children. He hoped Trevor wouldn't use them as a threat to interfere with the relationship Lamont wanted with Cassandra.

"It could get ugly," Lamont thought aloud as he cut off the water.

He needed to be one step ahead of Trevor. Sylvia's warning left a lot of unanswered questions. His only contact to what went on in the streets was the gossip that came by way of the customers and his workers at the shop.

He went to his closet and decided to check out the weather report before choosing his clothes for the day. Although Terrance said it would be close to seventy-five degrees, the summer tease didn't always bring constant warmth. The past few days brought plenty of sunshine but the temperature reading didn't go above the low seventies. Smiling to himself he thought about the conversation he and Sean would have regarding Mr. Trevor Black. The phone rang breaking his thoughts. Lamont looked at the caller ID that read, "Dearling & Moore Auto Repairs."

"Hey man what's up?"

It was Sean. It seemed since high school, whenever Lamont had a major issue Sean would call just when Lamont was ready to talk to him about it.

"You, man. Listen, Malik can't come in this afternoon. You know we got two on the lift and one in the bay. Do you want me to call in Jose' or what? I know we said, cut the Saturday hours down, but we need to move these three out of here by Tuesday at the latest. Jose' and that new kid can work on the Toyota, while Jeff and his sidekick finish the work on that truck. I think the parts for the other car will be here Monday."

"What's up with Malik? That's twice this week, didn't he take off Monday? Is he hitting the street again?"

Lamont wanted to talk with Malik. He and Jose' were known to have dealings with Trevor off and on. Lamont hired them because they were good mechanics and brought in a lot of business. They knew they couldn't bring their street dealings near the shop.

"Man, his girl is due any day now. You know how that is. Anyway he said her water broke. He rushed her into the hospital this morning. He said he'd be in early Monday to start on what was left from today."

"Yeah man, call Jose'. Tell him don't leave until I get there though. It's close to twelve. What time are you planning on closing today?"

"The regular time man three o'clock."

"Sean where will you be later? No, on second thought, I'll talk to you after I speak to Jose'."

"What's up? Talk about what? I don't have to call Jose' in. That's why I called and asked you what you wanted to do."

It was Lamont and Sean's goal to update equipment, remodel the offices and redesign the bays. After looking at their monthly profits and bills they agreed to cut the Saturday work hours and trim the staff to skeleton crew. Saturday's were there busiest days and at Dearling and Moore's there would be at least six to eight people working in the bay's; two more in the office and Sean or Lamont supervising. They paid their workers a decent hourly wage and although they all understood there would be a temporary cut back any one of them would come in to work for Sean or Lamont on Saturday's if needed. The staff size until all the renovations were done would be four in the bay and a supervisor on Saturday's. The staff agreed to rotate the Saturday's and be on call.

"No man, call Jose'. If I'm not mistaken we've got cars coming in the beginning of the week to get ready for the auction at the end of the month. I figured as long as I had to talk with Jose', I could see you while I'm there. If you have something else to do, man, call me later."

"Naw, it's cool. I'll see you this afternoon."

"Sean, let me know if Malik calls."

"Monty, man the brother is alright. His girl was admitted this morning."

Lamont and Sean laughed together. He knew Sean had checked the hospital already.

"The things people just make you do," He hung up the phone assuring Sean he would be there shortly.

With the start of his day coming to an end, Lamont knew it would be late afternoon before he would see Cassandra. He was determined he would wait for her to call. Lamont decided on jeans and a Pittsburgh Steelers jersey. As he reached for his Pittsburgh fitted cap his cell phone rang. .

"Hey, good morning Ma."

"Hey, good morning to you; you sound like you've been up for hours."

"Yeah, thanks to your daughter I have. I was on my way to the shop. What's up with you?"

"I was wondering how you and Cassandra made out. I mean did she move all her things into her mother's?"

"Yeah, we got all of her things last night. We finished unloading and getting her situated about eleven. I didn't know if you guys were still up."

Lamont didn't mention the note he found on his truck. Ma'Dear would have wanted to know what Sylvia wanted. He had no intentions on telling her what was going on.

"Your sister was here last night. I told her you were across the street helping Cassandra. I don't know what your sister has against her but something strange is going on between them."

Ma'Dear paused; waiting for her son to fill in the missing information. When he didn't reply she continued.

"So what's on your agenda for the day? You'll be going back to work Monday won't you?"

Lamont shook his head and smiled. His mother was fishing.

"Yeah, Monday I'll be back at the shop. I have to go there today though. One of the guys is with his girl who should be having their first child at some time today, so Sean called to let me know. I'll stop by to make sure he's not shorthanded."

"Well, that's what the owners have to do at times. I hope you don't have to work the rest of the day."

"No, Ma. Sean called another guy in. I won't be working, I'm just stopping by. I'll be checking out a few jobs and lining up the work for Monday, that's all."

"You know the Family Day Picnic is next week. Do you think you'll be attending?"

Ma'Dear needed to turn in a count for her family. She wanted to have an area for her friends and relatives. She hoped Lamont would come. She planned on inviting Laura, Mary, Cassandra and her children, and Earl. They could invite their families if they wanted to but she thought the day would do Mary some good. She also thought it would be nice for Cassandra's children and Cassandra. She wanted to invite them to the church as well. Lamont didn't go to church with her often but he attended most of their outings and functions.

"Is it on Sunday?"

"Yes, do you think you'll be able to attend?"

"I guess I'll be free. I'll let you know for sure by tomorrow. Is that okay with you?"

"I'll include you in my count. They want a count from the members tomorrow. If you can't attend let me know."

"If I wanted to bring a guest would it be a problem?"

Ma'Dear heard the question but didn't want Lamont to bring anyone else. She couldn't imagine who he would want to bring.

"I don't think it would be a problem. I thought you would be coming alone."

"I don't know maybe Cassandra and her children might enjoy the picnic. I mean they have a lot of activities for the children and Cassandra may see some of her old neighborhood friends."

Ma'Dear was relieved. Cassandra was her choice for him years ago. She was glad he didn't have intentions on bring a "date for the day".

"Well ask her and let me know. Terrance and Sylvia said they would be attending and I was going to invite Laura and Mary."

"Mama, how could you invite them and not invite Cassandra. You had planned on inviting her all along didn't you?"

"But I think she would love for you to invite her. I'll wait for you to ask her. Call me. I'll call Laura after you talk to Cassandra. Listen, I'm taking these cookies over there this afternoon, I'll mention it to Laura while I'm visiting. Call Cassandra early now and call me. I'll be going over there about three or four."

"Ma, I don't know if I'll talk to her by then."

"You will. Call her now."

The phone clicked. Ma'Dear had hung up. Lamont shook his head realizing his mother was playing matchmaker. He still didn't want to call Cassandra, he would wait.

Chapter 31

Trevor sat waiting for a call. His apartment was closing in around him as the hours passed. Carson promised he would have Sylvia call him, as soon as he heard from her. She hadn't returned Trevor's calls. Either Carson was lying, or she hadn't returned Carson's calls from earlier in the morning. Trevor was trying another angle to get back at Cassandra and her new found friend. Although it had only been a few days he didn't need his boys thinking he lost his girl to Lamont Dearling.

He looked at the couch where he had thrown Cassandra's coats. He would distribute them among the women he would see over the next few months. Cassandra would miss them when the weather turned cold. He picked up the coats to move them to his spare room. The smell of Cassandra's perfume teased his senses, and he sat on the bed as he laid them down. He ran his hands over the fur of Cassandra's favorite mink. The thought of losing her was tugging at his heart, but he couldn't dismiss the anger he felt.

Trevor jumped up from the bed, startled by the sound of his cell phone that was lying on the couch in his den. The room was his haven when he stayed home and the only room that looked as though someone occupied the apartment. The four-bedroom apartment satisfied his children when he kept them for overnight visits and that was its only purpose. He didn't want his children around when he did business, it kept down confusion. The phone rang again, the tone told him it was Carson.

"Yeah man, you ain't caught up with Sylvia's ass yet?"

"This is Sylvia. What do you want Trevor?"

"You know what I want. Where you been? I called you last night and this morning."

"I was with my family."

"I'm glad you were; just where I need you to be. Listen I need to know about your brother and Cassandra. What's up with this new relationship they seem to be having?"

Sylvia knew this would be the topic. She had no intentions of leading on she knew what he was talking about. Maybe he wouldn't involve her if she convinced him she didn't want any part of Cassandra's affairs.

"Trevor, I haven't seen or spoke to Cassandra in years. I don't think my brother would tell me his business either. Besides, I think he has a woman he plans on marrying."

"Is that so? Well, he was with Cassandra last night. Listen, your brother is stepping into forbidden territory. Territory I own and rule. If you don't want trouble for him, you'll warn him. By the way, what's been up with you? I haven't heard from you lately. That white boy can't be that good to you."

Sylvia didn't comment, she just listened. Her fears were slowly unfolding. Trevor would be calling her regularly as long as Lamont pursued Cassandra as a love interest.

"Trevor, how do you know that Lamont and Cassandra aren't just rekindling an old friendship?"

"Sylvia, cut the bullshit. They were never old friends. It was always more, but I was always there."

"So you and Cassandra are not together?"

"No, I mean, we deal, you know. But I don't want her involved with your punk ass brother. So just do as you're told. Keep an eye open for any signs of them getting closer than they should."

"Trevor, I'm not around Lamont like that. He'll know something's up if I start asking questions."

"Sylvia, listen baby, do what you have to do. Do I tell you I can't fulfill your needs when you want something from me? I even pass off to your white boy toy when you ask. When he can't satisfy you I give you a piece of my sweet meat. C'mon take care of me. I just want to know if they're getting close."

"I don't want to spy on my brother. If they're getting close I don't want to know. I don't particularly care for Cassandra, or what they do."

"Well I don't give two shits about your brother, and I plan on showing him if I catch him fucking around with Cassandra, or maybe I'll just tell him about us."

"What about us?"

"Don't play Sylvia. Lamont doesn't know about your addiction to me or the shit I offer you. Maybe you want to come clean to your family."

Sylvia heard the threat and knew it would lead to violence if Trevor thought a relationship between Cassandra and Lamont was ongoing. Her family knowing she was still on drugs and involved with Trevor would ruin the perfect picture of her life that they all thought she lived. She knew what her brother's response would be, and she didn't want to tell Trevor how she thought things would play out. Tears began to flow from her eyes. Sylvia knew the situation could get ugly.

"Sylvia, I'll tell you what, why don't you come over here and convince me that I don't need Cassandra? I told you before that if I had you as my woman, I would drop my teasers. I wouldn't be buggin' about your brother, and you could leave that boy you call your man alone too. Think about it, it's all fair in love and war. You and I would satisfy each other, and I promise you as long as you keep my interest, your brother and your secrets will be safe."

Sylvia thought about it while looking at Carson as he snorted another line of coke. He gestured for her to hang up the phone smiling as he held his crotch. Sylvia turned her back rolling her eyes. The best part of beginning a relationship with Trevor other than Lamont's safety would be getting rid of Carson.

Chapter 32

Earl spent the first hour of his visit talking with Kyle and Christopher about going fishing. He promised the boys they would go fishing often during the summer months. Laura, Cassandra, Tyler, and Cassie sat in the family room watching an afternoon movie. Mary was napping. Earl got up to look in on her again. He returned to the family room and sat on the couch putting his arms around Cassie.

"So I guess our sister didn't sleep well last night." He asked Laura as he tickled Cassie causing her to squirm.

"Earl, I don't know. When I got up this morning she was sitting up in the bed watching television. She said she had been up since five. Maybe she didn't sleep well."

Cassandra listened to her aunt and uncle before making any comments. She didn't quite understand their concern about her mother's sleeping pattern, but she was sure they would tell her what she needed to know.

"She ate well this morning. Aunt Laura said it was more than she normally eats."

"Well, her appetite changes from time to time but Cassandra is right she was hungry and in good spirits."

"I was hoping to talk with her, but I want to get back to the house and get some work done on my truck. I'll come back later or tomorrow."

"Earl you ain't coming back this way once you leave, who you trying to fool? It ain't me."

All was silent except the television. The children slowly began cheering for their grandmother who stood in the doorway. Earl got up, quickly helping Mary to the couch where he had been sitting. Cassandra and Laura watched as she reached for Earl's hand as she situated her body on the couch.

"Mary, why didn't you call me? I would have come and helped you out of the bed."

"I saw Earl peek in on me. I wanted to try to help myself Laura, and you know it took a minute but it worked."

"Mama, Aunt Laura is right, you should have called us. I mean its good you wanted to try to do it yourself, but we should have been close by just in case."

"Lord Mary, if you had fallen. Jesus, I don't know if I'm glad that you made it, or glad you could do it on your own."

"Laura, the therapist said I need to move around more. I think I've sulked enough. A bed will kill you if you let it."

Earl and Laura looked at each other. They knew that this new found strength was the beginning of what would be considered a miraculous recovery. A recovery from a terminal illness she didn't have.

"Earl come help me get some lemonade for everyone. Children don't y'all want to play outside?"

"Yes, Auntie. Please Ma, can we. Can we?"

Tyler loved going outside and the movie wasn't holding his attention. Cassandra wasn't comfortable with him being outside by himself yet, and if Kyle didn't go outside with him or the others they could only go as far as the porch. Cassandra sensed there was a need for adult conversation so as soon as she said the word all four children bolted for the back door.

"Mama, what do you want to watch? We don't have to watch this movie now that the kids are outside."

"Whatever you want is fine Sandra. You didn't have any errands to run today?"

"No I took care of everything yesterday. I'll go to the camp with the kids on Monday and start my classes next week. So far, everything is in place."

"That's good. You didn't make plans to go out? I figured you would be shopping with Trina or something."

Cassandra could tell her mother had no idea what occurred the night before.

"Not this weekend maybe next weekend. As a matter of a fact, I don't think we'll be seeing much of each other. Her schedule is different from mine as it is. Once I start my classes and begin dealing with the kid's summer schedule, I don't know how much time I'll have to spend with her."

"Cassandra, I know you're here for me. I don't want you to think you have to be in this house day and night. That's another reason why I'm striving to get around better on my own. I appreciate you and your Aunt's attention, but I can still do some things for myself."

"Mama, healing takes time. Take all the time you need. We're here for you. Trina won't miss me and for that matter, neither will anyone else. I have the ones who will miss me with me; your grandchildren."

"I just don't want you to feel trapped in this house. You're certainly too young for that. Feel free to invite your company here too. All but Trevor, I won't…."

"I know. He won't be coming here at all."

Mary was surprised her statement didn't bring the questions of why, and how long was she going to hold a grudge against Trevor. Earl brought in the pitcher of lemonade and glasses sitting them on the place mats on the coffee table.

"Mary, how you holding out girl? You got us wondering about the drugs you took last night. Was it a new prescription, sure seems like it gave you new strength?"

She didn't want to admit she was fatigued, but she would fight lying down as long as she could.

"Laura, fool, pour the lemonade. Y'all come on in here and relax."

Earl sat with his sisters and his niece enjoying conversation, jokes and laughter, something that hadn't been done in years. The atmosphere gave them all sense of peace in spite of the problems they all knew could surface later.

Chapter 33

S ean raised his head from the paperwork on his desk at the sound of Lamont's voice. The day's jobs were complete except for a Cherokee Jeep that was awaiting parts. It was close to three and everyone had begun cleaning up the bays, locking up the equipment and signing the maintenance logs. The conversations were lively ranging from what the balance of the weekend held for the hard working men to the vacations they planned to take later in the summer. Lamont had joined in the conversation telling them if all went well he would consider closing the shop for a week during the renovations.

"Man I hope that week includes pay."

Jose' spoke from under the hood of the 2002 Camry he was working on. He had an accent that was hard to ignore. The sound of his voice and the comments he made was usually enough to stir laughter, but Lamont could tell that this comment was said to stir the others to agree with him. Lamont decided to give him back a touch of sarcasm.

"I don't know man, if I count the hours you all sit around bullshitting I believe I could get a week from each of you."

"Go 'head with that man. We ain't that bad."

The men agreed with Jose's response by adding a couple of "yeah, with pay man", and the expected laughter.

Lamont walked over to the car where Jose' greeted him with a tap of the fist.

"What's up boss?"

"Man, I told you about that boss shit man."

"You got that. How was your week?"

"Man, went fast. How were things here? I hear your boy is finally gonna be a father today."

Jose' slammed the hood of the car and wiped his hands on the greasy rag that hung from his pocket.

"Yeah, sometime today I guess. You know, I think he'll be okay as a dad though. At least he seemed to be into the whole thing. You know the doctor's appointments, the shopping, and the proud father thing. The streets almost had him, til' he met his girl. They been together for the past three years now. It's all good."

"Three years? That's as long as he's been here. What you got three years on him right?"

"Yeah, about that. I've been here about six years. Man, time flies. Yeah, it's all good."

"Listen I need to talk with you. I need to talk to Sean a minute too. Finish here and stop in the office before you leave."

Jose' paused. He couldn't imagine what Lamont wanted to speak with him about. He knew if "the boss" was at the shop on his day off, it was usually because of a problem. Jose' didn't want any problems.

Sean was writing on the daily board the jobs to be done the next week when Lamont entered the office and closed the door.

"What's up?" The door was only closed when they needed to talk one on one. He finished the schedule listening as Lamont spoke.

"Sean, do you remember Cassandra Smith?"

"Cassandra, yeah, wait; no. I don't think she's who I'm thinking of. Does she live over on twenty Third Street or near there?"

"How'd you know that?"

"Jose' and Malik, I believe they knew her boyfriend or dealt with him. He came here asking questions about them and left her name and an address about a month ago. I thought she was the Cassandra we knew from back in the day, but I wasn't sure. The name must have stuck in my mind."

"Man, you don't remember her from our high school days?"

"So that was the Cassandra from back in the day? The one you were shot out over?"

"Man, keep that down. I wasn't shot out."

"Yeah, okay. What about her?"

"She's back on my mother's side of town. Her mother's sick, and let's just say we decided to get reacquainted. I spent some time talking and visiting with her."

"Okay and I know there's more to it than that."

"Well for now there's not, but there's some other issues."

"I can imagine. According to rumors and gossip, she was dealing with Trevor Black."

"Sean, you don't remember Trevor Black from school?"

"Man, you act like we were in school yesterday. No, I don't remember that nigga and I didn't remember him the day he left the address. Man, did he go to school?"

"Not often but that's who Cassandra was shot out over. Remember?"

"Naw man that ain't the same Trevor not that dude that came here. He didn't act like he knew me or nothing like that. He asked for Malik and never even gave me a second glance."

"That was him. And I bet he knew who you were. You know he knows who I am and everyone in this neighborhood does too. He knew where he was, probably hoped he wouldn't run into me. Anyway old boy saw me and Cassandra at her mother's house and again at her place before she moved out."

"Moved out? C'mon Lamont, you didn't move her in with you did you?"

"No man, keep up. I said she's with her mother. Anyway she went to get her clothes from her apartment and Trevor was laying up with her roommate."

"Lamont, man they say Cassandra brings drama. Trevor stays on top of her literally; from what I hear he's abused her. You might want to rethink the reunited thing. Did you say he was with her roommate?"

"Yeah, anyway Cassandra's at her mother's, and according to her, she doesn't want him in her life."

Sean took a deep breath. His friend always saw the good and didn't put much weight into the bad until he was faced with it.

"Look, Sean, I know what you're thinking. I've heard it from Terrance and Sylvia. But here's my dilemma. Trevor has made contact with Sylvia about me and Cassandra."

"With Sylvia, why Sylvia?"

"Exactly my question; I need to know how they're connected. She called me saying to stay away from Cassandra because Trevor would threaten her or use her in some way. I think Sylvia is seeing him or was seeing him."

"Lamont, not Polly pure bread; she wouldn't be caught with a corner boy."

"Sean, she's' with a corner boy. That white boy spends as much time in the street as Malik and Jose' would if they didn't have this job."

"Damn. It's like that. What coke habit?"

"You know it. Sylvia dips and dabs too. You knew that though. Anyway Trevor may be their supplier. I need to find out though."

"Okay, so you find out, then what."

"I stay a step ahead of his dumb ass. I want to see how far Cassandra, and I will go. I'm not looking for a romance, and if it's not there I can close another love chapter. For now I just want to know."

"Your love book is turning into a horror. First Gwen, now Cassandra and her skeletons; what you got a death wish in the love column?"

"Tell me what you know Sean."

"Me? Nothing, you need to talk to your boy."

Sean paused smiling. He now realized why Lamont wanted to talk to Jose'. Just as he was about to speak; there was a knock at the door.

"Who?"

Lamont went to the door and invited Jose' in. Jose' turned over the keys and the paperwork as he did each day. He had been promoted to floor supervisor and coordinated the daily work for the men in each bay. His position was new to him and Lamont only wanted a quick update.

The three men talked briefly about the business of the day and the upcoming week. Sean asked about Malik and how the work would be covered while he was out. He was guaranteed the work would be done. Jose' had begun to relax realizing there were no real problems to be discussed. Lamont knew it was his opportunity to question him about Trevor.

"Jose', do you and Malik still have dealings with Trevor Black?"

"No."

Jose's answer came quickly leaving Lamont to believe he was lying.

"Listen man, I told you when I hired you to leave the street in the street. Well, it seems that the street is stepping into my world, and I need to stay ahead of the game. Help me out here. When was the last time you dealt with Trevor Black?"

"I don't deal with that dude man. He's bad news. I've been straight since you hired me. Malik too, I told him he had to cut the strings before I introduced him to you. We've been working for you man. That's it."

Sean sat on the edge of his desk facing the chair where Jose' sat.

"Jose', we need your help here man. Come clean with us. How did Trevor know to come here and leave a message for Malik if you have no dealings with him?"

"Man, he's got his ways. We don't deal no more. Nothing, shit if I was dealing I wouldn't be stressing the pay. Not that it ain't enough. I mean the pay is good, but you know the life, and what it brings. I'm straight and so is Malik."

"Alright, alright you're straight. You ain't blind or deaf Jose', and you didn't move from the hood. You see and hear things, so talk. Is Trevor dealing with my sister in anyway?"

"Your sister? Lamont, how would I know?"

"You would know if you want to keep your job!"

"Shit man, I ain't nobody's snitch." Jose' began to stir in his chair. Lamont knew his employee was uncomfortable.

"Alright, so don't snitch. If I find out you know. You're done."

"Lamont, man. Your sister is a grown woman. What she does is her business man; talk to her. This ain't right man."

"I didn't ask you about what she did. I asked about Trevor Black. You got an alliance with him?"

"No, I ain't got no alliance with him. Okay look. I don't know what he wanted with Malik. I think Malik owed him some money. Some money, his sister, or somebody in his family owed Trevor. He looks for ways to get what he said we took from him back. We didn't take shit. We just don't work for that thug no more. Anyway that's what that was about. Your sister cops from him for that white boy she's always with. Sometimes she'll buy a little for herself but mostly for him."

Jose's accent was crisp. He was nervous and he rattled the information, which made Lamont start pacing from his desk to Sean's desk. Lamont took the time to repeat what he was being told in his head. It didn't take long for him to connect the conversation he was having to the information he already surmised. Voices from the bay indicated it was three o'clock as the men shouted their goodbyes.

"Jose', do you think they might be or were involved romantically or had a sex thing going on?"

"Who your sister and Trevor; or the white boy?"

"Her and Trevor."

"Man I know the white boy was all in but Trevor, well let's just say she's his puppet."

Sean twisted his face in disbelief and confusion. He began to speak but shook his head instead. He was baffled about her was dealing with Trevor at all. Then as though his thoughts bothered him, he asked his question.

"Did you say puppet? Sylvia is a puppet for Trevor?"

"Yeah man. Anything he wants, needs, or says is golden to her. She tries to stay away from him but she always returns."

"Jose', I thought you said you don't deal with him. Your information bro; where you get it?"

"Lamont, I'm just like you, staying ahead of the streets. I gotta know to keep that nigga away from me and mine."

Chapter 34

C assandra sat on the front porch watching the neighborhood traffic and thinking of the ways the neighborhood had changed. She allowed her memories to drift to those days filled with the fun she had as a child playing in front of the house with the Dearlings' and the other neighbor's children. The children she now watched as they played catch and chased each other calling out each other's names reminded her of a time of innocence she often missed. As her thoughts drifted on she remembered her friendship with Sylvia Dearling, Lamont's sister. In their younger years, they were inseparable.

Although Sylvia was older than Cassandra, they got along well as playmates. Sylvia would always tease her about the crush she had on Lamont and soon after, they labeled it "their secret". Sylvia knew the crush was mutual but neither of their parents would allow Cassandra to spend much time with Lamont nor Terrance. As they grew older Sylvia spent more time with her own group of friends leaving Cassandra to find friendship elsewhere. Trevor Black caught her attention and her friendship with Sylvia was soon forgotten.

Sylvia and her friends watched Cassandra from a distance. They always envied her beauty and were stunned by her relationship with Trevor Black. Some of them longed to be her friend wishing they could hang with some of Trevor's preferred crew. Cassandra had done what they all dared to do. Date a boy who wasn't their parent's choice.

Dating Trevor was always filled with unwanted excitement. Over the years, Trevor had drug deals go bad, arrests for possession, and the ongoing baby mama drama. Cassandra could see as she reflected over the years she didn't fit in the mold Trevor made for her.

No one else seemed to warn her about the dangers except the family she had run from. The glamour of their relationship wore thin when the news of her pregnancy got out. Then the whispers of envy turned to gossip and snickers. No one wanted to have children. No one accept Cassandra. Her desire to love Trevor grew stronger because she was carrying his child. Trevor had no intention of being her man exclusively, and he went on the hunt for anyone who wanted to be with him. Sylvia was one on the list of many.

Cassandra remembered the shock she felt the first time she found out Trevor was cheating on her. Now thinking back, he was always cheating on her. There was Pat who had her son, Kevin, three months after their son Kyle was born. Cassandra and Pat had heated arguments about who Trevor wanted to be with and who he loved. They called a truce when they happened to meet at the school where their sons were in the same class. The boys had become close friends and were pleased when they were told they were brothers. Pat and Cassandra grew to understand the problem was Trevor. Pat got married shortly after the boys turned nine and Cassandra was invited to the wedding. The two women continued their relationship. Kevin and Kyle spent many weekends with each other. Trevor saw Kevin only while visiting Kyle.

Then there was Robin, she moved with her daughter Stacey to Washington, D.C. The girl was the mirror image of her father. Trevor visited them in the summer. Robin didn't want him around longer than his money lasted, and she didn't waste time telling him to leave. She called constantly, telling him she would limit his visits if he didn't send money for her and Stacey. He sent the money every time she called. Stacey was eight and was Trevor's oldest daughter. Cassandra always thought he would leave for Washington and never return. Cassandra's new threat was Stacey not Robin. Trevor loved Stacey and was afraid he would lose her as he had Kevin. He accepted each of Robin's threats.

After Christopher was born, Trevor spent more time "finding himself", leaving Cassandra wondering more about their relationship. Although Robin's pregnancy was another slap in the face, nothing upset her more than to find out Sylvia was sleeping with Trevor too. Cassandra had come home early expecting to surprise Trevor for his birthday and walked in on the two of them in her bed.

Sylvia said something about Trevor lying about his relationship with Cassandra. Trevor blamed Cassandra for coming home without calling. The scene repeated itself with Carol, Sheena, and Lynn, the mother of his youngest son.

Cassandra fought back the tears as they formed in her eyes. She knew now, she should have left Trevor years ago. The abuse began shortly after she walked in her bedroom and saw Sylvia's legs in the air. Cassandra refused to have sex with him and when he forced her to, she would cry the whole time. After she got pregnant with Taylor, he accused her of sleeping with someone else giving him an excuse for his abusive outbursts.

Cassie was conceived two years later and until Trevor found out the baby was a girl, he continued to beat Cassandra, bruising her face and eventually breaking her leg. Trina came between them; often saving Cassandra from being beaten unconsciously.

Now Trina was on the list of women whom Trevor had as his pleasure. Cassandra didn't know why she was so deserving of his special love. It seemed he would always expect her to be there.

"Whew, I sure need a cure for this mess." Cassandra let her thought's speak aloud. As she stood to stretch her children ran past the front porch heading for the yard.

"Hey Ma, we're playing tag."

Taylor followed his brothers yelling and laughing. Cassie was last but was content just being allowed to play tag with the others. Cassandra could tell that the boys told her she was "it".

The afternoon was sun was fading an indication it was close to six o'clock. Laura opened the front door. In her hand, she held Cassandra's cell phone.

"It was ringing a minute ago. I didn't want to answer it. Are you okay? You've been real quiet this afternoon."

"Just thinking Auntie, I'm alright. Thank you."

"It's gonna be fine Sandra, you'll see. Your mother, you, and those kids are gonna be fine."

Laura handed the phone to Cassandra and went back inside. Cassandra heard her aunt's voice repeat the words, *"gonna be fine"*. The thought of finally being fine was a mental release. Cassandra checked her phone for missed calls. The phone listed two calls one from Lamont and the other from Trevor. Cassandra knew who she wouldn't be calling.

Chapter 35

T here were no messages left on her voice mail. After she dialed Lamont's cell number Cassandra put her ear to the phone expecting to hear the phone ring, instead she heard the wrong man's voice.

"So, let me guess, you were about to call me."

Trevor's sarcastic remark told Cassandra his game was still on, and he wanted her to tell him her next move.

"No, as a matter of a fact I wasn't Trevor. How are you today?"

"Oh, I'm fine. I guess I don't have to ask how you are. I mean I guess you feel you're sitting on top of the world. Your world now, huh Cassandra your world?"

"I wouldn't say all that, but regardless, you called, what do you want?"

"I could say I wanted you, but that would be a lie. Cassandra I want to know what you think you're doing. I mean, you don't expect me to accept this move you've made as a permanent thing, do you?"

"Trevor, you walked out on me before this move. I wasn't moving permanently until I saw you with Trina. I was getting some of my things to stay with my mother for a while. But you and Trina made up my mind to stay longer. Yes, consider it permanent, even if I don't live here. You and I are through. I'm tired of your shit Trevor. I guess I had enough of it all. Trina was my wake up call. You have hurt me for the last time Trevor. You and whoever you choose can play your games and enjoy them. I have too much going on right now…."

Trevor cut off her words in the middle of the sentence.

"Whoa, baby girl, whoa, me and whoever? What kind of shit is that? What you saying? Trina is a trick and you know it. Listen I just wanted you to know I understand you being angry and all. You take some time to think about what you doing. Lamont don't mean you no good, and you'll see that. What you think you got going on ain't shit. He don't know how to handle a woman like you. I mean I know 'cause I been with you for so long. You my girl, and don't nobody know what makes you feel good but me. Listen I didn't call you to cause no riff. I mean we got the kids and all, so we'll always be connected, but no thing, you do you. If you want Lamont you can have him. Play with him for a while. You'll be back. Just don't play into his shit about keeping me away from you and my kids."

"Trevor there is no me and you. You can have a relationship with your kids, but I don't want you to think I'm included in that relationship. We can make arrangements for you to see them or pick them up from Trina or something. I mean that's where you'll be and all."

Trevor didn't like the way the conversation was going. Cassandra was too calm. He needed her to be nervous about him being so cooperative. He needed to add insult to what he knew was her pain.

"Listen, once again. Trina was just a trick. Listen you're right. We can make some kind of arrangement. I'll talk it over with Sylvia. You know Lamont's sister. That's my piece. She'll be glad to see the children anyway, yeah that should work. I'll call you next week to set up something for the weekend. If you need to call me before then, call. Oh yeah, tell your boy, that nigga Lamont, I hope he enjoys you as much as I enjoy his sista. Later."

The phone went dead. Tears rolled from Cassandra's eyes. She slammed the flip cover on her phone and threw the phone on the bed. Just as she thought she was in control of her emotions, Trevor had rattled them again. Questions quickly flooded her mind. *'What will Lamont do when he finds out Trevor is screwing Sylvia? Will he want to end what we're starting? Does Sylvia know Trevor is using her? Why? Is she a part of Trevor's sick game? Does Lamont know about Sylvia and Trevor's past? What else could possibly go wrong?"*

She couldn't answer any of the questions that went through her mind. There was a way to get a few answers. She had to talk to Lamont.

Chapter 36

Earl sat with Laura and Mary enjoying his visit and their conversation. Laura began making motions to get his attention. Mary got up from her seat in the chair nearest the front hall. Her movement was slow and intentional but Laura knew right away she was headed for the bathroom.

"Laura, I'm going to get the hang of walking around here, and if I can't go on I'll call you." Mary stated emphatically noticing her sister was following behind her closely.

"Girl, you know I'm not going to wait for you to call, I'm right behind you."

Laura turned mouthing to Earl, *"Don't forget to ask her why?"*

Earl pretended he didn't understand, twisting his face, as though he was confused. Laura mouthed her message again slower than she had before. Earl nodded his head and waved his hand for her to attend to their sister's needs. Laura and Mary entered the bathroom with Laura praising her sister's efforts.

Earl didn't know where to begin the questioning. He wanted to tell Laura that the day had gone so well between them that he hated to spoil it. He knew Mary would immediately take the offense and the wall between them that seemed to be falling would quickly be rebuilt.

Laura and Mary returned from the bathroom talking about the children and dessert. Earl could tell from the conversation this would be Laura's reason to leave the room.

"Where did Cassandra go off to?"

Earl was reluctant to talk with Mary, and he wanted Laura to know it. He helped Mary to the couch and hesitated before sitting down.

"Sit down Earl, I'm gonna check on the children and Cassandra. Can I get you another pitcher of tea?"

"Yes Laura, if it's not too much. Make another pitcher." Mary smiled as she responded patting the couch for Earl to sit next to her.

Earl felt trapped. *"Laura told Mary I was gonna talk to her, I know she did!"* Earl was tempted to keep quiet but he had his own questions and he did want Mary to explain the reasons for her actions.

"Mary, I hope you don't feel I'm prying, but I need to ask you something."

"No, Earl go ahead and ask. I can only imagine the questions you may have."

"What you mean Mary?"

"Laura asked why I told y'all about the cancer spreading, and I explained it to her. I guess I should have told you both at the same time."

"Well, you already know she told me what you said. But my question is how do you think this will help your relationship with Cassandra? It may cause a problem."

"Earl, that won't happen if you and Laura let me handle it. I am not through with my therapy, my treatments, or my medication. The doctor said this will be a long process. Cassandra is here. That's what I needed. I'll work on everything else. I'll need your help and understanding, whether you agree or not. Laura thinks I'm being selfish. Well Earl, when death threatens to knock at your door, I guess you'll get selfish too. I want another chance with my child and her children and this may be the last one I have."

Mary placed her hand on Earl's hand and patted it gently with her other.

"I love you all Earl, but Cassandra is my only child. I need her to know that I love her too."

"Mary, we don't want Cassandra to feel we lied to her."

"Earl, I don't think it will matter. If God sees fit to spare me, he'll find a way for me to explain this mess. If God sees fit to call me home, well, Cassandra won't know the difference."

Earl shook his head. It seemed strange but he understood Mary's need a little better now that she explained it. Laura entered the room and put down the pitcher. Mary tapped the couch on her other side for Laura to sit down with them. Laura sat slowly not prepared for what Mary had to say.

"You both are a part of my reason for survival. I thank you. When the doctor said I had cancer I thought of you first, then it seemed I heard Cassandra's voice crying softly in my mind. I couldn't take the chance with the surgery, the treatments and all that without trying to wipe my child's tears. I need you both to help me. I can't leave my child without wiping her tears, holding her close and telling her how much I love her. It's been a long time, and we have to work our way back to each other, please help us. That's my last wish from you both. Please help us get as close as possible. I know I can be shrewd, but I'm willing to try to work for the sake of those babies of hers. Who knows it may help us all?"

Silence fell; neither Laura nor Earl said a word. They heard their sister's request as the tears rolled down their faces. They both kissed the side of her face and Mary smiled sitting back satisfied they understood her reasons.

Cassie entered the room and climbed into the chair across from the trio. Taylor, Kyle and Chris filed in laughing and pushing each other. Taylor crawled across the floor and placed his head on his grandmother's lap.

"Grandma, are you going to eat with us tonight?"

"Taylor, I think I just might. It's been a beautiful day, and we should share a meal together at least once a day, don't you think."

Laura told them to go watch the television in the den, assuring them dinner would be ready soon.

"Mary, are you sure you're up for dinner? You've been up most of the day."

"Well, that should mean I'll sleep better, Earl, join us won't you?"

Earl was still collecting his thoughts when Mary asked him to join the family for dinner.

"I'll need to call Reggie and Veronica, but I'm sure they won't mind me eating here. We usually eat out on Saturday's together."

"Well, tell me, how is Veronica and Reggie? And where is Kevin?"

Laura and Mary sat back as Earl spoke sharing his children's dilemma. It was the first time since Mary was diagnosed that Mary's condition wasn't the center of their attention.

Chapter 37

Cassandra called Lamont noticing it was close to eight thirty. She needed to get away and gather her thoughts. A ride with Lamont, or time at his house would calm her nerves. She didn't want to take the children with her. She heard her mother, aunt and uncle laughing near the front door. She needed to ask would they watch the children for the evening while they all seemed to be in a good mood.

"Leaving Uncle Earl?"

Cassandra hurried down the stairs to speak to him before he went out the front door.

"Yeah baby it's time I get home. I told Veronica I would call her, and I still haven't, messing around here with your Mamma and your Aunt Laura. They act like I don't have a thing to do."

Laura and Mary smiled saying, "You don't!"

They all laughed. Mary waved Earl out the door after each of them hugged him good night. Cassandra peeked in on the children, leaving her aunt to wave at Earl from the door. Kyle and Christopher were playing contently with their cars on the floor while Taylor and Cassie colored in their books. Cassandra knew not to disturb the peaceful moment they seemed to be enjoying, but she needed to leave them. She always told them when she was going out. Mary walked up behind her daughter giving her a loving push into the room.

"Go on in and sit child, why you standing here just looking?"

"They looked so content I didn't want to disturb them."

"Well come on in the living room with me and your aunt. They'll find you if they need you."

Cassandra saw the opening to ask her mother did she mind if she went out for a few hours, but she couldn't bear the thought of what the lectured answer would be. Laura was taking glasses to the kitchen.

Cassandra followed her, hoping her aunt would be easier to ask then her mother.

"Aunt Laura…."

"Sandra, did Lamont ever call on your cell? He called the house about an hour ago. I heard you talking on your phone, so I told him to call you back. He must have tried that cell of yours before he called the house."

Cassandra said a silent prayer. She would just wait for him to come and hope her mother and her aunt would throw them out.

"Yes, he did. He said his day was rather hectic and he would stop by for a little while. Is that okay with you?"

"Girl, you're grown with four children. Is what okay?"

"Well, I mean it's a little late for dropping in. It's almost nine o'clock."

"And? What do you want Sandra? Listen, I don't read minds very well and I hardly catch on to hints, so just say what you want to say."

"I was wondering. I need to talk with Lamont to clear the air of a few things that my past may have dug up. Would it be a problem for you to watch the children while we sit on the porch and talk?"

Mary entered the kitchen hearing only a part of Cassandra's question. She pulled out the chair at the kitchen table.

"Sit down child, we all need to talk."

Laura and Cassandra looked at each other. They obeyed Mary each taking a sit leaving the chair that was pulled out for Mary. Mary sat down giving Laura a smile. Laura had no idea what Mary wanted to say but she hoped the talk with Earl prompted her to tell Cassandra the truth about her illness.

Cassandra braced herself. The lecture she could stand, but she didn't want her mother questioning her about her intentions with Lamont, Trevor, or her future. She really wanted to handle those issues as she had done her other life changing moments, on her own. Although she wanted her relationship with her mother to be nurturing, she didn't want her advice without sorting things out for herself.

"Sandra, I want you to know that I am happy that you've come home to help me. I told your aunt and uncle, I don't want to be a burden to them or to you. I may be stubborn at times, but I won't allow you to do for me if I can do for myself. Although I am sick I won't stand to be treated as an invalid. I want to work through this illness or live with it, if I can. You and your children are now a part of this household. These are your children, we expect you to raise your children. Now I know we both are willing to help you in any way that we can, but we won't be used."

Cassandra knew it wouldn't be long before this speech was made. Laura sat across the table from Cassandra, speechless.

"Now you have four children and we all know their father cannot come here on any terms. I don't know if you should rush into anything so quickly. Please think about it before entering another dead end relationship. I don't want Lamont spending his time here just to dip and dabble and you wind up loaded again."

"Mary!! What's come over you?" Mary's comment struck Laura's nerve. She stood up pushing her chair in. Cassandra shook her head and sighed. This was the continuation of a bad dream, first, Trina and Trevor; then Trevor's phone call; and now this mess.

"Mama, I don't want to cause any trouble. I'll stay somewhere else if that would suit you better. I didn't come here to have you worry about my personal affairs. I have, and will manage them on my own. I have no intentions on having another baby. I plan on getting my life in order; moving into a home for me and my kids; and maybe one day I'll get married. But by no means will I or my children be a burden on anyone."

The doorbell rang. Cassandra got up, she and Laura knew it was Lamont. Mary saw the look on both their faces.

"Well, who is it?"

"It's Lamont, I'll get it."

Cassandra answered her mother as she headed toward the door with her aunt following close behind her. Laura reached for the door knob and gave Cassandra a comforting smile.

"Cassandra, ya'll go on get some air. I'll watch the kids. I'll talk to your mother."

"I think you're misunderstanding me Cassandra, we need to clear this up. Laura you answer the door for her this will only take a minute."

Mary's voice came from the kitchen where she sat and waited for her daughter to return. She was reaching in the cabinets for her medicine when Cassandra took her seat again at the table. Cassandra didn't know if continuing the conversation was best for either, her or her mother, but she took a deep breath and prayed.

"Cassandra, I know this is difficult for you. You're used to just doing things your way without much thought. You have four beautiful children, and you must think of them before you do anything. This may be the time in your life to make major changes and I want to make sure you don't make major mistakes."

Cassandra knew she wouldn't be able to take much of this "I know best" speech.

"Mama, I don't know what you think of my decisions in the past, but they were mine and I survived. Thank you for thinking my children are beautiful but with their beauty comes some of my input, my decisions. I have changed a lot in the past few years and this week has been an eye opener to say the least."

"Sandra, I don't want you to be used again, that's all. You said so yourself, look at what Trevor was doing right in your face. You're still naïve when it comes to his tricks. You haven't grown up as much as you think."

"I don't plan on being used Mama, no one plans on it. I'll admit I may have been naïve but who hasn't when they think they're in love. You and I need to get pass that. Trevor won't be coming here if that's your worry. I don't intend on using you or Aunt Laura. I do want to get my personal affairs in order, but I really don't need you to be a part of that."

Mary sat in silence. Cassandra couldn't tell if she understood or accepted what was said. Mary got up from the table and walked slowly out of the room leaving Cassandra confused, sitting at the table.

"Mary, are you okay?"

Laura and Lamont watched as she passed through the living room headed toward her bedroom. Mary entered her room and closed the door. Cassandra joined Laura and Lamont watching her mother's actions.

"Cassandra, what's wrong, what happened?"

"I don't know Aunt Laura. I thought we were having a decent discussion, and she got quiet on me. I told her my intentions, and she never responded. She got up and walked out of the room."

"Oh my God, did she take her medication. Sometimes she blanks out when she doesn't have her medication on time."

"She was taking it when I went into the kitchen."

"Cassandra that must be it, she'll be fine when the medication kicks in. It's been a long day for her, and she didn't take the medication on time. You and Lamont go on and have a good time."

"We were just going on the porch I don't think we were going anywhere."

Cassandra looked at Lamont for a confirmation.

"It's up to you Sandra; we don't have to go anywhere."

"I'd rather stay close in case my mother…." Laura cut her off.

"You've had a few trying days, you need a break too. Listen, I have your cell number. It's almost nine thirty. The kids will be in bed shortly. I don't know what young folks do, but you two go away from here for an hour or two and don't worry about things here. Cassandra, really I love watching the children, go on now."

"Thank you Aunt Laura, if we decide to leave the porch, I'll let you know."

Laura left the two of them standing in the living room as she headed toward Mary's closed door.

Chapter 38

Cassandra felt a sudden need for air. She couldn't remember when events in her life had been so full of drama. She no longer wanted to think of the past few days, she just wanted fresh air. She headed for the porch without inviting Lamont, who followed without speaking a word. The breeze of the evening gently touched her face giving her instant relief of her sudden pressure, stress and embarrassment. Cassandra couldn't face Lamont without breaking down. She chose to stare blankly from the porch onto the street.

Lamont recognized her need for a moment to embrace the silence and feeling of peace. He knew her days of stress had reached a peak. He wanted to be her shoulder of support but didn't want to push himself on her. Touching her gently, he approached her from behind.

"Sandra, let's get away from here for a minute. I think your Aunt had a point. Let me take you for a ride, and we can talk, you can talk or…"

Lamont paused. He didn't want to sound like he was pushing her feelings to the side.

"I mean, don't shut me out. Let me help you through this. Sandra, I'm here for you."

Sandra turned and faced Lamont. Tears were forming in her eyes. She couldn't hold her emotions any longer. Lamont took her into her arms and held her. She cried the tears she held since her arrival at her mother's home. Her fears of her mother's condition, the possibility of her dying; Trevor and Trina, and all her problems of her past rattled her emotions. Lamont held her close allowing her to cry in his arms without saying a word. His feelings for her were changing rapidly.

Cassandra didn't want Lamont to feel sorry for her. She wanted him to understand her situation. She didn't want pity. She agreed a talk would clear the air. She felt herself calming down and looked up at Lamont through her tear filled eyes. He wiped her tears and kissed her forehead.

"What's up girl? A ride, a talk, what?"

"I think a ride and a talk would be helpful. You don't mind, do you?"

"Not at all, let your aunt know. I'll wait for you in my truck."

Cassandra took a deep breath as he walked down the stairs toward his truck. Laura met her at the door as she turned the knob.

"I'm sorry sweetie; I was coming to tell you your mother was….Sandra you okay?"

"I'm fine Aunt Laura; I guess I had a moment. Lamont and I decided to take your advice, unless….is Is my mother alright?"

"Yes, that's what I came to tell you. She's sleeping. It was the medicine. Since the stroke, she has mini seizures, and they can scare you to death. She must have felt one coming on. When I got to her room, she said she wasn't feeling quite right. Anyway, she's sleep. She'll sleep through the night. Your children are getting ready for bed now. You and Lamont go on. Take your time you don't have to rush back."

Laura smiled at her niece. She wasn't ready for a night away from home and hoped her aunt didn't think that's what she wanted to do for the evening.

"Aunt Laura, I don't think our conversation will last too long, but I think I could use the fresh air."

"Baby, I can only imagine, but call if your plans change. Don't worry about your mother, she won't know if you're here or not. You deserve a moment or two. Besides your schedule is gonna be hectic the next couple of weeks with the kids in camp and you in school. Girl, you better enjoy the moment, even if it is just conversation."

"Okay, but it's my intention to come back tonight."

"Child, it's almost ten now. Here let me give you these keys. I'm going to bed too. You let yourself in. Like I said, take your time. If you start with a clear mind and conscious with Lamont, your relationship will benefit from it."

"Aunt Laura, what relationship? We're just friends."

Laura looked at Cassandra with a smirk that told Cassandra her aunt had her own thoughts about their relationship.

"Go on girl. You talk things through so ya'll will understand each other from the start. That man has been in the shadows for some time. It's been a long time Sandra."

Cassandra wanted to continue the conversation with her aunt but knew Lamont was waiting. She took the keys and kissed Laura on the cheek.

"See you in the morning. I'll be back though, in a few hours."

Chapter 39

Lamont got out of the truck as Cassandra came down the front steps of the house. As he opened the passenger door of the truck she couldn't help but smile. He remembered her first attempt at getting into his truck. She ignored his act of shivery allowing her thoughts to drift. She imagined that relationship, a romantic relationship with Lamont. *"I better learn how to get into this truck."*

The thought came and went quickly as she watched Lamont walk around the front of the truck. The headlights gave her a perfect view of the possibilities for the evening. She knew she wasn't ready to get involved in a relationship again, but if the moment presented itself, she wouldn't hesitate. Lamont's features and physique gave her a chill. Again she smiled, her life was in turmoil but there was an angel in the midst.

"Is your mother gonna be okay?"

Lamont put the truck in gear and pulled off turning the radio down so he could hear her answer.

"Aunt Laura said she was sleeping. She hadn't taken her medication on time and wasn't feeling well."

"Oh, well I'm glad she'll be okay. Sandra I want you to know that I meant what I said. Don't feel we can't talk about anything. Things haven't changed between us."

She was confused. *"What things is he talking about?"*

He continued to explain as though he heard her question.

"Remember when you were younger, and you always had something to tell me. I told you all the time I was waiting to hear what you had to say, and I guess I'm still waiting."

Cassandra remembered the times she would yell at Lamont as he would pass her porch, or she would see him from a distance. No matter where he was or who he was with, he would stop when she yelled, she had something to tell him. He would always yell the same answer. "I'm listening."

She wanted to be his distraction. She wanted to see if he would ignore her when he was with his friends. She never had anything to tell him. She just wanted to see if he would stop and wait for her to approach him. When Cassandra was in grammar school, she would run the other way after he'd stop. It was a childhood game. When she got to high school, her infatuation grew, and he loved her teasing him. Lamont would walk by her and whisper in her ear, he was "still waiting".

The thought of Lamont remembering the game they played pleased her. She realized what her aunt had said was true. It had been a long time. Although she still couldn't believe he could possibly accept her children, her problems and the drama it would bring. A relationship no matter who it was with would be difficult.

He drove slowly with the sunroof cracked and midnight love songs playing on the radio.

"Are you okay? I'm sorry I didn't ask you. Are you feeling a little better?"

"A little, I mean this week has been a bit much. I'm usually good at handling drama but this got to me, I guess."

"Some things don't happen every day Sandra. It's a lot for anyone to take all at once."

Lamont wasn't sure where the ride would take them. The peace of his yard was the relaxation Sandra needed, but he didn't want it to seem as though he was taking advantage of the situation.

"Lamont, can we go to your house and maybe sit in your yard? I mean we can sit in your house if you prefer, but it's such a nice night."

He replied with a smile, trying not to look too excited.

"Sure, if that's what will ease your mind. I have to warn you though. If you should want to stay, I'm not going to convince you to leave."

"Mr. Dearling, I will be coming back home tonight. I won't be staying."

"Whatever Ms. Smith, whatever."

The ride continued with Lamont and Cassandra making small talk about the music on the radio and the landmarks that had been demolished in the neighborhood where they spent their childhood days. As he pulled into his driveway, he noticed a black Yukon parked across the street from his house with two men in the front seat. It was eleven o'clock. Lamont didn't understand why Sean hadn't let himself in.

eleven o'clock. Lamont didn't understand why Sean hadn't let himself in.

Chapter 40

Sean approached Lamont's driveway and slowed his pace waiting for the driver's door to open. The look on Sean's face was questioning who the passenger was in Lamont's truck, although he never spoke a word. Lamont continued to the other side of the truck ignoring Sean's look and opened the door for Cassandra. Sean stood at the rear of the vehicle waiting for Lamont's next move.

"Cassandra, do you remember Sean? He was always with me when we were young. We've remained friends ever since."

Cassandra walked toward the rear of the truck as Sean walked to the passenger side. They both smiled seeing each other as old acquaintances would. Cassandra was surprised to see Sean had not changed much. He was taller and his baby features now had a manly overtone, but for the most part he looked like he had in high school. Sean was stunned to see Cassandra was still holding on to her beauty. She had always been a looker but the rumors that went through the neighborhood said she had been through abusive times. Sean expected it to show. He understood why Lamont still had an interest in his high school love.

"Cassandra, I'm glad to see you. Lamont said you were staying with your mother due to her being sick. How is she feeling? Any better?"

"Sean and I visit your mother together sometimes. He even visits when I can't"

Lamont didn't want Cassandra to think he told Sean everything about her mother's illness. Cassandra wasn't sure how to answer Sean's questions without the details.

"I don't know really. If you've been visiting you know how well my mother pretends to be alright. She's pretty sick. I pray she'll get better, but she won't let the doctor's do much for her. Thank you for asking and visiting. I didn't know you knew my mother that well."

"My niece goes to the school where your mom and Ma'Dear work at the after school program. My niece loves your mother, and I've grown to love her too."

"Thanks, it's good for her to have people around. I'm glad you're a part of her support system."

As Cassandra spoke Sean thought about the information he needed to give Lamont.

"Listen, I don't want to intrude on you two, Lamont, I need to talk to you a minute. I didn't want to call you with this info. Cassandra can you excuse us a minute. I promise this won't take long."

"Sandra, here's the key to the door. Let yourself in I'll be there in a minute."

She took the keys laughing to herself, *"I open the door, can't find the lights and then what?"*

Once again, Lamont read her mind. "The light switch is on the right side of the entrance."

He turned to Sean with a look of concern. Sean leaned on the back of the truck making him move closer to hear. They were out of the sight of Cassandra and Sean's passenger.

"Who's with you man?" Sean didn't answer. Lamont reworded his question. "In your truck, who's the brother in the truck?"

"It's Malik. We need to talk to him, but first I need to let you know what it's about. He called about eight o'clock to let me know his girl had the baby. I guess Jose' told him you were asking about Sylvia and Trevor. Jose' must have told him he needed to explain his association with Trevor to me and you. Malik called with all the information you needed and then some. I wanted you to hear it from him. You said you wanted to stay a step ahead of Trevor, so I brought Malik with the information."

"Man, I could have talked to him tomorrow or Monday. It really wasn't a rush man. Trevor and Sylvia ain't that important to me."

"Lamont, you know I know that man, but it's obvious Cassandra and Sylvia mean something to you. Trevor's been watching you and the shop for months. I didn't put it all together but something's up with that dude."

"Me and the shop, what's up with that? I just started talking to Cassandra, what, a few days ago. So this shit ain't about Cassandra. Maybe it's about Sylvia."

"Or Malik, listen to what he has to say man. We may have to step to Trevor."

"Listen, ya'll come in the house. Maybe Cassandra can shed some light on this mess."

"Man, maybe you ought to hear this first."

"Sean, Cassandra knows this man's motives like no one else does, besides, why not put it out there."

"Not this. Take my word, hear Malik out first, man."

"Tonight?"

"It's either now or first thing in the morning, before you go anywhere. We'll be here at seven in the morning."

"Man, bring breakfast dude."

Chapter 41

Cassandra made herself a cup of tea as she waited for Lamont. It seemed strange to be looking in cabinets and drawers for a cup, spoon and the other items to satisfy her need to relax. She found what she needed; herbal tea had a calming effect on her nerves. She stood waiting for the buzz on the microwave. She stirred the hot water and tea slowly as she added a little sugar. She carried the cup carefully making deliberate steps as she looked around the house. She took her first sip. Cassandra didn't want to go through anything that may be personal, so she simply stacked the papers that were spread on the countertop near the microwave. She changed her mind about standing at the counter and took a seat at the table. She closed her eyes and held head with both hands.

As she began to say a silent prayer she couldn't help but to begin to cry. Cassandra couldn't separate her emotions. The last week had been an emotional roller coaster. She didn't know if being angry with herself or Trevor would help, but she couldn't release her feelings without thoughts of her mistakes and his taking advantage of them. The front door open and closed as Cassandra wiped her tears trying to look as though she had not been crying.

"I'm sorry Sandra. Sean needed to give me some information that couldn't wait. I see you found what you wanted. I meant to tell you to make yourself at home."

"I'm good. I think the tea is helping to calm my rattled nerves. If you needed to talk to Sean it would have been okay."

"I got the gist of what he wanted. We'll talk tomorrow. You're more important right now. Are you comfortable in here or would you rather sit in the other room? Come on, I think you'll be able to unwind on the couch. Can I get you something else to drink?"

Cassandra smiled as she got up to follow him into the living room. He stopped at the couch and allowed Cassandra to sit first.

"If you're smiling because you think I'll try to get you to relax, that's my intention. You don't have to drink any alcohol or wine though, I just want you to be comfortable."

"No problem. I feel like I should be drinking. If I was drunk I probably would understand this mess surrounding me."

"Things will clear up shortly."

His thoughts drifted to his conversation with Sylvia and then Sean saying they might have to step to Trevor.

"Lamont, we need to talk. I don't want it to sound like I'm making assumptions, but before I can move on as your friend, I need to hash over some of this drama so you'll understand who I am now not what you may have heard or thought after the past few years. I'm not that person anymore and the reality of my mistakes has set in."

"What assumptions do you think you're making?"

She didn't want him to question her assumptions. She just hoped they were true. If Lamont wanted a relationship with her, she needed him to understand her feelings about the mess she was in and how she was going to handle it.

"I don't know. I'm confused, I guess. I just don't want you to think I'm using our friendship or your concern as a friend to avoid my problems. I think it's better if I just say what I need to say, and we go from there."

He let her words sink in and decided he would let her speak. He didn't want to tell her how he felt about her, but he didn't want to hear her say they couldn't deal with each other until she, "got it together". Those words would mean the relationship would never move on. Lamont realized he wanted a relationship with her. The drama wasn't running him away.

"Okay, hang on let me get a beer. Do you want more tea or anything?"

"Wine please, it doesn't matter what kind."

Lamont smiled, "Wino eh?"

"Wino! What do you mean?" Cassandra laughed.

"It doesn't matter what kind." He answered in a mockingly.

"Wino's drink anything. I understand though, the tea just doesn't have a kick."

Cassandra smiled and shook her head. Lamont had a sense of humor. It added to his character. She enjoyed his company. He returned with a Corona for himself, a bottle of Zinfandel Wine, and a glass with ice.

"I hope you like white wine; allow me to pour it for you. Now go ahead tell me what is it, I need to know about you."

Chapter 42

The atmosphere and the wine allowed Cassandra to speak without any inhibitions. There were paused moments between her time lines as she brought Lamont up to date on her life since her days in high school. She left out most of the physical abuse she suffered, but her tears reflected the story without the gory details.

She told him about her relationship with her mother and how over the years it had continued to deteriorate. She explained she had looked forward to reuniting with the woman she loved, but because of the years of arguments, and misunderstandings, she kept her distance. Her return to her mother's home, Trevor and Trina's fling, and being with Lamont shed strong light on unspoken realities. Cassandra admitted she wanted to be loved and accepted with her faults and new personal goals.

There was a faint beep that came from another room and Cassandra paused in the middle of her sentence.

"It's an alarm, it sets itself. It's for the house if I'm not home. The doors and windows are now alarmed my dear you can't leave without the code."

He smiled waiting for her response.

"And who said I wanted to leave Mr. Dearling."

She realized the wine had taken control of her tongue. If she wasn't careful she wouldn't be leaving.

"What time is it?"

"The alarm is set for four a.m., I was teasing, I'll take you home when you're ready."

"Lamont, I'm not worried about that."

"Good, can I ask you a question?"

"Sure, I've done enough talking, and I'm quite sure you have a few questions."

"Not really, I had heard things here and there about your relationship with Trevor. I guess I often wondered about us and how it would have been. I accepted the fact that you were with him, but what about now? I might want us to be more than friends, but I don't want to rush you into anything."

Cassandra didn't want to think the wine was playing with her emotions, and she didn't want to scare him with desperation. She decided to take a slower approach to their relationship.

"Lamont you and Gwen just broke up. You must need some time to sort out a few things about what happened and why. That's all I'm saying, I need to sort out a few things before involving a new romance."

Lamont shook his head.

"Since you've explained your life since high school let me just sum up my romances for you. I thought I found that everlasting love with Gwen. It took me a while to get into the whole thing of commitment and wanting to marry my second serious love interest. Girl, I know you won't believe me but, the first was you. I never told anyone how much I cared for you. I watched you from a distance. I thought I was over you until my mother told me you came home to take care of your mother. I respected what I thought you wanted. I need you to know Trevor never stood in my way. I understand what you're saying about your goals and a possible relationship between us, and it sounds like it doesn't include you dealing with Trevor. Don't get me wrong, I know you will have to see him from time to time regarding your children, and I would expect him to be in their life. I'm here for you, and I'm here to be whatever you feel comfortable with; me as your friend or your man."

Cassandra felt the water building in her eyes. Lamont took her hand and gently kissed it and let it fall slowly on her lap.

"I don't need time to sort out anything. Gwen played herself and I thank God it happened before we were married. It's been a minute since we broke up. I went from hurt to anger and I understand now you can't make someone love you. I won't pressure you. I just want to show my feelings for you."

Cassandra didn't have an answer. *No man wants a woman with a past like mine and four children. I've got to be dreaming.* The buzz from the wine wasn't enough for her to ignore the obvious.

"Lamont, can we take it a day at a time? I mean this is all new to me, more of a shock. I guess I never thought of me and you. Actually, I was preparing to raise my children and work long hours after I graduate from this program. Romance was the last thing on my mind."

"So can I be on your mind or what?"

"Sure you can, I just want us to understand each other."

"Well, there is one thing. I don't want Trevor to come between us. I've been told that's what he intends to do. It seems like he's been dealing with Sylvia off and on. Did you know about them?"

Cassandra took a deep breath before answering.

"I found out the same way I found out about Trina. They were going at it in my bed, in our apartment. Sylvia tried to say she didn't know we were still together, but I mean, damn, she knew I lived there. My pictures and my stuff was everywhere. I guess she didn't care."

"Well they're still dealing with each other. I don't know if they're bumping and grinding, but he has a hold on her. She told me leave you alone so he wouldn't hold it against her. Something's going on. I don't want him hurting her or you. He may use the kids as an excuse to be with you.

I just need to know when he's around."

"Not a problem. Personally, I don't think he'll come around if he knows we're dealing. He's always hated you, for some reason, even when we were together. It was as though you and him were competing."

"Yeah, unfortunately he's ahead of the game."

"How's that?"

"He won you over first. It should have been me."

"But who's winning now?"

Lamont leaned to meet Cassandra's lips. The kiss was long and passionate. Cassandra hadn't been kissed like that in years. Her thoughts went to the times when Trevor was his sweetest. His lovemaking was all she had known, he was her first and there had been no other. She pulled back slowly from Lamont's embrace embarrassed about her new fears. Could she truly love another man?

Lamont sensed her tension. Again Terrance's words of warning sounded in his mind. "She can't be loved, she's been abused." He refused to believe there was any truth in his brother's statement. If their relationship was meant to be it would just take time and Lamont knew it. He leaned forward and kissed her forehead.

"Listen, it's okay, we'll be fine. We need to be open with each other though. I need to know how you feel about things as the days go on. If you're uncomfortable with our relationship for any reason always remember we can discuss it before making any decisions. If it's to last baby, we've got to be able to talk to each other."

Cassandra realized he was saying this because of what happened in his relationship with Gwen. Just knowing he was willing to talk openly confirmed her thoughts. A relationship with him would be the start of her moving on.

"Are you ready Cassandra?"

"Ready?"

"Yeah, ready to be loved totally? Ready to be appreciated, cared for, and spoiled? Don't answer. Just get ready."

She could only smile. She hated to think about having to go home. As the morning light began to peek in the window, she knew it was time to get back to the house before her children got up. She looked toward the window and stared thinking of her mother's words the night before.

If anyone would object to their relationship, other than Trevor, it would be her mother. She wouldn't understand Cassandra's intentions. Her mother would see their relationship as Cassandra using Lamont for his money. As her thoughts began to unfold new problems Lamont's voice brought her back to the current time.

"Sandra, my mother's church is having a family day picnic next Sunday. I know your week will be busy but do you think you could squeeze a brother in on Sunday?"

"Squeeze you in? I better see you before Sunday."

They both shared a laugh. Cassandra got up and took her glass and the ice bucket in the kitchen. Lamont watched her walk away and smiled while he said a silent "thank you".

Chapter 43

L amont heard a truck pull into the driveway and remembered his meeting with Trevor and Malik.

He didn't budge from his position on the couch where he had been laying after taking Cassandra home. He took off his shirt and shoes and hadn't gotten any further than the living room.

Sean turned his key in the door and invited Malik to follow him into the home. The men entered the living room and their assumptions showed on their faces.

"What you smiling about?"

"Damn man it's like that? When was the last time you couldn't make it to your bed?"

"I chose not to. Didn't you tell me you would be here first thing in the morning? Let's just say you weren't the first thing. Malik man, welcome, don't pay any attention to Sean's bull, have a seat."

Malik looked around the room. He had been invited to Lamont's house often and never took the offers serious. He thought Lamont was just being an appreciative boss, having periodic barbeques for his employees. He tried not to look as though the home impressed him. The furnishings said that Trevor was right, Lamont's business brought in money. What Trevor didn't understand was Malik left the street and the game with no desire to return. Trevor had set him and others up once too often. Malik's last deal would be getting rid of Trevor permanently.

The men waited for Lamont, who returned with orange juice and glasses.

"Yo man, I told you to bring breakfast."

"We can go and eat if you want to."

Sean knew Lamont rarely ate breakfast unless it was a scheduled breakfast meeting. He didn't past up the opportunity to tease his friend.

"Shit. That means this must be business."

Lamont smiled and poured himself a glass of juice. He drank half of the glass and poured more for himself, then Sean and Malik.

"Lamont, don't take this lightly. Malik, man, go 'head you tell him what this shit is about."

"Right. Lamont, man I know what you said 'bout street deals and all but when you hired me, let's just say I had some unfinished business with Trevor."

"Malik, don't cut corners, what unfinished business."

The orange juice gave Lamont a jolt of alertness. He wanted to know all the details.

"Right. You know I used to deal with Trevor, I mean I pushed a lot of drugs, was involved in some other crimes and even did some jail time. Before I got hired by you some friends of mine got busted big time. I guess it was Trevor's proof he was in charge. See, he set the bust up. Yeah, the whole thing, just to throw the cops off him, my cousin was one of them.

Anyway I made a couple of promises to him if he got my cousin off. One was to set up another turf, new territory that the cops wouldn't suspect he was running. About a week later my cousin was out with no charges, I was expected to hold up my end of the deal. Jose' got wind of the deal and told me that's how Trevor set up most of his areas. He didn't deal at all. He capitalized on our sales and others picking up the goods. Trevor does all his business away from the inner circle. His payment to us was large but not as often as it was when we started. Sometimes we'd take ours off the top because Trevor just wasn't paying us back. He would always say we were short or owed him for something; seemed like he did it to most of us who was new to his game. Jose' told me there was a turf war about to start, brothers was sick of Trevor's shit. We would be the first hit, being we were on the streets working for him. Jose' got out with no strings attached. He said it was because of his family and I needed to consider doing the same being that my girl was pregnant.

At first, I didn't know what to do. I owed Trevor but Jose' was right. Those who didn't get killed would be arrested and Trevor was turning on his own peeps more and more. When one guy would drop out of sight, he'd just get another who was hungry for the fast money.

The shit was beginning to spook me. Jose' hooked me up with you. My debt to Trevor wasn't paid. I never set up a new turf. My cousin moved after he was released. Trevor started looking for us and found me at your shop. That's what he was looking for when he left the number for me to call."

Malik paused waiting for Lamont to ask questions. When he didn't he took a swallow of orange juice and continued.

"Right. I called him. He ran some shit down to me about me doing him wrong. I told him I had a kid on the way, I needed the benefits to take care of my girl and the baby. He told me he found another way for me to pay him back. Since I worked for you, he wanted to know when the shops deposits were made, when your safe was full. I told him if he was thinking about a hit, it was nearly impossible. He said nothing was impossible when you had inside help.

Man, I ain't about that kind of shit. It just showed me again how Trevor was treatin' his so called "boys". I mean, I know he would put all this shit on me if he got caught."

"Hold up man. You mean if you thought he could get away with it, you would have been down?"

"No, Lamont. No, dig. Right. I ain't no thief. I've sold drugs, you know and even had weapons charges, assaults, even well, I have capped a few brothers some are dead, but I ain't a thief. I'm just saying he played his self again. He was saying he was gonna hit the shop and blame me anyway with or without my help."

"So who's his boys then if it ain't you and Jose'? Where's he gettin' his info about the shop?"

"I'm not sure but if I'm right the fleet we're supposed to work on that's coming in from that dealership is Trevor's. I recognized the name of the dealer. It's one of his boys. If they start hanging around waiting on their cars to come and go, they'll get an idea about your business, you know, your intake, the daily time schedule."

The fleet was the new account Lamont spoke to Sean about. He was looking forward to the money which would be made from the repairs and detailing. It would pay for the renovation of the shop. It was one of the largest jobs he had in the ten years of business. It would take a few months to complete the job according to the specs. The dealership was said to be new but expanding. The cars were coming from auction blocks in the metro area and Lamont's contract included the pick up and delivery to the dealership locations. Malik waited for Lamont to respond when he didn't, he continued.

"Lamont they transport the drugs in their vehicles. The cars probably started overseas and worked their way up to this area. The detailing we do to the cars change how they look for the next run. Trevor's looking to pay you and set you up for drug trafficking without you knowing he's connected."

"Shit, once the cars leave the shop it ain't on us what they find."

After hearing the story a second time Sean could now visualize what Malik was trying to say.

"Wait Lamont listen to the way it would go. Malik tell me if I'm wrong. We pick up the cars from wherever. The drugs are in the cars already. Trevor tips the cops telling them we made a drop and are in the process of changing the cars over. The cops make the bust and the traces of the drugs are on the parts of the car or at the drop off point that Trevor gives them. We're also in the process of changing the cars appearances just like Trevor said we were."

"Okay, I kinda follow that bull but where does the robbery fit in?"

"Maybe he told Malik that to throw him off the real hit. Look it's a way to knock you down. We'll lose the business if we're busted for drugs. Even if we prove we weren't involved what car dealer will deal with us again. We'll be doing small handyman jobs from that point on."

"Okay, so that's our problem. This ass hole is trying to take our business. What does he gain?" Malik looked at Sean for the answer.

"Man, don't look at me. You know Trevor better than us. What does he gain?"

"Lamont man, like I told Sean. We all lose. Like I said arrested or dead, I feel like he's got me in a noose. I brought this shit from the street to your business. Ain't nothing for me to do but handle it. I just wanted you both to know what was up. I know what I have to do."

"Malik, man don't think about that kind of shit. You're a new father. I appreciate you telling me and Sean. Let me think about this. There's a piece missing. People don't just fuck with other people's money or business, unless they have something to gain. I need to know what he has to gain if I lose the business. He doesn't know Sean like that, there's no connection between them. He's threatened my sister too. He can't gain anything by hurting her or my business. I will go to jail 'cause, I'll kill him first. This nigga' keeps giving me more reasons to cross a line that I've never crossed."

Malik had never heard Lamont talk the way he was talking. He had heard Lamont was respected by the drug dealers and most of the gangs. He didn't know why but hearing Lamont talk, he knew he wasn't squeaky clean.

"Yeah, you're right, that's why I told you we might have to step to that nigga'. I mean it ain't like we didn't live in the same neighborhood. We grew up fighting and dealing on the same streets. Maybe he forgot about his boy, DJ you drew down on. If it wasn't for your relationship with DJ's brother you would have killed that dude."

"Don't remind me, 'cause, I still say I should have killed him. Like I said there's more to this."

Malik listened. He had heard about DJ's close call with death. DJ even talked about the night he was looking down the barrel of a gun. Malik didn't know it was Lamont's finger that would have pulled the trigger of the 357 magnum. The gun was chosen to kill DJ, the biggest dealer on the eastside of Philadelphia.

"Lamont, man whatever you need me to do I'm down. I mean I brought this shit to you, and I'm sorry man."

"Malik, listen, Trevor has some issues that may 'cause him to want revenge. I just don't know what they are."

"We've got to ask some questions on the street though Lamont and Malik might be the one to get us the answers."

"You might be right. Malik start asking questions and get the word on the street about Sylvia and Trevor. See if it leads to any conversation about me. Whatever you hear let us know, I don't know what would be good information or rumors. So don't think we can't use it. Tell us everything."

"Right. You got it. If there's anything else let me know."

Lamont stood up to shake Malik's hand. As Malik rose to his feet Lamont spoke.

"There is one other thing Malik. If you cross us, believe me you're dead. No doubt about it, you're dead."

Chapter 44

The week went by quickly for Trina. She had her job to occupy her mind during the day and Trevor at night. Although she enjoyed his company, she could tell he was there in body only. He told her he wouldn't be stopping by on Friday, and he would speak to her early on Saturday. The relationship she expected to have with him just didn't feel right.

Trina couldn't openly complain. Trevor had attempted to be attentive. He met her at her house just about the time she got home from work and ate dinner with her each night. Wednesday night he surprised her and cooked dinner. Tuesday and Thursday night he left about eight and came back about one. She knew he had street business to attend to so she didn't question where he had been. He hadn't asked about Cassandra and her name didn't come up in casual conversation. They made love less often, but she knew their romantic play wouldn't be as frequent once they were seeing each other regularly and not sneaking it in.

The transition from spring to summer was official with the weather reaching record highs. Children were playing on the streets while others sat on the porches, or stood around talking and laughing. The street dealers were out waiting on their buyers. There were people everywhere enjoying the warm weather, the preview of a hot summer.

Trina's ride home took her close to Trevor's side of town, but she was never interested in riding through "the block". He told her where he was staying, and she knew the area well. A couple of her co-workers lived in the same area. Curiosity got the best of her as she turned left just a few blocks away from Trevor's street.

"Damn, there's Trevor's car." She could see his car just past the next corner.

She hoped Trevor wouldn't notice her as she passed by. If he did, she would lie about her reason for being on his side of town. He was standing at the driver's window of a blue BMW with his back to the street talking to a white man. As Trina passed, she noticed a female in the passenger seat of Trevor's car. She frowned in disbelief.

"Who's that bitch?!"

Trina didn't stop. She circled the block not caring if Trevor saw her. As she passed the car the second time she slowed down trying to get the woman's attention without Trevor noticing. His conversation with the man held his attention but the woman turned and looked her in the face. She recognized Sylvia immediately. She remembered Sylvia and Trevor had dealings in and out of the bedroom. The story he stood by had been that Sylvia was a quick lay. He had only one reason for dealing with her; her white boyfriend had a habit and money. The white man Trevor was talking to fit the description of Sylvia's boyfriend, Carson, but Trina wondered why Sylvia was in Trevor's car. Sylvia's glare made the statement clearer. She had a claim, some right to be there.

Trina could feel herself getting madder by the minute. She convinced herself that loving Trevor would be a challenge, but she didn't think about any other woman. Cassandra wasn't really a threat. She could tolerate her. She wasn't secure enough to overlook him dealing with any other woman.

Trevor never looked as she cruised pass him and his client the second time. Trina waited until she was close to her home to call him. Her attitude would depend on what he had to say about Sylvia.

"Trevor, can you come here now?"

Trina knew the answer but she was interested in how he would avoid the issue of Sylvia.

"Uh, no not right now, I've got a problem I'm in the middle of handling. What's wrong? Can I get with you in about an hour or two?"

"What is it you don't understand about now? If it could have waited, I wouldn't be calling."

Trina wasn't good at disguising her feelings.

"Get rid of the bitch Trevor. I dealt with you and Cassandra. I ain't dealing with you and Sylvia too."

"Trina, what the hell are you talking about? Where are you?"

"I'm home Trevor. Get here if you can."

Trina hung up the phone. Trevor looked at Sylvia, licked his lips and smiled. She pulled down her shades feeling the rush from the last line of coke. He knew then, Trina would have to wait.

171

Chapter 45

K evin's attitude changed when the officer told him he had a visitor. He knew Reggie and Veronica were working to get him out. It was only a matter of time before they would get the information needed to prove he was set up. Kevin wasn't sure who set him up, but whoever it was, would wear it once he got out. He needed to talk to Trevor to let him know he had unloaded his goods before the cops got to him. The cops caught the guys Trevor sent with him. He didn't quite understand their purpose in the deal anyway. He did most of his pickups and drop offs alone. That's the way it was always done. Trevor told him he was sending the guys with him for his own protection. He argued the point but agreed if something went down, he would go with it and keep his mouth shut. He should have known they were crooked. Once he got out, he would talk with Trevor and get to the bottom of it all.

The officer led Kevin to a small room down the drab corridor. His escort waited with him at a door marked window visits. The large white painted letters moved to the left as the door opened slowly. The room reminded Kevin of a spacious phone booth. The only furniture was a table and two chairs. One chair faced the wall filled with scribbled phone numbers and the other faced a Plexiglas window with a phone mounted beside it. Kevin was confused. If Veronica or Reggie were visiting, they would be in the room with him, that's how attorney visits went.

"Take a seat. When your visitor comes, pick up the phone to speak. After you're done, just hang up someone will be back to get you." The voice over the intercom boomed. Kevin could hear background noises of radio transmissions in the control station.

Kevin sat down and waited. He heard muffled voices that he thought were more transmissions until the door opened on the opposite side of his window. Through the window, he could see the visitor was Trevor. Trevor took his seat listening to the instructions from the escorting officer. The men lifted the receivers to the phones mounted on the walls simultaneously.

"You alright man?"

Trevor started the conversation. A bad feeling came over Kevin when he saw Trevor enter the room. He decided it would be better if he just listened. Malik warned him about Trevor turning on his workers. Kevin expressed his doubts, knowing he and Trevor had run the street game together for years. He never thought that he would be a part of a double cross.

"I said are you alright?"

"Yeah, you?"

"I'm good. It's all good. Listen, your sister and them are working to get you out. The cops don't have nothing on you anyway. If I interfere, it will look strange you know?"

"Bail me the fuck out Trevor. My sister will handle the rest. But you bail me out."

"It ain't that easy. They set your bail pretty high. They think you know something. That's why I'm here. You know what to do. Like I said they don't have nothing if you don't tell nothing."

"So you thought you had to come and tell me that?"

Kevin could tell Trevor didn't trust him.

"Are you scared I might drop something on you 'cause you dropped something on me?"

"Cut the bull man. I told you they ain't got nothing. If they did you'd be on your way. Do you know how much that exchange was worth?" Trevor paused knowing Kevin had an idea of the money that had been exchanged. "Listen they caught the other two. How'd you get separated?"

"They went their way and I went mine."

Kevin played along. Trevor knew what the job was and where the drop offs were. There was no reason for his questions.

"I didn't carry no drugs or money. That's it. I was with them for the ride. When I got tired of riding, I got out the car and went my own way."

Trevor looked into Kevin's face. The conversation was a stale mate. Kevin wasn't talking. Trevor looked around the room. The cops might have been listening on the phone. He understood Kevin's hesitation to talk.

Kevin put the phone on the hook. He pointed his finger at Trevor indicating he was pointing a gun. He slowly moved his finger, as if he was pulling the trigger.

"Yo, man, that ain't right. Pick up the phone nigga'. Pick up the phone. Oh, it's like that!"

Kevin walked away from the window and sat at the table waiting for the officer to open the door. Trevor slammed his phone down causing an echo of anger. His door opened first and the escort officer led him out. Kevin waited for an hour before his door opened.

"Kevin Pearson, your sister's here to take you home. You're free to go your charges have been dropped."

Chapter 46

Veronica smiled when she saw her brother approaching the counter where she was signing his release papers. According to the paperwork Kevin was being held for questioning regarding the drugs that were confiscated when they made a local bust. There were drugs, weapons, and a confrontation with the police, all of which Kevin claimed from the day of his arrest, he was not involved in.

Veronica made calls and found out that one of the guys arrested used Kevin's name as an alias when he was booked. Kevin was picked up during the booking and brought in. The second man named Kevin as the mastermind. They stated they made the pickup of both the weapons and the drugs from him. After their fingerprints were run, they began telling the truth for fear of outstanding charges being brought against them. Kevin held on to his story throughout the interrogation. Even when questioned by Trevor, he maintained that he got out the car before he could be involved in any drug deal. The cops didn't find anything on him, they couldn't hold him. The bust was made; the cops were satisfied. The arrest of two runners, the drugs, and the weapons seized, made it possible for them to overlook any role Kevin played. They didn't have enough proof to hold him.

Veronica and Kevin walked out the precinct in silence. He had a few questions, but they would wait until he got to the car. Veronica wanted to apologize for the family doubting him but her apology would come with a warning. She really wanted an explanation. His excuses would lead to an argument. She decided not to apologize.

"I parked across the street. Let's cross the street here. Are you hungry?"

"A little thanks."

"No problem. Did they give you your belongings?"

"Yeah they did that before I got to you. It was all there. Veronica, what did they have as evidence?"

Veronica opened the doors on her Volvo and moved her papers from the passenger seat to the back of the car.

"We didn't get that far. I called this morning to say I was coming to collect the paperwork for your lawyer."

She put on her seat belt starting the car and turning down the radio. Kevin buckled himself in prepared to hear her response. He felt he knew the answer.

"They told me there was no need, they were sure you would be released; something about the dudes who they picked up using your name. The cops made it seem as though it was a story, they didn't believe at all. Your name was thrown in the mix for everything. First you had the drugs and guns for a delivery; then they picked up the drugs and guns from you. I don't know. Anyway they couldn't make it stick at all after one of them used your name as his own. I guess they picked you up just in case it was true."

"Veronica, I was with them earlier in the day. We didn't do no deals together."

Veronica turned into the parking lot of their family's favorite diner. The owner was an old friend of the family and had a great staff of cooks. They took their seats at an empty table and Kevin continued to talk.

"I told the cops that, and they still went on with their bull. I think I was set up Ronnie. That damn Trevor set me up. I just don't know why."

"Is he still dealing with DJ and those other jokers?"

"They still deal, but Trevor just started turning on his own. I just got on the street again, and I know that."

"Yeah Kevin you need to do something about that. If the charges would have stuck you would have been looking at some serious time. We can't keep getting you out so you can continue your shit, and get locked up again."

"I did one run to cushion my pockets. I'm good. I didn't want to borrow from y'all no more. I'm thinking about seeing Lamont for a job or something. Word is he's helping the brothers who are looking for work. You know he owns that auto body place. That's my next move, if that don't work I'll find something."

The waitress came to the table for their order. Veronica ordered a chef's salad and iced tea. Kevin ordered a cheese steak and fries. It came with an oversized soda.

"Lamont's doing his thing there. He's getting it renovated, expanding or something too. I like the way he handles his business. You know Dad says he's seeing Cassandra now."

"Damn, Trevor know that?"

"I guess he would. Why?"

"Well, him and DJ got beef with Lamont. That might keep Lamont from hiring me. I mean he may think I'm bringing Trevor and DJ's shit to his shop."

"So tell him you know about Trevor turning on his people. What could he say other than no? You'll never know until you ask."

"So what happened to Trevor and Cassandra? How did Dad find out about them?"

"Aunt Mary is real sick. Cassandra came home to help Aunt Laura and Daddy care for her. Lamont helped her move her things to the house. When they went to her apartment to get her stuff Trina and Trevor were there laying together when Cassandra walked in. I guess they hooked up from there. It's only been a couple of weeks, but they've been seen around town with the children. I think they're enrolled in the summer camp. Lamont picks them up from camp with Cassandra and whatever. They seem to be getting along."

"Damn, Trevor has got to be mad as hell."

"Why, he treated her like shit. Kevin she's been abused for years. I know you heard the rumors. I never told you 'cause you were too busy running your game but your boy should be in jail for domestic violence."

Kevin spent his time making drug deals happen for Trevor and serving time in jail. He didn't stay in touch with his family until he needed bail or help to get back on the streets.

Cassandra was Kevin's heart, his family favorite. She would always let him stay with her if he needed to lay low. He knew of the minor episodes of abuse. He had no idea how bad she had been beaten until Trina spoke to him once when she saw him on the street. Kevin listened with concern but he never approached Trevor about it. Personal problems weren't good for business. Trevor had given Kevin the first reason to confront him. Veronica had just given him the second. He needed to talk to Lamont about the job. He would need a new direction. His next conversation with Trevor would be face to face.

Chapter 47

Cassandra spent her week adjusting to her new schedule. The children enjoyed day camp, and she felt comfortable after their second day there. Cassie told Cassandra they didn't need their mother walking them to or from the school. She smiled thinking about her youngest child being the voice for her brothers. She continued to walk with them until her instincts told her different. All the children walked home together playing and teasing each other. She remembered her days of careless play. Cassandra gave her children all the rules she was given before allowing them to join the walk to and from day camp on Wednesday.

She was prepared for her class to start the next week. She received her information packet for school in the mail. There were forms and minor assignments that she had to have completed for her first day of class. She spent the next few days adjusting to what be her new schedule.

Cassandra's day started with her making breakfast for her children, aunt and mother. After meeting with the therapist for her mother's session, she followed their methods. Massaging her mother while periodically being sure to give her an uplifting conversation seemed to work well. Mary never complained and they both enjoyed the hour together. Lunch was simple and Cassandra, her mother and Aunt spent it watching television and debating over the talk shows. Ma'Dear had visited twice that week bringing the neighborhood gossip. During the afternoon Cassandra cleaned and washed clothes and relaxed before the children got home at four thirty.

Laura laughed to herself as she agreed to the schedule thinking Cassandra wouldn't last the week. Her shift didn't start until after the children got home. Cassandra spent time with the children, reading and giving them math and writing assignments. They worked until dinner was ready. Laura cooked dinner and cleaned the kitchen afterward. Mary told Laura Cassandra had made a good first week impression, but she wasn't sure it would last. The two sisters shared a laugh but Laura was keeping her comments to herself.

It was Friday and Laura needed to know how Cassandra planned to handle the schedule while she was attending classes. After looking in on Mary and the therapist, she found her niece in the kitchen.

"Mornin', Sweetie."

"Mornin' ", Cassandra replied smiling at her aunt in her flowered smock. Her morning outfit couldn't be one on the runway of Victoria Secret's Angel's tour, but it spoke of total comfort.

"What's up for today?" Laura returned the morning smile; she received seeing her niece's beauty with the sun's glare enhance her color.

"Nothing, I've finished all those questions for the school and most of the chores for today are done. So, I'll be looking through some of the books I bought for class. Just a day of leisure. What do you have planned?"

"Ma'Dear called. You know the church picnic is Sunday. She invited all of us to be her family guests. Ma'Dear's family lives in North Carolina so she chose us to go with her on Sunday. I believe Terrance, Sylvia and Lamont are going too."

"Lamont is going, I don't know about Sylvia and Terrance. He invited me last week. The children can't wait. He told them about it Tuesday when he came by. It sounds like it will be really nice."

"We didn't go last year, but the year before it was a lot of fun. Anyway, I told Ma'Dear, I had until the five o'clock hour to help her shop for the rest of the odds and ends she may need. Is there anything special you want for the children?"

"Aunt Laura you don't have to worry about them. Lamont and I are going shopping for a few things tomorrow."

"So things are going well between you two?"

"Day by day, I think I'm still dreaming. He pretends not to notice my tension, and I try not to seem so scared but Aunt Laura, I don't want to fall for him and be dumped."

"Dumped? Why would he dump you?"

"Why? Trevor, four kids, no job, I could go on."

"Cassandra move on; if Lamont didn't want to deal with the obvious he wouldn't have pursued you. You have to look to the future for your strength. Look at the goals you have set for yourself. Move on. Allow Lamont to be close to you, and if you're uncomfortable tell him. But first allow him. He has accepted you. You've got to accept you. Things will change for you if you allow them to."

"I guess you're right. I didn't think it would be this hard. I mean I don't want Trevor in my life on that level. I just want him to be a father for his kids."

"Cassandra, what if he's not interested in his role as their father without a relationship with you. Let it go, move on. Trevor's a grown man. Don't wait to see what he'll do before you make personal decisions for yourself. Lamont is a good man. His kind just don't walk into your life every day."

Laura took a seat at the kitchen table and waited for Cassandra to sit opposite her. Her concern, as always was about her niece's well being. Eager to receive words from her aunt that would give her the courage to move on; she stood behind the kitchen chair.

"Sit down child. Listen to me. You pray daily, I know you do. God hears all prayers, especially those when we are in despair. It's up to us to recognize when your prayers are answered. Your mother's illness has brought some reality to your life. Cassandra, God is working with you. Move on with your life, let it go and let God work."

"I see His work Aunt Laura. I'm just scared I'll ruin what could be my only chance for happiness. Lamont is the only other man I've dealt with. I don't know if I'll satisfy him. I've never been treated the way he treats me. I don't know how to react, and sometimes I don't know what to say."

"Say a silent prayer of thanks. You'll be fine girl."

"We haven't spent much time together, but I guess I'll have to get used to our schedules being full. Everything is so different. Trevor used to drop in during the day or night. Lamont hasn't been in my life long enough for me to have him around the kids daily. They know him but if they see him on the regular; what will I tell them about their father and me?"

"You tell them the truth. You don't want your children to think you're romancing two men. Your children aren't sleeping through this. They know you're not with their father. It's time for them to know the truth about love. The relationship between Lamont and your children will grow while your relationship with him grows. Make time for them to be included as well as time for you and Lamont to be alone.

Cassandra you've got to make up your mind what you want. Lamont is not Trevor. Allow yourself to be loved."

Cassandra sighed at the thought. She had gone over the possibilities in her mind. Talking to her aunt echoed the thoughts she tossed around earlier during the week. She leaned on her hands in thought before making another comment. Laura watched the young woman's gestures. She knew the problems love could bring. She knew her niece deserved better.

"Lamont said the same thing. We'll be arranging outings for the children as well as time for us. I was hoping Trevor would call early today. It's his weekend for the children, and I need them to be home early on Sunday to go to the picnic. I don't know if I want to tell him why or not. He's so spiteful he may not bring them back in time. My plans were set if he came, I would spend some time with Lamont before Sunday."

Laura smiled at the thought. Ma'Dear said Lamont invited Cassandra to spend the weekend with him. They both agreed the children should stay home. Laura was waiting for Cassandra to ask her to watch them. She wasn't aware of their visit with Trevor.

"Cassandra, contact Trevor. Tell him to switch weekends with you. Tell him you've got plans for the weekend and the kids are looking forward to it. He can't come here so he won't know where you are. Even if he drives by he can't stop here. I'll watch the children for you. You and Lamont have a nice time, and we'll see you Sunday. Let me know if they'll be riding with us, or you'll be meeting us at the picnic."

"Thank you Aunt Laura. I didn't want to deal with Trevor and his mess anyway. We'll be here Sunday to take them to the picnic."

"We need to look at next week. How are you going to get back and forth to your school? The children will walk to the day camp and back right?"

"Yes, they're straight. They love the camp and they're happy with walking. I'll catch the bus back and forth. It stops right in front of the school. I'll have to walk up the street to catch it from here. I'm going to save up some money and get a car eventually. My goal is before the winter sets in."

"So you think you'll be staying here after you graduate from the program."

Cassandra thought carefully before answering. She had given it some thought but without knowing how her mother's condition, she had to be truthful.

"I'm not sure. It depends on my mother, and how things go between us. I hope if all goes well to be here until I can get my own home."

The doorbell rang.

"That'll be Ma'Dear. You call Trevor now; tell him you've got plans. Don't let that man ruin your living. The kids will be fine."

"I'll see you when you get back. Tell Ma'Dear hello for me."

"Sure will. Tell Mary I'm gone now."

Cassandra started toward her mother's room and was stopped by the ringing of the phone.

"Hello."

"Hey, Cassandra. This is Veronica. How are you?"

"Hey, Ronnie, how are you?"

"Fine girl. My dad said you were on this side of town for a while. How have you been? How's the kids?"

"I'm fine. The kids are getting big. They're in summer camp so this summer will be one they'll remember."

"Wow, even Cassie?"

"Yeah, Cassie too. She enjoys it the most. I was worried at first, but she loves it. It's the first week but no problems. I think she'll be fine. Now I know she'll be ready for school in September."

"I would love to see them. Are you going to the picnic on Sunday?"

"Yeah, you know about the picnic?"

"My father and Ma'Dear, talk on the regular girl. I think there's something between them, but you know they won't admit to it. Anyway she invited all of us."

"So are you coming? What about Reggie and Kevin?"

"Reggie will be there too. I'm not sure about Kevin; you know he never was much on family outings."

"It'll be good to see you all."

"Kevin said he wanted to talk to you, maybe he'll come if I tell him you'll be there."

"Tell him to call me. If he doesn't want to go to the picnic, he can always call me."

"It's so good to hear your voice. How's Aunt Mary?"

"Ronnie, I don't know. It's up and down. They said if she doesn't get treatment she might die. I don't even know how to convince her that the treatment is needed. Then there's her recovery from the stroke. She has problems on one side. The therapist is here three days a week.

The doctor said most of her bad feeling is from the pain medicine she takes. Ronnie these past few weeks have been an eye opener."

Veronica listened as Cassandra gave her emotional details of the past three weeks. She told her about Lamont and her new love dilemma. Cassandra felt relieved to talk to someone it was something she missed not having Trina to talk to. They talked and laughed for more than an hour.

"Girl, you need to follow Aunt Laura's advice. Move on. Trevor is no comparison to Lamont. You deserve some satisfaction and I'm sure Lamont can give it to you."

"Ronnie, I know he can. I don't want him to think I'm rushing things."

"Well you don't have to wait forever either."

"I'm taking a step at a time."

"Run Forest, Run."

They both laughed. Mary called Cassandra from her bedroom, which let her know she was attempting to get out of the bed. Cassandra went to aid her mother telling her cousin, she would see her Sunday.

Chapter 48

Trevor didn't expect Trina to call him for the weekend visit after their last conversation. The children hadn't been with him since her move to her mother's, and although it didn't bother him, he needed to find out if Lamont was spending time with Cassandra regularly. He would use their time apart to fulfill his plans. Whenever Trevor spent time with his children it meant there would be no street business handled. He thought about loose ends that needed to be cleared up before their arrival.

He turned at the corner cutting off the driver who had the right of way. The woman in the driver's seat laid on her horn and gave Trevor the name of "Asshole" as she yelled other obscenities from her window. He smiled ignoring her fury. His thoughts drifted again to romp and play with Sylvia. He was headed to her apartment when he remembered Cassandra and his children. He decided she would be his weekend entertainment.

Malik hadn't called him in the past few days. He and Kevin would be a problem. DJ was right he couldn't take on any new jobs without getting rid of them. Jose', Malik, and Kevin had been his top dogs before DJ told him they wanted more. The way DJ saw it. They wanted to overpower Trevor's turfs, an internal takeover. He had to prove his alliance to sit at the table with DJ. He had been in the game long enough to sit back and collect. DJ would wait for Trevor to set each of them up and see what they would do.

Jose' walked away leaving most of the goods in the apartment for the cops to walk in and get. He claimed no cash exchange was made, but he kept what he got away with and sold it later to one of DJ's boys. Trevor decided to let Jose' walk, he would deal with him later.

Malik never brought in the new prospects he promised. Trevor couldn't trust that he hadn't started his own clientele. Then there was

Kevin, he would be the real problem. He peeped Trevor's game and now he would tell what he knew. Trevor and DJ had big plans and that didn't include Kevin, Malik or Jose'. Combining DJ's run of the eastside of town with Trevor's run on the westside, would give them the control a dealer could only dream about.

When they agreed to join forces and Trevor told him Kevin would be an asset. They would be able to run their area and a good portion of South Philadelphia with Kevin on board. Kevin controlled the streets of South Philly. The empire could grow overnight. DJ put the paper work for the cars in motion and set up the run. They needed Kevin to handle the cars they would send to Lamont's shop. Trevor told DJ about his problem with Mr. Dearling and the surge of revenge ran through DJ's veins.

The two had been setting up their plan for months. Trevor gave up a couple of leads for the cops to follow, and they would easily fall for a bust involving trafficking across state lines. Once Lamont was busted, they would buy his business and everything would fall in place. Then they would run the drugs from the auto shop. Jose' and Malik owed Trevor and his reputation wouldn't allow them to just walk off and not pay him, one way or another. Trevor was certain they would be the inside help he needed.

Lamont was at the top of DJ's hit list. The successful mechanic thought he was above running drugs and using women. DJ had his reasons to want Lamont to fall and fall hard. Trevor thought about loose ends again and decided to try to talk to Kevin once more before adding him to his list of problems he needed to handle. He was aware that Kevin was released so he dialed his cell phone number.

"Yo, Kev man. Are you going to let me explain?"

"What the fuck do you want Trevor?"

"So, you're still mad. Listen you took one for the team. I want to thank you."

"Trevor, you're talking to Kevin. Not one of those stupid bitches you deal with. You don't use me man. Don't include me in your bullshit games."

"Listen, it was a test. I got some big shit coming up, and I need to know where my people stand. I mean look at Jose' and Malik. They just walked off. They didn't even confront the issue. You, on the other hand, are a businessman."

Kevin cut Trevor off. He had made up his mind. He didn't want to deal with someone he couldn't trust.

"Listen Trevor, your actions showed me one thing. You don't trust me and I can't trust you. We can't work together like that. I did everything I could to show you I was down with your program. What did you do? Set my ass up! I'm trying to forget you crossed a line. A line that could get you killed. Don't push it Trevor. Obviously, you don't know me."

Trevor made one last attempt to gain Kevin's interest.

"What do you mean? I made you nigga! You wasn't shit until I showed you who you was! So I tested your ass. I test everyone I deal with, one way or another. You passed my brother. We need to talk and celebrate. Things are gonna get bigger for both of us. I want to include you in the bigger picture. Don't fuck it up for yourself."

"Trevor, find someone you can play with. No better yet do what you do best."

"What's that?"

"Fuck yourself!"

Chapter 49

Trevor slammed the phone on the receiver. Kevin was indeed a problem that would have to be handled before his plans with DJ were executed. His plans for the weekend would have to change if he was to stay on schedule. Trevor missed his children, and though he didn't want to admit it, he missed Cassandra too. He had spent most of the week with Sylvia so the gossip could get back to Cassandra. Sylvia even spoke to Terrance when he spotted the two of them shopping at a jewelry store downtown. She was getting the best of Trevor's arrangement. She didn't mind his public appearances but there had been no response from Cassandra or Lamont. They didn't even respond to any comments made about Sylvia and Trevor's new relationship. He was sure it got back to them. He paid well for the subtle conversations to be made in their presence. Trevor was becoming desperate. First his love life was falling apart and now the business deal was going sour.

The phone rang, which brought a smile to his face. He prepared his attitude to show Kevin he was glad he had come to his senses. Trevor knew Kevin had the tendency to be mad and change his mind after he thought about the money they could make. Trevor didn't look at the caller ID which would have told him Cassandra was on the other line.

"Man, let's just forget this shit and move on."

Cassandra shook her head realizing Trevor had no idea she was on the phone.

"I have moved on. How are you Trevor?"

"Damn, baby, what's up? I was just thinking about you. Are the kids okay?"

"Yeah, everything's good. Listen…"

"I was gonna call you the past couple of days, but I didn't know if my timing was okay. I mean I hear you've got a busy schedule now with the kids in camp and your mother. See I keep up with those I care about."

Cassandra could hear the lies mounting. She sighed as she listened moving the phone from her ear. It was talk like this that would make her long for Trevor's attention. Cassandra noticed she didn't feel the same and didn't want to listen to his game. He sounded pathetic. She would have told him so, but she wanted him to be okay about the children not visiting him for the weekend.

"Thanks for caring. Listen, I'm calling because I have been busy, and I made plans to make it up to the children this weekend. Would it be okay if we switch weekends, so I can take them out? I made the arrangements and told them about it, and then I remembered it was your weekend. I'm sorry."

Trevor knew he needed the weekend to settle the mess with Kevin, Malik and DJ, but Cassandra didn't need to know that. He could use this request as a favor granted and look forward to Cassandra repaying him.

"Well, can I ask if I may be included in the plans?"

"No, it's just a mommy and the kid's day. I promised them."

"What, no Lamont in the picture?"

"Trevor yes or no. I didn't call to talk about Lamont or your affairs. I need the children to be home for the weekend."

"I thought you had plans. What do you mean home?"

"I've planned outings for Saturday and Sunday. Yes or no?"

"So when are we going to talk Cassandra. You and me, when?"

"Talk about what? Trevor I just asked one question, if you don't want to answer…"

"Oh this question comes with threats?"

"No, if you don't want to answer don't, just remember I asked."

"What does that mean?"

"It means I'm trying Trevor, despite all you have done I'm trying. I don't think I should be trying at all, but I am."

"Okay and what the fuck does that mean?"

"Trevor, it means yes or no."

"Damn, you really don't want to talk about nothing huh?"

Cassandra didn't answer leaving Trevor wondering if she was still on the line.

"Sandra, Sandra…"

"Trevor. Yes or no."

"No! It's my weekend. If you and I can't even talk then I can't give up my weekend."

"Okay, thank you."

Cassandra hung up the phone with tears rolling down her face. Before calling Trevor, she knew he would want to talk or be with her just to agree to her terms. It was Trevor's blackmail. Cassandra knew matters between her and Trevor just wouldn't change.

Chapter 50

S ylvia was surprised when Trevor bought her a diamond earring and necklace set. He had the jeweler ship it from New York. She stood in the mirror admiring how the set added to her beauty. Sylvia fingered through her hair flipping it into different styles. A pony tail, bun or just letting it hang allowed the earrings to be shown. She walked over to her closet and pulled out two of her favorite dresses. Sylvia modeled in the mirror pleased with her new accessories. She chose another dress unsure which she would wear to thank Trevor for her gift. He had put the icing on the cake. She was willing to stay in a relationship with him after being showered daily with gifts and money. Carson had never bought her anything without being told what to buy and where to buy it. His solution was handing her his credit card. Sylvia thought Trevor was beginning to care more about her.

The week was filled with his apologies. Trevor explained he had business to take care of during the week that would keep him out all night, street business. Sylvia understood and didn't ask questions. During the day, they satisfied each other. She would prepare their lunch in the morning and meet him at her place to eat and play during her lunch break from the office. Carson never said much about them spending less time together or her extended lunch hour. Sylvia would bring him a goody package and spend time with him on the weekends to keep his interest on edge.

The employee's at Klien and Son's watched as the affairs and habits of Carson Klien grew worse. Sylvia got stares and mumbles whenever she entered an area but her new jewelry would ruffle all feathers when Carson took her to the company dinner later in the year. Sylvia was ahead of the game. She had the executive position in Klien and Sons she had always wanted. Carson was at her finger tips. His want for coke would be supplied by Trevor in exchange for her being there for him. Trevor never mentioned gifts being a part of the deal. Sylvia felt his feelings for her had changed indeed.

They didn't talk about any future plans, but Sylvia wanted the relationship to continue. She was convinced that Trevor's thoughts about Cassandra and Lamont would soon become a part of the past. There would definitely be problems with her brothers and family. Sylvia needed to let them know that he was not her supplier but her man. She didn't know what to say or when to say it, but it needed to be said. Terrance didn't question seeing Trevor and Sylvia together at the jewelry store. She didn't know whether or not Terrance told Lamont or Ma'Dear. She needed to talk to Terrance before the picnic just in case Trevor wanted to come along.

Sylvia had taken the day off, and it was close to twelve. Trevor hadn't called but if he followed their schedule, he would be at her door in an hour. Sylvia hadn't prepared lunch. Quickly, she took off her earrings and returned her dresses to their place in the closet.

The condo was small compared to most. The floors and wood work gave it an expensive flair. It had two bedrooms, two baths, a kitchen nook, living room and loft. Sylvia liked its location, the center of town. Most of the executives rented living quarters for their clientele to stay in when they visited. Sylvia had a lease with Klien and Sons. Carson would pay the monthly expense if she asked. Sylvia was enjoying the best of both worlds. The view from the second floor showed most of the Philadelphia highlights and was beautiful at night. Sylvia was content in her own world.

Sylvia walked through her condo thinking again about the possible protests her family would present. She decided to ignore the "what ifs", and any other questions she thought they would ask.

She opened the refrigerator realizing she would have to fix a salad to go with the grilled chicken from the night before. Sylvia started to prepare the salad and changed her mind. She would tell Trevor they should go out to lunch. They both would enjoy the change and maybe spend the afternoon together. Sylvia decided to relax until Trevor arrived.

When the phone rang, she was startled. It was obvious she had dozed off on the couch where she waited for Trevor. The clock on the wall told her it was three thirty. Sylvia glanced at the called ID which read "private number". It wasn't Trevor.

"Sylvia, this is Trina."

"Trina? Trina who?"

"Trina Slater, Cassandra's old roommate."

"Oh, yeah what's up?"

"You tell me. I saw you in Trevor's car the other day. You and him got something going on other than his dealing?"

"What are you talking about? Better yet what do you care?"

"Where do you think he is when you're not around?"

"What?"

"Cut the bull Sylvia, he spends his time here with me."

"How did you get my number?"

"His cell, listen, I know you know by now that Cassandra is no longer in the picture. I am though. I stepped in when she checked out."

Sylvia listened as Trina filled her with information about Trevor and Cassandra and her invasion of their lover's paradise, which created a love triangle.

"Sylvia that ain't going down no more, I'm Trevor's woman and there's no room for you."

"Trina, there must be room for me if you're calling. I mean you sound like you feel threatened by me being his friend."

"Is that what it is Sylvia, you're friends?"

"Friends before lovers, you can't go wrong if you get to know the man first. I mean before you play, make him pay that way he'll stay."

"Where'd you get that whacked shit. Sylvia, I'm fucking Trevor and you need to keep your uptight ass with that white boy, Carson."

"I think that's up to Trevor. Talk to him."

"I did. He said you were his way back to Cassandra. I'm not willing to have that either."

"Trina, what did you say?"

"You're his ticket back. He wants to make her jealous, so he picked you. He's been here keeping me warm, so I won't get mad while he uses you."

"I know, Trina. I know. I thought things would change, but if he told you, damn...." Sylvia's voice faded as she got up looking for the aluminum foil package. After the dose of reality Trina gave her she needed a hit. She tapped the foil onto the glass table and pushed the speaker on the phone. She listened to Trina waiting for the coke to dull the shocking blow that had been delivered.

"Stay away from him Sylvia. He don't mean you no good."

Trina had brought her to her senses. Wiping her tears she responded before hanging up the phone.

"I can't. He threatened to kill my brother."

Chapter 51

L amont's day was filled with meetings. Sean was careful about having any meetings with new customers. They were on the alert for any of Trevor's business coming through. Jose' and Malik were appointed escorts for anyone coming to meet with them. The four men were looking for any suspicious deals or people. Malik and Sean agreed Trevor wasn't stupid enough to send someone they knew or recognized. Jose' prepared a set of questions for each new client. The answers would indicate how much they knew about the area, the business, and if they were sent by Trevor. When Kevin showed up Malik and Jose' froze.

Jose' threw a signal with his head in Kevin's direction after he got Malik's attention. Malik looked up and wiped his hands on his oil rag. He walked toward Kevin smiling.

"Yo, what's up man? Trevor sent you after me?"

Kevin hesitated before answering. He sensed Malik's nervousness. As he scanned the shop noticing Jose' watching from under the hood of the car he was working on.

"Naw, that nigga didn't send me. I need to see Lamont, but first I need a minute with you and Jose'. Listen if it's not a good time I need to know when. Its business but I understand you dudes are working."

"Give me a minute, we're wrapping things up but, let me get Jose'."

Kevin remained near the bay doors. His back was to the shop as he watched the traffic and people walking by. He didn't know how long it would be before he would hear from Trevor, but he needed to know where Malik and Jose' stood with him. Malik walked up behind Kevin and tapped him on his shoulder.

"Come on man, we can talk in the conference room. Jose' will be there in a minute. I told Lamont you wanted to talk to him too. Did you want us to be together?"

"Uh, no, why you being so damn formal? What the hell is wrong with you?"

Malik didn't answer leading the way to the conference room. The entrance was off the bay area. The hall was lined with lockers and two vending machines. There were signs indicating "customer waiting area, employee cafeteria, restrooms, showers and the conference room". Malik opened the door and flipped the light switch.

"Take a seat man. Do you want something to drink?"

"No I want you to answer me? What's with the formalities?"

"Kev, man if I can explain later I will. For right now I need you to tell me what you want to talk with me and Jose' about."

"I can talk to you both together let's wait for your boy."

Kevin was getting angry. Malik never treated him this way before. As they waited for Jose' Malik looked out the window not saying a word to him.

"They don't trust me." As Kevin's thoughts ran through his head Jose' entered the room.

"Hey man, good to see you're alright. What's up, what's on your mind?" It was apparent, Jose' didn't feel the same as Malik about Kevin's drop by visit.

"Well before your boy here treated me like a disease I came to talk about this shit with Trevor. You tell me. I mean I heard about him turning on his peeps. I guess I thought me, you and Malik were above that. Anyway he turned on me last week. Cops picked me up on some old bogus charges. I think Trevor was connected though. Had some new dudes run with me, backwards ass dudes. Everything about them felt wrong. I dumped his shit long before the cops showed. Those asses didn't even know when or where. I got it off smooth though. They got stopped after they dropped me off. Used my name and shit, the cops ran down on me. You know usually Trevor is quick about getting us out. I spent a week trying to get out. My sister got involved and the shit charges disappeared. The lies began with Trevor as my visitor. Nigga said he couldn't get me out without the police looking at him funny. Ya'll know he don't come to the precinct. It was a set up. I just don't know why. Then I find out about him and Cassandra, Lamont and Cassandra, man, I know that ain't going over smooth. Trevor hated Lamont before he got with Cassandra. I just got a bad feeling about this shit man."

Jose' and Malik looked at each other. Malik decided to let Jose' pick Kevin about Trevor before either of them talked.

"So why are you here?"

"Trevor told me you both owe him, but you dropped out of the ranks."

"Yeah, pretty much. We don't owe him shit and if the nigga told the truth he would be telling you how much he owes all of us, including you."

Jose' told Kevin about the deals and sales that they hadn't been paid for. Trevor promised payment after the next deal and sales were made. After going through it with him again and again both he and Malik got out. They kept the profit from the last deal and pick up to make up for their lost. Trevor set up a few of their runners to prove he could get them busted, but he was showing his loyalty to DJ not the cops. DJ told him who to set up and get rid of. If they didn't get busted by the cops, they were shot down by DJ's boys.

Kevin listened realizing why Trevor was so apologetic. DJ didn't know Kevin ran most of the Westside. Trevor dealt with the spot checks only. Malik and Jose' worked under Kevin. Kevin didn't try to stop them when they said they had family to protect and wanted out, he didn't know there was more to it. If Trevor thought they owed him, he thought the same of Kevin. Trevor knew he owed them. Trevor thought Kevin was in on the cut or was taking his off the top. DJ and Trevor feared Kevin was setting up turfs with Malik and Jose' working for him.

"Trevor and DJ are working together?"

"Seems like it. DJ's boys are everywhere. I noticed they were hanging out near the club last week. That wouldn't happen if they weren't down with Trevor."

"So DJ's taking over Trevor's turf?"

"Naw, they're working together like you said more territory bro. The way I see it, me and Malik were expendable, and if he set you up so are you. It's either that or DJ is scared we wouldn't work under his terms, and maybe we worked with you. You would become their competition. We walked away clean, we're done with that shit."

"So am I. I'll wind up killing that nigga. Then I will be in jail. But man he's got to pay somehow for setting me up and for not paying us. I mean I understand you got yours, but it's the principle. I ain't letting that shit ride. You and Malik got out just before he got you. That nigga is headed to getting hurt real bad."

Jose' looked at Malik for him to speak. Malik just lowered his head.

"Malik, what's up man? What did I do to you man?"

"Nothing Kev. It's just, man, you come here with this story and if this hadn't went down you would have been down with Trevor hurting us or our family. That shit ain't settling right with me."

"You think I would have been down with setting you up or harming you and Jose'. Man I ain't about no hits now that's your thing. I hurt those who hurt me or mine. Man I came to be sure what I was assuming and heard was true."

"Well why you need to see Lamont?" Malik still needed answers.

"I need to check on Cassandra. I plan on talking to her, but I hope Lamont can give me a heads up on Trevor, and if he's still abusing her. I also wanted to talk to him about a job. If I'm not going to work with Trevor, I need to find a job somewhere. I don't know much about being a mechanic, but I have done detailing and some other odd jobs."

Jose' got up out of his chair and told them he would see if Lamont was free.

"Malik man, I know what it's like not to trust someone who you thought had your back. Man, I still have your back. Trevor is stirring up some shit both on the street and in his personal matters. The brother is causing serious problems. If I have to, I'll settle them."

Chapter 52

amont smiled as he saw Jose' coming toward his office door. He nodded his head letting Jose' know he would be in the conference room when he got off the phone. He saw Kevin enter the shop. He was waiting for someone to let him know about the unexpected visitor. Lamont continued his conversation with his mother hoping to rush her off the phone.

"She said they were coming Ma. I think she was talking for her and the kids."

"I know Laura, Mary and Earl are coming." Lamont could tell his mother was excited, but he needed to end their conversation and get to the conference room. Ma'Dear continued without hesitation.

"Earl said he wasn't sure about Reggie and Veronica. I didn't expect him to know nothing about Kevin, I think he said he was locked up or something like that. Anyway, I just wanted to make sure you and Cassandra were still coming together."

Lamont didn't mention Kevin wasn't locked up. He wanted his mother to explain what she meant by "still coming together" but he didn't have the time to hear her logic.

"Listen, I've got someone in the office. I'll come by when I pick up Cassandra. You'll be home later won't you?"

"I've done all my running around so I'll be here. Terrance should be home by then. Around what time are you coming?"

"I guess about six or seven. Listen, I've got to go. Love you." Lamont didn't wait for Ma'Dear to respond. After paging Sean on the intercom, he headed toward the conference room. Sean was already there. Lamont walked in closing the door as everyone took a seat.

"Kevin, I haven't seen you in years. What brings you here?"

Kevin could tell from Lamont's statement Jose' didn't tell him why he wanted to see him. He looked around the table at the four men waiting for his response. Jose', Malik, Sean and Lamont made him feel as though they were a jury, and he was on the stand.

"Somebody needs to fill me in. Lamont I came here to see about working for you but man, since I walked in the door I've felt like there's a problem, and I'm it."

"So why are you here Kevin?" Sean repeated Lamont's question ignoring his statement.

Lamont and Sean wanted to hear what Kevin had to say. He repeated the story he told Malik and Jose'. As he spoke, he felt his anger for Trevor building again. Jose' left the room and returned with bottled water for all. Kevin took the water from Jose', happy he could quench his thirst.

"Thanks, man. Lamont I wanted to see you about my cousin, Cassandra. I heard you and her might be an item now. I don't know if you knew about how Trevor used and abused her. She would never admit it, but she went through some shit with that brother. I'm glad she's breaking away from his spell. Is she okay or was it another reason she really came home?"

"Cassandra's fine. I forgot you guys were cousins. Anyway Trevor hasn't been a problem for her lately. He's a problem for me, and I'll have to handle that in my time."

"I was wondering man if I could get down with the guys here. I mean working here. I did some detailing and until I can set up something permanent I need to make some legal income."

Sean stood on his feet positioning himself next to Lamont. Jose' and Malik took their stance on both sides of them. Kevin noticed the four stood directly in front of him, as though they were a wall.

"You can't work for me here Kevin. I don't want that street shit on my premises, and I don't know if I can trust you yet. The men here regardless of their street activities in the past have worked hard to clean up their acts. I get a lot of business from work programs, not to mention state funding. The government monitors us on a regular. I can't let the streets kill my lifestyle. But you can show your loyalty and sincerity by taking on another job for me."

Kevin gave a puzzled look at the men standing at the table. He could tell the topic had been discussed among them. Kevin felt he was the last to know.

"So where's the job? I mean if it ain't working here, where is it?"

"Kevin you said you wanted to get Trevor back right?"

Jose' took a drink of water as he continued his thought.

"So do we. Me and Malik ain't really through with that brother. We've been laying low til' the time was right."

"Yeah, no better time than the present. The brother's got to know the shit he's pulling ain't gonna continue in his favor."

Malik paced back and forth looking out of the conference room window onto the street as he agreed with Jose's statement. He told Kevin about Trevor's plan to set up Lamont. As he spoke, he looked to Sean and Lamont for final confirmation.

"So you down or what?"

"Down for what Malik? I heard what you said but what's this job, I mean what ya'll got planned."

Lamont spoke before Malik could answer.

"There's really no plan. You just filled in the gap we had. We need one of Trevor's boys to go along with his plan. Set me up, and stand aside while he gets busted."

"Lamont man, what? How's that? I mean, I understand I'm the man but how does Trevor get busted."

"Kev, man it's simple. Trevor needs an inside man. Tell him I hired you, that you start working for me say next week, say Thursday. If Malik is right he'll tell you his plan, ask a lot of questions about what we do here and tell you about the drug run."

Kevin interrupted Lamont by shaking his head. "Lamont that's only if Malik is right, it may not be going down like that."

"Shit Kev. Either way it goes, we still need to know, and you're the man to find out."

Jose' yelled at Kevin trying to convince him he was needed to complete the plan.

"No, I ain't sure I'm the man. I just told the brother, I didn't want nothing else to do with him. I even told him I would kill him if he crossed me again. He won't trust me."

"Hmmn, maybe we shouldn't trust you either."

"Sean man, what the fuck you mean? I didn't know nothing about this until Malik told me just now. I wasn't sent here. I just don't want to get caught in the bull and the nigger walk off clean again. A lot of people can get hurt in the deal."

"Look Kevin, the way I see it, me and Sean got more to lose than any of you."

"That's just it Lamont. You lose a business. Malik and Jose' can lose their family, I could lose my life and who knows what else. They don't play fair. They play for keeps. You got to play the same way. I agree Trevor needs to be done. We have to get him to back up or understand he will be done."

"Awright Kev, you see the problem. What's your take on it?" Jose' and Malik took a seat waiting for Kevin to answer Lamont's question.

"You said Trevor has put in the paperwork for the cars to be picked up?" Sean answered placing the file on the conference table.

"Here's the details, they were faxed to us this morning. The final paperwork is to be signed and delivered by a courier this afternoon."

"Who's making the delivery?"

"Everything is on us; the pickup; the transport and the delivery to the next location."

"Wait Lamont, explain it to me, I'm confused."

"Listen, the way it works is we pick up Trevor's vehicles to be painted, detailed and delivered to an auction location. Trevor hooked up a fleet. He doesn't know we know he's behind the job. We're to pick up the fleet, bring the cars here, detail and paint them and deliver them. Sean did he give the address of the final drop off?"

"No, I guess we'll get that when the final papers are signed." Sean continued.

"Kevin, Malik told us what he told you. That's how we know Trevor is behind it. The drugs will be in the cars, but he needs someone on the inside to insure the drugs won't be moved from the cars before the cops make the bust."

"Or to plant the drugs while the cars are here."

Jose's words brought a new light to the discussion.

"Damn Jose' I hadn't thought about that. The inside man plants the drugs. Trevor would know everything was in place and the bust would be made here. I still don't understand how he makes out in the deal." Kevin understood Trevor's strategy.

"Damn, Lamont, listen. Let's just say I'm the plant. The cars get delivered. I stash the drugs throughout the fleet and contact Trevor. He calls the cops for the bust. He's been giving up big runners and deals lately they'll definitely respond. They bust your spot, you're out of business. You lose it, he buys it. The cops owe him one. Trevor and DJ run their drugs right from your door. The business becomes a cover."

"Yeah, that's the shit and Trevor needs a cap in his ass." Malik gestured shooting Trevor and smiling slowly.

"So Kev, you know what I need you to do are you game?"

"Man, I don't know if Trevor will even ask me. I told you I cussed that brother out just this morning. He'll be on my collar if I whimper up to him or DJ. I'm on to his game. I can watch from the outside. Let's see who he uses to come in here. Give me a few days. Who knows maybe his bitch ass will ask me to work with him again?"

"Lamont, listen, we don't have to sign these papers for a couple of days. Give Kevin the days he needs. We can say there's a delay with the contractors and the bays aren't ready yet. If he's as hungry as we think he'll wait."

"Yeah, Sean, that's cool. Alright Kevin that's what we'll do. You keep your ears open. Don't come here though. Jose' get my card for Kevin. You stay in touch with me by phone. Jose' and Malik are screening guys as they come through, they'll run the names by you."

Kevin took the business card from Jose' and rose to his feet. The men walked out the conference room in silence and approached the bay doors where Kevin entered two hours earlier. Kevin shook their hands saying goodbye.

"I don't know Lamont, Trevor might not make it to see this deal."

"That's up to him. We've got too much to lose."

Malik looked at Kevin and smiled slowly gesturing shooting a gun.

"He'll be dead long before we lose anything that's fo' sure."

Chapter 53

Trevor returned to his apartment to change cars. Since he wouldn't have the children for the weekend, he could sport his two seated BMW. His phone hadn't rung since his conversation with Kevin, and he left a message for DJ that he would be busy with his family on the weekend. The next two days would give Kevin enough time to cool off, and they could talk business on Monday. DJ didn't need to know the problems he was having with Kevin, he would handle it all on Monday.

Trevor pulled into the apartment complex parking lot and parked his Lexus next to the BMW. The heat of the day was at its peak and the interior of the sports car told him he needed to turn on the air conditioner before driving off. Trevor stood outside the car checking the scenes. There were children running between the playground and the basketball court which was designated for the apartments within the A through D complex. Trevor lived in the C complex. He picked the apartment so his children would have access to the playground and the other children. They didn't know about their father's drug deals or any of his abusive relationships. Trevor didn't want his children involved in his illegal activity. The complex was filled with families. This was the image Trevor portrayed for his neighbors.

"Hey Mr. Black, where's Kyle?"

"He's visiting his grandmother. I don't think he'll be here this week. Where's your mom?"

"Over there with my sister."

The boy was Kyle's friend, Craig. His mother was the beauty of the complex. She kept to herself, working and raising her two children. Trevor had spoken to her occasionally and thought she had an eye for him. Both her son and daughter had her features, bronze skin with jet black hair. Trevor told her she had to have a Brazilian bloodline. Cheryl never took their conversations any further than the children and discussing changes in the complex.

Trevor made several attempts to ask her out for a date, invite her into his apartment and when all failed, he decided he would settle for her friendship. As she approached Trevor carrying her groceries she smiled and shook her head.

"Why the smirk? We haven't talked in a while, why do you always treat as though I'm guilty of some wrong doing?"

"Mr. Black, that's because you are."

"Trevor, I thought we agreed we've known each other long enough to be on a first name basis."

"Trevor, you've had company. Two females, they left together. One was really upset. You might want to check your apartment before you leave."

"Cheryl did they say anything to you?"

"Me? No, why would they? I just live next door to you. But they did mention something about you can't live with both of them and not expect some drama."

Trevor used his remote to cut off his car. He knew Sylvia and Trina had paid him a visit.

Chapter 54

Sylvia opened the door to Carson's condo and put her suitcase down before calling his name. As she walked down the hall to the bedroom she noticed how clean it was. She scanned the apartment looking for the usual mess Carson left on the floor of the living room and the couch. She peeked into the kitchen noting it looked as though he called a cleaning service. She complained often about the mess he made. Now she wondered if he cleaned it to impress her. She recalled the arguments they had that caused her to leave. She moved into her own place because of the mess he made and his taste in the décor.

As she looked around she noticed he had changed the window dressings as well as putting coordinating pillows on the couch and chairs. The dining area was decorated with a beautiful centerpiece and table setting. Sylvia could only smile. Carson told her she was more than welcomed to come home.

When she called him crying about the call from Trina and the visit they made to Trevor's, they both decided she wouldn't be safe at her condo. Sylvia didn't know how long her stay with Carson would be. She needed time to think and talk to Carson and Lamont. Carson would be the easier of the two.

"Carson, are you here?"

Sylvia entered the master bedroom and saw that the room was clean as well. The huge pillows on the bed were an invitation to comfort. There were a dozen roses in a crystal vase on the table where Carson usually cut his cocaine. Sylvia was puzzled. She had been with him for two years and his habit as well as hers was their downfall, which had increased in the past four months. They often talked about getting clean but when the arguments ended, they got high, made love and slept it off. She walked over to the bed and sat down. The day was overwhelming. She began to sob. She fell back on the bed and closed her eyes. As her body relaxed, she felt herself dozing off until she was startled by Carson's voice.

"Sylvia, are you here?"

Sylvia sat up and wiped her eyes. She heard the front door close and the sound of keys falling on the table in the hall.

"Yeah, Carson. I'm here in the bedroom."

"I'm sorry I wanted to be here when you got here. I went to get us something quick to eat. Are you hungry? I got you that deli sandwich you like."

Carson put the bags on the counter. He entered the bedroom and walked toward the bed where Sylvia sat holding her head.

"Baby you look tired. Are you okay?"

Sylvia stood and greeted Carson with a smirk. He thought better than giving in to his urge to embrace her. He held his hands out offering to help her stand. She smiled and followed him as he led the way into the kitchen. He began to empty the bags putting the sandwiches and chips on two plates. Sylvia stood at the counter and watched as he motioned for her to take a seat. He was dressed in business attire. She could tell he had been at the office. Carson's appearance gave him a rush. She hadn't seen him dressed in business attire in months.

Carson was a handsome man. His olive tone skin and dark hair gave him an appearance of a wealthy executive. He was what Lamont called a functional addict. His appearance didn't hint that he had a habit that seemed to have increased during their relationship. His father and the other executives knew about it. Most tolerated his binges. After all he would be the heir to his father's business.

"Go sit down, I'll bring it to you. What do you want to drink?"

"It doesn't matter babe."

"Yeah, I told my father, I would call him at the office, once I was sure you'd be okay."

"I wasn't supposed to be at work today anyway."

"Yeah, I guess he was as worried as me. I was in his office when you called. I mean, I didn't know what to think. You're not going back to his place, are you?"

"No, I don't know what to do. Carson I need to tell you something. I just want you to listen."

"Sylvia, you don't have to tell me anything. It's all good I understand."

She looked him over as he set the plates on the table. He looked better than he had in months. His face wasn't drawn and he looked as though he had been getting the rest he needed. They had only been separated a few months and Sylvia took a moment to make mental comparisons.

"Carson, what's up with the apartment and you? Everything looks so different."

"I lost the only thing I loved when I lost you, and I didn't realize it until you called me crying today. I was on my way to being seriously addicted when you left me, I didn't care about anything else. I went and talked to my father after you left. For the past months, my dad has been grilling me about losing you, dealing with drugs and a lot of other shit. I just took it down. The last thing I wanted was to lose you permanently. The things you said were right. I wasn't ready for a long term relationship. So for the past month I've been avoiding the streets. It was hard the first week, but I think I can really do it. I think I spilled more coke than I snorted. Anyway, I'm trying to kick the habit. I haven't walked away from the game totally, but I won't be using and dealing. I've got to make it a business, not a recreational thing."

"It shows. Damn, I don't know what to say. I came to dump on you and get high to wash away my trouble."

"You can dump on me baby, but I don't have anything here to get you up. Sorry."

"Carson, this is bigger than me, and I can't handle it.

Trevor wants to kill Lamont. He used me to get Lamont to confront him. I thought it was real. I thought he was beginning to love me for me. It's still about Lamont and Cassandra. He still wants to kill my brother."

Sylvia began to cry. She wiped her face and continued.

"Trina told me about the two of them. He's a piece of shit Carson. I should have known he wouldn't change. I'm scared. Trina and I wrecked his apartment. I know he's going to come after us. I don't want to include you, he's already after Lamont."

"What did Lamont do to Trevor?"

"He's with Cassandra. Trevor wants Cassandra. He was using me thinking Lamont would leave Cassandra alone to keep him from dealing with me. I don't know what made him think Lamont even cared about who I was dealing with. Anyway it seems he was dealing with Trina during the time he was with Cassandra and then Trina found out about me. She told me everything. Carson I was a fool. I should have told Trevor to deal with Lamont and leave me out of it. I feel like a fool."

"So what's next? I mean, you can't go back to him Sylvia. You belong with me. I mean you're welcome to stay here. That's if you want to stay."

"I want to, but I don't want you to be hurt in the process."

"I would be hurt if you didn't stay. You need to call your brother though."

"Yeah, I guess I have to."

"You mean you were considering not telling him?"

"No, I mean I just don't know what to say."

"Sylvia, just tell him the truth. You can stay here as long as you like. We'll get the rest of your things over here later."

"Trevor may be watching for me to come there I don't want to see him."

Carson picked up the phone. Sylvia took a bite of her sandwich. Her nerves were beginning to settle.

"Yeah, Dad, listen, I need them to bring her things here. Yeah, we'll get the rest later. All of her personal belongings will be fine. Thanks. I will. Thanks." Carson placed the phone in the cradle.

"My father will have your belongings brought here."

"Carson, why is your father so willing to help me?"

"He said you're the best thing for me. I believe him and I love you. One of the managers will open the door. We'll have a few of the guys from the job pick up your things. Trevor won't bother them. We'll put a sign up that the condo is for sale. He won't come here or call here either."

"He might Carson. You were buying drugs from him."

"Trust me Sylvia, he won't call."

Sylvia heard what he said and took his tone to mean there had been some truth about the deal that went bad between them. Trevor and Carson had been arguing about a payment and no delivery when Trina spotted Sylvia in Trevor's car. Sylvia sat in the car listening to them arguing. Carson told Trevor he wasn't the typical junky and wouldn't be treated as one. Trevor told him his man had been busted and the drugs were confiscated, he would make up on the amount on the next buy.

"Did you get your money from him?"

"Yeah, he paid me and offered me more coke. I told him he couldn't be trusted. Trevor won't come here."

"I don't know, maybe I should stay with my mother."

"No, you should be here with me. Trevor didn't get away with what he did, trust me."

"What does that mean?"

"Sylvia, that coke wasn't for me. He'll pay for that delivery not being made."

Chapter 55

The children returned from camp laughing and running from the porch through the front door. Cassandra gave them a motherly look causing them to change their pace to a well postured march. They giggled as they passed her going into the kitchen for their afternoon snack.

"Make sure you wash your hands first."

She stood at the doorway as her children stopped and turned at the kitchen table. They followed each other to the bathroom. Pleased they didn't fuss, she went into her mother's room hoping the therapist was finishing the session with Mary.

"How's it going?" Cassandra entered the room prepared to ask her question while remaining at the door.

"Your mother's doing fine. Better than we expected. Isn't that right Ms. Smith?" The therapist spoke smiling as she gave her patient a tender pat on the arm. Mary waved her hand in agreement but the grimace on her face told Cassandra she was in pain.

"This is her last set of exercises; I believe we're making progress. If you have a moment, I can explain the next level. I've explained it to your mother already."

The therapist seemed excited about Mary's progress. Mary listened to the therapist talk hoping there would be no mention of the reduction in medicine as was previously mentioned. The therapist told Mary she would need to contact her medical doctor to continue any of her pain medication. Mary didn't want to talk to her doctor. She was sure her questioning about pain medicine would interfere with the surgery she agreed to have done. Mary changed her mind and arranged to have the surgery performed on Monday.

"I would love to talk with you. I'll be in the living room when the session is complete."

Cassandra had packed her clothes for the weekend and decided to put her overnight bags in the den. When Lamont picked her up she didn't want the children to notice she was leaving with luggage.

"Mama, where are you going?"

Taylor had spotted her luggage and questioned her with worry on his small face.

"I need to take a few things to Lamont's house."

"Are we going to stay at Lamont's house?"

"No, you and your sister and brothers are going to stay here. We'll pick you guys up on Sunday and take you to the picnic."

"Where are we going to be on Saturday?"

"Here baby, with Grandma and Aunt Laura."

"Mama, are you leaving us?"

"No Taylor. I'm just going to Lamont's house to visit until Sunday."

As Cassandra felt the pressure from her youngest son her other children formed a circle around her waiting to ask more questions.

"Why can't we go? Lamont said we could come over whenever we wanted to?"

Chris smiled awaiting his answer as the others nodded their heads in agreement. Cassandra's instinct told her she was about to lose her weekend of freedom. Just as she was about to explain her weekend getaway Laura and Lamont came through the front door.

"Ma'Dear said for you and Lamont to stop there before you go Cassandra. Kyle you come help me with these bags, I left a few in the car. I sure am glad I made it home before the traffic got bad. Is the therapist through?"

"Just about, Aunt Laura, Kyle you heard your Aunt. Chris you go help him with those bags."

Cassandra smiled to herself. Aunt Laura saved her from what she knew would be a long question and answer period filled with tears.

"Mr. Dearling, how are you today?"

Lamont smiled as he returned from the kitchen and headed out the door with the two boys.

"I'm fine Ms. Smith, just fine."

Laura set the bags she carried from the car on the kitchen table. As she passed Cassandra, she noticed Cassie and Taylor were silent looking at their mother.

"What's the problem with the children?"

"Aunt Laura, they want to go with me to Lamont's. I told them we would be here to pick them up Sunday, but I'm afraid that didn't sit well."

Laura smiled at the two youngest children. "Who wants popsicles?"

"I do," chanted Taylor and Cassie.

"Well you sure can't eat them if you go away with your mother for the weekend. Besides, there's things to be done to get ready for Sunday's picnic. Maybe some baking too. I might just need help."

Cassie waved her hand anxiously in the air. "I'll help. I want to bake a cake."

Cassandra walked to the front door and held it open for Kyle, Chris and Lamont. Each had a bag and headed for the kitchen. Lamont leaned and kissed Cassandra softly as he passed her with his bag.

Cassandra stepped out onto the porch realizing she hadn't been outside all day. The sun was fading but remained high enough to be seen. The humidity wasn't bad for a summer evening, but it left a promise to return the next day. Cassandra looked across the street at Ma'Dear's porch. She could see Ma'Dear through the screen door walking toward her kitchen. Cassandra imagined the cooking that was to be done before Sunday.

"Ms. Smith, your mother's session is through for today. I've given her the weekend exercises. I don't want to sound out of place but your mother really is doing a lot better than she wants anyone to know."

The therapist had stepped out of the front door onto the porch with her bags in hand. Her round face and soft voice reminded Cassandra of her grandmother. She was a soft spoken wise woman. The therapist wasn't old but her mannerism told she had been caring for people in their homes for years.

"What do you mean?"

"Well, Ms. Smith…."

"Call me Cassandra please. What is your name?"

"I'm Anne. Your mother shows signs of motion and movement that she just won't use. Maybe she's scared because of the stroke and all. Some patients become dependent of their family members and don't want to heal right away. Your mother really should be up and around more."

"Anne, my mother has had a stroke and suffers from cancer. Some days are bad for her. I'm sure she'll get worst before she gets better."

Anne gave her a puzzled look. The look told Cassandra she had the wrong information.

"Didn't you know about the cancer Anne?"

"Your mother has breast cancer, operable breast cancer. She's hoping the medication will curtail the spread of the cancer, but she just told me she's decided to have the operation. Didn't you know she was having the surgery done? I believe she's going to have it done next week."

The look on Cassandra's face told Anne she wasn't aware of the surgery.

"She'll have a few days for drainage if they take her breast. Of course we're hoping that won't have to happen. I won't be back for her regular therapy until the following week. She should be able to get up and down, you know out of bed. Exercise will be important so that she doesn't get stiff, nothing much while she's healing from the surgery, but she must move around more."

Anne hesitated before continuing. Cassandra was at a loss for words.

"Cassandra, please don't tell her I told you if you didn't know. I like your mother and as with all my patients, I want the best for her. I've been talking with her at each of our sessions about the surgery, her stroke and the effects it has had on her as well as her family. It's taken some time but she is willing to get the operation now. If you question her about her not telling you she may change her mind."

Cassandra wanted to cry. She had mixed emotions. She couldn't understand why she hadn't been told about the surgery, but she was pleased that her mother had agreed to have the procedure done. She hugged the therapist assuring her she wouldn't say anything to her mother about their conversation. Cassandra thanked her for her time. They agreed to talk again on Monday after the surgery was complete.

Cassandra stayed on the porch watching the woman get into her car. He forgot Lamont was in the house. Her thoughts and thanks were directed to God.

"Lord, it's been a while since I recognized your work around me. I know it was through prayer and your mercy that my mother has agreed to have this surgery. I want to thank you. Help me Lord. I want to be strong for her and for me. Thank you Father."

The door opened and Lamont stepped onto the porch.

"You okay, my lady?"

"Yeah, I can't tell you why now, but I'm a lot better than I was. I'm sorry I was caught in the moment, are you ready to go?"

"Whenever you are, your children told me my house was second to popsicles and baking a cake."

"Yeah, Aunt Laura promised them all but the moon. They wanted to come with me to your house."

"They could have come. I mean, if you want them to."

Cassandra smirked and shook her head.

"I don't want them to. I think I need this weekend more than they do. Aunt Laura will keep them occupied."

"Hmmn, that gives me a chance to keep you occupied."

"Mr. Dearling, I believe you're a mind reader."

Chapter 56

Trevor sat in his car and looked at his watch. After parking his car, he thought about what he needed Sylvia to understand. He knew that most of the destruction in his apartment was done by Trina. She had gone through his papers and tore most of the documents in half. The sheets on his bed and pillows had been slashed. His paintings on the wall throughout the apartment were smashed on the floor. Vases, lamps, mirrors, and dishes had been thrown throughout the apartment and broken. The place looked like it had been vandalized. Trevor could imagine the look on Sylvia's face as Trina wrecked his home.

Trevor's anger rose to a heightened level when he saw his stash of cocaine and marijuana was gone. He knew Trina wouldn't touch the drugs, unless she was trying to flush them down the toilet. Sylvia would have stopped her. Sylvia kept his drugs, and regardless if she used them or sold them Trevor decided to collect. She needed to understand his promise to hurt Lamont was still hanging over her head. She hadn't returned home. His watch told him he had been waiting over an hour. He got out of the car and walked around to the front of the condo complex.

He saw the for sale sign posted on the lawn. In a holder under the sign, the real estate company left a layout of the condo and a number for prospective buyers to call. There was no number listed for Sylvia. The number listed for further information was Klein & Sons LLC.

"That bitch is with Carson!"

Trevor walked the paved path to the front door. He leaned over the railing and looked into the grand room window. The room was empty. All the furniture was gone. He stood in shock. As he returned to his car, he thought about all his plans unraveling. Sylvia was his way to destroying Lamont's social life while Kevin would help destroy his business. He took out his cell phone and dialed Sylvia's number. A recording told him the number was no longer in service.

Trevor's phone rang, not recognizing the number, he hoped it was Sylvia.

"Yea, who's this?"

"Man, you hard to catch up with."

It was DJ. Trevor listened with no response. He didn't know what DJ could want. They weren't supposed to talk until Sunday.

"Look, I heard about that shit with Kevin and the cops. Where's the goods?"

"Kevin made the drop before he got busted."

"My boys say different."

"Your boys wasn't with him the whole time. Kevin ditched them. The cops caught up with him later."

"If Kevin made the drop, why is Carson's peeps sweating me about their goods? Man, this is the second time white boy didn't get his shit."

"DJ look I talked to Carson. That drop was large enough to cover the shit from the first drop and this delivery. Kevin said they got the shit. If he said he made the drop, the drop was made."

"I told you I didn't trust that nigga. Carson's connects run too deep for us to fuck with 'em. You know they get a part of each of our runs. That's how it's done. Now I don't know what your boy told you, but we can't fuck with Carson like this and expect it to be okay. Trevor you promised him to make it up, and YOU didn't. It's on your head. I don't know shit about your promises, you got that? If this shit falls, it falls on you, all around. Carson's people want answers. I gave them, you."

"What the fuck does that mean?"

"It means you'll be explaining where the drop went. It was your promise and your boy. Oh and by the way, it ain't advisable to do business with the man and fuck his woman."

"What is that supposed to mean?"

"Trevor, you play too hard brother. Sit back and look around you. Sylvia is his woman. You fucked him and his woman. Sounds like sudden death. You're walking a thin line brotha."

"That bitch was a part of the plan to trap Lamont, and you know that."

"All I know is the drop wasn't made. Who you fuck and why, shit man that's on you."

"DJ, so what did you hear?"

Trevor's nerves were beginning to stir. Carson was making moves,

moves Trevor never expected him to make. Carson always appeared to be a runner who dipped into the packages before delivery. He played the game better than Trevor thought.

"Trevor, Carson runs his own thing. You know, with those elites at that company his father owns and all. He ain't no Wall Street man, he's their connect to the streets. You just fucked up his business trying to stick it to Lamont, or whatever you're trying to do."

"So, you saying you ain't got my back. That's how you roll?"

"Kevin is your man. Who messed up the last drop?"

"It wasn't Kevin."

"It was one of your boys though. I'll assume another one you set up. What did you think? Set up your boys with the white boys shit and there wouldn't be no repercussions. Carson is the wrong white boy. You should have thought it through. I have no way to save your ass. I'm connected to that white boy's money. I told you when we got together, be careful who you do business with. You're on your own man. That shit about Lamont's business is on the back burner until you get clear with Carson. I can't see us losing another shipment just for a set up scheme."

"Man, I thought you had it in for Lamont too?"

"I ain't trying to put my name on nobody's hit list man."

"Carson is easy to deal with. I'll call him. I need to talk to him anyway."

"Yeah man well you do that. Later."

The phone went silent. Trevor replayed the conversation in his mind. He couldn't imagine Carson playing him, but apparently he had. Trevor started the car remembering he still had to clean his apartment.

Chapter 57

Trina woke up startled by a male's voice in the hall outside of her apartment. She recognized the voice to be her neighbor talking with his wife as they entered their apartment. She looked at the television. She missed the end of the movie she turned to. Sleep crept upon her as three hours passed since she and Sylvia trashed Trevor's apartment. She didn't mind trashing his belongings, but she was a little nervous about the drugs they found. Sylvia convinced her that it would take a while for Trevor to realize they had found the stash hidden beneath the floor boards. Trina was so frustrated with Trevor about Sylvia, she gave in and told Sylvia to treat herself and her white friend to a free high. Now reflecting about it, she knew if nothing else Trevor would deal with them about his drugs.

Trina and Sylvia talked for more than an hour after leaving his apartment. She drove to Sylvia's condo, so she could pack a few things before she went to Carson's place. They exchanged numbers promising to call the minute one of them heard from Trevor. Trina watched as Sylvia pulled off blowing her horn and saying goodbye. She knew she would have to call Cassandra and warn her of Trevor's threat to hurt Lamont. Sylvia cried off and on during their conversation. Trina remembered her feelings about Cassandra when she shed tears over Trevor. Now she had tears of her own to shed.

Cassandra was right Trevor wasn't worth it. She lost her friend thinking she gained Trevor's love. Sylvia was proof; she hadn't gained his love at all. She went in her kitchen got a glass of iced tea and returned to the sofa. As she picked up her phone it rang in her hand.

"Hello."

"Hey, Trina? It's Sylvia. Are you okay?"

"Yeah girl. Did he call you?"

If Trevor called, she would be able to tell what level his anger was on. The longer Trevor didn't call the angrier he would get. Trina learned from Cassandra, this brought on his violent outbursts.

"I wouldn't know, that's why I'm calling my cell has been cut off."

"What, Trevor was paying for your cell phone?"

"No Carson said it would be better if Trevor didn't know where I was or how to reach me."

Trina didn't speak. Sylvia had Carson. It was obvious now, Trina had no support.

"Trina, are you there? Hello."

"Yeah, I'm here. So you're staying with Carson?"

"Trina, I have a number you can call if Trevor contacts you. Like I said he won't be calling me." Sylvia was cautious about telling Trina where she was staying.

"What about at your job, he knows where you work?"

Trina's voice gave signs of desperation. She didn't want to be the only one Trevor contacted. Sylvia had taken herself out of harm's way now the weight would fall on Trina. Tears began to well in her eyes.

"Is the number you're calling from yours. I mean should I call this number?"

"No, this is Carson's cell number. Do you have a pen?"

"Hold on." Trina pretended to get a pen as she held back the tears. She knew Trevor would be furious when he couldn't reach Sylvia.

"Go ahead Sylvia. What's the number?"

Sylvia gave her the number and asked Trina to repeat it back. Trina recited the number as it was given and told her she would call if she heard from Trevor. They said their goodbyes and Trina hung up the phone. Trina sat for a moment feeling the need to talk to Cassandra. She had so much to tell her but her fear was that her friend wouldn't listen. She dialed Cassandra's number anyway and waited for her to answer.

"Hello."

"Cassandra, this is Trina."

"Oh, hey. What's up?"

Trina was surprised. She expected Cassandra to hang up after she realized who was on the phone. She decided that talking for a moment would be wise before warning her about Trevor's intentions.

"I was thinking about you and the kids and decided to call. How are you and the kids doing? How's your mom?"

"Things are getting better. At least I think they are. You know how my mother is. You never can tell when she's feeling bad. She's a lot better though. The kids are in camp and loving it, and I'm ready for my classes, they start Monday."

As Cassandra spoke her mind drifted for a moment. Monday was her mother's surgery. Trina didn't notice the pause and continued to talk.

"So things are going well for you. That's good. I know the kids are loving camp. I'm glad for you, you deserve it."

"Trina, what's wrong."

Cassandra's attention was on the conversation again realizing Trina's tone was strange, there had to be another reason for Trina's call.

"Sandra, its Trevor."

"Listen Trina, I told you when I left; I didn't want to know nothing about you and him."

"It's not me and him. I mean he's seeing Sylvia again, and we got together and trashed his place. I mean I got mad and Sylvia helped me."

"What?"

"Well that's me and his shit. I called to tell you Trevor plans on hurting or killing Lamont if you don't leave him alone. Sylvia told me that's why she was with him. Trevor threatened to kill Lamont if she didn't pretend to be his woman. He wanted Lamont to get mad enough to step to him, and then he was gonna hurt him or something like that. You know, say it was self defense."

Cassandra listened but she was confused. The only thing that wasn't confusing was Trina's statement about Trevor wanting to hurt or kill Lamont.

"Trina thanks for the warning. I'll let Lamont know. I'm on my way out. I'll call you over the weekend though."

Trina felt the pain of loneliness again. Her relationship with Cassandra would take a while to mend.

Chapter 58

T errance opened the screen door for Cassandra and Lamont to enter the house. Lamont shook his hand and Cassandra smiled timidly saying hello. Cassandra looked around the living room vaguely remembering the last time she had been in Ma'Dear's house. The smell of fried chicken was in the air and the muffled sound of the television from the den was in the background.

"So what's up bro, on your way out?"

Terrance asked his question as he took a seat in the recliner that held the scattered daily newspaper he was reading.

"Yeah, on my way home, Ms. Laura said for us to stop by. Where's Ma?"

"She just went upstairs. Have a seat Cassandra. How have you been? I've been meaning to stop over to see you and your mother. I've seen you coming and going though. Your children sure have grown up."

Cassandra took the seat offered on the couch as Lamont went upstairs to see his mother. She let Terrance continue to talk not really listening fully. Cassandra knew Terrance loved gossip and passed it off as part of his character. Since high school, she handled his gossiping by not telling him anything of importance. Nothing seemed to have changed. As Cassandra scanned the room, she noticed the mantel over the fireplace still held the childhood pictures that she remembered from their school days. There were additions made over the years but the old pictures were displayed throughout the room and stirred her memories.

Terrance couldn't get her to say much and after a few attempts he gave up. She answered most of his questions with yes and no answers giving Terrance the impression, he was prying.

"You're gonna have to loosen up if you're gonna be around us Cassandra. It's okay to talk to me, I promise I won't bite."

Terrance chuckled to himself as he lifted the paper to continue reading the sports page.

"There is something you can tell me Terrance. How often does the cross-town bus run, the one that goes by the Civic Center?"

"On weekdays it runs pretty regular, I'd say every fifteen to twenty minutes. They double up during the rush hour so it may be more frequent. Where are you trying to get to?"

"The cosmetology school, I'm not sure what the name of the building is. The bus stops right in the front of it though."

"I could find out for sure. When are you going there?"

"Monday I start classes but I'll get the information, thanks. I thought you might know."

Cassandra gave Terrance that information willingly. She knew it would become the topic of conversation on the bus. She smiled at the thought of her name being mentioned in conjunction with the cosmetology school, her dating Lamont and her separation from Trevor. The bus would be buzzing.

"Well if you don't reach anyone by calling information let me know I can call my depot for you and get it right away."

"Information on what?" Ma'Dear entered the room with her arms opened as she interrupted the conversation. Cassandra stood smiling as she walked toward Ma'Dear to receive a motherly hug.

"I just told Lamont how glad I was to see the two of you getting along so well. I guess you'll be making up for lost time."

"Ma, c'mon now. Don't go pairing them up just because of their friendship, right Lamont."

All eyes shifted toward Lamont. He knew that Terrance was putting him on the spot. Ma'Dear and Cassandra were looking for clarity about his feelings. Lamont would wait until later to have a word with Terrance.

"One day at a time. That's what we've agreed to, one day at a time."

"That's cool. Did you hear that Ma? You can hold off on booking the reception hall."

"There's hope with Cassandra and Lamont, Terrance. You and Diane ain't nowhere near the altar, and Sylvia and that Carson ain't nowhere near the church."

Ma'Dear went into the kitchen to check on the chicken. The top of the frying pan clanged as she lifted it to turn the sizzling chicken.

"Cassandra come here a minute. Let me show you what I'm baking for the children." Cassandra looked at Lamont, who smiled as she excused herself from the room.

"Speaking of your sister, have you heard from her?"

Terrance folded the paper and sat to the edge of his chair. Lamont waited for an answer. His brother answered, lowering his voice so Ma'Dear and Cassandra would not hear the conversation.

"Her phone is disconnected at the house and the cell says the service has been terminated. I called Carson's number and I got no answer. I haven't heard from her since last week. We usually talk at least once during the week. Maybe she'll call between now and Sunday. She said she was coming to the picnic."

Lamont listened but his thoughts drifted to his conversation with Malik and Sean. He needed to know that Sylvia was safe.

"Did Ma'Dear speak to her?"

"I didn't ask her. I didn't want to sound like there was a problem. You know Mama would have picked up on it just by me questioning her. You ask her and see what she says."

"Listen Sylvia is messing around with Trevor. I don't know why."

"You mean she's not with Carson?"

"I don't know if she's with both of them or not, but she's with Trevor. Anyway he's got it out for me. I haven't found out why, but I'm assuming that it's because of Cassandra. We've got to make sure Sylvia is okay."

"You think he'll do something to Sylvia? Man I told you this thing you got for Cassandra ain't gonna bring you no good. She's weak, man. She can't even talk to a man without feeling, you know, belittled."

"Where do you get your shit from Terrance?"

"You don't see it Lamont, but I do. There's trouble stirring around that girl and now Sylvia is a part of it."

"If Sylvia's involved with Trevor, she was headed for trouble before me and Cassandra got together. Look I can't get into all that right now. We need to know where Sylvia is though."

"Well I don't know what else to do. You need to think twice about this thing with Cassandra though."

"Anyway…." Lamont paused in the middle of his thought. There was no way around it. He would have to ask his mother if she heard from Sylvia.

"Ma, have you heard from your daughter?"

Ma'Dear and Cassandra came into the living room. Cassandra stood next to the couch where Lamont remained seated. Ma'Dear took a seat in the chair opposite Terrance.

"Yeah she called about an hour ago and gave me her new cell number. I meant to tell you Terrance, it's on the refrigerator. She said she needed to talk to you Lamont, but she would call you later."

Terrance fell back into the chair. Lamont rose to his feet.

"Look we've got to go; I'll call you later bro after I talk to Sylvia. Ma, I'll see you Sunday."

Both Terrance and his mother walked to the porch with them. Ma'Dear watched the body language between Lamont and Terrance. She could tell there was more to Lamont's early departure than was said. Ma'Dear went into the kitchen to take the last batch of chicken out of the pan.

"Terrance, what kind of trouble is Sylvia in?" Ma'Dear shouted from the kitchen.

"Who said she was in trouble?"

"I know something's going on."

"Huh Ma, what did you say?"

Ma'Dear walked back, into the living room where she found Terrance looking out the screen door.

"What's going on Terrance?" She asked wiping her hands on her apron. "I raised you and your brother. I know when something is wrong."

"Well you tell me then sweet lady, what is the problem with your daughter?"

"Terrance, I'm not falling for your game. If Sylvia is in trouble I'd like to know."

"Sounds like you know more than I do."

"Well Cassandra said something about Sylvia calling and then Lamont asked. I'd say that wasn't a coincidence. Then when I said I spoke with her you and Lamont's reaction told me that something just ain't right."

Terrance knew he couldn't avoid Ma'Dear's questions. As he thought about his answer, he wondered what trouble Sylvia was in. He didn't know how much Lamont knew, but he did know Lamont wouldn't back down from Trevor. Terrance tried helping his sister by telling Lamont that Cassandra meant trouble, but in reality, he could see the changes Cassandra had made. Terrance gave the best answer he could without disclosing Sylvia was already in too deep.

"I told Lamont about her phone being off and the house phone being disconnected. I don't know what's going on with her, she'll tell Lamont I guess."

"I sure hope they talk before Sunday. I want everyone to have a good time, which means we don't need no drama."

Ma'Dear shook her head as she went back in the kitchen to check on the rest of her dinner.

Chapter 59

L amont took Cassandra's overnight luggage and put it in his master bedroom as Cassandra unpacked the groceries they picked up on the way to his house. They agreed that Saturday morning would bring a crowd at the local supermarket that neither of them wanted to face. Cassandra was a little embarrassed when she found herself separating the W.I.C. items at the checkout. Lamont leaned over and whispered she didn't have to separate the items, and he would pay for them. There hadn't been a word exchanged between the two of them, since they left the store. She felt Lamont was embarrassed about the W.I.C. check and stopped her. She never looked up at the cashier or anyone else in line. She didn't want to embarrass Lamont, she wanted to contribute to the food bill, especially since most of it consisted of treats for her children.

Lamont entered the kitchen and without hesitation put the food in cabinets and bins where it belonged.

"Babe you can put the soda's and chips on the shelf by you. I'll put everything on ice Sunday morning, and you can pack the bags for the kids then too."

"Lamont, are you upset with me?"

"Upset, no. Why?"

She knew she had to say what she felt. There would be times when she would have to pay her way and right now her cash was by means of a government check.

"About what happened in the supermarket?"

"What happened? Cassandra I'm not being funny, but am I supposed to be upset?"

"You haven't said a word, since we left there. I thought you were upset because I was going to pay with my check. Remember you stopped me from separating the foods?"

"Listen, that's nothing. I mean you and I are together I already had planned to pay for the items. Save the check for…"

"Save it for when I'm alone," blurted Cassandra. "When you can't be seen with me paying with a W.I.C. check?"

"Cassandra, wait. Where's this coming from?"

"Lamont, I don't want you to be embarrassed to be with me. I am who I am."

"Who said I was embarrassed? Why do I get the feeling you're picking a fight?"

"Never mind Lamont, you don't understand. It's hard enough for me to accept my situation."

"Cassandra, your situation is behind you. I accept you and your children; you and your goal to become whatever you want. I told you, stop fighting me off. I didn't pay attention to your check. I wanted you to know I was willing to do what a man does for a family he loves. Keep your money, cash or check, for when you need it. Okay? "

Cassandra's cell phone rang in her purse and Lamont smirked as he passed her leaving her to answer the phone alone in the kitchen.

"Hello."

"Cassandra, it's me, Trina."

"Hey."

"Did you talk to Lamont about Trevor?"

"No. Why what's up?"

"Well, Sylvia changed her number because she's scared of what Trevor plans on doing. Sandra I should have listened to you, now I'm scared too. I mean, suppose he wants to hurt us all in some way. I haven't heard from him, and I don't want his going off to be my fault."

"Trevor does what he does Trina. He can't blame anyone but himself. But you're right I warned you. If Sylvia changed her number maybe you should too."

"What about you?"

"Trina, you didn't ask that when you and him were fucking around behind my back. I'm fine. As a matter of fact, I'm better than I have been in years."

Lamont's words were repeating over and over in her head. Cassandra was convinced their relationship could work. Trina's call brought light to another hurdle they would have to leap over. Trevor.

"Sandra, you need to warn Lamont about what Sylvia said."

"Thanks Trina, listen, I'll call you later, and we'll talk more. Don't answer Trevor's calls or your door and Trina, I'm going to say it one more time, stay away from Trevor."

Lamont re-entered the kitchen on Cassandra's final words. She led him back to the living room where they could talk. The look on his face told Cassandra now was the time to tell him about Sylvia and Trina's visit to Trevor's apartment. He listened looking at the carpet the entire time she repeated what Trina called and told her earlier that afternoon. Lamont's thoughts bounced between the conversations he had with Terrance, Jose', Malik, Kevin and Sean. He couldn't believe that since her return both his livelihood and possibly his life were in jeopardy. The trouble between Lamont and Trevor had always been Cassandra. As he listened to her speak, he realized Terrance was right. There was trouble when you dealt with a woman who was abused.

"Cassandra," Lamont interrupted her sentence as he pulled her closer to him.

"Cassandra, do you think you could ever love me. I mean all this mess with Trevor, him wanting to sabotage my business, and try to hurt me over you. I mean, do you think you could love me?"

Cassandra was stunned. If she answered yes, she wondered if Lamont would think of her as being desperate. They had only been a couple for a little over a month. If she answered no, she wondered if Lamont would feel uneasy about continuing the relationship.

"I'm not trying to force you into a permanent commitment. Listen, Trevor has an agenda that hasn't changed since high school. As long as Sylvia and you are fine I'm good. He's not running my life or my love for you. If we're gonna last, it's just something I need to know."

"Lamont, I don't want to be the cause of anyone's grief. I've had enough of that in my life and Trevor has always been the cause of it."

"Babe, that's not the point. Do you think you could ever love me?"

It was at that moment that they both knew that they loved each other without saying it aloud. Cassandra leaned in closer to say what Lamont needed to hear. Her lips barely touched his as she expressed her feelings for him. She moved her lips slowly speaking softly.

"Lamont, yes, I've always loved you."

Cassandra's phone rang interrupting the moment. Lamont stood gaining control of his physical desire for the woman he loved.

Chapter 60

"**H**ey Kevin. I'm surprised to hear from you."

"Why the surprise? You know you're my favorite family member. How's things going for you? How's your mother doing?"

Cassandra walked behind Lamont. He was going through his CD collection loading the player with music. She pointed to the phone and mouthed Kevin's name. Lamont nodded his head yes letting her know he didn't mind the call interrupting their conversation. She walked across the room and sat in the chaise lounge chair and relaxed back on the pillows, she was happy to hear Kevin's voice.

"Kevin things are as well as to be expected. Did your father tell you I've been home for a minute now?"

"No, Veronica did. I haven't talked to my dad yet. You know how that is. I'm not looking forward to his speech. I don't know Sandra, I'm trying but money on the street comes so much faster."

"Yeah but with so many problems."

"Fo' sure, fo' sure, so you and Trevor finally through huh?"

"Yeah, I can't do it. I mean I've had a chance to really take a look at the things we've done to each other and man, I must have been out of my mind. Anyway I'm glad I saw what was going on before it got worse."

"Cuz, it was bad enough. How's that leg coming along?"

Cassandra rubbed the leg that had been broken in two places by Trevor. The doctor's did what they could to reset the bone, but it had been splintered in two places causing it to take longer to heal. It healed with a scar that lasted for months and a limp that bothered her off and on.

"It healed. You can barely notice the limp. I can walk on it more days than none. When it rains it causes me some pain, but I deserve to feel the pain as a reminder."

"Cassandra, no one deserves pain. So, what's your plans? I hear there's a new love interest in your life."

"Did you now? What did you hear?"

"Veronica schooled me on what was going on. Lamont's a good man Cassandra. He's about family and business. His money is right too. No doubt. It can flow as slow as it wants, the brother is about business."

"Well it's not locked yet. I mean we've just started talking. But I like him a lot. I really do. You know he was my high school secret crush."

Cassandra started laughing. Lamont turned around from the stereo and smiled. The music had drowned out her conversation, and she continued to talk.

"Listen, you know it ain't sitting well with Trevor that you're with Lamont."

"Kevin, you didn't get that information from Veronica. Trina said the same thing. Did Trevor put a hit out on Lamont?"

Cassandra knew that a hit wasn't out of the norm for Trevor and his boys. Her fears brought tears to her eyes.

"No, Trevor hasn't said anything to me yet. He will though. Lamont told me."

"Lamont?"

"Don't say anything, just listen. Trevor and DJ got plans. I ain't letting it go down that way cuz. If I think it's getting close to your man, I'll put a stop to it."

Cassandra listened as Kevin told her about Trevor's plan to get Lamont's business. She told Kevin about the calls she received from Trina.

"Trevor is crazy Cassandra but I'm crazier. He's 'bout to cause his own life to be snuffed out. The word on the street has it that he's been setting up his own boys to get the spotlight from DJ. If he got Lamont's business he'd be in with DJ for life. You remember DJ don't you?

"I think I do."

"He's the one that Lamont promised to kill that night around the corner from your Mom's. We were all hanging out at that club; damn I can't remember the name of it. They turned it into that chicken spot.

Anyway, Trevor told you to get in the car something was going down, remember?"

"Oh yeah."

"Well Lamont drew down on the nigga. Took his heart and gained the respect of everyone else. DJ was disrespecting his sister Sylvia or something like that. I don't know why he didn't shoot him. Sylvia pleaded for DJ or told him she would leave him alone. I can't remember but he let DJ live and vowed to kill him if he ever crossed his path again. DJ is playing this one hiding behind punk ass Trevor."

"Kevin, I didn't know you knew Lamont as well as you do. Sylvia was dealing with DJ? You and him were cool like that? Did you and him talk about this?"

"Speak up girl, I can barely hear you. You playing music or something?"

"That's Lamont playing music."

"Why didn't you tell me y'all was together? Listen we'll talk later. I just wanted to hear your voice. If you're with Lamont you're fine. Hey, between us. Don't mention this to Lamont or family."

"No, it's all good. I'm good too. Are you coming Sunday to the picnic?"

"Yeah, Veronica told me about it. I'm gonna try to talk to my father tomorrow. If it turns out good I'll be there."

"Uncle Earl loves you man, it'll be fine. I'll see you Sunday."

"Tell Lamont I said hey. I'll see you Sunday."

Cassandra hung up her phone. She gave Lamont's house and cell number to her Aunt Laura, so she cut her cell off. She didn't want to take another call. She watched Lamont as he stood with his back to her pouring himself a glass of wine while swaying to the music. Cassandra approached him, just as he turned offering her the glass. She told Lamont she needed the drink, a warm shower and a soothing massage.

Lamont kissed Cassandra on her lips saying, "Who told you I was a masseuse?"

Chapter 61

Sylvia planned her day around a desired shopping spree. Carson promised he would spend a day shopping with her, something he never did. The prior evening ended with Sylvia crying in his arms, begging his forgiveness. Carson allowed her to believe he was as naïve as she thought. He never told her the part she played in his setting up Trevor and DJ.

Carson Klein ran his drugs through all of Philadelphia's corporate offices. He started as a runner for DJ but quickly learned the game and wanted his cut. After all white corporate America made the money for the bigger deals. DJ gave him what he wanted and introduced him to Trevor's side of town. DJ's interest was to have control of the city by bringing drugs in from New York, Washington, DC and the surrounding areas. Trevor had a run that came in through the airports and waterways. Carson was the man to get control of that. Neither DJ nor Trevor knew that Carson's connections ran the drugs up and down the east coast border, and it was only a matter of time when they would take over the turfs ran by DJ and Trevor. Sylvia was the bait and Carson used her to get Trevor to feed him his drugs. He played the dumb white boyfriend with a drug habit who had friends with bigger habits. As his demand grew Trevor started taking cuts from the profit and the supply, just what Carson needed to put the word on the street that Trevor couldn't be trusted by any of the larger sellers.

Carson alerted DJ. There was dirt in the game and Trevor was the dirt. DJ began watching Trevor set up his boys as they did the local runs. His trust for Trevor disappeared completely when Trevor told him of his staged set up. When DJ explained their plans, giving a reason for Trevor's misdeeds, Carson warned him that Lamont would retaliate on them both.

Trevor begged DJ to let him make the drops to Carson as a sign of his sincerity in the game. Trevor didn't bank on Malik, Jose' and Kevin taking the drugs from him and never making the connections. Now, DJ agreed with Carson, Trevor would have to be done.

Carson was waiting on a few phone calls but wanted to please Sylvia in any way he could. So shopping would fill his day because he did love her. While he played the dumb white boy, Sylvia used him for his money and not his love. It was time Sylvia dealt with Carson the man. DJ hadn't called, which meant Trevor would. Everything was working out fine, and he looked forward to having a serious relationship with Sylvia. DJ needed to save himself. He let it be known that Kevin, Malik and Jose' had Carson's drugs and Trevor knew this all along. Carson was waiting to talk to Trevor.

Sylvia stepped into the bedroom with a towel barely wrapped around her. Carson smiled from the bed knowing it was an invitation.

"Carson, you haven't gotten up. You promised you would be ready at ten."

"I'm ready now."

Carson's manhood stood erect as he rolled over to show her his naked body. Sylvia slid into the bed next to him and wrapped her legs around his waist. He rolled onto his back waiting for her to mount him and take a pleasurable ride. His phone rang just as his penis entered her vagina.

"Baby, I've got to get the phone. It could be important."

Sylvia had been trying to have sex with Carson since the night before. It seemed as though he was avoiding her, she didn't understand why. They had made love frequently when he was snorting daily. She could remember longing for more. When he couldn't perform she'd find herself in Trevor's bed. It happened more often than she wanted to remember. Sylvia felt she owed him a good lay, something to show her appreciation. After all, he always took her back. Carson went to his dresser to answer the phone. He fondled his manhood as he walked into the living room where the conversation could not be heard by Sylvia. The erection was bothering him, and he needed to release the pressure that was building. He continued to rub his penis. The call would have to end quickly.

"Yeah, who."

"Oh, you cool now huh?"

It was Trevor. Carson grunted to himself thinking of jerking off in Trevor's face.

"What's up man?"

"You, heard you looking to talk to me." Trevor was unaware of the tension building between them.

"Yeah, but it ain't a good time right now. Besides, where's my shit. I don't want to talk until my shit is delivered."

"Wow. You don't even sound like the white boy I been dealing with."

"Call it what you want, but I got some other issues waiting right now. I ain't trying to chit chat Trevor. I got somebody waiting for this white boy."

Carson was still satisfying himself with his hand.

"Sylvia's there with you?"

"Is she with you?"

"No. Listen enough of the games. That bitch and Trina took the stash I had in my house. That was enough for us to be squared. Get your shit from her."

"I didn't make no buys from Sylvia or Trina. Trevor don't call back, we ain't got nothing to talk about until you square up. But you were right my friend, I'm gonna get my shit from her. You know the shit she really didn't give to you. So bro, if you ain't gonna satisfy my needs now then I'll fuck you later."

Carson hung up the phone. He looked down at his throbbing penis glad he controlled his urge to climax. He returned to the bedroom where Sylvia was laying with the towel between her legs. Carson pulled back on his penis slowly as he massaged himself to his maximum length. He could feel the warmth in his hand as the veins in his penis enlarged.

Carson got a little angry at himself because he knew he was about to explode just looking at Sylvia as she spread her legs for him to gaze at her. She smiled as she saw the head of his penis glistening with moisture.

He refused to mount her. It had been weeks since his last sexual encounter, and he needed this one to last. She needed to be loved, and he needed to show her what he held back while playing the dumb white boy. He spread her legs and pulled her toward the foot of the bed. He could feel his warm sperm running down his leg as his penis pulsated.

Sylvia was surprised when he parted the lips of her vagina with his tongue. He never showed an interest in oral sex. She trembled as he took the time to explore her. Her moans of pleasure brought his penis to full size again as he rolled her over kissing her thighs and mounting her for what should have been their first time. The encounter was new to the both of them as they took their time slowly satisfying the other's needs. His hands found her breast, and as he motioned himself in and out of her warm cove, he touched her gently on each nipple as he kissed her back.

She wanted to scream but knew the time would come for them both to shout together. As she repositioned herself onto her back, she raised both of her legs in the air. As her knees rested beside her ears Carson kissed each leg from her toes to her pleasure. He couldn't wait. He fondled himself pulling back and forth as he touched her with each of his finger tips. He played with her clitoris putting the tip of his penis on it and moving in and out slowly. He started to penetrate Sylvia deeper and deeper until her warmth turned hot and his penis started pumping sperm into her. He stopped only to get deeper and exploding again. She moaned his name as her body trembled its thanks.

"Carson, oh Carson."

"Baby, it's all good. Shit!"

"What's wrong?"

Carson rolled on his back as he felt his body tingling and his sacs filling again.

"That ten o'clock deadline won't be met this morning."

Carson buried himself into Sylvia's breast licking her nipples and fingering her vagina. Sylvia gave in.

Chapter 62

Trevor slammed the receiver of the phone into its cradle. He couldn't believe the past few weeks. Now Cassandra was the least of his worries. He had to get Carson off his back. He knew the streets, and his name would be on the black list if he didn't square up with the white boy. He had no idea that Carson was "the white boy" that the street dealers talked about. As long as DJ had his back, he didn't have to look over his shoulder. DJ didn't want to deal with Carson. His alliance was to the streets. Trevor thought about it. There was no way he was going to lose everything, including his life.

Trevor had to deal with each of his problems separately. After talking to Carson, Trina and Sylvia would be first on the list. He went to his kitchen table and snorted the line of coke that was there from the night before. He would have to persuade Malik, Jose' and Kevin to join him in getting paid. They would be more than willing to help move the drugs at Lamont's garage after they heard the money they could make. Trevor decided to pull a few runs without DJ and show him the profit. When he made enough money to tease Carson and DJ, he would put the sting on Lamont in motion. He would have Lamont's garage and eventually Cassandra. The thought of Lamont laying Cassandra down raised his anger, but as he leaned back he imagined her movements were all for him.

As the coke began to take effect Trevor dialed Trina's number. Trina's answer machine picked up his call after the fourth ring and the voice made Trevor sit up.

"The party you are trying to reach has blocked this number; please state your name or the company you're with for acceptance of your call."

Trevor let most of the day pass. He enjoyed the rest of his stash before he dialed Sylvia's number again he heard the same message. He hung up the phone and dialed her job. The number in her office gave the number to her cell phone. He waited for her new cell phone number to be recited by the recording.

"Hello."

The voice on the other end was Carson's.

"So you screening her calls?"

"No, what's up?"

"Put the bitch on the phone."

"I can't man. She ain't here. I thought I told you that earlier."

"Bullshit Carson. Put that bitch on the phone."

"Listen man, what she had I gave her. That's right, the condo and all that was in it, her cell phone and her job. Well, Trevor, I took it all back. I'm in charge. I needed to show you that bro. Now get my shit or else. Sylvia won't be needing your black ass for nothing. The white boy is giving it all to her as usual. The difference is you're on notice. Stay away from what's mine. Bring me my shit Trevor or they'll be problems waiting for you."

"She can't hide. I'll see her and you on the streets."

"Not if I see you first."

The phone went silent. Trevor went to the bathroom and took a shower. As the water ran over his head and face, he decided he would get Trina to take him back. If he acted as though he understood her actions, he could find Sylvia and his drugs. He would threaten Sylvia and release her only when she promised to bring him his drugs. Once he got the drugs, he would beat Sylvia until she couldn't see her way home. Trina would pay soon after he fulfilled his last sexual pleasures with her. Lamont would want to step to him after he beat Sylvia's ass and Carson would be looking for him too. That was the excitement of it all. The buzz from the coke and the shower painted a picture of chaotic bliss.

Trevor stepped out of the shower and dried himself as his thoughts gave him the solutions to his problems. He would call the police and arrange for the bust. When Lamont and Carson approached him, it would be at Lamont's garage.

Trevor would play the victim, and explain to the officers that he came to pick up his drug money. He would produce the paperwork for the fleet. Kevin or Malik would have planted the drugs an easy bust for the cops. Carson would see it all come together and tell DJ how well the plan worked. He'd be willing to deal with Trevor once he saw the operation had been in progress for about two months. At least three shipments would have gone through before the bust. Trevor realized he would have to be patient and not let his anger blind him.

He looked in the mirror smoothing his eyebrows and hair with his hands. He decided he would get a haircut before visiting Trina later in the day. Trina owed him. The thought of her body caused him to rearrange his plans. He would handle some other runs during the day and go to Trina's apartment later to spend the night.

Chapter 63

Terrance sat in his car waiting for Sylvia to park. She called saying she needed him to meet her, so she could get a few of her belongings from her office. He didn't understand why she couldn't wait until Monday, but he didn't ask questions and promised his sister, he would be there waiting.

Sylvia walked toward his green Acura looking from side to side. Her steps quickened as though she knew someone was watching her approach the car.

"Hey, Terrance thanks, we're going around to the back of the building."

"Why? The security guard is at the front door. What or who are you looking for?"

"Listen, I don't know when I can come back to the office. I've got some important papers to get from my desk."

"Again, why can't we go to the front door? Security knows who you are."

"For once Terrance, let me do this my way."

"Where's the white boy? He could have escorted you in the building. "

"Terrance! Please do this."

Terrance turned the key in his ignition. He put the car in gear and slowly went through the parking lot to the rear of the building. Sylvia went into the building and returned with a briefcase and a box ten minutes later. The box was crafted with fine art work and caught his eye.

"What's in the box?"

"Personal items and protection from Trevor. I won't be returning to work for a while. I'll need these things at home."

"Home and where is that these days?"

Terrance was grateful for the opportunity to ask questions about her personal life.

"Terrance, you know, I don't really know. I'm staying with Carson but I don't think I want to call that home."

"So what's up with your spot and the job? I mean you don't have to live with Carson do you?"

"No it just would be better, for the time being. Trevor may be looking for me."

"And?"

"And, it could become physical. Things got ugly Terrance. I went with Trina and ransacked his apartment. I don't really want to talk about it. What's done is done and Trevor is upset about it."

"Shit, I would be too. Why would you tear up his apartment? What was on your mind?"

"He was fucking over me and Trina. I guess the same way he did Cassandra over and over. I couldn't see myself going through it as many times as her. He was dealing with me and Trina and God knows who else. Anyway we tore up his shit until it felt good. Now I am waiting for him to come back at me."

"What about Trina?"

"She's gonna call me if he should show up. I know he called her a few times, but she didn't answer the calls. We took his drugs, a stash he had in the floorboards. I flushed half the shit in the toilet. The rest I put away."

"You should have flushed your head too. What are you thinking? You say you don't want to deal with him yet you take what you know he'll come to collect on. Damn, girl. Now you got to travel with a bodyguard. So where are you staying."

"I don't need a bodyguard. I needed an escort to the building. I'm staying with Carson. I wrote the information for you. I'll be away from the job for about a month. Carson said in a month the air should be cleared."

"What does he know about Trevor that we don't? I mean you were close to Trevor, what do you think?"

"Terrance, Trevor wants Cassandra. He told me he will hurt Lamont if he has to. Whether Cassandra wants him or not is a different story, but it's a story I don't want to read. I can't wait for Trevor to make up his mind. This is about the third round with him, Cassandra and me. This round he included Trina and whoever else. My feelings count too.

I thought I could fall in love with him again and convince him to forget about Lamont. It didn't work cause; he didn't give a damn about us. Carson isn't a genius but he does care about me."

"Sylvia, if Trevor was gonna hurt Lamont, why didn't you tell us?"

"I'll tell Lamont."

Sylvia had to call Lamont before Trevor stepped to him. If Sylvia's thoughts were right after Trevor couldn't reach Trina or her by phone he would carry out his threat and step to Lamont.

"Will Lamont be at the picnic on Sunday?"

"Yeah, where are we going now? Are you leaving your car here too?"

"No, a sister needs her wheels."

"Sylvia what was the purpose of me coming here with you. You mean I just did the security guard's job from the car?"

Sylvia rolled her eyes. "No, Terrance really, maybe we could get Lamont to stop by so I can talk to both of you at the same time."

"Maybe, call him. No, we'll be together tomorrow, if you can wait that long. But in the meantime, why did I play parking lot security?"

"I don't want anyone to say it was possible they saw me, and I know Trevor would ask."

"Yeah I forgot your ass is in hiding. Where are you going now?"

"To Carson's apartment."

Terrance pulled up next to Sylvia's car and watched as she put her belongings in on the passenger's side. Sylvia came back to Terrance's car with the box in her hands and sat in the front seat. She looked at her brother and sighed.

"Sylvia, what's wrong. Don't give me that shit that it's all good either. Listen we can call Lamont and the three of us can talk about it now."

Terrance watched as Sylvia talked holding on to the shined handcrafted box.

"Terrance, I was a fool to think I could be different. I tried. I mean, you know the corporate world bull. I worked hard to erase the past, and I realize today, I'm no further than I was years ago."

"Listen we all slip up every now and then. Nobody is judging you but you."

"But Terrance, I have been so critical of others. You, Lamont, Ma'Dear, and others, I've always tried to be the better one."

"You thought you was better than us?"

"Yeah, to a certain point. But today I know better. I mean we all have unique qualities but for the most part I thought I held it together better than any of you."

"Yeah right!"

"I did, really. I mean a good job, living in a condo, eating those expensive lunches and dinners, credit cards with the minimum sitting on the roof. You name it, I had it."

"Had it?"

"I don't really want it anymore. It ain't the same no more."

"Sylvia, what are you talking about?"

"Terrance, I thought about only me. I didn't think about the consequences. I saw another way for me to get more, when I had all I needed. I can't run away from what I did, but I refuse to cause more problems for anyone else."

"You're talking in circles. Listen we could talk about this until we're blue in our faces, but we'd have to repeat it all for Lamont. Can this wait until tomorrow?"

Sylvia wasn't ready for the round of true confessions, so she agreed to call Lamont and let him know she was alright. They talked for another fifteen minutes about their mother, Cassandra, and Lamont. Sylvia watched a car slowly pass them in the next row of parked cars, and she decided to leave after it passed. Sylvia got out of the car still clutching her box of keepsakes.

"I'll see you tomorrow around two thirty?"

"I'll be there early, Ma'Dear is cooking."

"Love you Terrance, call Lamont for me."

"Hey, you call Lamont. I love you too."

Chapter 64

"**E**arl I don't know what to think. She just told me while I was in the room helping her with her medication. I noticed one of her prescriptions was low. She told me don't worry about it, said it would probably change on Monday. So I asked what was going on Monday. I knew there wasn't no doctor's appointment or nothing. She said she was scheduled for the surgery. Earl just like that, surgery!"

Laura was upset. She couldn't control the tears that flowed from her eyes. She was certain that Mary changed her mind knowing that it was urgent she had the operation. After her conversation with Mary, she excused herself saying she wanted to check on the children. They were comfortable in the den watching television. Laura went upstairs where she knew Mary wouldn't hear her talking on the phone.

"Laura we don't know that the doctor told her any different than she told us. Maybe Mary finally decided to have the surgery done. Does Cassandra know?"

"I don't think so. She's with Lamont until tomorrow, I'm sure she would have spent the weekend with her mother knowing she was having this procedure Monday."

Earl shook his head. Again he was caught in the middle he didn't know what Laura wanted him to do. He took the receiver from his ear and leaned back to say a silent prayer.

"Earl, you there, did you hear me?"

"Yeah, Laura I heard you. That gal don't know this either. How is she supposed to feel when this is all said and done? Mary ain't right Laura. This ain't fair to Cassandra. Did Mary say why she changed her mind?"

"No, just said that she needed to face what the Lord put before her."

"Maybe she ain't in the right frame of mind Laura. Have you talked to the doctor? She seemed willing to answer any questions we had. Maybe she's talked to Mary about the surgery and convinced her it was best."

"Yeah, maybe, she's not that sick Earl. It comes and goes. She's in her right mind. I'm sure of that. I just don't know why she won't tell Cassandra about her plans. She told me don't open my mouth to her."

"What about to me?"

"She knew I would tell you."

"Laura, I'll tell Cassandra. I think Mary knew I would."

Earl said his goodbye as he looked in his cell phone for Cassandra's number. He dialed her number and was connected to her answering machine after the fourth ring. He left the message for his niece to call him.

Chapter 65

Cassandra closed her eyes as the smell of body oil entered the room. Lamont was in the shower. They slept in late and spent the morning watching on demand movies. The warm shower and massage ended when they both hit the bed. Neither tried to fulfill any of their fantasies their first night together. Cassandra had become frigid and was scared Lamont would feel her fears as he got closer to her tense body. He never said a word and held her close to his bare chest as they drifted off to sleep.

He woke up at ten o'clock with the sweet smell of her hair beneath his nose. He smiled as he got out of the bed gazing at her bronze body in his king size bed. Cassandra was beautiful, but as Lamont thought of loving her fully, Terrance's words crossed his mind. "She's an abused woman…." Lamont had seen signs of that the night before.

Lamont went into the kitchen to prepare her a nice breakfast and start another day in love. His thoughts made him laugh to himself. He would truly have to love her, one day at a time. Cassandra couldn't see a future because she hadn't believed in the future for a long time; the results of abuse. He cooked breakfast thinking about how it could be. Cassandra's youngest was five. He didn't know if she wanted more children, or a husband. He didn't know if she wanted him. He knew Cassandra felt the physical attraction, but she didn't react at all. "She's an abused woman….."

He brought her food on a tray to the bed, and kissed her forehead. As she opened her eyes, he saw Cassie in her smile and returned the smile. Lamont left her in her thoughts and went into the shower. Cassandra came to the door of the bathroom and watched his silhouette through the shower doors.

"Lamont…"

"Yeah."

"I've got to go to the house today. Uncle Earl called. He wants to talk with me and Aunt Laura about my mother."

"Is everything okay?"

"I hope so."

"I'll be right out. Will you be coming back tonight?"

"Yes, if you'll have me."

Lamont stepped out of the shower. His naked body dripped water onto the floor. Cassandra reached for the towel on the rack behind her and turned him around to dry his back.

"I didn't mean it that way Cassandra. I didn't know how serious it was. You can stay here if you want. I told you that and I meant it."

Lamont turned around allowing her to rub the towel down his chest. She stopped at his waist and handed him the towel. Lamont let the towel fall to the floor. He stepped closer to kiss Cassandra on the lips. Cassandra put her arms around him allowing the kiss to give her an arousal. Lamont smiled knowing that the night ahead would be different than the night before.

Chapter 66

Terrance brought two beers to the porch and sat waiting for Lamont to take in what he was told about Sylvia. His brother stood, leaning over the banister looking at the front lawn. Lamont was also worried about the news Cassandra was receiving across the street from her aunt and uncle. A neighbor yelled his name, and he waved as he turned to Terrance to continue their discussion.

"Terrance, I'm not running from nobody, you know that. I've known about Trevor's threat for a minute now. I haven't stepped to him because I know that's what he wants. If he gives me a reason I will, until then he's just another Lamont Dearling hater."

"Lamont, how many of your haters really want to kill you?"

"I don't know and don't give a damn, as long as they don't bring it."

"Yeah, anyway, Sylvia seems to think she can deal with Trevor by herself. I don't know Lamont. I think she's thinking all wrong. It ain't easy to love someone who wants to kill a member of your family."

"She told you she loved him?"

"Yeah, she loves him or loved him. He shot her a raw deal. Trevor ain't the loving kind. Look what he does to the women he supposed to love."

"Man, I only know of one, Cassandra. I think Sylvia and Trina thought he loved them. In his own way, he's always loved Cassandra. I don't know when she woke up, but she doesn't love him and that's all that matters to me."

"Love is tricky. I mean look at you and Gwen. Shit look at me and Diane. You never know man."

"What's up with you and Diane?"

"I don't know if she's even coming back. I don't know why either. Just like that, left to visit family and called saying she was staying there for a while. So what am I supposed to do? Sit around and wait?"

"No go and find out what's going on. I learned that from that shit with Gwen."

"Shit, I can get over her right here. I ain't going where her family is and possibly another man to find out what I already know. You want another beer?"

"I hear you. Where's your sister? I thought she was on her way?"

"She said she was on her way when I called her. I told her you were on your way. How long are you gonna be here?"

"Cassandra said she would call when she was ready. Mr. Earl pulled up when we got here."

Terrance went into the house to get them both another beer. Lamont followed and took a seat on the couch. Ma'Dear was at the church finalizing the picnic arrangements. Terrance returned with a smile on his face.

"What's so funny?"

"I was thinking about that damn Trevor telling Sylvia she better be with him or else. He didn't have to threaten her, she would have been with him just 'cause he asked. That brother is stupid."

"So was Sylvia. How could she think he loved her when he was threatening her from the door?"

"Love, man I'm telling you, love."

"She's abused too."

Lamont walked to look out the screened front door, peeking again across the street. The afternoon breeze was welcomed, though he could barely feel it. The house was warmer than usual. Lamont ignored the warmth knowing they would be walking in and out of the front door. Ma'Dear would have words with both of them about "swinging her door open" if they turned the air conditioner was on.

"What? That nigga put his hands on her?"

Lamont turned to his brother with an explanation knowing Terrance wouldn't fully understand.

"No, his words, his actions, man abuse comes in many forms. Sylvia is just as tired of Trevor as I am. Just as tired of him as Cassandra and Trina. Shit even his boys are tired of him."

"Don't leave out the white boy. I think he loves Sylvia and didn't want to compete with Trevor. Word is Trevor did him dirty too."

"Terrance, that's what Trevor banks on, nobody wanting to deal with his ass.

Terrance thought about Sylvia and her handcrafted box. Her words of protection came to his mind.

"Lamont, have you ever known Sylvia to have a gun?"

"No, I don't think she knows how to handle one, why?"

"She picked up her briefcase and a fancy box, big enough for a gun from her office. She said it was a few things to protect her from Trevor. Paperwork wouldn't protect her, unless she went to court or filed charges, but a gun would protect her immediately."

"Terrance, don't jump to conclusions. Call Sylvia again, see where she is."

Chapter 67

E arl told Cassandra he would pick her up in front of her mother's house. She explained she didn't want to go in the house and upset her children. Laura waved at them from the window. Earl drove in silence for what seemed like forever. Cassandra began to recognize the neighborhood as Earl parked curbside in front of his house.

"Things look the same. I expected some changes. Do the Simons still live next door?"

"Their children do. They moved four years ago to Florida and left the house to their oldest, Elaine. She's married now with two children, stair steps. Cute kids though, but who knows how they'll turn out. Her brother is sickly and lives with them."

They both got out of the car as the front door opened. Veronica stepped onto the porch smiling with open arms.

"Sandra, girl look at you, I told daddy to bring you over for a minute. Girl you look good!"

The cousins hugged and held hands going into the house. Reggie stood in the middle of the living room waiting for his turn to compliment the cousin he hadn't seen for years.

"Reggie, look at Cassandra. She's looking good, right? Daddy was it hard to convince her to come over?"

"I didn't tell her. I just picked her up, and we drove here. We have a few things to discuss anyway. I knew you and Reggie were here so it was easy."

Cassandra was happy to see her family and welcomed their display of love. She looked around the room trying to catch a memory or any resemblance to the past when she and her mother would visit. The house was painted another color on the outside and the rooms had been renovated on the inside. Cassandra's memory told her that the comforting living room was blue and white where she played on a carpeted floor. She remembered her dollhouse, the adults playing bid whisk, and her older cousins teasing her. The floor she walked across now was beautiful. A polished wood that showed no signs of the years that had passed.

"Wow, you've done so much with the house Uncle Earl. It's beautiful. Reggie where do you live these days?"

"Here and my home in East Philly. Some days I make it home others I don't even try. Dad doesn't mind the company and its closer to the office I work out of."

"And Ms. Ronnie, when's your big day? Word is you're getting hitched."

"Yeah, well it's a lot of work. Picking the hall, the arrangements, a menu, girl between that and keeping your boy out of jail I don't know if I'm coming or going."

They talked about Kevin, her uncle's youngest, and his dealings with Trevor Black. Cassandra never let on that she was aware of what was going on between Kevin and Trevor.

"Where is Kevin? I mean it seems you knew I was coming. Why didn't someone invite Kevin?"

Reggie and Veronica looked at their father. Cassandra could tell by the silence that Kevin had not talked to his father. Earl didn't want Kevin's trouble in his home.

"He promised to be at the picnic tomorrow, I'm sure we'll see him there?"

Veronica spoke not looking for a response from her father or Reggie. Lately, Reggie was avoiding any conversations about the family's relationship with Kevin. She talked to Kevin daily.

"He called me yesterday. He told me he would be at the picnic. I just assumed he called here after we talked, he said he had to talk to you, Uncle Earl."

Earl nodded his head but didn't confirm if he received the call from Kevin. They talked for more than an hour. Kevin said he would respect the wishes of his father's home. He promised his troubles would soon be over. Earl didn't ask any questions he just repeated his request for respect. Kevin ended the conversation stating he would be at the picnic on Sunday.

"Well at least he's not in jail. Maybe he's turning the game around."

Reggie spoke as Veronica brought out chips and sodas for them. Cassandra smiled at the thought, but she knew different. They all understood that Kevin liked the adrenaline rush of the street game.

Cassandra knew he would respect his father's home, but turning his life around would take more than his father's wish.

Veronica and Reggie knew the real reason Cassandra was brought into their father's home. So Veronica made her excuses for leaving after an hour or more of reminiscing, and Reggie left shortly after. Reggie went in the kitchen and returned to say his goodbyes.

"I left the buffalo wings on the stove; the potato salad is in the fridge. Sandra it was good seeing you let's make sure we don't become distant relatives. I don't think I'll make the picnic tomorrow."

"Reggie, you know your friend is welcomed."

Earl's voice had a touch of pleading. Cassandra wondered why.

"She's asking for some time alone Dad. We'll see though maybe I can convince her to come. Y'all be good."

Reggie walked over and kissed Cassandra on the cheek and shook his father's hand before walking out the front door. Cassandra's stomach grumbled, she decided to get the food from the kitchen.

"Uncle Earl, do you want a plate?"

"Yeah baby, I'll come in there. We can talk and eat at the same time. Lamont must be wondering where you are."

Cassandra made the plates and poured iced tea for the both of them. Earl took a seat at the kitchen table and waited for her to sit before he spoke.

"Pass the salt baby."

"Uncle Earl what's wrong? You haven't been yourself today. And what's up with Reggie's girl?"

"Nothing, she's paranoid about our family. Ain't nobody thinking about that girl. She thinks she has to be a lawyer or a scholar to be accepted. I told Reggie she has issues. When he does stay here she accuses him of being with someone else. Listen, Cassandra, your mother doesn't know you're here. Let's keep this between us, okay?"

"Keep what between us? What's this about?"

"Your mother agreed to have the surgery done, Monday. She didn't tell you and Laura, and I thought you should know."

"I already knew. The therapist told me Friday. I didn't tell anyone because she felt Mama would change her mind if we talked to her about it. When did she tell you?"

"She didn't tell me. She told your Aunt Laura last night. Laura told me and I thought it was only right for you to know. Why didn't you tell us you knew?"

"Uncle Earl I didn't want anything to change her mind. My mother told the therapist about her decision before she told any of us. That says a lot about our relationship. I don't know why our love isn't on the level it should be, but she needs the surgery. Her health is more important than anything else right now."

"I've been thinking maybe there's more to her decision than we know."

"What do you mean?" Cassandra questioned, reaching for a napkin.

"I always wondered about people having surgery for cancer. It seems that as soon as they have the surgery the cancer gets worst. You know that's a chance she'll be taking. Maybe she didn't want us to worry about that."

"I didn't think about that. I mean Uncle Earl, what other choices does she have? I thought the surgery was her only option."

It was then that Earl remembered Cassandra didn't know Mary wasn't in the danger she portrayed. He ate more of his food not answering the question.

"I'm glad she's made the choice. I just don't know what changed her mind."

"I think you did; you and the kids. She wants to see them grow; you accomplish your goals and settle your life. That's what all parents want. Cassandra your mother loves you, even if she doesn't always show it."

"Uncle Earl I take it one day at a time. Until lately I felt I was a burden to her heart. I stayed away cause, bruised love never heals. I know about that first hand."

"Trevor. Yeah, I guess you do sweetie. I sure wish things were different between you two. You have such beautiful children and years wasted."

"What's that saying? You live and you learn? I'm a slow learner I guess."

"It takes time to recognize real love. We've all been bruised, one way or another. You and your mother have a lot of lost time."

"Just like me and Trevor, huh?"

"You're not thinking of going back to Trevor are you?"

"No, but in comparison it's all the same. He never knew how to love me either. Maybe he'll realize it just like my mother did and want to reunite with me."

Cassandra spoke the words and her thoughts fell into a newfound reality. Mary and Trevor didn't care whether she knew they loved her or not.

"Cassandra, love is confusing at times. A love between a parent and child is different than the love between a man and a woman. But love never abuses, it never disrespects those involved, and it never lies. Your mother prefers not to tell you why you're so distant, which tells me she loves you too much to tell you. Trevor hurts you every chance he gets. Trevor doesn't love you Cassandra, not like your mother does."

"If I hurt those who hurt me calling it love, Uncle Earl, I would be in jail. It hurts to know my mother is so distant to me. I can't get over that. Trevor is the father of my children, I can't get over that. I will always be connected to this mental abuse."

"You can't change who your mother is or who the father of your children is, you're right. But you can change how you deal with them. Trevor is the easier of the two. Aren't you seeing Lamont now? Do you still pray?"

Cassandra nodded. She knew that her uncle's next statement would be "Let go and let God". He was right she

had prayed to be released from misguided love and the abuse. God answered her prayer. She was free to love Lamont. She prayed more than once about her relationship with her mother. Although it was sickness that brought her home, it was also a second chance for her and mother.

"Your mother may or may not admit to you that she loves you. You'll have to accept that. Sometimes love is underneath the hurt and pain that we don't know anything about. Trevor is in your past. Move on Cassandra."

"You're right Uncle Earl. I'll never get ahead tying myself to the past."

"Girl you've grown so much since you lived with your mother. I'm proud of you and I have all the confidence in the world that you'll be fine. Keep your head up. God has your spirit, let Him work through you. Listen we could talk all evening about this, but that would only worry Lamont. Call him and tell him you're on your way. Your Aunt Laura and I didn't want Monday to come and go, and you not know about this surgery."

"So on Monday what do I do? I mean my mother didn't tell me, and I'm not supposed to know. My first day of class is Monday, but I want to be at the hospital."

"Laura and I will go. You handle your class and we'll call you when the surgery is done. You and your mother can talk about this when she's home and feeling better. You'll see it will work itself out."

Cassandra had a bad feeling come over her as Earl told her things would be better. She wanted to protest and give her reasons for wanting to be there but decided her presence may upset her mother. She called Lamont and told him she would be at his mother's in twenty minutes.

They cleaned the kitchen together and rode across town talking about the children and their expectations for an upcoming fishing trip. As they approached Ma'Dear's house Cassandra couldn't contain her smile.

"You know it's rumored that you have a thing for Ma'Dear."

"That ain't no rumor child. Your mother and your aunt been trying to set us up for years. We do our thing. Now you go do yours."

Chapter 68

It was close to nine o'clock and the early part of Cassandra and Lamont's evening was filled with phone calls. Lamont spoke to Sean and Jose'. He invited them to the annual picnic. Ma'Dear's promise of sweet potato pies was enough for them to purchase their tickets. They told him they would definitely be there. Malik would only stop by the park for a minute or two. They didn't think the new family planned to join the festivities. Jose' was certain that Malik still had other women in his life. The men began to talk about his female visitors who stopped by the shop. Lamont's conversation with Jose' ended when Sylvia called on the other line.

Cassandra left the room when she heard Lamont say Sylvia's name. She decided to give him some privacy. She would use the time to take a long shower. Lamont went to the bar and poured himself a drink.

"Lamont, I owe you an apology."

"Why's that?"

"You were right. I mean I should have told you the truth from the beginning. Maybe things wouldn't have gotten this far."

"How far have they gotten?"

"Trevor is after me and you now."

"Sylvia, stop it. Start from the beginning and don't leave anything out."

She told her older brother everything beginning with the day Trevor called her with the initial threat. She also told him of their past affair, the drugs, Carson and the drugs. Sylvia admitted her fear of Trevor carrying out his threatening promises.

"Trina hasn't called. I'm really worried about her. She still loves him. I can tell. When she gets enough of his shit, she'll feel like me. I changed my address, my phone, and I won't be going to work until things die down. I don't want him to know where I am."

"And how will you know when things have died down?"

"Carson said in about a month. Lamont I believe Carson knew Trevor before I introduced them. Seems strange but Carson has been different lately. Trevor was supposed to bring him a package and Carson claims he never got it. Since then he has been treating Trevor a lot different, me too for that matter."

Sylvia had a flash back to the bed, she and Carson shared earlier. Carson was different in more ways than one.

"Carson isn't as naïve as you thought. I guess he did have a reason for being in the hood."

"Anyway like I told Terrance, I'm staying with Carson at his place for a while. I'll be fine. But Lamont you need to know he has it in for you and now probably me too."

"Sylvia, I'm not gonna say I told you so. But I will repeat this. If Trevor hurts you or Cassandra, I'll kill him. Did you tell him that? I mean since you're always telling me what he said. It seems to me, you have more faith in his words than mine. My threat is just as serious as his. I'm glad to know you're safe. Stay out of Trevor's way, and let the streets deal with him. He's on his way out. Are you guys coming to the picnic tomorrow?"

"I told Carson about it. I hope he remembers."

"If you need someone to come and get you, call me or Terrance."

"Okay, I will. Thanks Lamont. I should have listened."

It's okay. You never did listen to me."

Lamont's drink took the edge off the anger he felt. He knew there was nothing to do but wait for Trevor to make his move. Cassandra entered the living room and saw his look of defeat. She sat next to him on the couch and pulled his head over to her breast and stroked his temple. He welcomed her comforting hands and the warmth of her embrace. He sat back on the couch letting out a deep sigh.

"Baby I don't know how long I can live like this."

"What do you mean Lamont? There's nothing you can do."

"I could kill that bastard. I don't want to live day by day waiting for him to make a move or someone to off his stupid ass."

Cassandra held her thoughts. The desire to be free from Trevor was coupled with the desire for her children to have their father in their lives.

"Cassandra he's threatened you, me and Sylvia. That's well beyond my limits as a man. I just don't know when my emotions will become rattled enough to react to this bullshit."

"I understand Lamont, but he's the father of my children."

"That didn't stop him from whipping your ass from time to time. He knows you're in a better relationship, and he's threatening that too. What's next? He's driving you crazy 'cause you still love him."

She started crying. Lamont's words hit her inner core.

"Lamont I love you."

"You say you do, but then you defend Trevor in his shit. Stop protecting that nigga."

"Lamont I just don't want…"

"What, Cassandra what, you don't want to live a fulfilled life, one that includes true love? Don't your children deserve someone that loves their mother and them? I need to know that you understand my love for you. Otherwise, we won't have a foundation in our relationship. I know I'm not their father. A father doesn't hurt the mother of his children."

She heard his words and remembered saying the same thing to Trina. Lamont was right. It was time to let go of her dead love for Trevor. She relaxed on Lamont's chest. He wrapped his arms around her. They left the living room and headed for the bedroom. The night's sleep would be well deserved.

Chapter 69

Trina checked the locks on her apartment door three times and still didn't feel secure. As she went to her bedroom past the front door, she checked the door again. The past few days were what she considered the most unnerving. She had limited her travels to one route; to and from her job. Her mother met her for lunch twice during the week but Trina waited in her car until she saw her entering the restaurant. She was sure Trevor was watching her from some corner or in the distance, from his car. Her fears had taken over her daily routine.

She turned down her covers on her bed earlier and was more than ready to close her eyes for the night. She unplugged her phone, which had become a habit each night. Trevor hadn't called after she'd unplugged the phone the beginning of the week. She cut off all the lights and turned on the bedroom television. It was close to two thirty in the morning when Trina thought she heard someone in her kitchen.

The light from her front window provided dim lighting to the living room. She entered the room hoping she was just being paranoid. She looked toward the door attempting to see if the chain was still in place. As she walked closer to the door a hand from the darkness covered her mouth.

"Yeah bitch; it was only a matter of time. Now I'm gonna let you go, but if you scream you won't get a chance to scream again. Do you understand?"

Trina shook her head rapidly. She understood saying no wasn't an option. Trevor took his hand off her mouth and pushed her on the couch.

"So, you weren't smart enough to move huh?"

"Why would I move?"

"Why wouldn't you? That's what Sylvia did. I mean when you're guilty you avoid the punishment."

"Trevor, what am I guilty of? Wanting to love you? That's all I wanted?"

"You showed me plenty of love. I saw evidence of it when I walked into my apartment."

"Trevor, you played me hard. I was hurt. I just wanted to show you how it felt. I know you only gave a shit about your belongings so with a little help, I wrecked it." Trina was pleading, hoping he would see her point of view.

"Where's my shit Trina?"

"I never touched it. Sylvia did. I don't know."

"You don't know. You don't know. Trina, do you know how much shit that was?" She felt the warmth of his breath as he leaned into her face.

"I didn't see it. I told Sylvia to take it and do whatever with it. Trevor I knew you would be mad about that."

Trevor stood up. He began unzipping his pants and leaned forward putting his crouch in her face. He pulled out his stiffened penis and rubbed it across her face. Trina turned her head fighting not to take his penis in her mouth. She looked at him with confusion as she realized his plans included rape. His pants dropped to the floor as he reached down and ripped her camisole exposing her breast. She tried to contain herself hoping she could change his violent rage into an aggressive round of love making. He punched her in her face causing her nose to bleed.

"You don't understand Trevor I don't have your shit. Please don't do this. I know you love me." Trina squealed spitting back her dripping blood.

"Nah bitch, I love Cassandra. I'm just addicted to your ass. I want some before I kill you."

Trevor beat Trina and she couldn't fight back. Blood soaked the sofa but it only caused him to enjoy her more. She couldn't speak, her jaw was broken. Her thighs were burning from him punching them for her to spread her legs. When she refused to open her mouth, he ejaculated in her face. He held her arms down with his legs and body weight. Trevor knew beating her first would allow him to use her as he wanted.

As he finished the final round of pumping in and out of her vagina, he decided he wanted to use his fingers too. Trina cried the entire time he stuck his fingers in her ass. Her painful moaning caused another erection, and as he felt another climax come on, he shouted slapping her until she finally fainted.

"Bitch, is this what you wanted, my love? Is this enough for you? I'll give it to you all the time baby."

Blood began to run from Trina's ears. He stood over her limp body allowing sperm to drip over her stomach. He pumped his penis back and forth releasing the last of his excitement. He smiled callously as he urinated over her motionless body before he pulled up his pants.

"If you live Bitch, call me when you want my love again."

Trevor walked out the door not caring enough to look back.

Chapter 70

C assandra tossed and turned most of the night. At the peak of dawn, she had to get up. Lamont was lying next to her. He appeared to be in a peaceful sleep. She sat up trying to ease her way from under the sheets.

"What's wrong?"

Lamont held on to her elbow as she pulled back the sheets.

"I'm sorry did I wake you?"

"No, I was just laying here with my eyes closed. Are you okay?" He let her go and she laid back down.

"What time is it?"

Cassandra turned looking at the clock on the nightstand on her side of the bed.

"It's early, ten of six. I guess I just couldn't sleep."

Lamont wanted to make love to her but didn't want to push her into it. She snuggled close to him and kissed his cheek. The kiss was enough to start a reaction. They both felt they needed to display their feelings. Lamont wanted her to enjoy every moment of their lovemaking. He caressed her breast and began kissing her neck. As he felt the warmth of her flesh against his Cassandra began to massage his penis through his pajama pants. He felt her relaxing as they massaged each other. She pushed him onto his back and straddled his body lifting her gown slowly. He took off his pants and waited for the pleasure he had longed for. Cassandra spread herself allowing him to enter her body slowly. It wasn't long before their pace increased as their hips rotated. She put her breast in his face and his tongue found her nipples. He coupled her breast with his hands as he felt the first of multiple orgasms. Cassandra rolled over onto her back and Lamont was glad to take the lead. Her moisture excited him with each movement. He couldn't believe how relaxed her muscles were. It was as though they had made love many times before. She moved enough to keep him hard as she found herself reaching a peak.

"Lamont, oh right there."

He moved faster. Hearing Cassandra's whisper his name caused his penis to begin to pulsate. Lamont knew he was ready to explode.

"Baby is it okay?"

"Oh it's so good, Lamont, please give it all to me."

Lamont didn't know whether to cum in her warm vagina or pull out. He arched his back as Cassandra wrapped her legs around him pulling his body closer to hers. As Lamont's penis found a new depth he exploded. Their juices combined as they both moaned in pleasure. Lamont continued to rotate his hips hoping to find new warmth and depth. She lifted her legs and opened them wider for Lamont to fulfill his wish. As his penis grew in size, he felt his sacs tighten. He was ready for round two.

Cassandra began to tremble beneath him. Lamont wasn't quite ready for the next climax, but he enjoyed watching her as he fulfilled her pleasures. He wanted to slow things down, but it was too late. Her movements caused his body to react. He tried to pace himself and make the moment last. Cassandra rolled over on her stomach and positioned herself on her knees. Lamont mounted her back and immediately began to pump in and out of her vagina. She wanted more and guided his fingers to her clitoris. He fingered her as his penis grew to another explosion. She began to tremble. Her clitoris grew receptive to the stimulation of his touch.

"Lamont, Lamont oh Lamont, please baby please."

He pumped faster giving her all he had left and they both rolled on their backs satisfied that they had pleased each other.

"Are you okay?"

She didn't answer. She was enjoying the feeling while still trembling. A feeling she hadn't had in years. Sex with Trevor had become routine. Cassandra always enjoyed sex but she didn't know what to expect when renewing any of her needed pleasures. She was glad Lamont didn't spoil the feeling by wanting to wear a condom. She was always cautious and used birth control, but she preferred not using condoms.

"Lamont, do you always ride bare back?"

"No, babe. I usually wear a condom. I'm sorry I didn't think about it."

"I'm glad you didn't"

"Well, I will if that's what you want."

"I use birth control always. My children were planned by me. I thought about tying my tubes, but I haven't got around to it yet."

"Don't." His words caused her vagina to throb.

"Why?"

"You never know, I mean we may want children later."

Before Cassandra could respond to Lamont, he got out of the bed and went into the bathroom. She watched him walk across the floor and said a prayer of thanks.

Chapter 71

Evansburg State Park had begun to fill with those attending the fifth annual Zion Hill Baptist Church picnic. The committees for the picnic were all in place to welcome the members, their families and guests. There were those assigned to perimeter parking. The elderly and handicapped were given assistance to their tables. There would be plenty of activities during the day for all ages. The youth of Zion Hill Baptist suggested a time schedule, so they could participate in more than one activity. Signup sheets were available at the information tables close to the food area. Sister Costly was in charge of announcing each activity fifteen minutes prior to its start.

Ma'Dear was the head of the food committee and was proud of her volunteers. This was the first year that they all arrived early. It gave them plenty of time to set the tables and with time remaining to check for any missing items. Ma'Dear wanted them to be ready for the arrival of their guests.

"Ma'Dear, I think we've got everything ready. I'm gonna start the grills and put on the hot dogs about eleven o'clock."

"Robert, put the burgers too. I think you're right, we're ready. Scott and Franklin went to get another table from Brother Jones for the cups, napkins and things. That table ya'll brought wasn't long enough. They'll use that for something else, maybe the fifty-fifty jar and prizes."

"Okay, that sounds good. So eleven is fine then?"

"Yes, thank you. Y'all keep the meat on the grill going if you need more pans just let me know I brought plenty."

Robert was Ma'Dear's right hand in preparing the food for most of the Zion Hill Baptist's events. He called her earlier that morning telling her he would be at the park by eight-thirty. Ma'Dear had Terrance bring her to the park at nine. Although all picnic committees and volunteers weren't scheduled to be there until ten o'clock, a few others were there when she arrived to get things started. The picnic was scheduled to begin at eleven. The church reserved the park for the entire day.

Evansburg State Park was of good size and those who enjoyed fishing could go out on the boats or fish from the shore. There were baseball fields and basketball courts and plenty of space for volleyball, horseshoes and other activities. There would be dominoes, chess, checkers, and card games being played. The community enjoyed the Zion Hill Baptist Annual picnics and the church made large donations to various community based organizations each.

Ma'Dear had three tables set aside for her family and friends. Terrance used his arrival time to set up that area for his mother. Lamont, Sean and Jose' brought their coolers with them as well as the sporting equipment. The picnic was a reunion for those who didn't see each other during Sunday services or those that hadn't seen each at other since the last picnic. The men who lost in basketball and baseball couldn't wait for their revenge while the winners couldn't wait for another opportunity to brag.

It was a beautiful day for a picnic. The sky showed no threat of rain or showers and the sun promised to give warmth without humidity. By twelve thirty the tables were filling in and people had begun to eat the hot dogs and burgers as they came off the grills. The children were playing together running from table to table.

Cassandra and Lamont unpacked the truck and the children ran to Ma'Dear's table when they spotted Laura and Mary, who were seated there.

"Aunt Laura, Lamont's went back to his house to get the fishing sticks."

Everyone at the table laughed at Cassie's description of the fishing poles Lamont picked up at his house.

"So are you going fishing Ms. Smith?"

Cassie looked at her mother and then her brothers.

"No, I don't think I want to kill the fish. Did you know the fish die when they're out of the water?"

"They die later Cassie. Not when you catch the fish. When you catch them, they wiggle like this."

Tyler began to shake and wiggle, imitating a fish on the hook.

"Well your Uncle Earl will probably want to fish with you guys. Lamont do you fish much?"

"Ms. Laura I have to make the time. I usually take a vacation just to fish, I enjoy it though."

"Well you, Earl, and the children can keep fishing, I just enjoy eating them. Mary that's something we should suggest to Ma'Dear, frying fish at the picnic."

"Well you can handle that committee. I'm sure Ma'Dear won't mind you helping out."

Mary shook her head laughing as she watched the people mingling at their tables. The sight of the children, their families and friends brought on a good feeling. At the last three picnics, she attended Ma'Dear had one table consisting of Terrance, Laura, Earl and herself. She was glad that Ma'Dear invited everyone and they all accepted her invitation. It was good to be among friends and family. The first announcement came over the bull horn interrupting her thoughts.

"All children wanting to do face painting, please follow our friendly clown to the face painting tables."

Cassandra's children looked at her with pleading eyes, and she nodded her head. Kyle grabbed Cassie's hand and they all took off running. Sean and his girlfriend, Joyce joined the table saying hello and asking about Jose' and his family. Lamont gave a gesture toward the parking area where Jose', his wife Maria, and their children were getting out of the car. Mary, Laura, Ma'Dear, and Earl moved to their second picnic table leaving the third table for the children. Veronica welcomed Jose' and Sean introducing them to her fiancé Derrick. She sat at the end of the table with Cassandra and watched the men as they talked about their jobs and sports. It was obvious after an hour everyone felt as though they had known Derrick for years. Kevin arrived around one o'clock and shortly after the last of Ma'Dear's expected guest, Sylvia and Carson showed up.

Cassandra checked on her mother off and on from her table while talking with Kevin. She got her up excusing herself to make a plate of the food for Mary. She returned to Mary's table with a plate for herself. She sat eating with her, watching for signs of pain or fatigue.

"Cassandra, I'm fine girl. Go on over there with the young folks. Laura and Earl are here if I need them. Believe me I'm fine."

"Well I don't want you to think I forgot about you."

"No, you enjoy yourself. You and Lamont seem to get along well. I am glad you're having a nice time. How do the children like him?"

"They like him. We haven't really spent time a lot of time dating. I didn't want them to get attached to him like that. I mean maybe our relationship won't work out."

"So, how's it going? Don't get me wrong, I'm not trying to pry."

"Ma, it's okay. Lamont is different. I mean this all is different to me. But I'm enjoying it. I hope my classes go as well. Things are looking better."

"Well, I told you that damn Trevor....."

Laura heard that part of the conversation and redirected Mary's attention.

"Mary, come with me over to Sister York's table. I think her family is here from Virginia. We haven't seen them in years. I see Jeanie too. Come on walk over there with me."

Cassandra smiled letting her Aunt know she had done the right thing. Mary agreed to take the walk stating she saw a few people she knew from the day camp. Another announcement was coming across the bull horn as Cassandra walked back to her table.

"All men interested in the annual three on three basketball challenge, please sign up."

Terrance stood up and smiled. Jose', Sean, Kevin and Derrick looked up at him and gave a manly shout of barks.

"You know that's our call. Sean you know we've got to defend the title. Lamont and Uncle Earl need to park that fishing boat 'cause the game is about to begin."

Lamont and Earl had fulfilled their promise to the boys. Tyler, Kyle and Chris were happily fishing on the water. Cassie found her friends from the day camp and busied herself with arts and crafts.

Sylvia and Carson sat at the end of the table holding small conversations with Joyce and Maria. Carson hadn't moved from Sylvia's side. Terrance didn't want Carson to feel left out, but he preferred for him to remain at the table with Sylvia. Jose' got up as did Sean stretching before they went to the basketball court.

"Yo' Carson, you play man?"

Jose' tossed the basketball to Carson. He caught the ball and smiled knowing his game was better than most.

"I play a little. I mean for a white boy, I can handle my handle."

Carson figured he would rate himself before they did. Sean didn't let his answer get him out of the game.

"We all handle our handle. Listen you'll add balance to the team c'mon. Lamont and them are coming now. If you can't play you can cheer us on."

Terrance and Sean laughed. They all taunted and teased Carson, who gave in, following them to the courts. He was grateful that he was accepted. Derrick grabbed a couple of waters out of the cooler and followed the other men as they walked to the court waving Lamont over to join them. Cassandra could see Lamont talking to her boys and pointing

to the basketball courts. They smiled and followed her uncle to their table.

"We caught two fish. Uncle Earl made us throw the little ones back."

Tyler was smiling from ear to ear as he handed his mother the pail with the fish in it. Cassandra shook her head and frowned as she watched her Uncle pack up the fishing poles and remaining bait. Christopher and Kyle helped carry the equipment to the car while Tyler went to the restroom to wash his hands. Cassandra put the pail with the fish under the end of the picnic table.

The afternoon was near perfect by four o'clock. The men were now playing football after winning two rounds of basketball. The children ate off and on and Cassandra had begun telling them no when they asked for more food. Veronica, Mary, and Laura told her they had eaten so much they would pop. Sylvia avoided talking to Cassandra unless it was necessary and that was fine with Cassandra. Maria kept the conversation at their table going. They talked about employment, children, cooking and men. Cassandra thought about bringing up cheating men and the women they deal with.

"Does anyone have aspirin?"

Veronica felt a headache coming on. Joyce raised her hand, searching in her bag, but came up empty handed.

"I thought I put them in this bag, but I don't see them."

Everyone checked their bags and Veronica asked her aunts did they have anything to help her with a headache.

Sylvia remembered putting Tylenol in her glove compartment.

"Veronica I've got something in my car. I'll go to my car and get them for you."

"Thanks girl. I don't even think I have any in my car."

"If Sylvia doesn't have any, I think Jose' has some in the car. Sylvia let me to walk with you. I can look in my car while we're there." Maria stood from the picnic table before Sylvia answered.

"Yeah walk with her."

Cassandra spoke out feeling better that Sylvia didn't walk to the car alone. It wasn't until that moment that Trevor crossed her mind. Although most of the cars in the park belonged to those attending the picnic there were other cars riding through the park. Sylvia and Maria didn't have far to go but it would take them a few minutes to get to the cars. Veronica continued the conversation starting with finally finding the right man. Cassandra scanned the park spotting Lamont and the other men in the open field playing football. Tyler and Kyle were on the sidelines with their Uncle Earl cheering them on. Kevin was sitting at another table talking to a female he remembered from the neighborhood. Mary and Laura were at the table with the Minister and his wife. Terrance was headed toward the football field with waters for the guys playing. All seemed calm.

Ma'Dear approached the table holding a plate of sliced watermelon. She had been serving each table and stopped to sit where Cassandra, Veronica and Joyce were getting louder with their laughter.

"So you girls seem to be having fun. Would you like a slice of watermelon?"

"Ma'Dear why are you still serving people this late? You should let them get their own watermelon."

"Veronica, there's so much desert over there girl. They looked clean past the watermelon. I'm just putting their taste buds in order. The watermelon is already sliced they really need to eat it up. I can pack up the cookies and cake. Hey, is that Sylvia arguing with that guy in that car? He's blocking the road. The park traffic won't be able to get by."

Everyone turned to look at the scene that was now drawing attention from others at the picnic. Cassandra recognized the car. There was definitely an argument going on, but their voices couldn't be heard over the other conversations and music in the park.

Sylvia and Maria got the aspirins from Sylvia's glove compartment and walked close to the edge of the road before crossing the grass to return to their table.

"Sylvia, let me see you."

Trevor was riding slowly alongside the ladies as they walked.

"Trevor, not now this is not the place for us to talk."

Maria moved to the opposite side of Sylvia letting her be closer to the car. Maria didn't want to interfere in their conversation. Although Trevor didn't know Maria, she was well aware who he was, the drug dealer that Jose' had trouble with.

"Bitch any place I choose is the place. Get in the car."

Sylvia continued to walk. Trevor stopped the car and got out. He walked around the car and stood in front of Sylvia blocking her way. Maria stepped to the side looking around frantically for help.

"Listen, I don't know when you got your fucking nerve up but don't let me have to beat it out of your ass. Now get in the car!"

"Step the fuck off Trevor! I ain't going with you nowhere."

Sylvia let her voice get louder hoping someone would notice the conversation wasn't normal. Maria got nervous and began yelling out Cassandra's name. Trevor heard Maria's cry and turned to Sylvia with anger.

"Bitch, I want my shit. You got 'til tonight. Don't make me look for you."

"Mother fucker…."

Before Sylvia could finish her statement Trevor punched her in her mouth. He threw two more blows at her head and face. Everyone at the picnic was drawn to watch the beating Trevor was giving Sylvia. Men had begun to run to her assistance. Trevor got in the car and drove off.

The crowd around Sylvia was so large it took a minute for Lamont, Terrance and Carson to see what Trevor had done to her. Blood was all over a towel someone had given her. The church nurse yelled for someone to call 911. Mary and Laura were consoling Ma'Dear, who had fallen trying to run to Sylvia's aid. After reaching Sylvia and seeing her face Ma'Dear collapsed into one of the Deacon's arms.

The park police arrived clearing the people around Sylvia and trying to get information. Maria gave as much information as she could before she broke down crying. Sylvia's left eye was purple and closing. The gash above her eyebrow would require stitches.

The children were at the table with Veronica and Joyce. Cassandra was pleading with Lamont and Terrance to go to their mother's side and see about Sylvia before tracking Trevor. Lamont's anger had reached the breaking point.

"Cassandra, there's no doubt about it. That nigga is done!"

Sean and Jose' began packing the cars. They would be ready to go with Lamont and Terrance. Carson came over to the table and pulled Lamont to the side.

"Listen, we need to make sure Sylvia is alright. I mean she's your sister, but I love her too. Your mother is not taking this well. I've got some connections that will seek that mother fucker out and hold him for us."

Lamont looked at Carson in a new light. Maybe the rumors on the street were right. Carson was the big time dealer in the hood. He was right and Lamont needed to know that both his mother and sister were stable.

"Alright make the call."

Carson stepped further away and pulled out his cell phone. Lamont began helping Jose' and Sean. Mary and Laura watched Ma'Dear as she and Sylvia got into the ambulance. Laura told Terrance they would follow them to the hospital. Earl gave Terrance a nod of approval and joined the family in packing the rest of their items for their departure.

Cassandra's cell phone rang and everyone at the table looked her way. They all held the same thought. Trevor was calling to explain his actions to her. Cassandra didn't hesitate to answer.

"Hello."

"Ms. Cassandra Smith, please."

"Yes, this is Cassandra."

"Ms. Smith this is the emergency room at Thomas Jefferson University Hospital. We have a Ms. Trina Slater in our trauma unit. She's been beaten and raped. We've tried to find out information on her but other than her identification, we haven't had any success. Your number was written on her medical card as her sister and one of her emergency contacts. We have tried to reach the number listed for your mother, but she hasn't called us back."

"Oh my God! Who beat her? Oh my God! Is she okay? Did you say rape?"

"Yes Ms. Smith if you could get here. She's slipped into a coma."

Cassandra dropped the phone and fell to her knees. Veronica and Joyce screamed bringing the attention to their table. Earl backed the children up to make room for Carson and Lamont, who helped Cassandra to her feet. Kevin ran over to the table as he saw Cassandra falling to her knees. He picked up her phone and told the caller they would be there shortly. Kevin repeated the information he had been told.

"Trina's been raped and severely beaten. She's in a coma. Cassandra is listed as her emergency contact."

Lamont looked at Kevin and Carson. They all had the same thought.

"Cassandra, did they say if she knew who did it?"

Cassandra answered between sobs. "No, but I know he did it. He raped and beat her and beat Sylvia in the face. Trevor did this shit. She's in a damn coma. Somebody get me to the hospital."

Chapter 72

Sylvia didn't respond to Ma'Dear's questions or statements and that worried Laura and Mary.

"She hasn't said a word to Terrance or her mother. Ma'Dear keeps talking to her but she hasn't said a word."

"Laura, she's probably in shock, the doctor's will make sure she's okay before they release her."

Mary got up from her seat and walked over to Terrance who sat across from the women with tears rolling down his face.

"Baby, she's gonna be alright."

"Ms. Mary, my mother can't take this. I know she can't. Sylvia has to snap out of this. She won't even talk. Her jaw ain't broke, why won't she talk to my mother?"

"I don't know sugar. They'll check her out though. They're waiting for the test results now."

"I think they ought to keep her for a few days, you know to make sure."

"I know Terrance. I know."

"Ms. Mary, can you and Ms. Laura stay here with them? I mean, I need to catch up with Lamont at the hospital with Cassandra. I'm not gonna leave now but as soon as they say she's okay I'll need to leave okay?"

"Ms. Dearling? Come with me please."

The orderly led Sylvia in the door marked x-ray and Ma'Dear turned to her friends for comfort.

"Laura, I don't know what's going on. Why would Trevor fight her like that? What the hell was on his mind?"

"How many stitches did she have to get?'

"I think they said ten or twelve? Terrance how many stitches did they give her?"

"Twelve mama. But she has to wait for the swelling to go down before they look into her retina. It may cause her some trouble. They're checking the bone around the socket and her jaw now."

Ma'Dear sighed reciting a silent prayer for strength. Laura and Mary held her hands and consoled her as they waited for the door to the x-ray room to open.

Terrance dialed Lamont's cell phone and got his answering machine. His phone rang right back before he could hang up.

"Hey, how's she doing?"

"Twelve stitches. They aren't sure about her retina. She's in x-ray now for the orbital socket and her jaw. Lamont she's not talking. She's not even acknowledging us talking to her. I'm gonna suggest they keep her to monitor her. She may have snapped."

"Listen let me know what's going on before you leave there. We're leaving now to go to University Hospital to check on Trina. Carson made a call for his boys to find that ass hole until we get to him. Anyway call before you make a move."

"Lamont, suppose they want to release her."

"Then make sure she gets home."

Chapter 73

Four hours passed before Carson drove Sylvia to his apartment. The test returned with negative findings, and they gave her medication for pain and swelling. It was suggested she schedule a follow up visit to her private eye doctor regarding her retina. Laura drove Mary and Ma'Dear home in her car, Terrance left them saying he was meeting Lamont at University Hospital. Carson made sure Sylvia was situated and comfortable in bed before he left her. He explained to he promised to meet Lamont at University Hospital. Sylvia closed her eyes without saying a word.

The calls had been made to Kevin, Terrance, Carson, Jose' and Sean. Lamont gave them an hourly update regarding Trina's condition and at nine o'clock they agreed to meet at the hospital by ten o'clock to talk about Trevor's fate. Cassandra paced the floor between her ten minute visit intervals on the Intensive Care Unit. Trina's mother was in Florida visiting family and would be on the first plane she could book back home. Cassandra never told the staff she was just a close friend.

"Ms. Smith would you and your friend like some juice or water?"

"No thank you."

It was the floor nurse who had been helpful in giving them the information about Trina's condition. She was in a coma. Her nose and her jaw were both broken. Her ear drum was damaged. There was the fear of a blood clot on the brain, but they would be testing periodically to make sure it wasn't just bruising from the blows she received to the head. The police were still there when Cassandra and Lamont arrived. Kevin, Sean and Jose' decided to wait for the call from Lamont later so not to draw attention to their plans. To Lamont's surprise Cassandra told the police that she thought Trevor Black was the suspect. She told them about the assault on Sylvia in the park and all she knew about the reasons why. Though Cassandra pleaded with them to pick Trevor up for questioning, the police assured her they would get to him sooner or later. There didn't appear to be any rush to track him down.

Trina was motionless in her bed attached to intravenous tubes for constant medication. Her head was bandaged and her jaw was wired. Although her eyes flickered slightly there were no signs of her waking. Cassandra came out of the room looking for Lamont. She found him staring out of a darkened window.

"Do you have my cell phone?"

"Yes, Kevin picked it up in the park."

"Has it rung?"

"No. Who are you expecting to call?"

"Trina's mom. She said she was trying to get a flight out tonight. I don't know if she got one."

"How's Trina? Any signs yet?"

"None. Did you call Terrance? How's Sylvia?"

"She's at Carson's. He called; she's got to go to the doctor for her eye in a few days. The swelling has to go down first. I'm gonna go there and check on my mom in a few if you don't mind."

Lamont didn't mention the guys would be meeting him in an hour at the hospital. Cassandra looked at her watch.

"You should leave now. It's getting late."

Lamont thought about it. He could ride by his mother's and Carson's and still be back before the other's got there.

"You're right. Call me on my cell if you need anything."

Lamont decided to go to Carson's apartment first. The address was closer to the hospital. He pulled into the drive attached to the condo. There was no sign of Carson or Sylvia's car. The garage was closed. Lamont parked, walked onto the front porch and rang the bell. After waiting a few moments he was convinced he had missed Carson leaving to meet him at the hospital. He rang the bell again. After the third attempt he left concluding Sylvia had dosed off after taking her medication and Carson was on his way to Thomas Jefferson University Hospital.

On the way to his mother's Lamont decided to call first. After the phone rang three times and the answering machine picked up Lamont dialed Cassandra's mother.

"Hello."

"Ms. Laura, this is Lamont. Is my mother there with you or at home?"

"She's here Lamont. Terrance said he had to meet you at the hospital. Ma'Dear didn't want to be alone. How's Trina doing?"

"She's resting but there is no change. Is my mother okay?"

"Yes, she's fine. Aren't you meeting Terrance?"

"Yeah I thought I could stop by before he left."

"He left about an hour ago. Is Cassandra okay?"

"Yes Ma'am she's fine. I'm going back there now."

"Okay, keep in touch."

Neither Terrance, nor Carson were at home. It all seemed strange.

Chapter 74

Trevor returned to his apartment without a thought about the night before or the incident in the park. He popped the lid on a beer can and cut on his television trying to find a movie he hadn't seen. In the morning, he would call Cassandra and apologize for his rage. Lamont would step to him after his call and Trevor would be ready for him. It would be days before the cops would bother him about Trina or Sylvia. He assumed Cassandra would tell the police he was responsible for the assaults. It was almost nine thirty and too early for him to go to bed.

He thought about calling his neighbor, Cheryl and thanking her for letting him know about the raid on his apartment. Maybe if he talked right they could watch a movie together. The thought of a roll in the bed with the bronze beauty gave him an immediate erection. He closed his eyes to relax and decided it would be better if he pleased himself. He turned the channel to the playboy station and opened his pants waiting for the sexual acts to begin. The girls began kissing each other and moaning and Trevor turned up the sound and cut off the apartment lights to get a better effect. He returned to his sofa and repositioned himself.

As he got deeper into the televised activity, he began to feel himself reaching his peak. A muffled voice came from the darkened corner across the room near the hall.

"Trevor, fuck you!"

Shots hit Trevor pinning him to the sofa. Before he could cry out, more shots were fired. The only sound in his apartment was that of a silencer and the moans of the women reaching ecstasy. The front door gently closed as the shooter left the apartment. Trevor had been shot nine times. Six shots were in his chest and three were in his forehead. The reports later revealed the first shot to his head killed him.

Chapter 75

L amont returned to the parking lot at Thomas Jefferson University Hospital at ten fifteen. He told Sean and Jose' to meet him in the lot across from the emergency room. After parking, he saw no sign of their vehicles. Terrance, Carson and Kevin hadn't arrived either. Lamont glanced again at his watch and dialed Cassandra's cell phone.

"Hey babe."

"Hey, how's your mom and sister?"

"They're fine. Sylvia was sleeping and my mother is with your Aunt and mother."

"Really, I thought she would be resting too. Today was long for everyone. Is your mother feeling better?"

"Yeah, your mother needs to rest too."

"My mother? Oh, damn Lamont I almost forgot my mother's surgery. Is Uncle Earl with them?"

Lamont hadn't asked about Earl.

"I didn't go there. They were at your mom's house, so I just asked your Aunt how my mother and your mother were doing. Did anyone call you back?"

Cassandra paid no attention to Lamont not knowing whether Earl was there or not. She had been in touch with Veronica and Maria. They both told her they would keep in touch throughout the night. She hadn't bothered to ask Veronica about her father. Cassandra didn't want to leave Trina's side until her mother arrived. The plane was scheduled to leave Florida at eleven o'clock. She calculated her arrival to be about six in the morning. It would be enough time for her to go home, shower, and go to class.

Their conversation was ending as Lamont noticed Sean's truck pulling into the lot. Jose' and Malik were with him.

"Do you want me to bring you anything tonight, clothes, food, anything?"

"Lamont I'll be fine if you just stop by before going home for the night. Where are you now?"

"I told Sean I would meet him for a minute. Terrance is coming by too. I'll be near Sean's. You can reach me on my cell though. Listen Sean just pulled up. I'll call you back."

"Thanks, I'll talk to you later."

The phone silenced. Sean, Jose' and Malik walked up to Lamont's truck as Carson rode pass them.

"So Lamont, how's your sister and Trina?"

"Sean man, Trina's in a coma. She's the worse case. Sylvia is home. I guess sedated. Carson can update us on her condition. I know her eye is closed and purple. They're worried about her retina. She got twelve stitches. Terrance said she hadn't spoken to anyone since it happened."

Carson walked up to the group of men shaking their hands and thanking them for their words of support.

"Did your boys run down on that joker?"

Malik knew Carson from the street and recognized him immediately when the parking lot lights hit his face fully.

"White boy, that you?"

"Yeah, Malik. What's up?"

"Damn, I didn't know you were the infamous white boy, Carson!"

"Yeah Lamont to answer your question, they went to his house but no sign of him, or his car. So they've been hitting a few of his spots. DJ claims Trevor called him to say he was on the run. My call came after that."

No one said anything knowing according to the streets that meant he left the state. Terrance was the last to arrive and the swelling of his eyes told them he had been crying before coming to meet them. He parked his car right where they stood.

"This ain't no parking spot man. Park your car."

Lamont shook his head and sighed.

"You want to draw attention to your vehicle."

"What Lamont? What we doing here anyway? That nigga is done and we all know it. So what we doing?"

Lamont ignored his brother and continued to talk to the others. Terrance sounded as though he had been drinking.

"Trina may not make it. They haven't said it but the girl is in a coma with tubes running everywhere. Sylvia may have problems with her eyes the rest of her life. So we know what the outcome should be. Carson we can't wait for your boys to find him. We need to start looking ourselves."

"That's cool man. I'm down. I'll call them when we need to get rid of things."

"Alright so I say first we check his place and see what's there. Then move on with any tips your boys or the street may have."

"That nigga ain't home I know he ain't Lamont. He can't think he can go home and get a good night's sleep after this shit."

Malik had begun pacing while Terrance was kicking pebbles on the ground.

"Malik if he's not there we can tell if he's coming back. He might be waiting until the early morning hours to sneak in and out."

"So what are we doing? Splitting up or what?"

Sean's truck could hold them all, so they loaded up and headed over to the east side. The conversation focused on the condition of both Trina and Sylvia. Every now and then, Malik would look at Carson and repeat how surprised he was to know the famous "white boy".

"So Carson, tell me what's your claim to fame man?"

"What you mean, Terrance?"

"You know what I mean. You've been running this game with my sister for close to a year pretending to be a junkie, drug addict, or whatever, and now we find out you the dealer. What's up with that?"

"Man you know everyone has a game. My father never accepted me as the corporate son. You know the one he would leave the business to so I made my own business within his business. Drugs sell in the corporate world."

"Yeah and they bring this bullshit."

Lamont didn't like the way Carson was bragging about his business. Sean agreed with Lamont before changing the subject.

"This shit has got to stop. I mean look at the innocent people this affected. Damn, Lamont where's Kevin?"

"Did he call you Malik?"

"No, I don't know where he is. Jose' call him."

Jose' dialed Kevin's number and they all sat in silence waiting to hear why Kevin didn't meet them at the hospital.

"Yo' man, where are you? Yeah, we're on our way to his house. Oh, okay yeah we'll be there in about ten minutes. Okay, we'll see you there."

Jose' hung up the phone and raised his eyebrows at Malik.

"So what he say?"

"Kevin is a strange dude. He said he'll meet us there. He's on that side of town. He said he had a stop to make before coming to the hospital."

"Well damn, it's almost eleven o'clock what time was he gonna come?"

Terrance was right it was an hour pass the meeting time, and he was at least thirty minutes away. Lamont pulled into Trevor's apartment complex where he spotted Trevor's truck but his black car wasn't there.

"There's his truck. Anybody see the car?"

"No, but that don't mean shit. One of his boys may have the car. The nigga could be home."

They got out of the truck and noticed the lot was well lit. There were a few people were standing around their cars and homes talking. Most of the noise was coming from the playground where the teens were playing music and dancing. Windows were open and the sound of televisions airing late night news could be heard. Kevin's sports car turned the corner turning the heads of the men.

"Okay, I see your work. Nice ride."

Sean walked over to the car as Kevin got out and shook his hand. As they huddled by Lamont's truck the decision to walk through Trevor's front door was agreed upon.

Chapter 76

Carson knocked on the door and found with little effort the door slowly opened. The television was the only sound the men heard as they entered the darkened apartment. Terrance looked across the room where Trevor sat on the sofa riddled with bullet holes.

"Aw shit. He's fucking shot up! Get out, back out, don't touch nothing."

Sean backed out and the others followed hurriedly scattering as they ran. As they got near the parking lot, they heard the words of the police.

"Stop right there, what's the rush?"

Lamont looked around and noticed they were outnumbered. Kevin, Malik and Jose' were missing. Carson looked at Lamont shaking his head, an indication that they didn't come out the same way. Terrance immediately began talking about what they had seen.

"We walked in on that shit. We didn't do nothing."

The officer waited for the word from his partners as they checked the apartment and the surrounding area.

"A shooting. He's been dead longer than an hour."

"Where's the rest of your boys? We saw six of you enter the apartment."

Lamont didn't know what to say but he sure knew what not to say.

"They weren't riding back with us."

"Well Mr. Klein, you know what's next. We'll need to question you all downtown and get the names of your friends. If there's nothing to hold you on you'll be free to go. Any disagreements?"

Terrance looked at Carson. Lamont didn't respond, so Carson did.

"Not a problem. I need to call our lawyers."

Chapter 77

Carson made a call and they waited for the lawyers to come to the station. The police explained the scene. According to the Sergeant in charge, the officers arrived shortly after Lamont and his friends got out of the truck. Once the police knew they were going into Trevor's apartment. They waited to run down on Trevor with the assault charges. When they saw the men retreating from the apartment and three of them take off running in the opposite direction, they stopped them for mere suspicion. It was easy to see Trevor was shot hours before their arrival but there were questions that needed to be answered.

After talking to Lamont, Terrance, and Carson for three hours the police were convinced they didn't know what happened, and if they did the evidence would prove it. The shooter left no dispelled shells or any other evidence. There was no blood splatter or fingerprints on the door. Prior to the entrance of the six men no one in the complex witnessed any unusual visitors or heard any unusual sounds. There was a neighbor who said Trevor had a problem with two women a week or more prior, but she couldn't identify them. Trevor hadn't said who they were. It was apparent to her that he knew them the way he laughed and wasn't angry about their intrusion.

Jose', Malik, and Sean were asked to come to the precinct the next day to answer the same questions. Carson's lawyers would be there to meet them. The lawyers were told that the investigation would continue and if any of their clients were needed, they would be notified. Lamont, Carson and Terrance were free to go at four o'clock the morning after the picnic.

Carson walked out the door and shook the hands of the two lawyers who showed up on the spur of the moment. They left giving their regards to his father.

"Carson, thanks man, I mean I don't like your type business, but you know your shit. I thought we were gonna sit in holding until the morning."

Lamont shook his head in disbelief. He hugged Terrance, who was at a loss for words.

"Lamont, my business is not who I am. It's just what I do. Anyway as I said, I love your sister, and I'm about her and her family. I respect your walk and I wouldn't cross your path with mine."

"It's all good man, I hear you. Listen we need to get my truck, I want to check on Cassandra. Somebody has to tell her about Trevor."

Terrance spoke, thinking about Cassandra's new troubles.

"Damn, Trina, then Trevor, and her mom has surgery this morning. Talk about emotional turmoil."

Carson was on his cell making contacts to get them to Lamont's truck while Terrance and Lamont talked about the chaos of the day.

"She starts that class tomorrow too. I'm gonna try to convince her to stay home. Maybe we can talk to the people or something. There's got to be something she can do. Terrance you know her mind won't be with her."

"Damn man, who shot that nigga up like that. I mean that looked like some old professional shit."

"Could have been Carson, he ain't no joke."

They both looked at Carson, who gave them the thumbs up signal.

"I'm glad he loves Sylvia."

The brothers laughed and waited for the ride.

Chapter 78

L amont could feel that the events of the day had taken a toll on him. As he walked to the elevator in the hospital on his way to the Intensive Care Unit, he felt a sudden need for sleep. The elevator doors opened and Lamont walked down the corridor headed for the closed doors marked with instructions to visitors of the unit. Cassandra was seated in the visitor's waiting room near the nurse's station with two police officers. Lamont pushed the silver button that opened the automated doors, they closed slowly behind him.

"Lamont what did you do? Where did you go with Carson and Terrance? What happened?"

The thought of Lamont's original plans came to his mind. If Trevor wasn't dead when they arrived, Cassandra's assumptions could have been right. The question came to Lamont's mind. *"Would they have killed him?"* Lamont ignored the police who told him to remain where he was standing. The officer who was standing grabbed Lamont's wrist attempting to cuff him.

"Get the fuck off me. What are you doing? I just left the police station. Touch me and I'll fucking sue your ass. Cassandra, Trevor was dead when we got there."

The officer paused while his partner called for more officers to meet them on the fourth floor. The Sergeant call came across the radio asking what the problem was.

"Sarge, we may have a potential suspect here."

"I'm no suspect. Cassandra, are you okay?"

"Lamont who killed Trevor?"

"We don't know. We got there and the door to his apartment was opened. We walked in and he was on the couch. He was shot when we got there. Somebody killed him. We ran out the door and the police surrounded us."

Lamont turned to the officer who was still transmitting on the radio.

"Contact the precinct; we were interviewed by Detective Madison."

The officer repeated the information to the Sergeant on the radio. The Sergeant told the officer to stand by.

"What were the cops there for?"

"Babe, I don't know. They saw us when we went in and came out. They said he had been shot at least a couple of hours before we got there. Whoever shot him knew what they were doing."

Cassandra sat back in her chair and allowed her tears to flow. The officer who was taking information from her backed away. The other officer who was anxious to arrest Lamont, held his radio to his ear for the Sergeant to tell him to proceed. Lamont took a seat next to Cassandra ignoring both officers.

"Sandra, you can't possibly go to your class like this."

"Oh, damn. Lamont I can't skip the class. If I miss the first day I'll have to sign up for the next course."

"Cassandra, it's too much baby. Trina, your mother, Trevor and not to mention the dumb ass police questions; you need your rest. Did Trina's mother call yet?"

"She's on her way from the airport now. My class starts at nine what time is it?"

"Five thirty. Listen let's go there at say eight thirty and talk to someone. I don't feel comfortable that you'll be okay in that class."

"Ms. Smith do you have a number where we can contact you?" The officer interrupted their conversation ignoring Lamont's facial gestures.

"I gave you my cell number."

"Do you have another number?"

"That's the best number to reach me. I won't be home much today."

"Ms. Smith…."

Lamont was tired and the police were not helping the situation.

"Listen man, you've got the number where you can reach her. Would you like mine? We'll be together today and nowhere near a home number."

The officer looked toward his partner. "What did the Sergeant say about this joker? Sir, I was talking to Ms. Smith. Your intrusion can be cited as interference in an investigation."

"Call it what you want. You've got the only number she's to be contacted at."

"The Sergeant said he's good for now. There's no other questions for her either. Homicide has the case now."

The officer closed his note pad and gave Lamont a look that said he wanted the chance to deal with him one on one.

"Yeah right." Lamont turned his concerns to Cassandra ignoring the officer's audible complaints as they walked out the door.

"Cassandra, what did they ask you?"

"I guess they thought I knew he was gonna be shot or something. They wanted to know why I insisted that the cops find him. You remember at the park when I told them to question Trevor. Stupid shit, if they had found him then, he probably would be in jail and not dead. Lamont, what am I gonna tell the kids."

"The truth, they'll hear people talking anyway. Just tell them the truth, and if they have questions we'll answer them."

Cassandra felt a headache coming on. She was beginning to get sick. Her nerves were finally reacting. She had been in and out of Trina's room. Although nothing had changed, she held her hand and prayed. She was exhausted. Lamont was right she wasn't up for a class.

"When Trina's mom gets here we'll leave. You're right. I need to deal with this mess before taking on school. Do you think the investigation will be long?"

"I don't know. They talked to me, Terrance and Carson. They told us that Malik, Jose' and Kevin had to come to the precinct later today."

"Malik, Jose' and Kevin? They were with you too?"

"Yeah, they went the other way when we left the apartment. The cops knew they went in with us though, they were in the parking lot."

"You didn't see the cops?"

"They were in plain clothes, probably in an undercover van or truck. Didn't you say they were there to get Trevor? I don't think they'd pull up in squad cars."

"Yeah, I guess you're right. So what happened?"

"It happened so fast and Terrance saw more than any of us. We went to the door, Carson knocked and the door was ajar. We went in. His kitchen is to the left of the front door the dining room was straight ahead. You have to go to the right and around a bend to the living room. You've been there right?"

"No, um, I haven't, the kids have though."

"Oh, anyway we separated into the three rooms. Terrance was the first to enter the living room. As soon as he got there, he yelled that

Trevor was shot. He told us to back out and don't touch anything. We backed out and ran back to the truck."

"Why did Kevin, Malik and Jose' go the other way?"

"Instinct? I don't know but the parking lot is on the side of his apartment you have to walk out of his courtyard and around the side to get to the parking area."

"So where did they run to? Did you see the cops when you came out?"

"I didn't. Maybe they did, I don't know. Anyway the cops stopped us and went into the apartment. They saw Trevor was shot, and I guess because the blood wasn't fresh, they knew we didn't do it."

"Did they ask why you were there?"

"I think they knew. I mean you had told them about the assaults. When they questioned me, they knew Sylvia was my sister. They also knew I was dealing with you, and I guess since you're listed as Trina's sister they thought I had a connection with her. They asked what my connection was with all the guys and Carson."

"Lamont is Carson who they say he is?"

"Yeah, seems to be true. I don't know if Sylvia even realizes who he is."

The thought of Trevor's death silenced Cassandra. The description of the shooting did sound professional. It had Carson's name, or someone he knew, written all over it. Cassandra thought of Malik, Kevin, and Jose' running in the opposite direction. Questions crossed her mind about their sudden disappearance. They dealt with Trevor and Carson. In Cassandra's mind the questions were never ending. Kevin had promised her Trevor would not hurt her relationship with Lamont. Lamont looked over his clasped hands in her direction. He left her in her thoughts.

Lamont entered Trina's room. He was instantly overwhelmed at the sight of all the tubes and machines connected to her. She was now connected to a respirator. The monitors and the machines made a rhythmic sound that told any listener that Trina was barely hanging on. Her bruises had darkened over night and Lamont knew each marking was a sign of intense pain. Visualizing each blow that contorted the face of the attractive girl he met weeks before, brought tears to his eyes. The nurse entered the room with a chart and Lamont stepped to the side for her to get a reading from each monitor.

"I'm sorry. I'll be out of your way in a moment," said the nurse softly. She reached for Trina's wrist, feeling for a pulse.

"No, go ahead by all means. Can I ask a question?"

"Sure."

The nurse, whose tag read RN Candice Sommers, took off her glasses, and they fell to her chest hanging from a beautiful eyeglass chain. She turned to Lamont giving him her full attention.

"How often do patients recover from this type of trauma?"

"That all depends on their physical condition prior to the trauma. Some that we think are strong have other physical conditions that prolong or hinder their recovery. Others that we think won't make it do, call it a will to live. It's hard to say. But I always say that support helps. Her sister, and you being here, your touch, when you're in the room, and prayer; it's really too soon to make any predictions."

"I was here earlier and she wasn't on a respirator."

"Yes, that's to help her body rest. She can breathe on her own, but it is hard for her to rest and breathe. We're allowing her to rest and the respirator is breathing for her. It's like medication. We'll take her off later and see if she appears to be any stronger."

"Has a doctor been back to see her?"

"No they'll check in on her in a few hours."

"Thank you."

Lamont left the room allowing the nurse to finish her assessments. Cassandra was sitting in the room with Trina's mother when he returned. She stood escorting him to Ms. Slater's seat. The woman who looked older than her possible age was searching through her purse. She pulled out a pack of tissues before looking up.

"Ms. Slater, this is Lamont. He's been with me most of the night."

"Hello, thank you. I came as quickly as I could. I don't understand this. I mean Trina and Trevor. How could she let it get to that level? What was she thinking? And Trevor was killed? My God! I don't know what to think."

She talked through wiping the tears from her face. Her visit to her daughter's room would be delayed. Ms. Slater looked toward the doors where nurses and doctors could be seen. She began to cry again, and wipe her eyes. Cassandra's phone rang. She excused herself and went to the opposite side of the room to talk.

"Hello."

"Ms. Smith, this is Detective Madison. I'm trying to piece yesterday's incident in the park to the killing of the assailant you provided us with, Mr. Black. I've just been told that your friend Trina Slater was possibly assaulted by Mr. Black on Saturday evening. I need to talk with you concerning these matters. When do you think you could come to the precinct?"

"Detective Madison, I'm at the hospital now with Ms. Slater. I have a class, I must get to by nine and my mother is due in surgery for cancer this morning as well. I still have not seen my children, who Mr. Black is the father of. I mean was the father of…."

Cassandra collapsed into the chair and began crying. Lamont came to her side and took the phone from her hand.

"Hello."

"Hello, who's this?"

"This is Lamont, who's this?"

"This is Detective Madison Lamont. What happened to Ms. Smith?"

"Reality just set in. Can she call you back sir?"

"I was explaining to her, I need to ask a few questions. I really would prefer it not be in a stressed environment."

"How about my place? We have to make a stop and pick up her children. Can you come there after one?"

"Lamont, Lamont Dearling?"

"Yes, that's me. Is that time fine?"

"Yeah, I have your address and number. If anything changes I'll call."

"Detective Madison?"

"Yes."

"Do we need a lawyer?"

"No, I'm just wrapping up a few things."

Chapter 79

Lamont turned on the radio to a jazz station as he drove to Cassandra's mother's house. Cassandra let her seat fall back, and she closed her eyes hoping to get a little rest. They left Ms. Slater holding Trina's hand. Nurse Sommers took Lamont's cell number in case Trina's condition changed. Lamont took his time as he drove through the neighborhood. His mind drifted off as he thought of the incidents that happened during the last two days. He shook his head in disbelief, turned off the ignition, and tapped Cassandra.

"C'mon, we're here."

Cassandra looked at him with bloodshot eyes. He smiled and kissed her on her lips.

"You look like Cassie."

"Hmmn, I wish I was sleep like her."

"Listen we'll pick them up and take them with us to the house. It's seven now, you can shower and change, and I'll run you to the school."

"Yeah, that's cool. What time do we have to see Detective Madison?"

"He'll be at the house about one."

"Okay, okay," she answered as though she was taking in what had to be done during the day.

Lamont looked across the street. He wanted to stop and talk to his mother and Terrance before going to his house. His brother's car was in the driveway and the front door was closed. Ma'Dear would open it once she was downstairs for the morning.

Cassandra opened the front door to a quiet house. No one was stirring. Lamont walked into the living room and sat on the couch. Cassandra went upstairs to the bedrooms. Laura was coming out of the bathroom. She hugged her niece and gave her an affectionate kiss on the forehead. She began their conversation barely above a whisper.

"How's Trina?"

"It doesn't look good. She hasn't responded at all. They have her hooked up to a respirator now and all kinds of other tubes. Her mother showed up though."

"Everyone here went to bed pretty late. Your mother forced herself to bed about ten thirty. She told us she needed to rest before her procedure today. Ma'Dear volunteered to go to the hospital with us but of course with Sylvia's condition, she may change her mind."

"How is Sylvia? Lamont is downstairs waiting for me. We came to get the children and take them with us."

"Veronica and your Uncle Earl were coming by this morning for them. Earl was going with me and your mother Veronica said she would take the kids with her."

"They need to be with me today Aunt Laura."

Cassandra's voice dropped lower as tears rolled from her eyes.

"Sandra, what's wrong baby?"

"Their father is dead Aunt Laura. Somebody killed Trevor."

"What, do they know who killed him?"

"No, they're investigating but what would that matter. It could have been anyone on the street. Trevor crossed everyone."

"Your uncle said he'd be dead before the week was out."

"Why would Uncle Earl say that?"

"Baby I don't know, he said it when he left last night."

"What time did he leave here?"

"He left about eight thirty or nine. Ma'Dear was here until eleven, when Terrance didn't call she went home. We all were beat. The children watched television with me until close to twelve. Do you want me to help you round them up?"

"Can you call Veronica for me? I don't know how many times I can go through the questions and answers. I have to go to the school and find out about missing days or registering again."

The thought of her dream going down the drain brought more tears. Cassandra sighed and went into the bathroom. She looked into the mirror while turning on the faucet. Cassandra looked worn; she was tired and emotionally drained. She closed her eyes and splashed the warm water on her face letting it drip into the sink. When she opened her eyes a reflection of Trevor was standing behind her in the mirror. Cassandra turned screaming in fear and burst into tears. Laura ran into the bathroom after hearing her scream. She let her niece cry on her shoulders. She realized the tragedies would be an emotional setback for Cassandra.

Chapter 80

L amont ordered picked up breakfast for himself, the children and Cassandra. Cassandra tried sleeping as they rode from the restaurant. The children were quiet but their conversations buzzed in the seats behind her head. She hadn't told them about Trevor. She put that off until she dealt with her school business.

It was close to eight forty five on Monday morning when Lamont drove Cassandra to the school to speak to the program director. It was then that she remembered she would have to speak to Ms. Johns, her representative at the Unemployment Office. She shook her head in annoyance. She said a silent prayer hoping they would not deny her unemployment payments because she wouldn't be enrolled in the class. Lamont told her he was going to stop by the shop, and he'd be back in thirty minutes. Cassandra told the children to be good and listen to him.

Cassandra entered the office and waited for the lady behind the counter to notice her waiting.

"Good morning, may I help you?"

"Good morning. I'm here for the cosmetology class. I registered two months ago, and I don't think I'll be able to attend."

As Cassandra heard the words come from her mouth tears welled in her eyes. The lady noticed her emotions taking over. She went to another desk and got Cassandra the box of tissues.

"Let's talk about it. Come into the office dear."

The woman went to the end of the counter and waited for Cassandra to walk to the end. She followed the woman into an office in the rear of the reception area. The woman offered her a seat across from the desk and then took her seat behind the desk. Cassandra wiped her tears and straightened her skirt sitting up ready for the dreaded conversation.

"I'm Mrs. Pickens. I'm one of the supervisors for the work programs here. I'll be more than happy to work with you. What is your name?"

The woman wrote all her information on a legal pad on the desk. Cassandra told her about the representative from the unemployment office and the date she signed up for the program.

"Okay, your class begins today. I'm assuming you can't attend this course?"

"Yes, there's been some family problems, and I don't see it clearing up before the end of the week."

"What kind of problems are you having, if you don't mind me asking? The woman put the pen down preparing herself to listen to the excuses she had heard over the years.

"My children's father was killed last night after he assaulted my girlfriend and my boyfriend's sister. My girlfriend was raped and beaten by him night before last, she's in the hospital now in a coma. My boyfriend's sister was assaulted by him yesterday at the church picnic. She received twelve stitches, and she may have permanent damage to her retina. Today in about two hours my mother is undergoing surgery to remove the cancer in her body. I don't know if my girlfriend will live, I don't know what the outcome of my mother's surgery may be, and I have to be at the funeral of a man that abused me for more than twelve years."

Cassandra used the tissue to wipe the tears flowing from her face before she continued. The woman sat silent. She listened attentively trying to find the usual lie in the excuse Cassandra made. She said a prayer for the strength Cassandra would need. She said another prayer asking for angels to look over Trina, Cassandra's mother, and children.

"I don't know if I can be focused in this program right now. I don't know how long my mother may need me, or what my children will need after their father's funeral."

"How are your children taking it?"

"I haven't told them yet."

"How old are they?"

"Eleven, nine, seven and five, three boys and the baby is a girl."

"Did they have a good relationship with him?"

"He would come and get them from time to time. We haven't been together for a while. I lived with the girl who is in a coma until a month ago. He wasn't able to visit them, but they didn't seem to miss him either."

"I see."

Mrs. Pickens flipped the calendar to October and tapped her pen on the desk. She walked over to the file cabinet and took out forms bringing them back to the desk.

"Ms. Smith, would you be interested in entering the program in October?"

"Yes, but what about my unemployment. They won't pay me without my actively seeking a job or being enrolled in a program."

"You're right. I'll call Ms. John's. She and I are close friends. Your situation is unique to those who just make excuses for not attending or participating in the program. You call me at the end of this week or when you know what the arrangements for the funeral are. It may be longer since you said he was shot. You're right to believe it may take a while for your problems to be handled. You will still have your children to deal with after the dust settles. I'm going to have Ms. John's continue your unemployment checks. You and I will set a date for you to see me after the funeral." Cassandra was feeling better. Her concern for the class was minor in comparison to her concern for her checks. She needed a way to take care of her children.

"Thank you. I really appreciate this."

"It's okay. Do you type or file?"

"Yes, I've worked as a bank teller and reports clerk."

"Good, we may have a job here for you. You can still attend the school in October but the pay is better than your unemployment check, I'm sure."

Cassandra smiled in relief. Mrs. Pickens stood indicating their meeting was over. They left the office and said goodbye, agreeing to talk soon. Cassandra told Mrs. Pickens, she would call her by Friday. She walked out the reception area into the hall and for the first time she sighed, thank God for answering her prayers. Lamont was waiting in front of the building. She could see her children cheering as she approached the car.

Chapter 81

Terrance drove Ma'Dear to Carson's condo to visit with Sylvia. She barely got through eating breakfast worrying about her daughter's condition. Carson opened the door and welcomed them in while offering them juice, fruit and cheese. The table was set. Extra glasses and plates were on the kitchen counter. Terrance accepted the offer, pouring himself a glass of juice. Ma'Dear declined and walked into the living room looking around. She was impressed with the artwork and flower arrangements that accented the room furnishings. Terrance remained at the counter taking a seat on one of the kitchen stools.

"Sylvia is awake. I tried to convince her to sleep longer. She's fidgety, must be her nerves or maybe the medication. Ms. Dearling, would you like to go to the bedroom to see her? I'm sorry Terrance you can come with your mother if you'd like."

Carson paused waiting for Terrance to join them.

"No she can visit with her first."

Terrance waited in the kitchen for Carson's return. He wanted to talk to him alone before seeing Sylvia. Carson returned moments later to sit on the stool next to Trevor's.

"Would you like more juice?"

"No, man thanks. Did that detective call you again this morning?"

"No, did he call you? He shouldn't have that's what the lawyers are for."

"What about Malik, Kevin and Jose'?"

"They'll meet the lawyers at the precinct this morning. After the initial questioning the police will have to reach them through the lawyers too."

Terrance understood that the lawyers were working for Carson. He was curious as to why he would pay the lawyers for all of them.

"Hey, what do you think made Kevin and them run the other way?"

Carson shrugged his shoulder as he answered Trevor's question. "I don't know maybe they spotted a car they recognized."

Terrance was sure Carson knew more.

"Just seemed strange they would go a different way. I mean the cars were parked in the opposite direction and Kevin had a sports car. I wonder how Jose' and Malik got back to the hospital."

Carson went to the refrigerator and got another container of juice. He didn't respond to Terrance's comment. Carson gestured, offering Terrance more juice.

"No, I'm good."

"Listen, those guys know the area. Could be they knew someone close by. Anyway Trevor was done before we got there."

Terrance helped himself to the fruit and cheese.

"Yeah you're right he was done, nine shots. They said they didn't find no shells. That's some shit there."

Again Terrance looked for Carson to show he was surprised about the evidence or the lack of evidence. Carson didn't show any expression Terrance's conclusion did faze him.

"Trevor did a lot of people in. Anyone could have bumped him off. I'm just glad we didn't get a chance to touch him. Then we might have needed the lawyers to bail us out."

"Carson, did you have something to do with the shooting?"

Carson smiled and chuckled. "I was with you and your brother, remember? I could ask you the same question. Damn, for that matter, we could ask each of us the same question. Trevor's done, that's all that matters to me."

"Were you down with that shit he was trying to run on Lamont?"

"No. I heard about it. Kevin told me. Another reason Trevor deserved to die. Lamont's a good brother. The people in the neighborhood know it, even the drug dealers."

Carson's answer led Terrance to the second set of questions he wanted to ask.

"So what's with DJ and his beef with Lamont?"

"DJ has no beef with Lamont. It was Trevor's beef. DJ was down with the movement of the drugs. He wasn't willing to risk my drugs for Trevor's shit. Like I said he was crossing a lot of people"

Terrance was surprised Carson was so open with what was going on.

"So they were your drugs?"

"Listen; let's leave that business to me. It's all good. Trevor is done. The shit is over."

Sylvia and her mother were entering the room. The men stood meeting them in the living room where they all could sit and talk. Terrance looked at Sylvia and smiled slowly. Sylvia had a patch over her damaged eye. The stitches weren't covered but they were greased with medication. On the left side of her face, she had a large bruise near her mouth and jaw. Terrance was surprised; she was up and walking without any help. Other than her facial injuries she was doing fine. He listened as she spoke about Trevor's death. She stated she was surprised the media hadn't run it on any of the news stations.

"Terrance, have you spoken to Lamont? How's Cassandra and the children? They've got to be upset about their father. Cassandra may feel bad too, I mean for her children."

Terrance couldn't understand his sister's reaction. It was as though she didn't have an emotional tie to Trevor. He wasn't sure what to say. He told her that Lamont said they were all fine, but they were in concerned about Ms. Mary's surgery and Trina's condition. Terrance was concerned about Sylvia and the temporary shock she went through. He looked at Ma'Dear to see if she was thrown off by Sylvia's demeanor. Ma'Dear was patting her eyes with tissue, glad that Sylvia was feeling better.

"Carson, please make sure she takes the medicine. They said it would help the swelling. Sylvia you know you don't want your face to be puffy."

"I'm okay Ma, just a little sore. That medicine puts me under; I haven't taken much of it. Terrance, tell Lamont to call me. I need to see him or at least talk to him. I would go to the hospital to see Trina, but I don't want to upset Cassandra."

Ma'Dear gave her daughter a confused look. She couldn't believe Cassandra would be upset with Sylvia. "Cassandra wouldn't be upset about you visiting Trina, why would she?"

Ma'Dear still didn't understand the relationship between the three women. Terrance realized if his mother continued asking questions, Sylvia would have to tell about her dealings with Trevor. Terrance looked at his watch, which told him their visit had reached two hours.

"We need to be getting to the hospital. The surgery should be over. Carson, Sylvia we'll call you guys later."

Terrance rose to his feet and waited for Ma'Dear to do the same. Ma'Dear told Sylvia and Carson, she would visit later. The men hands and promised to stay in touch. Terrance kissed his sister and whispered he loved her.

"Terrance don't forget to tell Lamont to call me."

Terrance assured Sylvia he would give Lamont the message. He also made a mental note to talk to Lamont about their sister's new attitude.

Chapter 82

Cassandra was exhausted when she finally laid across Lamont's king sized bed to rest until Detective Madison arrived. They returned to the house and explained to the children the death of their father. The news brought tears to Christopher and Kyle while Tyler and Cassie stood by in silence. Cassandra knew the questions would come later. The children asked to watch the television in the den and after an hour wanted to play in the yard. Lamont showed them how to enter and exit from the deck. He went in the den and scanned the television channels for the local news.

Cassandra told Lamont about the class in October as well as the job offer. He could tell by her sense of accomplishment it wasn't the time to tell her she didn't have to work. He was more than willing to help her reach her goals. Sleep was creeping upon him but the sounds of the children laughing and playing kept him from completely dozing off. He was grateful when the phone rang. He didn't want to talk, but he knew the conversation would keep him awake.

"Hello."

"Hey, Lamont."

It was Kevin. He sounded as though he was in traffic.

"Hey man, where are you?"

"Coming out of the precinct. How's Cassandra?"

"She's sleeping. Did Detective Madison question you?"

"Yeah, he tried to pin it on me and Malik. They ain't got no proof though. The place was clean. No prints or anything. The lawyers talked rings around them."

"How'd you find out about the place being clean?"

"Inside information, they told us they didn't find no shells. Stands to reason, if the shooter took the time to collect the shells they wouldn't leave no prints."

"Hmmm. I guess you're right. Is Jose' and Malik with you now?" Kevin continued his conversation while sitting in his car.

"No, they went to the shop. Sean knew they were coming late."

"Yeah, he did mention that. I stopped by there this morning."

"How's your sister?"

"I haven't talked to Terrance, but they would have called if there was a problem. I guess she's fine."

"Lamont man, listen, if you need me to do anything for you call me."

"I hear you. Are you still looking to go clean?"

"It's too soon to say. I mean with all that went on it kinda turned the tables."

Lamont didn't quite understand Kevin's response. "Well you think about it. I mean with all the mess this weekend over drugs you might want to think twice about leaving that kind of living alone."

"Hey, you're right. But that's how it goes. I don't know man. But I do know I want to be in touch with my cousin and her kids, my family. I've got some things to sort out with my dad and all. It's a big change for me Lamont you wouldn't understand. But I'm gonna take your words into consideration."

"Listen, Kevin. I can't tell you what to do, or what's right for you to do. But your contact with Cassandra's kids can't include that world touching their lives. The closest they got to that world was their father, and now he's gone. Cassandra may not tell you this, but I've seen it over and over again. Kyle and Chris are at a vulnerable age. You know it's easy for them to take to cousin Kevin, hang out with him, and the next thing you know they're in the game. That's not fair to them or Cassandra. So when you visit them the game is shut down. That's the only thing Trevor did right. He kept the game from his kids."

"You're right and I can respect that. No problem. Lamont when and if I decide to walk clean I'll let you know. Don't hold it against me if it's not right away."

"That's fair. You keep your end of the deal. Keep the kids out of that business and I won't judge you."

"Cool, has anyone called about Cassandra's mother?"

Lamont looked at the clock it was close to twelve. He was beginning to wonder why no one called.

"No. I'll wait for Cassandra to wake up. If they haven't called we'll make the call. I'll call you when we hear something."

"So did Carson say we're done with the cops?"

Lamont was confused again. Carson and Kevin were closer than he and Carson. He didn't understand why Kevin was asking him about the cops.

"Kevin, I think they're fishing. That detective should be here around one to talk to Cassandra. I'll get a better feel about the situation then. I think you're right, they don't have much to go on."

"That's what I told Carson."

"What did you tell Carson?"

"I told him the cops can ask all the questions they want. They won't find anything or the killer."

Lamont heard Kevin's final words for the next hour. *"How did Kevin know what they would find?"* Lamont wasn't convinced that Carson didn't know any more than he led everyone to believe. *"Why did Kevin, Malik and Jose' run the other way?"* The phone rang again as Lamont went to the deck to check on the children who had become silent. Tyler and Chris were at the far side of the backyard looking in the dirt. Cassie and Kyle were running to the area to see their discovery. Lamont grabbed the phone on the fourth ring.

"Yeah."

"Lamont, how's Cassandra and the children?"

It was Sylvia. Her speech wasn't slurred and she didn't sound like she was in a lot of pain.

"Hey, how are you?"

"Well I can't say that I haven't had better days, but I'm feeling better than yesterday. I think I'll get better day by day."

Lamont knew that Sylvia wasn't talking about her physical bruises. He shook his head in agreement as his sister continued.

"I heard about Trina when Kevin called Carson while we were in the hospital. Terrance, Mama, and Carson talked about it while I was waiting for my x-rays. All I can think of now is Trevor laying in his own blood. His murder was the first time in my life that a wish came true. He died as he lived, cold."

Lamont was surprised Sylvia had taken his murder so calmly. "I'm glad you're okay with his death. I was worried you would take it pretty hard. Sylvia I know you loved him."

"Lamont he didn't love me. He didn't love Trina either. I don't know that he even knew how to love without hurting those that loved him. Whatever made us happy he wanted to destroy. Lamont he wanted to kill you. Just to get at you, he was willing to hurt Trina and me. It wasn't gonna end Lamont until he got to you."

Lamont thought Sylvia was getting ready to tell him what happened to Trevor. He sat down slowly on the couch listening without interrupting her.

"Trevor didn't deserve to live. Once I understood that I felt better. So today, I'm fine. The bruises will go away. But if you had killed him, or he had killed you, I couldn't live with that. Trevor's done and I'm glad. How's Cassandra, and the kids?"

Lamont didn't answer right away. Sylvia asked her question again.

"Cassandra's sleep, the children are playing in the yard. They're fine. We're waiting for the detective to come and question her. Trina is in a coma and Ms. Mary is in surgery. It's a lot to deal with Sylvia. You've had a lot to deal with. You should be resting."

"Lamont, I'll be fine, better than ever. Carson loves me, he always has, and I've finally accepted that. I should have loved him all along. But now he's given me more than enough reasons to be with him."

Lamont was stunned again. *Was Sylvia saying that Carson had Trevor killed, or that he killed Trevor?* Lamont hung up the phone moments later understanding what Terrance meant about Sylvia's new attitude. Lamont called the children in for lunch. After they ate their sandwiches they went into the den to watch television. Cassie fell asleep right away and Lamont knew the others would be following her within the hour.

Chapter 83

Terrance left the floor where his mother, Laura, and Earl were waiting for Mary to come out of recovery. He told them he was going on the fourth floor to look in on Trina. As he entered the Intensive Care Unit the nurse directed him to the visitor's area to the left of the nurse's station. Terrance walked in the room where there was a woman holding tissues and crying softly. He sat on the opposite side of the room waiting for the nurse to allow him into Trina's room. As the door opened both, he and the woman looked up.

"Ms. Slater."

"Yes."

The nurse looked in Terrance's direction. "Sir I understand you're here to see Ms. Trina Slater also?"

"Uh, yes."

Terrance looked across the floor realizing the reason for the woman's tears. His eyes followed her as moved closer to the door. He felt an uncomfortable twinge watching her trying to disguise her emotions. The nurse held the door open for her checking the chart in her hand.

"Sir what is your relationship to the patient."

"A friend, I stopped by to see how she was doing."

"Yes, Ms. Slater Dr. Clemons is requesting to speak with you before you visit."

Ms. Slater needed support and she felt any friend of Trina's would help her through the moment. She reached for Terrance's hand. He understood her gesture. They were led to an office in the opposite direction of Trina's room. The diplomas on the wall indicated they were in a doctor's office, one who graduated with honors.

"Ms. Slater. I'm a friend of Trina's my name is Terrance Dearling."

"I heard that name earlier today. Yes, Cassandra's friend Lamont mentioned your name."

"That's my brother."

"How's Cassandra doing?"

"She's okay. I haven't talked to them today. I was here with her family. Her mother is having surgery today."

"Yes she told me that. How is her mother doing?"

"She's in recovery. How's Trina?"

"I don't know Terrance. I went for breakfast and when I came back, they said the doctor's were with her. I haven't been in there since."

A man, wearing glasses and scrubs entered the room displaying a somber mood. He excused himself as he walked past Terrance and Ms. Slater going to the chair behind the desk. He took his seat and removed his glasses.

"I'm Doctor Clemons. I've been with your daughter and friend Trina Slater in an attempt to stabilize her. For the moment, she is stable. We believe the clot is causing problems for her. She's still in a coma and may not recover from this state. We'll have to evaluate her brain activity to determine if she is brain dead. Ms. Slater does Trina have a living will?"

"I don't know." Trina's mother answered as she closed her eyes fighting back the tears.

"Ms. Slater I don't know who else you may want to consult with but if Trina is brain dead we don't suggest keeping her on life support. She's no longer breathing on her own."

Terrance felt a thud hit his heart as Ms. Slater screamed a shrilling "No". The doctor stayed with them answering all the questions Ms. Slater asked. The nurse continued to comfort her as they sat listening to words that confirmed their worst fears. After a call came over the intercom, Dr. Clemons hurriedly left the office with the nurse in tow. Ms. Slater and Terrance walked slowly to the visitor's waiting room. There was a crowd of doctor's, and nurses going into the Intensive Care Unit.

"Ms. Slater can I get you water or anything?"

"No Terrance, thank you. This is so much to take in. I don't know what to do."

The door to the visitors' waiting room opened, Dr. Clemons stood at the door.

"I'm sorry Ms. Slater. We couldn't save her."

Chapter 84

E arl and Laura drove home after the doctor told them Mary would have to be in the hospital for a few days. They were silent, occupied by their own thoughts. The doctors removed the lump from Mary's breast but there was a mass that was found on her intestine. After tests were taken, the mass was found to be cancerous and malignant. The doctor suggested removing the mass as soon as possible. Mary was in and out of sleep and was not aware of her fate. The family decided to leave. Earl and Laura would come back later. Laura broke the silence.

"Terrance said Trina died before he could see her."

Laura's comment didn't distract Earl's thoughts. He questioned Laura about the matter at hand.

"Laura, do you think Mary can handle another surgery?"

"I don't know. This is what she feared, the continuous surgeries and all the radiation treatments. Earl she may not let them operate."

"What about Cassandra? This will tip her over. I mean, all that has happened and then Mary needing another surgery? Did the doctor say they told Mary?"

"I don't think they did this afternoon, but they may before we visit this evening. Mary might not say anything if she decides one surgery is enough. Earl you are going back with me tonight, right? We'll have to talk her through this."

"I don't think I have a choice. Mary needs to know that we are there for her. I'll pick you up about six thirty.

I'm going home to rest for a couple of hours. You should too."

Earl rode home praying for strength, and the healing of his sister. When he pulled into his driveway, he heard the doorbell ring as he entered the kitchen from the back door. He walked through his home to answer the front door.

"Mr. Smith?"

"Yes."

"I'm Detective Madison and this is Detective Davis. I have a few questions about yesterday's incident in the park. I'd like to take a moment of your time."

Detective Madison and Davis stood looking through the screen door. They presented their identification before making an effort to enter Earl's home.

"Sure, come in. We can talk in the day room."

The detectives followed him into the day room. The detectives were well dressed. Earl thought they looked more like insurance agents but the guns on their hips and the identification confirmed they were police. The afternoon light brightened the room. The men made themselves comfortable as they pulled out their pads and pens. Earl prepared himself for their questions and despite his emotions, he was glad to talk about the events of the day before. It would take his mind off Mary, and what they would later face.

"Mr. Smith this will only take a few moments of your time. As a matter of fact, we're on our way to talk to your niece."

Earl didn't respond giving the detectives the impression that he wasn't concerned about their questioning Cassandra. They hadn't made Earl relax with their cordial opening.

"Are you questioning everyone that was at the picnic?"

"No, no we have a list of people who were close to Sylvia Dearling and Trina Slater."

"And where do I fit on that list. I mean Sylvia is my sister's friend's daughter and Trina was a friend of my niece."

"Mr. Smith you said was?"

Earl didn't understand why police didn't know that Trina had passed. The mention of her name caused Laura's words in the car to repeat. Since Trevor was connected to her assault it seemed they would want to know what her condition was.

"Yes, update your records detectives Trina died this afternoon."

Detective Davis sat to the edge of his chair. He looked directly in Earl's face as he questioned him.

"Mr. Smith you seem to have an attitude."

"Well, it's been a long trying day. You know your side of the events, and I know mine, which include my sister's surgery and the need for another surgery. Emotionally, I'm drained and I guess you could say tired."

"I see. Well, we'll try not to push you to the edge."

Davis sat back in the seat looking around the room trying to get a feel of the man they were questioning. Earl Smith's name came up when they questioned a few people at the picnic. One person remembered him saying that Cassandra was doing so much better without Trevor, and he deserved to be killed. Earl made the comment shortly after Trevor had the confrontation with Sylvia, later he was found dead. Detective Madison started the questioning.

"Mr. Smith do you own a gun?"

"Sure I do."

"Is it registered?"

"Yes."

"When's the last time you shot it?"

"About a month ago, I shoot at the indoor range once a month."

"Recreational shooter huh?"

"No. Just a shooter."

Davis saw the opportunity to dig in. "Why do you have a gun Mr. Smith?"

"I live alone, inner city, crime, protection. I have my reasons."

"Trevor Black one of them."

"Hell no, I've owned a gun all my adult life."

"I see. Where were you about eight thirty or nine o'clock last night?"

"Leaving my sister's house."

Davis began writing on his pad as Madison took over the questioning.

"Where'd you go from there?"

"Here, I knew what today would be like minus the two of you. I had been fishing, and was with my niece's kids most of the day yesterday. I came home to go to bed."

"Was anyone here who can verify that?"

"I live alone."

"Okay, Mr. Smith I think that's all."

Davis had another question as Earl escorted them to the front door.

"Did you like Trevor Black?"

"No, I didn't care for him."

"What kind of gun do you have?"

"I have a Smith and Wesson, forty caliber."

Davis and Madison thanked Earl for his time. They assured him they would be in contact if they need him to answer more questions. Earl smiled as they walked out the door.

"I'll let my lawyer know."

Chapter 85

The detectives left Earl's home with information they already knew. The investigation was becoming just another formality. The Philadelphia Homicide Unit had been dumped a dead file. No one in the department cared to investigate the murder of a well known drug dealer. Trevor Black was just another dealer on the list of many. Trevor's home had been swept for drugs and weapons none were found. Other than Trevor's body and the surrounding blood there was no evidence of a crime. The reports gave no signs of forced entry and without any evidence the case would go cold. Detective Madison called his office and notified the unit that he had information that Trina Slater was dead. Trevor had been accused of assaulting Trina, and now that case would go cold as well.

"Dave, do you think we'll find a killer talking to the ex-girlfriend?"

"Seems like she's the only one with valid information. I think she might know something. It could tie up the loose ends. If she doesn't know any more than we already have, then we start on another case tomorrow."

"I guess you're right. Dave, what's the number of that house? I think that's Dearling's house over there."

"Yeah that's the right address, park behind his truck in the driveway."

It was three o'clock. Cassandra was taking more Motrin for a headache that seemed to be lingering on. Terrance called when he got home to tell them about Trina. Lamont relayed the information to Cassandra right away. He told Terrance he couldn't talk long. He knew the information about Trina would set in shortly.

"Lamont, man how much more can Cassandra take? I mean this is a lot for anyone to deal with."

"You're right man. As soon as I can get these detectives out her face, I'm gonna make sure she takes it down."

"Did Ms. Laura call you? Ms. Mary has to have another surgery. They're going back at six thirty to see if Ms. Mary will let them operate."

"What choice does she have Terrance? Well, I don't know. This is a lot of shit to deal with. And oh man, you were right about your crazy ass sister, something just ain't right. Listen, I'm gonna check on Cassandra before the cops get here, they said they were on the way. We'll probably be going to the hospital after that. I'll call you later."

"Are they coming to your house to question you again?"

"No, Cassandra. They wanted to talk in a different environment. I don't know what they think she knows, but I'm sure she wants to get this over and done. Hey man that's the bell gotta go."

Lamont hung up the phone to answer the door.

"Detectives, you're rather late."

"Mr. Dearling, we've been very busy. I'm sorry we have to put you folks through this. Mr. Smith gave us a brief run down on how your day has been going."

They stepped into the living room and took a seat. Detective Davis kept quiet as he watched Lamont closely as he talked.

"Cassandra will join us shortly. Can I offer either of you water, or something to drink?"

"No, thank you."

Lamont recognized Davis from the hospital. He was with the officer that wanted to put him in cuffs. His attitude changed instantly.

"I'll get Ms. Smith for you."

The detectives looked around making mental notes about the home. Cassandra entered the room shortly after their arrival. Her appearance told them she made an attempt not to look emotionally drained. Her read eyes and apparent nervous movements told the true story. She was at a breaking point. She took a seat on the couch and Lamont sat on its arm.

"Ms. Smith, as I've explained we just need to tie up some loose ends. I'm Detective Madison and this is Detective Davis. I understand you told the police in the park that you had reason to believe Trevor Black was responsible for the condition of your friend Trina Slater."

"What difference does it make now? They're both dead."

"I understand your feelings Ms. Smith, but we have to take your answers for the reports."

"Get it from the cops who didn't want to go on my hunch; a hunch that would have Trevor Black in jail and not in a coffin."

Davis couldn't help his desire to question Cassandra's motives. Madison had told him earlier in the day that Cassandra wasn't a suspect but Davis didn't believe it.

"Ms. Smith, how did you know Trevor assaulted Ms. Slater?"

"I know Trevor. Trina called me about Trevor's threats, his dealings with Sylvia, and the fact that they both were scared of what he might do to them."

Madison listened. Davis' line of questioning might give them a lead to the killer.

"What was he threatening them for?"

"It was more like blackmail. At first it was the threat of him hurting Lamont. He didn't want me to be with Lamont. He used Sylvia to get at Lamont. He told Sylvia that he would kill Lamont straight up if she didn't act like she was his girl. Trevor figured Lamont would confront him, but he was sleeping with Trina while he was pretending to be with Sylvia. I guess he was with Trina to make me jealous. Trina found out about Sylvia and they both decided to raid his apartment to get back at him. The raid caused his rage to hit the ultimate they took his stash and flushed it. It must have been a lot because he wanted to kill them over it. When he saw Sylvia, he had been looking for her for a week or more. He raped Trina and beat her the night before, and if he had the chance, he would have killed Sylvia."

Davis turned to Lamont. "Sylvia is your sister right?"

"Yes, she's my sister."

"I know we asked you this but Mr. Dearling do you own a gun?"

"I told you earlier that I owned two guns and a shotgun."

Davis looked around the room, as though he could see the gun boxes. He continued to probe.

"Yes, you did. Are they registered Mr. Dearling?"

"Yes."

Madison stepped in seeing Davis was picking with Lamont. "Ms. Smith do you own a gun?"

"No."

"Do you have access to a gun?"

"No."

Davis interrupted Madison's chain of questions, showing a different reason for his questions. He wanted Cassandra in his net of suspects.

"You live here Ms. Smith?"

"No, I live on Grape Street with my mother and aunt."

"What time did you leave the hospital last night?"

"I never left the hospital. Detective Madison asked that earlier."

"Yes," answered Madison, "but the nurse said she came into the hall about nine o'clock, and you weren't there."

Lamont remembered his leaving the hospital at nine. Cassandra walked him to the elevator.

"She was at the elevator with me. I remember because I was meeting the guys at the hospital about ten. I left at nine to check on my sister and mother."

So you weren't with your friends between nine and ten."

"No I wasn't"

Davis wrote in his pad while Madison remained silent. The story connected well with the information they already had, too many suspects with no evidence. Madison wasn't looking to dig any deeper. He had seen trash like Trevor Black get what they deserved in the past. Davis had a few more questions.

"Ms. Smith you said Trevor didn't want you to be with Lamont. Did you still have feelings for Trevor?"

"No, he's the father of my children. That's the only reason for me telling them to pick him up for questioning."

"Well Ms. Smith had the police picked him up, he may have had to do jail time for assault. Well, now murder."

"That would have been better than my children's father being murdered."

"So you knew he would be murdered."

"Detective Davis, did you see Ms. Dearling's injuries or visit Ms. Slater before she died?"

"No, I looked at the pictures that the investigation folder has."

"Then you know for what he did he deserved to die. It was just a matter of time."

"So who do you think killed Mr. Black?"

"How would I know that?"

"You knew he would assault your friend and your boyfriend's sister. I think you knew he would be killed. Maybe you know who did it."

"That's your job detective. I've given you all the information I have."

Davis wasn't satisfied. He wanted to leave Lamont angry enough to react. Davis pegged Lamont as the killer.

"Ms. Smith, would you tell us if you knew who killed your ex?"

"For years I wished I had the nerve to kill him. I didn't because he was the father of my children. Today I'm relieved he's gone. My children will learn to survive without him."

Lamont's reaction was to end the questioning and escort Madison and Davis to the front door. He was subtle about it but both detectives knew they wouldn't be questioning either Cassandra Smith or Lamont Dearling any further without a lawyer present. Lamont stood and gestured toward the direction of the front door.

Chapter 86

Sean called Lamont shortly after closing the shop for the day. Throughout the day people had stopped by to talk about the shooting of Trevor Black. The rumors were in the street with Lamont's name at the forefront. Someone thought Lamont used Malik and Kevin to make the hit. Malik gloated all day about his name being a part of one of the biggest hits in the neighborhood. Sean didn't say anything to Malik, but he told Jose' to talk to his boy.

"Malik and Kevin, that's a fair thought?" Lamont questioned, wondering if they had been a part of the killing.

"Yeah, man, especially after they ran the other way." Sean still couldn't believe the story they told about why they went the other way.

"Sean it's a done deal Trevor's dead. They can't prove a thing. They asked again about my guns. They even asked Cassandra did she own a gun. They don't have a clue. Kevin told Carson that shit."

"It figures Kevin would know something. Malik knows something too. I don't know what he knows, but I'll be glad when this shit is over. How's your sister and Cassandra doing? I heard Trina didn't make it."

"Terrance called and told us. Cassandra is taking it all in. We're going to visit her mother in a few, she needs another surgery. Sean this girl has had nothing but bad news for the past two days. Terrance called to say Sylvia is acting strange, but she's so phony that she may be faking her attitude too. I talked to her for a while. Yesterday she acted like she was in shock, but today she repeated everything she heard about Trina. Sean, if I took a wild guess, I would say Carson ordered the hit but Sylvia knew about it."

"Wow, I didn't think about that. Listen man; call me if you need to talk."

Lamont heard Cassandra screaming from the bedroom.

"Lamont, you alright? What's that noise?"

"It's Cassandra man, gotta go."

Lamont ran to the bedroom. Cassandra was paralyzed with the phone in her hand. Lamont spoke into the phone.

"Yes, this is Lamont, who's this?"

"This is Thomas Jefferson Hospital; we're calling about Ms. Mary Smith. She's had a heart attack. Her daughter needs to get to the hospital as soon as possible."

Lamont called his mother and asked her to watch the children for them. He knew Laura and Earl would meet them at the hospital. Cassandra would need him with her.

Two Months Later

Terrance was relaxing. It was his day off. His schedule was empty and he wanted to keep it that way. He and Lamont helped Laura move all of her belongings back to her apartment as well as pack Mary's things for charity. Ma'Dear assured Laura and Cassandra the church would pick the boxes up before the end of the week. They found a letter with a list of requests and instructions on Mary's dresser waiting for them after the news of her heart attack. Laura cleaned her room daily and never opened the envelope with the list. It was written and left there that Monday morning when Mary went to the hospital. She wrote the letter, in case she never came home.

Terrance popped a beer can while surfing the channel guide on the television. Ma'Dear went out the front door leaving it opened.

"Ma, what's up with the door? It ain't summer no more."

The air from the door was cool for early September.

"It ain't quite winter either. I was looking for Earl's truck. He said he'd help with those things for the church."

"I thought the church was picking them up. Mr. Earl don't need to be moving that stuff by himself."

"He said Kevin was coming with him, both him and Reggie. They'll get it. Cassandra has just about changed the house over. She was right. She needed her mother's things out of the house, so she could breathe. It's funny how a spirit will linger on if it can."

"Lamont tried to get her to move with him. She didn't have to stay at her mother's."

"Terrance she needs time baby. I can understand. She loves Lamont and Lamont loves her, but they can't rush into anything while nothing has been settled. The death of people she loved was enough to send her over the edge. It ain't time for a full time relationship. She's got to deal with her children and their understanding of it all too. And then there's the police constantly calling. Terrance, Cassandra is a strong woman."

"Well I guess you're right ma. A lot stronger than I thought she was. Lamont is hanging in there. I really hope they can make it."

"They will. Lamont isn't pushy and that's what she needs. He spends a lot of time with her and her children. They truly love each other. They'll do fine. He's still closer to the altar than you or your sister."

"You're right again. I ain't looking for a wife and Sylvia is content to live with Carson without being married."

"What time are you picking up Sylvia?"

Terrance looked at the clock. It was close to eleven o'clock.

"She said about one o'clock. Carson is out of town, so he couldn't go with her after all."

"I thought she went to the doctor a week ago? Oh, there's Earl and them. Lock up good when you leave."

Terrance was glad Ma'Dear had to leave. Sylvia lied about the doctor's appointment. She was receiving treatment for her eye every two weeks. Terrance knew she would be tracking Sylvia's appointments. He didn't mention where he and Sylvia were going. Trevor's apartment was officially released it had been sealed since the murder. Sylvia had been notified that if she wanted to pick up her belongings, she could do it while the officers were there.

Terrance picked up his sister as he promised. They went to Trevor's old apartment. Officers met them at the door telling her any items removed had to be signed for on a police inventory sheet. Any large items would not be released without receipts or proof of ownership. Sylvia was one of the several women who had come to claim their property.

She walked into the apartment slowly. She came went through the rooms methodically. She returned with the items she had in the bedroom. A few dresses, a makeup case, shoes and a garment bag. She went into the kitchen and picked up a wooden handcrafted box. The box looked as though it was used to hold bills or notes. It didn't appear to be an odd piece for the kitchen counter.

Terrance watched his sister as she opened the box checked for contents and closed it. As Terrance focused more on the box, he remembered where he saw the box before. It was the box, she picked up at her office the day he drove her there. He remembered the box with its fancy handcrafted artwork and a briefcase. Terrance followed the time line of events. It didn't include Sylvia returning to Trevor's apartment. She hadn't seen Trevor until the day of the picnic.

His thoughts were carrying him so fast that he began to feel dizzy. He stepped outside to get some air. His blood was pumping faster than normal. Terrance had a clear picture now. Sylvia changed her number and moved when he took her to the office. Carson told her to live with him from that point on. Sylvia said the briefcase and the box would protect her from Trevor. Terrance's thoughts held a major question. *Did Sylvia go back to the Trevor's apartment, would she?*

Terrance stepped back into the apartment. Sylvia was signing the sheets for the items she was claiming as hers.

"What's in the box ma'am?" The officer reviewed the signed pages. He pointed to another line for her signature.

"Oh, nothing officer. It held some paperwork."

"Where's the paperwork?"

"I had removed that earlier. I lived here temporarily."

"Open the box please."

Terrance watched as Sylvia's unlatched the gold hinge. The box was lined in red satin. The satin made no definitive pattern but Terrance had an idea what had been the box. The officer took the box from Sylvia and touched around the edges feeling for anything that may have been under the satin lining. Terrance knew the contents were removed the night of the shooting.

"Thank you ma'am. We're sorry for the inconvenience."

"No, problem. Terrance can you help me carry the rest of these items to the car."

He moved looking at the box. Sylvia's nonchalant attitude didn't arouse any suspicion. Terrance wondered was she hiding something. He smiled, trying not to appear to be nervous and thanked the officer for his time. He walked behind his sister as they approached his truck. Sylvia took her seat on the passenger side keeping the box on her lap. Terrace put the rest of her items on the back seat. They drove in silence for two blocks. She seemed relaxed, content. Her brother thought the visit to the murder scene would have been emotional for her.

"Sylvia, where did you get that box?"

"Carson had it crafted for me."

Terrance had another question he needed to ask.

"What do you keep in it?" He wanted to retract the question before she answered.

Nanette M. Buchannan

"Protection, Terrance, protection."

Other Novels by Nanette M. Buchanan

Family Secrets Lies and Alibi's

A Different Kind of Love

Purchase Your Copy Today

www.ipendesigns.net
www.amazon.com

Rising Sonz Books
Willingboro, New Jersey
Urban Knowledge Bookstore – Maryland

Nanette M. Buchannan

www.ingramcontent.com/pod-product-compliance
Lightning Source LLC
Chambersburg PA
CBHW051608100726
47898CB00001B/276